D1624883

14
DAY
LOAN

Donated in memory of
Dolores Wallace
by
Joe and Gloria Weisberg

IMPOLITIC CORPSES

IMPOLITIC CORPSES

Paul Johnston

This first world edition published 2019
in Great Britain and the USA by
SEVERN HOUSE PUBLISHERS LTD of
Eardley House, 4 Uxbridge Street, London W8 7SY.
Trade paperback edition first published
in Great Britain and the USA 2020 by
SEVERN HOUSE PUBLISHERS LTD.

British Library Cataloguing in Publication Data
A CIP catalogue record for this title is available from the British Library.

ISBN-13: 978-0-7278-8908-9 (cased)
ISBN-13: 978-1-78029-640-1 (trade paper)
ISBN-13: 978-1-4483-0339-7 (e-book)

All Severn House titles are printed on acid-free paper.

Severn House Publishers support the Forest Stewardship Council™ [FSC™],
the leading international forest certification organisation.
All our titles that are printed on FSC certified paper carry the FSC logo.

Typeset by Palimpsest Book Production Ltd.,
Falkirk, Stirlingshire, Scotland.
Printed and bound in Great Britain by
TJ International, Padstow, Cornwall.

To Neil 'Eric' Swan,

Iuvenes dumb eramus

ACKNOWLEDGEMENTS

Here I go again. Mega-thanks to Kate Lyall Grant and her team at Severn House for their habitual excellence in every regard. Ditto, with a *coup de blanc*, to my longstanding and ever supportive agent, Broo Doherty, of the DHH Literary Agency. And glasses raised – maybe not so often, so quickly, the next time – to David 'Destructor' McDowell for essential Embra information. Great gratitude, too, to Claire and Chris for various vital forms of backing. And love eternal to Roula, Maggie and Alexander for filling my life with, well, stuff.

PROLOGUE

November 2038. Snow time.

The three-year-old reconstituted state of Scotland – that name had prevailed over the old chestnuts Alba, Scotia and Caledonia – is doing remarkably well. So much so that sceptics such as I are beginning to get suspicious. Of course, living in Edinburgh, confirmed again as the nation's capital, has its benefits. I doubt the farmers up to their oxters in climate-change-induced drifts of the white stuff that has been covering the country's hills since mid-October are dancing the fling, Highland or Lowland. Baa, baa, black, white or black-faced sheep, have you any wool? Yes, sir, yes, sir, but you're not getting your clippers on it for many a month.

The government, in power for two years now after free and fair elections – *really* – has turned out to be progressive, competent and serious. Given that I tangled horns in the past with both the presiding minister, the opposition leader and several other members of the cabinet, never mind numerous people's and municipal representatives, especially those from Edinburgh, I've been kicking myself on a daily basis. Still, a capitalist state, even one with a decent number of checks and balances, creates many an opportunity for dishonest behaviour. Which is good news for private investigators like me. ScotPol, the national public order organization, needs all the help it can get. There's also an increased interest in reading about bad men and women, as well as in those who do the writing. Yes, one has become a published and lionized author. Put out more saltires and roaring big cats, but ditch the unicorns: we don't need any more mythical creatures, human or otherwise, in our brave new republic.

Then again, life isn't completely cloudless. My hair's gone as white as the braes, the Enlightenment-era fillings keep falling out of my teeth, and I'm heavier than my wife, adopted daughter and son standing on the scales together. When Edinburgh was independent, badly fed and either drenched by the Big Wet or sweating in the Big Heat, we had more pressing problems. Like staying alive, avoiding arrest, nailing our nefarious leaders . . . Maybe I took the latter more seriously than I should have.

But hark, the doorbell rings and, after I press the button, heavy boots thunder up the tenement stairs – sixty-four of them – with no reduction in speed as altitude is gained. My partner in battling crime. If not, my many enemies have finally decided to give me a terminal battering. The way I often feel, it would be a mercy. Like in the Sunnyland Slim song 'Be Careful How You Vote', you never know what's round the corner in a democracy creating more wealth than it knows what to do with.

At least in the benevolent dictatorship that used to run this city you knew whom to trust. No one.

ONE

After looking through the spyhole, I opened the door a split second before a large fist shivered my timber. Davie Oliphant stumbled over the threshold – I having neatly stepped to the side – and nearly went his length on the parquet floor.

'Bastard, Quint,' he said, regaining his balance. His large frame loomed over me, though the intimidation was leavened by his clothing. Davie hadn't got over not having to wear a City Guard uniform and his pale-blue herringbone jacket and grey trousers were ill-fitting and crumpled.

'Good afternoon to you too, big man. I think there's some shortbread.'

His expression lightened. 'How much shortbread?'

'An unopened tin.'

He headed for the kitchen. 'Sophia and the kids not around?'

'Violin lesson.'

Davie stopped rooting around in the cupboards. 'Heck's not even four yet.'

'For his sins, which are many, he's having to listen to Maisie.'

He grinned. 'She's great. Best eleven-year-old in Embra on that thing.'

'So they say. I still prefer the guitar.'

'Aye, right.' He ripped the lid from a red tartan tin. 'When are you going to put that blues band together?'

I was filling the kettle. 'When I have time.'

'I.e. never,' he said, spraying crumbs.

I shook my head despairingly and made coffee. You could get decent beans these days and I could afford them, but the memory of Enlightenment beverages was still hard to shift. Davie, my loyal sidekick for eighteen years, deserved the best, though I wasn't going to tell him that.

He ran a hand through his thick locks. 'I know,' he said, catching my eye. 'There are a few grey ones. But nothing like your white-out.'

'Detective Leader, I don't like your tone.' I put Maisie's *Beethoven is God* mug in front of him. 'Amend it or you'll get Hector's Highland cow drinking cup.'

'Yes, sir, right away, sir. Wait a minute – you're not my boss any more.' He inserted more shortbread into his maw. 'Away and boil your—'

'Who solved that bank robbery last month?'

Davie looked out of the window. The watery sun was failing over the New Town and lights were coming on in the windows across the garden space.

'According to the report, *I* did,' he said, avoiding my eyes.

'Uh-huh. Does your boss know you consult me?'

'I haven't said so, but of course she bloody does. Muriel's a bright spark. Helps that you're not on the payroll, mind.'

I poured the coffee. 'And my lack of security clearance?'

Davie laughed. 'You think she cares? Results are all that matter.'

'No change there, then.'

I shepherded him into the sitting room. Sophia had decorated and furnished it tastefully. Although we were on the highly desirable Great Scotland Street – originally Great King Street and, under the Enlightenment, Great Citizen Street – the place had been in a mess when we bought it. My first novelized memoir, *The Body Politic*, was published eighteen months back. It had been an instant success all over Scotland and soon after in the Scandinavian countries, followed by the German Federation (not including Bavaria, which was otherwise engaged trying to take over what remained of Austria) and those states of the former US and Canada that had returned to a degree of prosperity and literacy. Most of those were on the upper east and west coasts.

'Finished showing off about your second book?' Davie said. 'What's it called again?'

He knew very well it was called *Bone Yards*, not least because it was dedicated *to* him and featured a loosely disguised version *of* him.

'Yes, thanks. Sell-out crowd in the biggest theatre in Aberdeen.'

'Ooh la la, mon brave,' he said, in an execrable accent. Foreign languages had never been an Edinburgh strongpoint, except in the Tourism Directorate. Steps were being taken to rectify that, as Edinburgh was even more of a tourist attraction now.

'And the purpose of your visit is?' I inquired.

'Ah. You'll like this.'

'A murder?'

'You fiend. No, but not far off it. Laddie in Leith strangled. The paramedics managed to save him.'

'Gang-related?' Edinburgh's port had been a stronghold of violent criminals even under the Council's supposedly iron grip.

'Not sure. A witness said the aggressor was a tree with a fishtail.'

'You've got my attention. Let's go.' I was interested all right but, with the year-round festival even more all-encompassing than under the Enlightenment, people dressed in silly costumes was an Edinburgh way of life.

Davie gulped down his coffee. 'Aren't you going to tell Sophia?'

I wrote a note. The prospect of calling her late on Saturday afternoon wasn't enticing. It was supposed to be family night. The truth was, she and I hadn't been getting on for some months. I could spend time with the kids tomorrow. I loved them, especially wee Heck, but I got bored easily. That's what came of being a writer – I always want to be alone. Then again, I was currently blocked worse than the side roads across the country.

Davie was driving the ScotPol Korean four-by-four at his usual breakneck speed over the setts. 'Nice flat, that. I still don't understand how you can afford it. You can't have made that much from the writing.'

'You're wrong, my friend,' I said, putting on the wire-rimmed glasses I'd recently been prescribed. Presbyopia, the optician said. Most older people got it. I said I was only fifty-four and he smiled sympathetically. I almost broke *his* glasses. 'Advances from here and other countries, radio, film and TV rights, merchandising . . .'

He guffawed. 'Don't tell me there's going to be a Quintilian Dalrymple action figure?'

I gave him a sharp look. 'If there is, his slob of a sidekick will have to appear too.'

That got me a glare. 'I didn't agree to that.' There was a pause. 'Anything in it for me?'

I laughed. 'You know fine well that my number two in the books is called Andy and he's got red hair – nothing like you.'

'Bastard.'

'If you call me that again . . .'

'You'll what? Piss on my foot?' He grunted. 'I suppose that thieving bawbag Billy Geddes is doing the deals.'

'Aye, but he takes a hefty percentage.'

'Poor, poor pitiful you.' Davie had recently become a fan of the long-late, magnificent Warren Zevon, whose music had become popular since censorship was lifted. At least I hadn't become Quint the Headless Thompson Gunner. Yet.

On Goldenacre we passed what used to be Scott, one of the twenty barracks for Enlightenment bureaucrats and Guard personnel. It had been sold to a Finnish bank which gutted it and replaced the cladding. Everything was up for grabs in Edinburgh and across the country. The government took its cut. Since the oil and gas fields off the northwest coast had come on stream, the country was awash with money. Finland was one of many states buying various kinds of fuel. The irony was that Scotland itself was fully supplied by renewables. That technology was sold too, but at very high prices. There were those – not only in the ScotGreen Party – who said it was a disgrace our leaders were selling resources that made the effects of climate change worse. I sympathized. On the other hand, wealthier Scots, Finns and many others bought my books and I had a family to look after. Sophia would dispute that. She didn't like me raking up the past and she had a decent enough salary as one of the city's few pathologists – though she'd had to learn a lot about contemporary techniques and equipment since the modern world and its cadavers entered the morgue.

Heavy drizzle was now falling in the glow from the streetlights.

'At least it isn't snow,' Davie said, as he turned on to Ferry Road.

'Give it time,' I said, leaning back in the seat. I was thinking about Sophia's view of my books. Maybe she was right. Digging up the ghastly remains of the city's thirty-year experiment with supposedly benevolent totalitarianism wasn't good for the soul, let alone the body. I was eating too much and getting through substantially more whisky than before. Even expensive single malts did your head in, eventually. I'd lost myself with the end of the Council and writing about old cases was a desperate attempt to regain my identity. Why wasn't my new and successful life in the thriving reunified country enough? Why did I feel the need to dash off with Davie every time he brought me a case? It wasn't just a desire to help him. My family wasn't enough for me. Sophia wasn't enough.

'That bad?' Davie said, nudging me with his elbow.

I held back from answering.

'You miss it, don't you?' He paused. 'I do too, even though we lived like dogs and the Enlightenment lost its way in a big . . . you know what I mean.'

I nodded. 'The party was a necessity when the country fell apart and the drugs gangs ran riot. Firm control. It's happened all over the world. We were just quicker off the mark.'

'But there were places that loosened their grip on people earlier than we did.'

'There were.' I turned to him. 'I believed in Enlightenment principles – guaranteed work and housing for all, free lifelong education, no personal wealth. Now we've got thirty TV channels and our own cars and mobile phones, how much better off are we?'

Davie stopped at a red light. 'Look at them,' he said, nodding towards the people crossing the road. 'Their lives have improved and you know it.'

I sighed. 'Yes, I do. And we were responsible for denying them all but the basics.'

The aggrieved faces of Edinburgh citizens at the Truth and Reconciliation Hearings in the gothic Assembly Hall three years ago rose up before me . . .

'. . . Quintilian Eric Dalrymple, we will first hear the accusations against you,' said the elderly South African convenor, a black man with white hair. 'You will then have the opportunity to explain your actions.'

At the table to the judge's left, I breathed in deeply, trying to calm my pounding heart. The fact that my middle name had been made public for the first time didn't help, nor did Davie's wide eyes and expanding grin from the front row. My maternal grandfather had been given the 'E' name after the Olympic gold-medal-winning runner Eric Liddell. I'd always hated it. QED my backside.

'Bell 03 was your barracks number before you were demoted,' said my accusers' lawyer, a fleshy Glaswegian in an expensive suit.

The Council's Edinburgh had done away with his kind, the Public Order Directorate making what were called 'informed judgements', and our new breed were still in training.

'It was,' I confirmed.

'And you were the author of the City Guard bible, *Public Order in Practice*.'

So that was his angle of attack. 'The first two editions only,' I said. 'After I left the Guard, amendments that I wouldn't have countenanced were made.'

The advocate, one Peter Adamson, looked at me dubiously. 'There were still plenty of harsh directives in your versions. For example, in the first edition, citizens who used firearms against the Guard were to be executed.'

I couldn't deny it. 'That was during the war against the drugs gangs. Most of them weren't Edinburgh citizens.'

'My brother Richie was!' shouted a red-faced middle-aged woman from the second row.

'Indeed,' said Adamson. 'Richie Elliot was born and brought up in Portobello.'

'He was also a known drug dealer who joined one of the most vicious gangs – Howlin' Wolf's.' I felt a twinge of apprehension. The gangs were all mad blues fans because the Council had banned that music as subversive. That was why I liked it too. But the Wolf and his people were merciless.

'According to the Public Order Directorate archive, your squad came under fire from the gang in Barnton.'

I nodded. 'The Wolf operated near the city line. His men slaughtered hundreds of citizens in the outer suburbs.'

'But after you returned fire,' Adamson said, moving on swiftly, 'nine of your assailants surrendered and threw down their weapons.'

'Which meant nothing.'

'I beg your pardon?'

I raised my shoulders. 'Guard personnel were often killed or injured by criminals who had reserve weapons behind their backs.'

The advocate looked at his notes. 'But these nine did not. Some time passed after they were searched and then you had them lined up against a wall and shot.'

I didn't feel great about that, I never had. 'You have to understand. The city was at war. There weren't the facilities or provisions to keep prisoners. We tried at first, but they would escape and rejoin their gangs. Our casualties were high and we had to fight any way we could.' I was careful not to say that I was obeying Council orders. The responsibility as commander on the ground was mine.

'Murderer!' the woman screamed, getting to her feet. 'Monster!'

The convenor looked over his half-moon glasses. 'Madam, this is not appropriate. You will have an opportunity to speak shortly.'

'To hell wi' you! What dae you ken aboot Embra?' She only sat down after a glare from Adamson.

In fact, the convenor, whose identity had been kept secret to avoid recriminations, was well aware of what had gone on in the city, having led a group of his own staff through the archives for six months. The new Edinburgh Municipal Board had given him full access. He'd been involved in South Africa's Truth and Reconciliation Commission as a young man and had unrivalled experience of the relevant procedures.

'Madam,' he said patiently, 'the governing principle of these hearings is that people said to have committed crimes are brought face to face with their accusers and given a chance to explain themselves. If they accept responsibility and display contrition, they will receive an amnesty. This is a procedure that was proposed by your own elected representatives and overwhelmingly approved in a municipal referendum.'

'Amnesty?' the woman shouted, on her feet again. 'Travesty more like.' She pointed at me. 'That man's a killer, pure and simple.'

The advocate waved at her to sit down. 'It is in everyone's interest that we comport ourselves in a civilized fashion,' he said. All that got him was a pair of V-signs, which he ignored.

To my relief, he moved on from Richie Elliot. I'd had the worst of dealings with the Howlin' Wolf gang and a particular piece of shit in it. I blinked to dispel a vision of the psychopath in question.

I was examined for two weeks. I'd made a lot of enemies during the years I was in the Guard and there was no shortage of citizens who hated me from the subsequent years when I acted as a freelance investigator for the Council. On the other hand, my refusal to maintain hardline directives when they were no longer necessary and my subsequent demotion from the rank of auxiliary impressed people, as did the many cases when I'd cleared out corrupt guardians and their adherents. The advocate whom I'd recently sacked advised me to have the faded DM tattoo on the back of my right hand inked back in. No chance. It was my body now, not the city's. There were citizens prepared to put in good words for me and the fact that I showed regret for many of my actions eventually stood me in good stead. But it was a close-run thing.

It was the final accusation that nearly did for me. I'd ridden a storm about my mother, who had been an uncompromising senior guardian – though it helped that my father had resigned in disillusion from the rank of guardian. I'd even got away with being a school and university friend of Billy Geddes, who'd been behind many of the illicit money-making schemes that had brought down his superiors; at his own hearing later, he managed to show sufficient fake repentance that, to my astonishment, he was amnestied and went straight back to his old ways. Then came my nemesis.

We were supposed to be told in advance of our accusers, but sometimes – deliberately – we were caught on the hop to see how we reacted. I knew as soon as I saw the wizened young man limping painfully into the hall that I was in a vat of excrement. Davie didn't look too chipper either.

Peter Adamson, who had become more and more frustrated by my slipping off his hooks, licked his lips. It was cold in the former council chamber that day and I remembered numerous occasions when I'd had strips torn off me by various guardians who were either dead or had long departed the city. There had been a crew of young idealists known as the Iron Boyscouts who had conducted meetings while walking around in true Platonic style – the ancient philosopher had been the Council's inspiration. They denied he was the ur-fascist, of course. I wished I could have walked around now – around to the exit.

'Quintilian *Eric* Dalrymple' – the advocate had registered that I didn't like my full name – 'you are accused that, on November the ninth, 2033, you brought about the crippling of Michael Joseph Garden and failed to investigate adequately the disappearance of his sister Amy.' He gave me a scathing look. 'Her mutilated body was found in the basement of number twenty-three Bruntsfield Place over a month later. How do you answer?'

Every investigator fails on occasion, but this one had been

particularly hard to bear. We'd been tipped off that Garden, who was only twenty-four at the time, was working for the Dead Men, a gang of brutal Glasgow smugglers. Firearms they'd brought in had led to the deaths of several innocent citizens. Davie had insisted that his team went in fully armed. I had a Hyper-Stun, a recently introduced device that could deliver electrical charges of varying strength. Not that I used it.

'That was . . . a mistake,' I said, trying to catch Michael Garden's eye. He was looking intently at the convenor. 'A set-up. Citizen . . . Mr Garden had refused to let his sister go out with a member of the Portobello Pish . . .'

'One of the most violent gangs in the city,' said the old judge.

I nodded. 'They decided to do the dirty on him. Told us he was a dangerous subversive, responsible for the deaths of two people, including a nine-year-old child.' I paused, recalling the scene at the Garden family flat in Newington. It was well looked after, with ornaments and wallpaper that had recently become available after the Council's loosening of trading regulations. His parents, both teachers, were at work at evening classes.

'Before the door was smashed down, Mr Garden heard you order Guard personnel to shoot on sight,' said Adamson, with a look of disgust. 'Can that be true? This was years after the drugs wars. Edinburgh was safe.'

I could have argued that Newington was equidistant from the centre and the still ravaged suburbs, but I didn't. The case had kept me awake for weeks before and after we found Amy. Plus, Davie and I had come straight from a shootout in Silverknowes in which a guardswoman had been killed and one of her male comrades seriously injured.

'I did give that order,' I said. Actually, I hadn't. Davie had, but I wasn't going to drop him in it – he had his own hearing coming up. I blinked in his direction to stop him jumping to his feet. 'I'm sorry I did. Mr Garden quite reasonably ran in the opposite direction and was shot above the knee.' He was still refusing to look at me. 'I regret the incident immensely and ask forgiveness.'

None was forthcoming. I couldn't blame him. He'd been in hospital for months and had lost much of the stricken leg. I'd contributed to a collection for a decent prosthesis – everyone in the squad had – but, again, I kept that to myself.

'That's very big of you,' said the advocate. 'And what about Amy Garden?'

An image of the seventeen-year-old flashed before me. She was a slim, blonde girl with striking blue eyes whose only mistake had been to fall in love with a scumbag. Michael Garden's shooting hadn't been enough for the Pish. They raped and murdered her, only telling us where she was after we'd searched half the city. The wrong half, it turned out.

Davie's voice boomed out. 'It's not true that we didn't look for her the best we could! Citizen . . . Mr Dalrymple was not responsible. I was.'

I raised my hand and eventually he sat down. 'No. The decision to reallocate some personnel after two weeks was mine.' In fact, it was the Public Order Guardian's but that individual wouldn't be appearing at any hearing because he was dead. In any case, I hadn't objected. There was an upsurge in crime in the period before the overthrow of the Council. 'Again, I regret it enormously and offer my deepest sympathies to Mr Garden.'

Finally, he turned his eyes on me. 'Fuck your regret and sympathy, you piece of shite,' he said in a low, venomous voice. 'You know what happened to ma parents? Dead, both of them, two weeks after Amy was found. Hanged themselves together in the bathroom. Can you live with that, Dalrymple? Cos I cannae.' He pulled a knife from his pocket and ran it along his throat in a single, blurred movement. People pushed away from him, screaming, as the blood fountained.

The hearing was immediately adjourned.

The following week, the convenor called me to appear again.

'Mr Dalrymple, you are in no way responsible for what that poor, misguided man did.'

'Yes, I am,' I said firmly.

The judge shook his head. 'I am minded to offer you a full amnesty because of your indubitable contrition. But it can only apply if you accept it.'

Sophia was in the front row, paler than ever. She knew that other Council operatives who had refused amnesty were in jail. That morning she'd told me I had a duty to her and the kids – wee Heck was only a couple of months old at the time – to stay with them. But I had some kind of death wish, as if the weight of all the violence I'd perpetrated on behalf of the Council had hit me at last.

'I will not accept amnesty for this,' I said, catching the convenor's eye.

There was loud whispering in the hall. Sophia was looking down, her ice-blonde hair pointing at me like a featureless, ghostly face. From that moment things were never the same between us.

'You will,' came a firm voice from behind me.

The noise stopped immediately.

I turned to see Lachie MacFarlane, provost of the Municipal Board that had taken over from the Council, standing on a chair. Although he was only four feet seven inches in height, he dominated the space. Behind him stood his deputy, Rory Campbell.

'Quint Dalrymple was one of the saviours of this city,' Lachie said. 'Without him, the revolution would not have succeeded and countless lives would have been lost.' He smiled at me sadly. 'I know how much he is haunted by the decisions he had to take, both as a member of the City Guard and as an often-unwilling servant of the Public Order Directorate after his demotion. I am here to publicly offer my support and to beg him to accept the offer of amnesty.'

'As am I,' said Rory, his actor's voice carrying to the four walls.

I looked at Sophia. She nodded once, her lips set in a straight line.

So I buckled. But I couldn't get the sight of Amy Garden's ruined body from my mind for months. It still comes back, one of the legions of revenants from the Enlightenment Party's well-intentioned but ultimately tainted regime. Of course, for some Edinburgh citizens the fact that the two most powerful men in the city intervened to keep me out of jail made me even more unacceptable. Even now, they turn up at bookshop and library events and heckle. Good for them.

'Quint? Hallooooo?'

I opened my eyes and took in the scene. The orange glow of streetlights, not all of them operational, was obscured by heavier rain. I could make out tenements a lot less salubrious than those in the New Town.

'Where are we?'

'Madeira Street.'

'Brilliant. Our family dentist was round the corner. I still hate this area.'

Davie handed me a blue-and-white ScotPol umbrella. 'Come on. Time to be mystified.'

I followed him to the door of number thirty-five. A pair of junior officers, one male and one female, stood on either side of the entrance. Both were in high-visibility jackets, the peaks of their uniform caps making the icy water cascade in front of their faces.

'Sir,' said the woman, with a faint smile.

Davie returned it. I might have known. He'd always been one for putting himself about. Ironically, that was more likely to get him in trouble now than during the Council's time. Hel Hyslop, the less-than-user-friendly director of the nation's police force, had made it clear that fraternization between officers of different rank was a sacking offence.

'Anything to report?' Davie said, turning his gaze on the male officer.

'No, sir . . . nothing, sir,' he stammered. He couldn't have been on the force for more than a month.

'No one showing any interest,' confirmed the woman, whose name badge identified her as C. Badenoch, a good Highland name. ScotPol regulations required fifty per cent of officers in each city or region to be non-local. The idea was to avoid over-familiarity and the corruption it could engender.

Davie led me inside. There was an unusually large common area on the ground floor. The bicycles that every citizen had during the Enlightenment were still numerous, but at the rear a white crime scene tent had been erected. The shadow of a bent figure was visible in the powerful lights.

'Your favourite Glaswegian,' Davie said, in a loud whisper.

'Detective Leader,' said the man wearing white coverall and bootees. He was tall and thin, his face disfigured by a ludicrous Zapata moustache. His name was Graham Arthur, a mixture of first and surnames that made me smile. Graham Arthur What? He glanced at me. 'Ah, Mr Bad Penny.'

'That'll do,' Davie said, 'or you'll be on the next train to the great green place.' His tone expressed what he felt about Glasgow, which had been known as the Wild West until the authorities managed to overturn the open-carry law. Glaswegians were still allowed to own personal weapons but had to keep them in their homes. Which didn't stop Saturday-night not-at-all-OK gunfights. 'What have you got for us?'

Arthur pointed to the array of sealed evidence bags on the table in the tent. 'There's no lack of material, but I gather twenty-three people live on this stair, so most of it will turn out to be irrelevant.' He gave a smile that revealed gleaming white teeth. Those, more than his accent, distinguished him as an outsider. 'These are the business.' He picked up two bags. 'Care to show off your skills, Mr Dalrymple?'

I could never resist a challenge and took out my pocket magnifying glass. 'Bits of tree bark in this one,' I said. The second was hard to make out in the light. 'Fish scales. A large cod, perhaps?'

'Perhaps?' said Arthur, unimpressed by my lack of certainty. I'd never claimed to be an ichthyologist. 'So the individual who dressed up as a tree and fish took his costume seriously.'

Davie gave him a dubious look. 'That'll be my area of specialization. Anything else?'

'What was the assailant wearing on his or her feet?' I asked. 'I assume the fish made up the bottom half?'

The SOCO nodded. 'I don't deal in assumptions, but that was what the witness said, was it not, Detective Leader?'

'Aye,' said Davie. 'Makes sense – fish go deep and trees go high.'

He was right, in his inimitable way, but an image I couldn't identify was floating at the edge of my consciousness.

Graham Arthur gave another of his blinding smiles. 'And fish don't walk. There are numerous footprints and the rain hasn't exactly made it easy to separate one from another. However, I have good prints from the victim, who was wearing a pair of trainers with a complicated pattern.' He found a photo on his camera. There was a mass of knots and crosses.

'So anything near those, ideally behind them, will be the assailant's,' I said.

The SOCO found another photo. It was a mess of different prints, many of them smudged. 'I'll see what I can do in the lab,' he said.

'You do that,' Davie said brusquely. 'Come on, Quint.'

'Hang on,' I said, kneeling down. 'What are these marks? Looks like something's been swished across the floor. Like a narrow tail?' Arthur nodded. 'My initial conclusion too.'

I followed Davie up a staircase that was well worn but didn't have the stench of Enlightenment times. People didn't boil cabbage and turnips much these days – ready meals, mostly made in Fife, were the thing. Money had been invested in the sewage system too.

Davie nodded at another female officer, but she responded by standing to attention. One who resisted his charms, such as they were. He was in his forties now and carrying plenty of weight, though most of it, unlike mine, was muscle. She must have been about his age, but was whiplash thin.

'There have been no visitors, Detective Leader,' she said, ignoring me. I suspected she knew who I was and didn't approve of civilian involvement in ScotPol cases. Not many officers did.

'I take it the witness has stayed inside,' I said.

She – T. Fabianski – kept her eyes to the front. 'My instructions were to keep her here and I have fulfilled them to the letter.'

I smiled at her, having remembered she was a former member of the City Guard. Many of them never got past the fact that I'd been demoted. ScotPol wouldn't have found enough volunteers to fill its ranks in Edinburgh if it hadn't allowed in former members of the Enlightenment. They had to go through a rigorous process of de-auxiliarification – only a former auxiliary could have come up with that term, let alone pronounced it.

Davie knocked on the door. It was opened by a youngish woman with thin brown hair hanging loosely on both sides of a pockmarked face.

'Ann Melville?' Davie said, holding up his ID.

She scrutinized the embossed card and then looked at me. 'Quint Dalrymple? What an honour!' Irony dripped from her words. Yet another citizen holding a grievance. I thought of the Truth and Reconciliation Hearing again. So much for amnesty.

'You don't have to invite me in,' I said.

She laughed. 'I know how you and the big man here work. Besides, I've got nothing to hide. Just don't expect me to make tea or open a bottle.'

We followed her down a dim hallway and entered a living room that was lit up like a Christmas tree. The Council had banned

Christmas so, like everything else that had been absent from Edinburgh for thirty years, it was now extremely popular.

'It's not even Advent,' I observed.

'Every day is Christmas Day in the new Scotland,' Miss Melville said. This time the irony was restrained, but present all the same. Some people were already disappointed by the way the state was operating. Me among them, though as a practising sceptic I'd never had the greatest expectations.

We weren't invited to sit down. That suited Davie, who wasn't keen on intimate interviewing.

'Tell us what you saw, please,' he said, pulling out a recording device.

I was still using a notebook, in which I jotted down what had happened. After I'd got to five question marks, I raised a hand.

'Miss Melville, I'm having trouble making sense of this.'

The young woman gave me a disparaging look. 'Too hard for you? Stick to making up stories, then.' She angled her head to the bookshelf behind her. I saw copies of my books. 'Those are called novelized memoirs, eh? But really they're just novels, right? Made up, I mean.'

'They're whatever the reader wants to make of them,' I said, reluctant to carry on the conversation about the genre I was experimenting with. 'You say the aggressor was already in the entrance hall when you came in.'

She raised her shoulders. 'So?'

'But that you didn't notice him or her till you were halfway up the first flight of stairs?'

'Right.'

'I've seen the lighting. It's remarkably bright. Is there somewhere the tree-fish could have been hiding? Is there a back door?'

'You can't get out that way. There's been a sinkhole in the garden for a couple of months and the door's blocked up.'

I glanced at Davie, who nodded confirmation.

'Maybe he was hiding behind the bikes,' Ann Melville said. 'Or in a corner. I don't know.' There were spots of red on her cheekbones.

'But you *did* see the victim.'

'Jack Nicol? He was bending over his bike, chaining it up. I said "hi" to him, even though he's a piece of dung.'

She didn't like the guy who had nearly died – that was interesting.

I kept at her. 'If you were only a few steps up the stairs, why didn't you run back to help?'

'Are you mad?' she said, voice shrill. 'There was a gun on his belt, a big pistol. I'm no' stupid.'

'So you called for help?'

'I . . . yes, I did.'

Davie took a step towards the witness. 'Nobody else heard anything. You didn't contact ScotPol either.'

'Aye, I did!' Ann Melville's eyes were bulging, as was a vein that ran down the middle of her forehead.

'At five thirty-seven,' said Davie. 'Just over an hour after the assailant was seen getting into a Land Rover outside.'

'Any photos?' I asked.

She shook her head, eyes down. 'My phone's rubbish, I never use the camera.'

Davie frowned. 'So you were frit and ran up here, leaving Jack Nicol to what was very nearly his death.'

Ann Melville shrugged. 'None of my business. Nicol's lowlife; I hate his guts.'

'Can you expand on your description of the tree-fish?' I said. 'Height?'

'The top of the vertical branches would have been about six foot, I suppose. No horizontal ones. The fabric looked like bark and there were holes cut out for eyes, so it could have been anyone. Christ, it stank.' She shuddered. 'And the hands that were holding the rope had long, spiky fingers. Not five – only three.'

I broke off from the sketch I was making. 'What kind of footwear?'

She stared at me. 'I don't . . . oh, I see what you mean. Well, the tail, it wasn't wide, stuck out like a snake. I can't remember seeing feet.' She grinned mockingly. 'Anyway, fish haven't got feet.'

I finished my sketch and showed it to her.

Ann Melville's eyes widened. 'That's exactly right. How did you know?'

'Let's go,' I said to Davie. 'I don't think you need to keep a guard outside.'

'What?' said the woman. 'I'm under threat here.'

I held the sketch before her eyes. 'Something you haven't told us?'

'I . . . well . . .' Ann Melville's bravado had disappeared. 'That monster – it saw me. It'll know I'm talking to you.'

'So what?' said Davie. 'It's not like you've identified him or her.'

'It doesn't know that.'

'How could you have?' I asked.

She grabbed my arm. 'Keep the guard, promise me!'

I raised my shoulders. 'If you can add to your statement . . .'

'It . . . it spoke to me.' Now she was shaking like a leaf. 'High voice, slow, really creepy.'

'Well?' said Davie, after a pause. 'What did it say?'

'The . . . the end of the world's coming for you . . . soon.' She sat down hard on the sofa.

We left the officer where she was.

'Let's see what you drew,' Davie said, as we went downstairs. I handed him my notebook. 'Very artistic. What is it?'

'It's a detail from *The Temptation of St Anthony* by Hieronymus Bosch.'

'The guy who did hell and the demons?' Art history had been a feature of Enlightenment learning, so he wasn't completely out of his depth.

I nodded.

'And what was it doing here?'

'Detective Leader, I haven't the faintest idea.'

In the street, we crossed to the other side and spoke briefly to the witness who had seen the Land Rover. He was old and doddery, the lenses of his glasses in serious need of a clean. He confirmed that the figure had been a tree-and-fish hybrid and that it had climbed into a Land Rover, but he hadn't seen the driver, never mind noted the registration number. The City Guard used to run Land Rovers, but since they had been kitted out with the Korean four-by-fours still used by ScotPol in Edinburgh, the city was full of clapped-out old machines that had been sold on.

'Your people are canvassing about the victim?' I said, as we got back into the vehicle.

'Aye, Jack Nicol's got to be the centre of interest now. Why was he attacked by that thing?'

'Have your people checked if there are any Bosch-themed shows in the festival?'

'No,' he said, turning the key in the ignition. 'Yes. There aren't.'

'That would have been too easy.'

'And there are no reports of similar in the ScotPol database.' He pulled away into the gloom. 'Where to now?'

'The infirmary. Maybe our suspicious victim will have woken up.'

I thought of Sophia and the kids. I should call. The fact that Sophia hadn't rung showed how little she approved of what I was doing on a Saturday night.

Then I remembered another detail – or rather a major point – about the tree-fish in the painting: it was carrying a swaddled infant.

I rang Sophia immediately and confirmed that she and the kids were all right. Wee Heck wasn't an infant, but the idea was close enough to the bone.

It wouldn't have been the first time a case had turned out to be about me.

I needed to puncture the Enlightenment-inflated sense of my own importance. In any case, a tree-fish wasn't so bad. Bosch had come up with many more horrific creatures.

So had Enlightenment Edinburgh. So too, I suspected, might the reconstituted state of Scotland.

TWO

The chill rain was horizontal by the time we got to the infirmary. The city's main hospital was still in the Victorian buildings in Lauriston Place, though the new facility out in Little France was nearly ready. Just as well. After thirty years of Council spending restrictions, the old place was coming apart, and not just at the seams. There had been a battle there during the revolution; Sophia, who, as Medical Guardian, had refused to leave her patients, had been wounded.

Davie and I ran across the courtyard, past a pair of brand-new ambulances. The money from the oil and gas reserves in the open sea beyond Cape Wrath in Sutherland was being allocated all over Scotland – hence the new hospital as well as the bright white body-mobiles.

'Nearly blind,' he said, sleeve over his eyes. 'That rain's like bullets made of ice.'

'Mainstay of many a crap crime story, especially ones set in locked rooms.'

'Aye, right.' He went to find out where Jack Nicol was. 'Second floor,' he said, heading for the stairs.

The lifts were slow. People not in the know stood hopefully at the doors. Although there were fewer evening clinics than there used to be, the medical staff still worked long hours to improve the health of Edinburgh folk. The Council had done what it could, but the city missed out on decades of progress in equipment and drugs. That was changing for the better.

A nurse took us to a small room with two male police officers standing outside.

'Visitors?' Davie asked.

'No one at all, sir,' said the broader of the men, his accent local.

'Either a saddo or a bad boy,' said the other, in the guttural tones of the central belt.

If it was the latter, none of his associates would show their faces, to avoid being linked to him. Then again, one of them – women included – might have been the aggressor. But why dress up as a creature from Bosch?

The patient was awake, a neck brace restricting his movements. His eyes made up for that by darting all over the room. They didn't stay on us for long.

'Right, ya piece of dung Hibee,' said Davie, leaning over him, 'who wants you deid apart from me?'

The young man had a shaved head with a football tattooed on it in the green and white of Hibernian. Davie's heart belonged to that team's deadly rivals, Heart of Midlothian. There was a Scottish Championship now and the Edinburgh teams were up against serious opposition. Football had been banned until the last years of the Council so a lot of fast-forward catching-up was having to be done, much to the amusement of the five Glasgow mega-teams.

'Naebody,' Nicol muttered, eyes down.

'Did you see your attacker?' I asked, with a smile. Soft ex-cop.

He tried to shake his head and immediately regretted it. 'Nuh. Didnae see nothin'.'

'So you don't know who it was?' Davie roared into the patient's right ear.

'Nuh,' the patient said, putting a hand to his ear. 'Leave us alone.'

I took out my notebook and found the sketch.

Jack Nicol stared at it blankly, but I was pretty sure there was a flicker of recognition. 'Whit the hell's that?'

'A tree-fish, obviously,' I said.

'Tae hell wi' that.' He shifted his eyes away.

I nodded. 'Hell is where it's from, all right.'

'I dinnae ken nothin'.'

Davie was close to detonating, but he managed to stay within ScotPol guidelines for dealing with people under suspicion if they had been hospitalized. The shaved one's lawyer was no doubt on his way, ready to make the most of his primary status as a victim.

'Suit yourself,' Davie said. 'But we're looking into your professional activities, son. I don't think you'll be seeing your own bed for a while.' He scowled.

I watched him stomp over to the door and then went up to the bed. 'Give me a name,' I said. 'I can help you.'

Nicol laughed. 'Quint fuckin' Dalrymple, the Council's toy boy. You're no' even a cop now.'

'Which is why you can trust me more than the big man.'

'Fuck ye.'

I held up the sketch again. 'You've seen this before, haven't you? Where?'

He closed his eyes.

After about a minute, I turned away.

Then, as I reached the door, the patient said three words that piqued my interest.

'Theatre of Life.'

The trip had been worth it.

It was after ten when I got back to the flat. I tried to make as little noise as possible opening the door. Sophia often went to bed early with Heck. She wasn't the only female in the place, though.

Maisie, eleven in body but sixty in mind, stood in the hall, arms akimbo. 'And where do you think you've been, Quilp?' She called me after Dickens's malevolent dwarf when she disapproved. Which was happening more and more.

'Case,' I said. 'Interesting one. I'll tell you about it, if you like.'
'Spare me,' she said, turning away. 'You were supposed to be with us.' The door of her bedroom closed behind her.

Sophia appeared from the adjoining room, hair in disorder, rubbing her eyes. She peered at me dubiously, presumably having taken out her contact lenses. There had been no such thing in the Council's Edinburgh. I hadn't been as brave as her – the idea of something on my eyeballs made me squirm – so I used glasses, admittedly much higher quality than those issued by the Medical Directorate. And I had to pay for them.

'For goodness' sake, Quint,' Sophia said, wrapping her arms round herself, not that it was cold in the flat. 'Heck was asking for you all evening. He cried himself to sleep.'

I took a step forward, then stopped. Her expression didn't invite greater proximity. I took in her lined face and the rings under her eyes. She was thinner than she used to be and the veins in her hands stood out.

'I'm sorry,' I said, hearing the inadequacy of the words. 'Davie had . . . had a case he needed help with.'

'Stop it, Quint!' she said, her voice loud enough to wake the street, never mind Heck. We waited, but there was no crying. Sophia went into the kitchen and took a bottle of white wine from the fridge. 'Just stop it.' She poured herself a glass, hand shaking. 'Davie doesn't need your help – he knows what he's doing by now.' She gulped wine. 'We've been over this a thousand times. Weekends are for family. No exceptions – unless you're writing.'

That had been a hard-won concession and it only gave me two hours each Saturday and Sunday, but, though I should have been, I wasn't writing these days. Writer's block in pyramid dimensions.

I wasn't going to make excuses. 'I'll take them out tomorrow,' I said, moving towards the bottle.

Sophia took a step back. 'You're bloody right you will. I have a job, remember? One that requires me to bone up on new research. I need time in the study too.' She emptied her glass and brushed past me on the way to the bedroom.

So much for family time, but I wasn't brave enough to say that aloud.

I poured wine into a glass with *Frida Kahlo, Legend* printed above an image of the Mexican artist's face that emphasized her monobrow and moustache. Maisie was a big Frida fan. She was keen on her politics too. I'd had to escort her to several meetings of the Edinburgh branch of the Scottish Communist Party. They hadn't done well in either the municipal or national elections. People were into individual liberty – too much so, I was beginning to think. Strangling people dressed up as monsters from Bosch?

Which prompted me. I had a tattered volume about the artist that I'd found in one of the many second-hand bookshops that had sprung up after the Municipal Board cleared out old books from the city's libraries. It had even found the funds to buy new ones, including mine, which were often returned with profanities scribbled over the deathful prose.

Our study was a small windowless space connecting the sitting room with Heck's bedroom. With Davie's help, I'd put shelves on all four walls. They were almost full, with Sophia's medical text-books taking up just over one. My main hobby nowadays was building my library. For research purposes, of course. The Scottish Revenue (ScotRev – someone in the administration had a deep love of Scot as a prefix – ScotMad, perhaps) allowed me to claim the cost back as expenses, though getting receipts out of some of the dealers was difficult. My burgeoning collection of art books was in the tall shelf on the longer wall. The guardians had encour-aged citizens to study fine art, but in typical fashion had restricted works by artists they did not approve of – no Pop Art (I wasn't rushing to change that), ancient Roman statuary (too derivative of the Greek) or religious painting – Bosch had been allowed, though not much taught, because his work was deemed to be sufficiently questioning about religious belief. Although religion itself hadn't been banned, the regime was atheist and there were only a few surviving members of the Church of Scotland. In the new Scotland, there was freedom of religion, but that hadn't exactly led to a stampede back to the churches, many of which had been turned into night-clubs and carpet shops. I could remember the latter from when I was a kid – some things always come back.

Overtly religious art I could take or leave, but the creations of the masters were impossible to ignore. I had books on Michelangelo, Leonardo, El Greco and so on. But I found artists who depicted the essence of men and women more interesting – the elder Brueghel, for one, Rembrandt and van Gogh for two more. Hieronymus Bosch fell between the sacred and profane. His religious figures were often surrounded by ordinary people engaging their baser instincts. This was the case with the Lisbon triptych of *The Temptation of St Anthony*. St Anthony himself is located in the centre of the middle panel, but he is almost a minor player, surrounded by monsters and demons in numerous bestial forms. The tree-fish is to the right, carrying a baby in swaddling clothes and sitting on a red robe on the back of a giant rat – presumably not, in pre-Sherlock Holmes days, from Sumatra. In the background a village burns and the sky is filled by hybrid beasts and a strange armoured ship. If you didn't know that St Anthony eventually prevailed, you wouldn't give much for his chances.

But what had this to do with the attempted strangling in Leith? Ann Melville hadn't mentioned any baby, and it would be difficult to strangle someone while carrying one, even in the marsupial pouches that were currently a craze among Edinburgh parents. And anyway, why dress up like a tree-fish when there were any number of more vicious, arms-bearing demons on display? Was Bosch the point? He was best known for his visions of heaven, earth and hell? Did someone think that Edinburgh was going to the underworld in a supermarket trolley? Was that evidence of a hankering after the Enlightenment? There was a local political party that propounded some of the Council's more benevolent views, but no one paid much attention to them.

I turned on the desktop computer. It was much smaller and faster than those that the City Guard used to have, and there were even so-called laptops to be bought now – but they were beyond my pocket. The national government's aim was to connect every home to ScotNet, the official web provider. That was going well in the big cities, but I doubted many people in the remoter parts of the Highlands and Islands were hooked up. I tried to access scholarly articles on the painting, but there were only a few that you didn't have to pay for, and they didn't mention the tree-fish. It was a disturbing image – the sinister face, probably female, inside the tree trunk with its narrow scaly tail didn't look to have the baby's best interests to the fore. Tree? Fish? What was Bosch getting at? And what was the failed strangler implying? All I could think of was change, metamorphosis, mutability. Those applied to the process

Edinburgh and the rest of the nation were going through, but the specifics made no sense. Maybe the victim had fathered a child and abandoned it, so this was nothing more than a case of revenge. I doubted it.

My eyes strayed over the rest of the painting. Horror and disgust were the emotions it evoked, with its grotesque rotten fruit, freakish figures and their miasmic malevolence.

Then, with the ease of a man much older than I was, I fell asleep . . .

. . . to wake with my face on *The Temptation of St Anthony*, jerking my head back when I saw the pig's snout of a man with an owl on his head. I hoped I hadn't caught a plague of monsters. Then I was invaded by two.

'Dadda, dada, dada!' said Heck, embracing my leg and biting it.

'Ooyah,' I said, lifting him up. 'We said your teeth are only for food, didn't we?'

'And toothbrush, dada, dada, dada,' the wee smartarse said, with a wicked smile.

A pair of fingers pinched my neck. 'And didn't *we* say no sleeping on desk or sofa?' said Maisie, leaning closer. 'You're not making Mother happy. And you know how that makes me feel.' She let go and walked away. Never one to hide her feelings, my daughter wasn't someone I wanted as an enemy. By the time she was ten, she'd given up calling Sophia 'Mum' and I could count the times she'd called me 'Father' on the fingers of my right hand.

Maisie was busying herself in the kitchen.

'What are you up to?' I asked.

'Making breakfast for Mother,' she said sniffily. 'I don't appreciate you drinking wine from my Frida glass.'

I could have blamed Sophia, but there was no mileage in that. 'Sorry. Though Mexicans like booze.'

She gave me a withering look. 'Beer and tequila, I think you'll find.'

Given that, last I heard, Mexico was ruled by a cartel of cartels, I reckoned the population would be lucky to get anything to drink that didn't contain narcotics, but Maisie was undoubtedly more up to date on the politics of Latin America.

'How about a walk to Princes Street Gardens?' I said.

Heck started leaping around like a kangaroo on heat. Maisie was less effusive, finally nodding as she went to the mistress's bedroom with a tray.

By the time a rucksack had been filled with pieces of equipment that Heck might want once in a year and Maisie had chosen three books, almost an hour had passed. Sophia appeared, still looking weary, and gave the wee man a hug before she wrapped an adult scarf around his neck about ten times.

'At least it isn't raining,' she said. 'If it starts, I want you back straightaway.'

'Don't worry, I'll hide them under my coat,' I said, with a hesitant smile.

'Don't be a dick.'

Maisie sniggered, prompting laughter from Heck. I picked up the buggy and headed for the door. The kids came down the stairs behind me, hand in hand. My son was talking non-stop in his personal Creole, of which about a third was comprehensible. 'Pancakes' was the most frequent word.

We walked up Dublin Street, me pushing the buggy. For a three-year-old, Heck was bloody heavy. Maisie was already reading a book.

'You'll walk into a lamp post, love.'

'No, I won't.'

She almost certainly wouldn't. Although she was wearing glasses, her peripheral vision was better than most of the Guard personnel I'd served with. She often caught me making faces.

'What's the book?' I asked.

'*Leviathan.*'

'Levia-thing,' said Heck, belting laughter soon turning into hiccoughs.

I put the less than trustworthy brake on the buggy, found a bottle and got him to drink. Eventually, he spluttered to silence and gave me a wide smile.

'Hobbes, eh?' I said. 'Not exactly a beam of sunshine on a winter's morning. "The kingdom of darkness . . ." and the like.'

'There's so much more to it than that,' Maisie said, eyes still on the page. 'The commonwealth is made of the citizen bodies, and depends on a social contract—'

'Citizen bodies,' I interrupted. 'That sounds familiar.'

'The Council's body politic is gone for ever – you of all people must know that, Quint.'

I was panting on the slope. 'Why me of all people?'

'Because you were involved in the revolution that put an end to the Enlightenment.' She gave me a searching look. 'Though you've been wasting your time since.'

I would have remonstrated but I was about to throw up from the exertion. Maisie had made it clear that she agreed with Sophia about my books: they both thought the future was more important than the past.

We went past the newly refurbished National Portrait Gallery. It had been a rooming house for citizens who worked in the tourist zone under the Council, its paintings in the big hotels or stored away. The Education Directorate concentrated on Edinburgh rather than Scottish history.

By the time we crossed St Andrew Square – the garden now graced by something called an infinity pond – Heck was demanding pancakes so loudly that passers-by burst out laughing.

Fortunately, there wasn't a queue at the kiosk. It was about twenty metres beyond the Scott Monument. What had been the largest memorial to any writer in the world had lost that distinction some years back when a large section at the top had collapsed and flattened a group of tourists. The Municipal Board was consulting about rebuilding it, but there was a feeling that leaving it as it was would be a fine symbol of the Enlightenment's ultimately gimcrack social structure. After all, Sir Walter did write *The Heart of Midlothian*.

Heck was engaged in stuffing a chocolate pancake into his ravening maw, while Maisie was daintily nibbling at one filled with mango and papaya. A few years ago I'd never seen either of those fruits. I was drinking coffee on an empty stomach, asking for trouble. You take what risks you can as a family man. And seven Scottish poonds for that lot was risky enough.

'Quint, what a surprise,' came a voice from the level of my left hip.

'Billy,' I said neutrally, as I attached the reins to Heck. The last time we were at the gardens, he managed to run down one of the steep slopes between the levels. I didn't like the odds of his pulling that off again without severe cranial damage.

My former school and university friend, William Ewart Geddes, sat in the electric wheelchair with his usual sardonic smile. It wasn't far from here that he'd been run over by horses on the race track covering the former train lines back in 2020. He'd had his finger in many of the indigestible pies the city's major thieves and murderers – often guardians and senior auxiliaries – had baked before the revolution. I still wasn't sure how he'd managed to become my publisher, so subtle was he at dangling carrots, negotiating and manipulating. The sleek dark-blue coat he was wearing must have cost thousands.

'Family day out?' he said, looking at Maisie. She was sitting on a bench with her nose deep in Hobbes. 'Your parenting skills are a bit random.' He laughed as I tugged on Heck's reins. My son went red-faced in rage. He stomped over to us and kicked Billy hard on the shin.

'Ow, ya wee bugger,' he said, clutching his lower leg.

'Thought you had no feeling down there,' I said, trying to restrain the rabid boy. Fortunately, he spotted a pigeon and went on the hunt.

'It comes and goes.' Billy grinned. 'Massages help.'

'I'll bet they do.' The Municipal Board licensed sauna clubs providing 'special services' to keep prostitutes off the streets in the centre.

I took off my woollen gloves to get a better grip on the reins. 'No way is this a chance meeting.'

'Correct. You owe me something.'

'Correction. *You* owe *me* something.'

'You'll get your royalties at the end of the year. Anyway, stop dodging the bullet. Where the hell is *Waters of Death*?'

Ah. I'd ground to a halt two-thirds of the way through the third book of my fictionalized memoirs about a month back and had signally failed to relocate my mojo. I'd been stalling Billy for weeks.

'You've dried up, haven't you?' he said, watching apprehensively as Heck headed towards us at speed, arms stretched towards a scrawny avian rat. 'Catch him, Quint!'

I did, then swung the wee lad within inches of Billy's face. The skin was drawn back behind his ears and he should have been wearing a hat that went lower than his Homburg.

'Have you had work done?'

He scowled. 'What's wrong with supporting our local plastic surgeons?'

'We got by perfectly well without them for three decades,' I said, wiping a waterfall of snot from my boy.

'This isn't purely cosmetic,' Billy said. 'As you know.'

I had a vision of his small form getting under the fence. He blamed me for chasing him there, overlooking the fact that he was carrying a briefcase full of illegal cash. I'd also screamed at him not to go.

'All right,' I said, trying to keep the little that remained of my right forefinger from Heck's grasp. He found the stump endlessly fascinating. It wasn't that he hurt me – his clutching made me remember how I'd lost the digit. That was one story I'd never be putting in a book.

'Don't worry, Quint,' Billy said solicitously. 'I'll put my best editor on it. She'll help you finish the book.'

'Protecting your investment? No, Heck, not Uncle Billy's nose.' If Sophia had heard me making Billy a member of the family, I'd be in the seagull-proof rubbish sack that every household received. I glanced at Maisie, but Hobbes was far too interesting.

'I can manage,' I said.

'But when? I've got overseas deals riding on publication in Scotland no later than May.'

I watched a dark cloud louring over the castle.

'Snow on the way,' I said. 'Got to go.'

'Keep in touch,' Billy said, reversing away and almost running over a small black child, who started to howl. 'And nail yourself to your desk before I do.'

'Better hit the accelerator,' I said, too late.

A large woman in brightly coloured robes ran after the wheelchair and landed a heavy blow on Billy's shoulder. He screamed abuse.

'Not your day, is it?' I shouted after him.

It turned out not to be mine either.

I got the kids home in a taxi and ushered them inside the street door. It wasn't till I'd struggled to collapse the buggy that I realized there were people on the steps above.

'Wow,' Maisie said. 'It's the presiding minister and the director of ScotPol.' Even she, who disdained authority figures, was impressed. Mildly.

'Quint,' said Andrew Duart, extending a hand. The leader of the Scottish government was called presiding minister because he had almost presidential powers. The conservative opposition, led by the Lord of the Isles, had suggested chief minister to create a link to the clan system. They wanted to take the country back to the sixteenth century, when it had been completely separate from England and the rest of the now disunited kingdom. Of course, now there was no England in toto.

I was busy with Heck, so managed to avoid taking the hand. I'd had dealings with both Duart and his one-time lover Hel Hyslop, the country's top cop. Both were from Glasgow and had been – and doubtless still were – promoting that city's interests above the other urban and rural districts. They also had substantially looser conceptions of truth and morality than I did. Still, at the worst I could use them for research. If I ever got *Waters of Death* finished, the next book would be largely set in their city.

'What are you doing on the stair?' I said, hoisting Heck on to my shoulders.

Hel's eyes flashed. 'Your wife declined to admit us any further.'

I laughed. 'You should have made an appointment.'

'There wasn't time,' Duart said, his goatee beard and the hair that remained on his cranium dyed blacker than pitch.

'This is potentially a national emergency,' Hel said, taking off her fur hat. I wondered which animal she'd skinned to get it. 'There's no time to lose.'

We made it to the second floor, though my neck was killing me, and got the kids inside. I directed the visitors to the sitting room as Sophia appeared from the kitchen. The smell of roasting beef made my mouth juice up.

'You refused to let them in?' I said, grinning.

'Not my types.' Sophia had met them when she was Medical Guardian. She'd always had impeccable taste.

'I'd better talk to them,' I said. 'Sorry.'

She turned away. 'At least the kids saw a bit of you.'

'Yes,' said Heck, bursting into raucous laughter. 'His not-finger. I saw his not-finger . . .'

I left her to it. After closing the sitting-room door behind me, I went over to the sideboard.

'I have several malts, not all from the south.' Distilleries had set up all over the country due to huge demand for the best whisky from Scandinavia and other functioning markets.

'Not for us,' the presiding minister said imperiously.

I poured myself a large measure of Lagavulin and dribbled water into it from a cut-crystal jug Maisie had found in a junk shop.

'Pardon my incredulity,' I said, leaning against the mantelpiece and looking down at them on the brown leather sofa, 'but don't you have the people you need for every kind of emergency?' I wasn't bitter – well, I'd got past the worst – that Hel Hyslop had shown no interest in finding a place for me in ScotPol. The truth was that I would never have fitted in.

'In theory,' said Duart. 'Maybe I will have a small whisky.' He glanced at Hel, but she shook her head.

'You've got about ten minutes till my son does his main battle-tank impression, using you as grass-free knolls,' I said, handing the presiding minister his dram. 'Speak.'

They did so.

I drained my third large Lagavulin.

'You can't be serious,' I said.

Hel's brown curls had sprung up after being confined by the hat. Not for the first time, she made me think of the Gorgon. I looked rapidly away.

'Neither of us is smiling,' she said. That was true, but she'd never been good at happy faces.

Andrew Duart's expression was forbidding. 'I don't have a high opinion of Angus, but parliament will be in chaos if he isn't located quickly.'

'Why me?' I demanded, resisting the temptation to refill my glass.

It was Hel Hyslop who was looking past me now, points of red on her cheeks.

'Because I'm the best,' I said, milking the situation. 'And you feel guilty about not offering a job to the best.'

'Would you have taken it?' she demanded.

'We'll never know.'

'Of course, we have the highest regard for your capabilities, Quint,' said the presiding minister. 'And the fact that the Lord of the Isles was last seen in Edinburgh makes you the prime candidate.'

'So you don't have the highest regard for ScotPol personnel here?' I said. 'Assistant Director Findhorn?'

'Muriel is a manager, not an investigator,' Hel said. 'And your friend Detective Leader Oliphant is—'

'Otherwise engaged,' Duart put in before Hel expressed her dislike for Davie in terms that would have led to me showing her the door and the stairs. 'This tree-fish case is very odd.'

'Is it?' I was surprised that the country's leading politician was aware of that. 'Do you know something about it that I don't?'

He glanced at Hel Hyslop, who frowned.

'Of course not,' she said. 'I read about it in the daily reports and mentioned it on the way down here. Typical piece of Edinburgh lunacy.'

I wasn't convinced. 'You know of no connection between the tree-fish and the disappearance of the Lord of the Isles?'

'Absolutely not,' said Duart, while the police chief shook her head.

She eventually said, 'No,' after I gave her my best interrogator's gaze.

'To the pressing case in hand?' the presiding minister asked.

'Not so fast. I need you to agree to certain . . . conditions.'

'Here we go,' said Hel. 'Citizen "I'm A Very Special Person" Dalrymple strikes again.'

I smiled. 'No, just "Mr The Best". One, I will share everything I find with the municipal authorities.'

Duart raised his hands at Hyslop, who was almost at boiling point. 'Very well, but confine yourself to informing Lachie MacFarlane. I'll let him know.'

'You mean you haven't already?'

Duart looked at his perfectly manicured nails. 'We wanted to get you . . . on board first.'

'Uh-huh. Two, D.L. Oliphant will work the case with me. Three, we will decide on all investigative and support staff.'

'Very well,' said the presiding minister after a lengthy pause. He took an envelope from his pocket. 'Here are the details you need.'

'Call me every evening at six,' Hel ordered.

I shrugged. 'Timekeeping's never been my strong point.'

'Just find him, Dalrymple,' Duart said, getting to his feet. 'Without causing another revolution.'

'You were both involved in that a long time before I was.'

But I was talking to myself, the pair of them having departed as if I'd lit their blue touch papers. At least I hadn't been retired.

Then the door banged open and Heck came barrelling towards me. Sophia was to his rear, almost smiling as he hit my legs and thumped me back on the sofa.

'Dadadadadada-down,' Heck said, digging his fingers into the flab above my belt.

'They've just hired you, haven't they?' Sophia said, sinking into an armchair.

'We didn't talk about money, but yes, I have to do this. The Lord of—'

She raised a hand. 'I don't want to know, Quint. Knock yourself out. We'll be here when you've finished. Probably.'

My stomach flipped. I would have spoken, tried to assure her that things would change, but I didn't have it in me.

I was well and truly hooked by the case of the missing Macdonald.

THREE

Davie picked me up twenty minutes later. I managed to read Heck two pages of a book about a cave boy. He wailed when I left. Sophia and Maisie weren't vocal, but their faces made it clear how they felt.

'I'll see you when I see you, then,' I said, leaning forward to kiss Sophia and making contact with her cheek for a nanosecond. Kissing Maisie was definitely not on the cards. She was avoiding my eyes and using *Leviathan* as a particularly bulky shield.

'Look after yourself,' Sophia said, as I turned away. 'Please.'

'It's only a missing person case,' I said, fully aware, as she was, that many of those had turned into horror shows in the past. I glanced round, but she was concentrating on the dinner I was going to miss.

Davie was waiting in the four-by-four. 'What's all this about, then? Sophia kicked you out?'

'Might has well have. You mean you're still in the dark?'

He looked around. 'The streetlamps here are fine.'

'Dickhead. They haven't told you about the new case?'

'Not more of Bosch's weirdoes?' he said, pulling away.

I shook my head. 'Go to Ainslie Place, number twenty-five. The Lord of the Isles has gone missing.'

'Shit.' His phone rang. 'Hang on.' He swerved to the kerb and listened. 'Got it, Director. Quint . . . Mr Dalrymple's in the car with me now.' Pause. 'Aye, ma'am, will do.' He cut the connection and drove on.

'Will do what?'

He grinned. 'Will make sure you observe regulations.'

'Good luck with that.'

The sleet had let off, but the roads were treacherous, cars skidding on the setts. We were only a few minutes from our destination and Davie was avoiding collisions. Most Edinburgh locals hadn't learned to drive under the Enlightenment as there were no private cars, so there were a lot of inexperienced drivers around. Dodgems Central was what Glaswegians called the city. Among other things.

'So, I'm officially on the case,' Davie said. 'The tree-fish has been passed down to one of my people. I've been told to leave her to get on with it, at least till we find the Puce Emperor.'

Angus Macdonald's face was that colour and he had definite delusions of grandeur. Then again, he'd been involved in the initial exploitation of the oil and gas fields, so he had power and influence beyond those of leader of the opposition.

Davie headed round the curve of Moray Place where the guardians used to be quartered. 'Something to do with rigs and pipelines?'

'You're not as thick as you look.' I yelped as a bear paw closed around my thigh. 'Which isn't thick at all . . .'

He let go after he parked in Ainslie Place down from the Lord of the Isles's house. There were other ScotPol vehicles in the vicinity.

'Watch your mouth, Eric,' he said with a guffaw.

I followed him to the tape barring the pavement.

'Detective Leader,' said the grizzled officer with the clipboard. 'Citizen Dalrymple.' He smiled. 'Always a pleasure.'

I nodded, pretty sure he wasn't being ironic. I still had a few fans from the old days.

'Right,' Davie said, striding to the steps that led up to the ornate white door. 'Who's in charge here? Or, rather, who *was* in charge?'

A tall man wearing a kilt stepped forward from a group gathered in the opulent hall. His red hair reached his shoulders.

'Hamish Macdonald, the Lord of the Isles's chief of staff.' He extended his hand to me. 'Mr Dalrymple. It's an honour. I've read your books.'

'Don't believe anything in them,' Davie said, introducing himself. 'You'll remember we're in Edinburgh, Mr Macdonald. I'm ScotPol's local detective leader.'

'Of course.' The skin on Macdonald's face was stretched tight; in fact, he was epidermis and bone all over.

'Are you a relation?' I asked.

He laughed. 'No, there are thousands of Macdonalds in the northwest.'

'Uh-huh. Stupid question, given the government's crackdown on nepotism.'

The chief of staff gave me a sharp look.

'What happened?' Davie asked. 'In detail.'

'Come into the lounge,' Macdonald said, leading the way.

There were several portraits of Highlanders in full costume on the walls, one of them the missing lord, his hair much less snowy than now.

I sat on what I thought was a Georgian chair. Davie consigned his bulk to a more modern sofa, a Macdonald tartan throw over the cushions.

'Drink?' The tall man was at a well-stocked table.

'No, we need to get on,' I said.

Hamish Macdonald went to the fireplace and tossed another log on the blaze. 'I've been briefed by the relevant staff members. It seems his lordship took to his bed here just after two o'clock this afternoon.'

'Does he normally have a nap?' Davie asked.

'Not every day.'

'"It seems",' I said, taking out my notebook. 'You weren't here?'

'No, I was at parliament.'

That institution was housed in what had been George Heriot's School, a building that was a citizen education centre under the Enlightenment and had been recently refurbished. The pre-2003 Scottish government's seat in the eccentric new building at the foot of the High Street was considered tainted by its use by the Council of City Guardians.

'His lordship made a speech in the debate on expanding trade with South Africa this morning,' Hamish Macdonald continued, 'and I was dealing with the aftermath.' He frowned. 'The press habitually make inferences bearing no resemblance to what is said.'

'So you didn't know where he was?' Davie said, eyeing the tall man dubiously. He had little time for bureaucrats.

'I knew he'd departed because he told me he was going to. I left the details to his chauffeur and security detail.'

'We'll be talking to them,' Davie said. 'Did he say anything out of the ordinary?'

'Did he say he was going to rest?' I added.

The chief of staff rubbed his chin. '*Yes* to both questions,' he said, brow furrowed. 'I thought nothing of it at the time, but his last words to me were "Come to the house at seven – I should be back by then". I should have queried where he was going, but a scrum of journalists surrounded me.'

I glanced at Davie. 'So where did your lord and master go?'

'That's just it. He never left the room. His valet was sitting outside the whole time.'

'Let's see the room,' I said.

'And talk to this valet,' Davie said. He wasn't keen on flunkies either, never mind lords.

We were led up a marble staircase with gilded iron balusters beneath the smooth wooden rail. The first floor contained ornate reception rooms, the doors all open – presumably because the staff had been running around looking for the missing man. On the second floor, by comparison, all the doors except one were closed. The door to the room at the rear was lying on the floor.

'You didn't,' I said.

The kilted man looked at me. 'What . . . oh, I see. I gave the order for it to be knocked down. I was worried about his lordship's health. His heart . . .'

'It was locked?' I kneeled by the heavy, panelled door, which was surrounded by fragments of wood and marked by what looked like sledgehammer blows. The key on what had been the inside was turned, and the bolt – now bent – was visible.

'We had some trouble breaking it down,' said Macdonald. 'I knocked for a good while and called him on his phones. No reply.'

'Has anyone been in the room?' Davie asked.

'Yes . . . but only me. I wanted to see what had happened to his lordship.'

Davie glowered at him. 'You've contaminated the scene. Don't move until the forensics team arrives.' He made the call.

I held off going in but could see the layout and contents clearly enough. The Lord of the Isles slept in a large four-poster bed. The curtains were drawn back and the quilt undisturbed. The wallpaper was in the missing man's Macdonald tartan, which was too red for anywhere except a knocking shop.

What really caught my eye were the windows. The two facing the street were shuttered, while those facing the gardens behind the terrace of high houses were uncovered. Outside both were bars too close together to allow anything but a slim pigeon to pass through.

It seemed I had a locked-room mystery, but one with two differences – there was no functioning lock and no body. If the SOCOs confirmed that – there were two large wardrobes and three trunks – I was living my own Golden Age crime novel. Thing is, I've always been a noir man; Hammett and Chandler didn't do locked rooms. What would the Continental Op, Sam Spade or Philip Marlowe have had to say about this?

Davie and I put on white coveralls and bootees, then pulled the hoods over our heads when the SOCO leader, my not-friend Graham Arthur, waved us into the bedroom.

'Well, there's no body,' he said, casting his eye over the open wardrobes and trunks. 'And before you ask – yes, we have checked under the bed.'

'Are those bars all secure?' I said, watching a technician at one of the windows.

'So far, yes. I take it someone was in here.'

'You take nothing,' Davie said, looming. 'This is a no-assumptions, no-surmises, no-gossip case – got it?'

Arthur smiled under his moustache. 'Of course. I hope the Lord of the Isles doesn't mind that you broke his door down.'

'Watch it,' Davie said, stepping forward. That wiped the smile from the Glaswegian's lips. 'What else have you got?'

'Fingerprints – we're collecting what we can find and also taking the prints of everyone who comes in here. The room is very clean and there's nothing obvious on any of the surfaces.'

'Including the floor?' I said. A Persian carpet took up most of the space, but there was about a yard of black-painted boards at the door.

'I've already matched those prints' – he pointed to an area that was sectioned off – 'with the chief of staff's shoes. Then again, there was dust and debris from the smashed door, so they stuck out.'

'Any blood?' Davie asked.

'Nothing obvious, but we're still checking.'

'Other fluids?' I said.

Arthur's teeth blossomed. 'Mr Dalrymple! We're talking about the leader of the—'

'We're talking about my boot going up your arse,' Davie said. 'Answer the question.'

The SOCO swallowed hard. 'As I said, the room is very clean. That includes the bedding, the towels in the en suite, the curtains round the bed . . . and there are no soiled clothes in the laundry basket.'

Angus Macdonald had never struck me as a sex addict, but you never could tell. I'd asked Hel Hyslop if we could access his medical file in case he had any life-threatening conditions and was told she'd get back to me. There was a quicker solution.

'Come on,' I said to Davie. 'Time we interviewed the chief of staff.' We'd already had a go at the valet, a timid Skye native, who said he'd never moved from the dressing room, hadn't dropped off, hadn't seen or heard anything out of the ordinary and couldn't imagine what had happened to his lordship, who had been behaving normally in recent days.

'Mr Macdonald,' I said, after we'd sat him down in the kitchen. Basement rooms are best for interrogations, although, apart from the magnetic strip on the wall with eight knives attached, the room was warm and unthreatening. The range was new and the cooking equipment both expensive and spotless.

'I'm at a loss—' he began.

'Quiet!' Davie roared. 'Speak when you're spoken to.' Sometimes he forgot he was no longer in the City Guard.

'Was your boss well?' I asked.

The tall man, now wearing different clothes as the SOCOs had taken his earlier outfit, looked surprised. 'As far as I know, yes. He's over seventy now, but he sees the best doctors.'

'I'm sure he does. So it's unlikely he'd have wandered off or collapsed?'

'I don't understand. He couldn't have left the room—'

'Just humour me, Mr Macdonald.'

'He was well, apart from his heart, but he took pills.'

I'd seen them in the en suite. I wondered if he had others with him. The label said one pill three times a day.

'Known enemies?' Davie said, licking the point of his pencil.

'Some, but he has a security detail.'

'Who were down here when he was upstairs,' I noted. 'Not exactly standard practice.'

The chief of staff raised his shoulders. 'I know nothing about that, but Jim and Andy have been with his lordship for over five years. They're loyal clan members.'

'Uh-huh,' I said. We'd be talking to them. 'Those enemies?'

'Brigands up north, though we've got rid of almost all of those; oil and gas explorers and their backers who want in on the Sutherland fields; crofters and fishermen whose property has been purchased by compulsory order or whose livelihoods have been affected. I suppose politicians from the other parties, not that I'm accusing anyone.'

'Aye, right. Plenty of potential assailants, then.'

'In theory, I suppose, but he should be safe in Edinburgh.' Macdonald looked at me and then at Davie. 'Shouldn't he?'

I shrugged. 'The aristocracy isn't exactly the flavour of the century here, even after the Enlightenment. Depends who he runs into.' I gave him a slack smile. 'Speaking of which, your boss is a businessman as well as leader of the opposition. Has he been doing any deals he shouldn't have?'

Hamish Macdonald's eyes opened wide. 'Certainly not! I'm party to all his lordship's commercial activities. I can assure you—'

'Yeah, yeah,' said Davie. 'Details, man, we need details!'

'That's impossible.'

'Is it now?' Davie got to his feet, shoving his chair back. 'Something else that's impossible is me stretching your neck from here.' He moved round the table and stood behind the tall man, putting heavy hands on his shoulders. 'It's not looking so impossible from here, though.'

'Just give us an idea of what's going on,' I said. 'It's in his lordship's best interests.'

'Very . . . very well. As you know, the bulk of shares in the Sutherland field and the ancillary plant and equipment have been sold to the Scottish state.'

'But your boss still makes plenty from ground rents and the like.'

'True. He also uses the knowledge he gained of the oil and gas businesses when he was in Texas to ensure that Scotland's deals with other countries are as beneficial as possible.'

'Any kickbacks?' I asked.

'No! His lordship is not that kind of man.'

I remembered his lordship in the years before Edinburgh had rejoined the nation. He had his fingers in a lot of very rancid pies. Then again, so did some of Edinburgh's former leaders. And Andrew Duart. Were they still playing us ordinary people for fools?

'Details!' yelled Davie into Macdonald's right ear.

'For the love of God,' said the Highlander, shaking his head. 'Very well, but this is confidential. His lordship has recently been negotiating with Norway's state energy company about sustainable technology, with the Finns – who recovered their country from Russian gangs last year – about oil and gas, and with the German Federation about computer technology.'

I remembered reading that the old capitalist had got his hands on shares of the leading companies in the Silicon Belt. What had been Glasgow's hi-tech sector had now expanded eastwards and was being met by Edinburgh's burgeoning online gaming industries.

'Might one or other of those countries resort to underhand methods to obtain the best deal?' I asked.

Hamish Macdonald slumped. 'I don't know. Maybe. It wouldn't be the first time, though things have been much better since Scottish reunification. Besides, the National Party's ministers keep an eye on the negotiations. Angus . . . his lordship acts in an advisory capacity.'

I noticed how he referred to his boss.

'We'll need names,' Davie said. 'Any trade representatives in Edinburgh at the moment?'

'Yes, there are Norwegians and Finns, I believe.' The tall man looked distracted. 'Oh, and some Nova Scotians.'

We'd have to check them out, but I couldn't see them being involved in the disappearance of the opposition leader – as his chief of staff said, Andrew Duart and the economy and energy ministers were also involved.

'What about organized crime?' I asked.

Hamish Macdonald's eyebrows almost reached his hairline. Which struck me as a dead giveaway. 'What . . . what do you mean?'

Davie could smell the man's fear. 'You understand English, don't you?' he yelled, avoiding the government advice to apply the term 'Scots' to the language. 'Has your man been threatened?' He grinned slackly. 'Or has he been up to nae good at all?'

'This is outrageous!' Macdonald pulled himself up to his full height. He looked like a tartan giraffe.

'I think we'll continue this discussion at ScotPol headquarters,' Davie said. The City Guard had been based in the castle, but the national force was in a purpose-built edifice opposite the former parliament building.

'I'm calling my lawyer,' said the tall man.

'That's your right,' Davie said, 'but it doesn't make a good impression.'

'I don't give a turd,' said Macdonald, which made me smile.

But not for long.

There was a kerfuffle at the kitchen door and Graham Arthur burst past the ScotPol officer Davie had posted.

'Look what I've found!' The SOCO had a beatific expression that was marred by a worrying smile. 'This one's for you, Mr Dalrymple!' He extended a latex-covered hand.

I felt my stomach gyrate like the high divers in the municipal swimming pool.

Lying on Arthur's palm was a human finger, the width suggesting it came from a male and the blood on the cut beneath the lower joint a dark crust of red.

'It's a forefinger,' the SOCO said, confirming my suspicions. 'From a right hand?'

He nodded at me animatedly. 'What do you think of that, then?'

Much was running through my mind, but I kept the barrier of my teeth well and truly shut. That didn't stop my heart thundering like a runaway train, nor the acid level of my stomach reaching critical.

Hamish Macdonald, pale-faced, was led away by Davie, who gave me an inquisitive look that I ignored.

'Where was it?' I asked.

'I'll show you.' Graham Arthur's delight was hard to take, but I played it as cool as I could as I followed him upstairs.

'Care to estimate how long ago the finger was removed and with what?' I said, hoping my voice was steady.

'I don't do estimates,' the SOCO said caustically. 'All I'd say is that the wound was inflicted between eighteen and twenty-four hours ago. As for the weapon – a device with two blades set close together. Possibly secateurs.' He looked round. 'Mrs Dalrymple will no doubt have an opinion.'

'You mean Miss McIlvanney.' Sophia had never taken my name. Women in Edinburgh generally didn't.

I put on bootees again outside the master bedroom and went to the four-poster. A drawer under the front part of the bed had been pulled out and its contents laid on a plastic sheet. Socks, mainly; a wank mag – I'd have to revise my take on Angus Macdonald's sexual activities, although he was married; and, in a plastic evidence bag, what looked like a stainless-steel cigar tube that was wider than the digit.

The SOCO held it up. 'See the blood on the rim?'

I nodded. 'Strange place to hide it.' I looked around the room. 'No ashtrays.'

'And no ash,' said Arthur. 'According to the valet, the Lord of the Isles gave up smoking when his heart condition was diagnosed.'

'Fingerprints?'

'Nary a one. The tube's either been wiped clean or handled by someone wearing gloves.'

I took another look at the finger, now in an evidence bag. The nail was bitten to the quick and there was what looked like the top of a tattoo above the cut. I'd seen Angus Macdonald's hands several times.

'Not his lordship's,' I said.

'No. I doubt there's enough of the tattoo to enable us to identify it, but we'll have a go.'

I decided to sweet-talk the SOCO – they always knew more than they volunteered.

'So, from your experience, what do you think went on here?'

Graham Arthur looked at me suspiciously. He knew what I was up to, but eventually couldn't resist showing off his talents.

'I've checked the chimney and looked behind all the walls. As you see, we've lifted the carpet and underlay. There's no secret chamber or exit. Ditto the ceiling.' He pointed to the smooth expanse of plaster above. 'No way out. No place to hide.'

I could have asked questions, but the SOCO was doing fine on his own.

'The bars over the windows, front and rear, have been put in recently – the cement's almost pristine. You should follow that up.'

'We will,' I said, with an encouraging smile.

'Also, I've examined the door.' He gave me a knowing look. 'I take it you're familiar with John Dickson Carr's *The Hollow Man*?'

'Was that on the reading list for forensics where you studied?'

'Certainly not. The Clyde University is a highly rigorous institution.'

'I'm sure.' There was world-class vanity in Glasgow, not to mention Edinburgh. 'So you read the ur-locked-room novel in your spare time.'

'Indeed. Chapter Seventeen's the one.'

'The famous "Locked Room Lecture". Any help in this case?'

Arthur flashed his teeth. 'Locked rooms usually contain a body. Of course, crime novels are far removed from reality, yours included.'

'Right.' So much for soft-soaping him.

The SOCO moved to the entrance. 'It didn't help that it was smashed down.'

'Suggesting that . . .?'

'The key was turned in the lock and bent after the door was broken in.'

'So his lordship may not have been there in the first place.'

'Correct. In which case, at least one but more likely several members of the household must know. I take it you've restricted their movements.'

'We did think of that. I'll be talking to those I haven't already questioned shortly.' I cast my memory back to John Dickson Carr's famous novel, which I'd reread earlier in the year. 'No body most likely means no murder, no suicide, no weapon, no victim dead earlier or later than presumed, no illusion – except with the key and that's hardly a good one – no stunning plot twists—'

'But maybe an accident or a misunderstanding,' said Arthur. In the novel, there were several of both.

'Such as?'

The SOCO smiled. 'That's your job, Mr Dalrymple. But would you like a piece of advice?'

'As long as it's free.'

'Perhaps an acknowledgement when you write your version of the case.' His teeth glinted in the high-powered lights that had been set up in the bedroom. 'If I were you – which thank the Lord I'm not, sir – I'd concentrate on the severed finger. It, rather than the object in the door, is the key.'

That was the last thing I wanted to hear, but I suspected he was right on the button.

Downstairs, I called Davie. He'd got nothing useful out of the chief of staff. I asked him to have everyone who'd been in the house in the afternoon taken into custody. I was about to cadge a lift to ScotPol HQ when a black Volvo drew up on the other side of the police line. The kerbside rear window opened.

'Get in, please, Quint.'

I did as I was bid.

'Evening, municipal leader.'

The short figure to my right was sitting on a raised seat.

'I've told you, call me Lachie.'

'Lachie.' I raised my eyebrows quizzically.

'What am I doing here?' MacFarlane nodded. 'Andrew Duart told me to keep my distance and the demon Hyslop said I wasn't to contaminate the crime scene.' He smiled. 'Naturally, I came straight down.'

The driver was executing a three-point turn, the twenty-year-old car's axles complaining. Lachie's father had owned a similar model before the Enlightenment and he'd sourced this one from Sweden when trade boomed after reunification. In my experience, revolutionaries frequently had a sentimental streak.

'I'm not sure it deserves to be called a crime scene,' I said. 'The Lord of the Isles is absent, but there's no telling why. He might have arranged his own departure. That might be more likely than that he was abducted. In both cases, someone singular or plural in the house knows. We'll squeeze that out of them.'

I watched as Lachie took a cigar tube from his jacket pocket. It was smaller than the one Graham Arthur had found, and there was writing on the silver casing. The cigar turned out to be a cigarillo.

'What?' Edinburgh's shortest citizen said, after he'd lit it.

'Small cigar for a small—'

His left hand grabbed my forearm and squeezed hard. 'Discriminatory talk like that's illegal now, Quint.' He laughed and released his grip. 'Smartarse. I don't have many vices, but these I can't give up.'

I waved the smoke away ineffectually. 'Are they made from randomly collected horseshit or do you have a city nag?'

He ignored that. 'Tell me about the finger.'

My gut had another go at twisting and shaking.

'Not much to say yet, except that it's not his lordship's.'

Lachie stared at me. 'Not much to say? What was it doing in Angus Macdonald's bedroom? Who collects fingers?'

He was very well informed. Probably one of the ScotPol officers on site was his spy, though he or she hadn't picked everything up.

'The said digit was severed quite recently. I doubt Macdonald even knew it was there.'

The municipal leader took that in, his eyes on me. I realized what he was looking at. Shit.

'It was a right index finger, was it not?' he said. 'Like the one you lost.'

I paused to calm myself. Lachie was famous for not missing a trick, which was why he was running Edinburgh.

'The one I lost a long time ago.'

'A coincidence, then.'

I kept my mouth shut, unconvinced that he meant what he'd said.

'Can I give you a lift?' he said, still watching me.

I met his gaze. 'Depends where you're going. I should get to ScotPol HQ. We have a lot of questioning to do.'

Lachie instructed the driver accordingly. 'I'm glad you were brought in by Duart and Hyslop.'

'Do I have you to thank for that?'

He blew a smoke ring. 'Andrew asked me. I told him he'd be insane not to make use of our renowned local expert.'

I laughed. 'And Hel went along with it?'

'He didn't give her a choice. Besides, you make it easy for them. If you screw up, they're not responsible.'

I looked out at the slushy pavements on Queen Street. 'Great.'

'What do *you* think's going on? Has Angus lost his mind and gone walkabout, or is it something more sinister?'

'That's what the questioning's about. Someone in the house knew he left. The business with the locked door was a distraction.'

'Not a very good one.'

'True. Even the lead SOCO spotted it.'

'Why did the culprit bother?'

'Delay, I suppose. It's possible he's been kidnapped – with the assistance of one or more people in the house – and they wanted to make sure they got far enough away before making contact. I suppose I'll hear if there's a ransom demand.'

'Hyslop will tell you. She's under orders from the presiding minister.'

That didn't warm my cockles. She'd done what she liked in the past, though usually in cahoots with Duart.

'You aren't aware of any suspicious deals the Lord of the Isles is doing, are you?'

He stubbed out the cigarillo in a portable ashtray. 'You know how it is. The oversight system means central government can't keep the cities and regions completely out of the loop.'

Scotland's pre-reunification states had been run in numerous different ways – Glasgow as a democracy, Stirling a feminist collective, Dundee a bastion of anarcho-syndicalism, Inverness having reverted to the ancient tanist tradition and so on. That was one reason why Edinburgh had voted 'yes' in the referendum – we weren't the only area with a curious form of government. Although there was now central administration, local government was up to local voters. The system had only been in operation for a couple of years and it wasn't clear how successful it was on a national level. I'd heard that Andrew Duart wanted the Glasgow system to extend across the country, but there were plenty of problems with his home city's politics.

'You've heard something, then?' I asked.

He nodded. 'You're aware of the energy contracts that have been endorsed by the national government.'

'The Scandinavian countries, northern Germany, some states in the south of France . . .'

'Aye.' The small man's face was grim. 'There's a new one that Angus Macdonald's been handling personally. He has contacts from before reunification.'

'Where?' I said, getting a bad feeling.

'Think south, but nowhere near as far as France.'

I stared at him wide-eyed. 'You're kidding.'

'I'm not. In the last six months, neighbouring states have come together and they want our oil, gas, whisky, fish and so on.'

'The English?'

'The northern part. Nor-England, they call themselves.'

I remembered the devastation I'd seen on the way to Oxford ten years back. Warring gang bosses, absence of government at any level, chaos, mayhem and slaughter. Glasgow had been Enlightenment Edinburgh's bogeyman, but England wasn't far short. My experience in Oxford did nothing but confirm that impression, even though there was a hyper-organized state there.

'So what are you saying, Lachie? The English have got hold of Angus Macdonald? That's not going to get them any trade deals.'

'You'd think they'd have worked that out themselves. Maybe the Lord of the Isles – who, let's face it, has an inflated opinion of his worth – has overstated how important he is.'

'Duart won't authorize a ransom. He'll probably pay them to keep the old toff.'

The man who ran Edinburgh smiled. 'Probably not, but there's a Nor-English delegation in the city as we speak.'

'What?'

'Don't worry, they're civilized enough. Only their bodyguards have weapons and they've surrendered them to my people.'

I sat back in the Volvo, which was now approaching ScotPol's concrete block. Behind it, the light from the watchtower on top of Arthur's Seat shone out like a beacon. What kind of people had it lured to the city of my birth?

'Not before time, Quint,' said Davie, coming out of an interview room. He was in shirtsleeves and there were patches of sweat under his arms. Even though the building was new, it smelled of unwashed bodies, urine and excrement.

'Any news?' I asked.

He shook his head. 'Hamish Macdonald's sticking to his story
– he was in the house all afternoon but saw and heard nothing out
of the ordinary until his lord and master failed to appear. I'm getting
the same from the officers who are questioning the others.'

'Someone's lying.' I took out my notebook and looked at the
layout I'd sketched of the rooms on each floor.

'Did you ascertain when the bars outside the bedroom windows
were put in place?'

'Aye. In September. The Lord of the Isles told Hamish that he
wanted to sleep safely.'

'Interesting. Maybe he sleepwalks.'

Davie raised an eyebrow. 'I can ask.'

'Later. The windows on the floors above and below don't have
bars. Get Graham Arthur's people to check them for signs of ropes
or other means of egress.'

'You're thinking he may have been got out without anyone
noticing?'

'Anyone except whoever was in on the plan. Have you talked
to the valet yet?'

'No. He's next on my list.'

'I'll take him. Tell the officer with him that I need to be alone.'

Davie registered shock. 'You'll be breaking ScotPol regulations.'
He grinned. 'In fact, you'll be breaking the law.'

'I can live with that if you can.'

He gave me a saucy wink. 'I'll have a go at the deputy chief of
staff. I've been keeping him on ice. He looks decidedly shifty.'

'By "on ice" I presume you mean you've turned the heating off
in the room?'

He guffawed. 'Don't tell Hel.'

'I promise. Where's the valet?'

He directed me to a door at the end of the corridor. As I walked
there, I heard raised voices from the interview rooms on either side;
in one there was even a full-blown slap. When it came to the crunch,
ScotPol wasn't so different to the City Guard. That made me smile.
I wasn't really hankering after the bad old days, but it was good to
know that regulations could be stretched to within a millimetre – the
Council's imperial measures no longer in force – of breaking point.

FOUR

There was a blue-and-white paper file in the slot on the door. I ran my eyes over the few pages it contained and then knocked to alert the officer before opening the door.

'Mr Dalrymple,' the middle-aged woman said, frowning.

'You've heard from the detective leader?'

She nodded, her expression troubled.

'Don't worry, I won't lay a finger on him.' I realized what I'd said too late.

Thanks a lot, subconscious. The stump of my right index finger was already tingling.

Still, my words had the desired effect. The valet had gone whiter than the Pentland Hills.

'Douglas John Dinwoodie,' I read, 'born Oban, January twenty-eighth 1989. Parents bla bla bla. Worked as steward on inter-island ferries – that must have been fun when the pirates were around – entered service with the Lord of the Isles, June 2027, initially as footman. Promoted to valet, 2034.' I looked up and smiled at him. 'Enjoy the work?'

'Oh, aye,' he said, 'I love his lordship. I'd do anything for him.'

There was an admission, but I wasn't going to use it yet. 'You must know a lot about your employer.'

The skinny man gave me a dubious look. 'What d'ye mean?'

'Well, you help him dress, you collect his dirty clothes . . .' I paused meaningfully. 'You go through his pockets.'

Dinwoodie looked outraged. 'No, I don't!'

'Calm down,' I said emolliently, then dug my heels in. 'But you do.'

He looked down, displaying thin hair and a pockmarked scalp. I wondered if he'd been in an explosion. There was nothing in the file. Then again, most Scots had been through the wars one way or another over the last thirty-five years.

'Well, it's my job. I didnae like the way you put it. I'm no thief.'

I'd got to him. Time to row back. 'Of course you're not, Dougie. But you see things, don't you?'

He shrugged.

'Did you see anything that would help us find your beloved master?' I leaned over him. 'Do you know what happened to him?' The valet started quivering like a terrified rabbit. 'No, no,' he said. 'I was outside his room till they came and broke the door down. He never came oot.'

I held his gaze. He was scared, but I wasn't sure if he was lying. 'Did you not have a cup of tea at all? Make yourself some toast? Go to the toilet?'

Now he looked guilty. 'Well . . . aye, but I wasn't away for more than five minutes.' His head went down. 'Twice.'

Bingo times two. I held off for a while.

'So his lordship could have slipped out or been abducted without you noticing?'

Dinwoodie started to sob. 'Find him, Mr Dalrymple, please, find him.'

'I need your help, Dougie. Is there anyone in the house you've got suspicions about? Is everyone loyal?'

He wiped his eyes with a very clean handkerchief. 'I don't know. The political types dinnae pay attention to me. They were all with his lordship before we came to Edinburgh, but that disnae mean they haven't been corrupted in this city of vice.'

'What about your master's pockets? Did you come across anything that would help? A piece of paper with a name or address or phone number?'

He kept his eyes off me.

'What about his mobile phone?'

Dinwoodie looked up. 'He had two. I had to plug them in to recharge overnight.'

'Did you hear him say anything suggestive when he was speaking on them?'

He gave me a puzzled look. 'Suggestive?'

'Well, did he get angry? Mention names? Sound as though he was being threatened?'

He thought about that, then shook his head.

I repeated the piece-of-paper question. This time he cracked.

'All right, Mr Dalrymple. One day last week . . . I think it was Friday – aye, it was definitely Friday, I remember because . . .' He broke off when he realized he was wandering. 'I found a card, one

of thae index cards with lines on them, in his inside jacket pocket
before I hung the suit up.'

'What was written on it? What did you do with it?'

Dinwoodie scratched his head. 'I didn't register it at first, then I
realized it was a name and address – in his lordship's handwriting.
He always uses a fountain pen and green ink. Matthew, it said. And
the address . . .' He squeezed his eyes shut and then raised a finger.
'Aye – seventeen Craigs Road, Drum Brae South.'

'And—'

'What did I do with it? Put it on his lordship's dressing table. It
had gone when I went in after he left on the Saturday morning. He
was playing golf at Gullane.'

'And you didn't see it again?'

'Naw.'

I looked at my notes. Drum Brae was a longish road that
ran north/south in the far western suburbs – an area that had
only become adequately crime-free for people to inhabit in
the Enlightenment's later years. The houses were a far cry from
Ainslie Place.

'I don't suppose the Lord of the Isles mentioned visiting the
address?'

'Naw. Hey, can I get a cuppae tea?'

I nodded and left, passing his request to a surly uniformed officer
in the corridor. I went to the room where Davie was interviewing
Hamish Macdonald, tapped on the door and went in.

'Mr Dalrymple,' the tall man said, his face wet. 'Thank God.
This madman's accusing me of involvement in Angus's – in his
lordship's – disappearance.'

I sat down next to Davie. 'Bad detective leader.'

He grinned.

I looked at the chief of staff. '*Matthew*,' I said. 'Mean anything
to you?'

His eyes dropped. 'The gospel?' he said quietly.

'Would that be relevant to your boss?' I asked, remembering
that there was a copy of the Bible on a bedside table.

'Matthew the gospel-writer doesn't live off Drum Brae,' Davie
said. 'If he ever lived at all.'

'His lordship is a practising member of the Church of Scotland,'
Macdonald said, 'as am I.' The church had reformed nationally in

the last couple of years, having fared better than its rivals in the Highlands and Islands in the stone years.

'So what goes on at that address?' Davie demanded. 'Sermons on the Craigs?'

I stifled a laugh.

The tall man looked at Davie in disgust. 'Freedom of religion is sanctioned by the new constitution, and worshippers are protected from bigotry.'

'I know the law,' Davie growled. 'Did his lordship go to the address? Did you go with him?'

'I don't know to the first question, no to the second.'

'He never mentioned it to you?' I said.

'He didn't – doesn't – tell me everything he does. I'm not involved in his private life.'

That seemed unlikely, but I let it go. We needed to get out to the western suburbs pronto.

Davie drove on to Princes Street and took advantage of the ban on all traffic except buses and official vehicles like ours to cut across the city centre quickly. Snow was falling but the asphalt and pavements weren't cold enough for it to lie. Although it was past one in the morning, there were plenty of clubs and restaurants still open, people wandering about in the state of inebriation that turns legs to rubber.

'Bloody hell!' Davie said, swerving round a large man in a bright yellow tartan coat who gave him the finger. 'Tourists!'

He was right. No Edinburgh local would wear a tartan over-garment. Glaswegians would be wary too – their city was a longstanding hub of the fashion industry. I didn't know about other Scottish cities. Perth, run by survivors of the landed gentry that had held sway before the UK fell apart, might be hot on the kilt. I hadn't been anywhere in the reunified country since road links were restored. The two Forth Bridges were due to reopen in 2039, although it was said that the laying of new railways was behind schedule. Those who could afford it – such as the Lord of the Isles – flew. Which made me think.

'Get someone to check the airport,' I said. 'Maybe old Angus is hundreds of miles away.'

Davie grunted. 'Already done. His name isn't on any flight lists and my people are scanning the security camera footage – nothing so far. I think he's still in Embra.'

I nodded. Under the Enlightenment, local dialects and vocabulary had been banned to reduce nationalist sentiments, and the city had been called Edinburgh, along with 'the perfect city', 'Garden of Edin' and other such propagandist handles. Embra was popular now.

Street lighting, which had been patchy to non-existent the further you got from the centre, was better now and there were plenty of cars on the roads. The capital of Scotland ran on a twenty-four-hour basis, which was great for night owls like me and hellish for people – the overwhelming majority – without double-glazing.

Davie's phone rang and he listened. 'Barker,' he said to me, 'Matthew Barker is the registered owner of the house we're heading for. My people are digging for more about him.'

I looked to the left. What had been Murrayfield stadium, home of Scottish rugby, was now a rusted ruin awaiting development as the biggest ice rink in the country. The Council had been keen on rugby's ethos for both male and female auxiliaries – Davie had been a fearsome player till his knee had said *that's more than enough, thanks* – but even before the regime fell, football had taken over.

The traffic began to thin as we got further west. ScotPol four-by-fours were stationed at potential trouble spots, usually pubs and clubs. Drum Brae was a dormitory area and there weren't many people about. Davie turned off the main road and then into Craigs Road. I counted the house numbers.

'That's it,' I said.

He pulled in smartly behind a battered German estate car. Glasgow car dealers had offloaded their superannuated stock on to Edinburgh citizens with their limited budgets.

I got out and looked at the semi-detached house. The row was new, as was often the case in the suburbs. Many buildings had been destroyed during the drugs wars. This one was solidly middle-of-the-range – not the kind of place you'd expect the Lord of the Isles to visit.

Davie joined me on the pavement. He was holding an extendable truncheon. The electric Hyper-Stuns used by the City Guard had been banned and only special units carried firearms. I was glad the big man was with me.

He walked up the paved path and looked through the round piece of glass in the front door. The curtains were tightly drawn on all the upstairs and downstairs windows.

'What do you think?' Davie said. 'Polite knock or thunderous hammering?' The former was ScotPol's compulsory method, but former Guard personnel struggled to forget the past.

I walked up and knocked three times on the glass. No one came, though there was a light on in the hallway. I looked in. The place was tidy, with a multicoloured rug on the floor. The stairs had been varnished and there were Rothko prints on the walls. Abstract expressionism had been frowned upon by the Enlightenment – too much freedom of, well, expression – and was having a rise in popularity. We'd put up a dark-red Rothko print in the sitting room.

I knocked again. 'Mr Barker? Anyone at home?'

We waited but there was no response.

'Bugger this,' said Davie, lowering his shoulder.

I opened my mouth and then thought again. Sometimes it was best to give him his head. I knocked one last time.

We stood in silence, waiting for a response. Nothing.

Davie gave me a baleful look. 'I smell a trap.'

'Call back-up.'

'Not yet.' His hand went inside his jacket and came out with his City Guard knife, its blade well honed.

'Glad to see senior ranks paying attention to ScotPol regs.'

'Screw you.' He pulled on a latex glove and put his left hand on the door knob next to us. 'One, two . . . three!'

He burst in. I waited before following.

'Clear!' he called. 'Jesus Christ!'

I looked at the bizarre sight before us.

'No,' said Davie. 'It's the other guy, or one of his sidekicks.'

Standing by a black leather sofa was a clarsach, a triangular Celtic harp. I knew that because there was one in the newly refurbished Museum of Scotland. But this version was larger, as tall as Davie, and a spread-eagled human form, naked with its back towards us, was attached to the strings.

Davie circled round the object. 'That's not a real man,' he said. 'It's a plastic figure, Quint. What's going on?'

'It's for the Theatre of Life,' said a deep voice to my rear.

I turned and saw a muscle-bound man of below average height walk into the room.

'Matthew Barker?' Davie said.

'Aye. Who the hell are you? What happened to my door?' His tone was irate, but I had the feeling he was putting it on. The sly smile that appeared on his thick lips suggested I was right.

Davie identified himself. 'We knocked, called your name. Are you deaf?'

'I was in the back.'

'Knocking up another exhibit from Hieronymus Bosch?' I said.

'Very good. Then again, *The Garden of Earthly Delights* is pretty well known, even in this benighted city.'

I ran my eye over the man. His hair was black and curly, his eyes dark brown, and his nose had been broken more than once.

'You're not from here,' I said.

'Heaven forbid.'

Davie came up. 'Where, then?'

'Have you got a warrant? I'm going to call my lawyer.'

'I wouldn't,' I said in a low voice. 'This is a high-priority case. Your house is about to be searched from top to bottom and side to side. Is there anyone else in?'

Matthew Barker shook his head, glowering at me. 'Who are you?'

I told him.

'I know you. I've read one of your books.' He grinned. 'Shite, I thought. Still, it confirmed my worst fears about Edinburgh. Can't understand why it got made capital again.'

Davie's phone rang. He listened and then laughed humourlessly. 'So, you're Matthew Duncan Barker, born Stornoway, December the fourth 1986, maker of theatrical props.'

That was interesting. Stornoway, centre of the oil and gas industry in the northwest, was the biggest city in the Lord of the Isles's domain.

'You make stuff like this?' Davie said contemptuously. 'Surely it doesn't pay well enough for you to afford this place.'

'I have a patron who looks after me. If it's any of your business.'

'Oh, it is, my friend. What's his or her name?'

We waited while Barker chewed his lips.

'Not telling,' he said.

I shrugged. 'Doesn't matter. We know who he is. The question is, when did you last see him?'

For the first time Matthew Barker looked worried. 'What's happened?'

'You tell us,' said Davie.

'I haven't seen him for a week.'

Davie's expression was neutral. 'How long have you known him?'

Barker turned to me, but I wasn't giving him any encouragement.

'We're . . . friends. Have been since Angus – his lordship – and his clan warriors drove the gangsters out of Oban. Nearly fifteen years.'

There it was – confirmation that Barker knew the missing man. I wasn't sure how long it had taken the Lord of the Isles to extend his rule to the north-western Highlands and Islands, but I'd heard he started on Mull and crossed to the nearest town on the mainland.

'A week?' said Davie, turning up the volume. 'Details!'

'Like I say,' Barker replied nervously. 'Last Sunday. He came round about four – we had high tea. I found some kippers – not that they were up to much.'

'Just for tea?' Davie said, with a leer.

'Fuck you! It's nothing like that. I'm an artist and Angus likes my work.'

I looked at the human form on the clarsach.

'Into bondage, is he?' Davie said.

Barker looked down and kept his mouth shut.

'What's that piece of art about?' I asked.

'Whatever you want,' its creator muttered.

'Don't get cute, shithead,' Davie said, fingering the handle of his truncheon.

'I told you, I want my lawyer.'

'Why have you got a lawyer?' I asked. People in Edinburgh were still unused to instructing the inevitably expensive professionals who had flooded the city since reunification.

'My contracts need vetting.'

That might have been true, but would that kind of lawyer be able to help him now? And if Barker was as pure as the driven white stuff, why did he need help?

Davie was on his mobile, calling in a SOCO team. I decided against pre-empting the experts.

'You say this piece is for the Theatre of Life,' I said.

'Aye. They're rehearsing a play about the hell that was Edinburgh over the last thirty years.' Barker gave me a snide smile. 'You'll love it.'

'The hanging figure's in the right-hand panel of Bosch's triptych, isn't it? The one showing the tortures of the damned. What sin had the man on the strings committed?'

'I don't know – composed terrible music?'

'Or allowed himself to be tempted by the devil? It used to be said he had all the best tunes.'

'Still is by the Bible thumpers where I come from.'

'I've heard the Lord of the Isles is a practising Christian.'

'Aye, but not that kind. We had a good malt with our tea.'

Davie had finished his call. 'Did you, now? Where is it?' He glanced around the room. There were bottles on a small table in the corner.

I went over. 'No malts, here. Not even any blended whisky.'

Matthew Barker shrugged. 'We finished the bottle.'

Davie got in the man's face. 'See, I don't believe you, pal. The Lord of the Isles is no friend of yours. For a start, no one in his staff has mentioned your name, let alone any visits out here.'

'He came . . . on his own.' Barker's eyes were down again.

'Very likely,' Davie said. 'No official car, no chauffeur, no security detail. He could no more slip away unnoticed from Ainslie Place than fly over here on a magic carpet. You're a liar!'

I couldn't make my mind up. I motioned Davie to the hall and told him where I was going. He gave me the keys to the four-by-four, saying he'd get a lift back with the suspect, who'd be interrogated with extreme prejudice, lawyer or no lawyer.

I drove on to St John's Road and headed back to the city centre. If I was lucky, Rory Campbell, Big Lachie's deputy on the Municipal Board but also director of the Theatre of Life, would be in his office behind the stage. I tried to remember if I'd ever seen him with the Lord of the Isles. I reckoned I had, on the TV news – Edinburgh politicians inevitably rubbed up against their national counterparts at events. The question was, did Rory know the old aristocrat better than that? Could he have had something to do with Angus Macdonald's disappearance? Surely not . . .

*   *   *

My mobile rang as I was only a couple of minutes away from the theatre. It was Sophia. I pulled in, prompting a horn blast from a bus, and answered.

'Quint, are you coming home tonight?' Her voice was soft and sleepy.

'Hope so, but you know what it's like on big cases.'

'You aren't meant to be doing this any more.'

'I know.'

'But you don't care.' Her tone was sharper.

'Of course I care. You know I do.'

There was a long pause. 'To be completely honest, I don't. Even if you don't want to spend time with me any more, you have to with the kids.'

I sighed. 'Who says I don't want to spend time with you?'

'When did we last have an evening together?'

'That's not very easy with Heck.'

'There's no shortage of babysitters. Come home when you can.'

'Sophia?' I said, before she cut the connection. 'Tomorrow morning you'll find a finger in the morgue. Can you check the night pathologist's report on it?'

'A finger?' She was fully awake now. 'Which one?'

I swallowed. 'Right index, belongs to a male.'

'What on earth?' She'd made the connection with my own missing digit instantly.

I kept quiet.

'Quint? What is it you aren't telling me?'

'Nothing,' I said, realizing that I'd responded far too quickly.

'You're forever saying you don't believe in coincidences.'

I laughed, which was a mistake. An empty beer barrel would have sounded less hollow. 'They happen from time to time.'

'So why do you want my expertise?'

Shit: good question.

'I'll see you later. Love you.' I hit the red button.

At least any conversation with Rory Campbell couldn't go worse.

The Theatre of Life had been a cinema when I was a kid and was then disused until the last years of the Enlightenment when Rory started putting on rabble-rousing plays as a front for his and Lachie's revolutionary movement. Currently, a revival of David Lyndsay's

Thrie Estaitis was running – satire was still very popular in Edinburgh. I banged on the glass doors and a burly security guard appeared in the gloom.

'Mr Dalrymple,' he said, after he'd unlocked the chain. He'd been a freedom fighter and we'd met during the last days of the old regime.

'Is he in?' Rory was notorious for the long hours he worked. These days he had to catch up with the theatre at night as he spent the daylight hours, and more, running the city with Lachie.

'Aye. Ye ken the way.'

I went down the side of the auditorium and through the door to the left. After a series of steps that went down and then up again, I came to his office. He'd removed the door to enable rapid access to members of the company – it was hyper-democratic by nature and all the staff owned shares – and I saw his bare feet hanging over a tattered sofa.

'Rory,' I said.

He looked to the left of the papers he was reading.

'Quint. What's up?'

I moved the chair from the chaotic desk and sat facing him. His head was shaved – supposedly so he could wear wigs more easily when he appeared on stage, though I reckoned he liked the hard-man look – and his features were delineated by the single light behind him. The roots of his popularity were in his politics, but his enviable good looks also played a big part.

'Don't tell me you've tracked the Lord of the Isles down already?' Rory said, sitting up, reaching for a bottle of Glenlivet and pouring large measures into glasses that might have been washed since reunification.

I shook my head. 'We're following some leads.' I took a sip. 'One of which ends here.'

The actor-director ran a hand over his glabrous scalp. 'Is that right?' He looked worryingly unconcerned, but unsurprisingly he was good at hiding his emotions.

'Your upcoming production – the one about hell.'

'*The Garden*?'

'Is that what it's called? Fan of Hieronymus Bosch, are you?'

He smiled. 'Any right-thinking person who isn't?'

'Wonder if Angus Macdonald is one.'

'Probably not.' Rory drained his glass and tipped the bottle again. 'So he's not involved?'

He stared at me. 'You're pulling my sporran. That old reactionary?'

'He wasn't a fan of the Council.'

Rory laughed. 'You think? He did business with them and no doubt would have continued to do so if we hadn't prevailed.'

'He's surely making more money now.'

'Marginally. Do you think everyone in Scotland's over the moon that Embra's capital again? There are plenty of markets for oil, gas and everything else the old bastard peddles. South Africa for one. Their economy's booming, largely because of Scottish oil.'

'Is that right? To get back to *The Garden* . . .'

'You a fan of Joni Mitchell? Thought you were a blues man.'

'I love Joni, not least because she was banned by our former leaders. "Woodstock" was far too subversive for them and none of us was stardust. But, at the risk of becoming monotonous, to get back to . . .'

'*The Garden* is a revue that combines visions of Bosch's underworld with a love story,' Rory said proudly. 'Take my word, it'll be our biggest hit yet.'

'Even bigger than *Spar/Tak/Us*?'

He raised his shoulders. 'That was revolutionary theatre. This is just entertainment.'

'Uh-huh.' Everything was political, as Rory Campbell knew very well. 'What can you tell me about Matthew Barker?'

'The prop-maker?'

I smiled. 'I think he locates himself on a higher artistic level.'

'True enough. He's right up himself. Good work, though.'

'You paying him?'

Rory frowned. 'I'll have to check payroll. Why wouldn't we be?'

'He claims he has a patron.'

The Scots ten-pence piece – the smallest denomination of coin – dropped.

'The Lord of the Isles?' Suddenly, there was a note of panic in Rory's voice.

'Aye. According to Barker, they had high tea together the Sunday before this one.'

Rory got to his feet and stretched his well-exercised arms. 'I'd have heard if he was offering to work for free. I wouldn't like to think Angus Macdonald had anything to do with the Theatre of Life. He's the nearest Scotland has to a robber baron.'

It struck me that Rory Campbell might have found out about Barker's affiliation and decided to teach the Lord of the Isles a lesson. On balance, I thought that was unlikely. They were both democratically elected representatives and the days of violence had passed in most of the country.

'You know what Barker's making?'

He nodded. 'Man on the harp – we decided that the clarsach was more appropriate.'

'I've seen it. Pretty terrifying. What else are you planning? A bird that eats and shits people? Ears with a knife blade protruding?'

'The latter, yes.'

I caught his eye. 'What about a tree-fish?'

'A what?' This time he seemed genuinely taken aback. 'Is that in *The Garden of Earthly Delights*?'

'No, *The Temptation of St Anthony*.' It was possible that he hadn't heard about the attempted strangling in Leith, but I wasn't convinced. Then again, what reason could he have for playing dumb?

I told him about the incident, watching for any giveaway reactions, but I caught none.

'How can that be connected to the Lord of the Isles's disappearance?' he asked.

'Apparently, via the Theatre of Life,' I said, getting up and heading for the door. 'See what you can find out about Barker, will you?'

'Aye, Quint.'

'Are there more props like his man on the clarsach?'

He went to his desk and opened a file. 'Seven,' he said. 'All from *The Garden of Earthly Delights*. We've got two other prop-makers working on them.'

'I'll need their names. Where are the pieces? Not here?'

He laughed. 'You're kidding. We've hardly got room for the current production. We rent warehouse space in the Pleasance.' He scribbled on a notepad, tore the page off and handed it to me. 'There's a security guard round the clock. People will nick anything these days.'

'Not like the old days?'

'Piss off.'

So I did. As I walked back to the glass doors, I felt mildly nauseous. Rory was as good a man as any in Edinburgh and I was harbouring doubts about him – worse, I'd shown him that I was.

I wished I'd stayed in my study and stuck to fiction.

I thought about going home to bed but, as always in the early days of big cases, I was running on adrenaline and knew sleep wouldn't come. I hadn't forgotten that Jack Nicol, Tree-Fish's potential victim, had pointed me to the Theatre of Life.

Back at ScotPol HQ, I tracked Davie down. He was in the senior officers' canteen, eating a very large late dinner.

'One thing about reunification is that we get Stornoway black pudding,' he said, looking up from his platter. 'Want some?'

'In a minute. Where are you with the questioning?'

'Matthew Barker clammed up straightaway. He's waiting for his lawyer.'

I sat down opposite him. The room had a low ceiling and reeked of fried food. Only one other table at the far end was occupied, by a pair of uniformed computer crime experts. They were deep in conversation.

'Doesn't suggest he's got a clear conscience,' I said, taking a piece of his burned bacon.

'Get your own,' he rumbled. 'The staff from Ainslie Place have all talked, at length. We've compared notes and their stories hook up. They could have learned a script, but they're bloody good actors if they did. There's a change of shift at four p.m. Hamish Macdonald thinks his lord and master could have slipped out then.'

I raised an eyebrow. 'Doesn't seem very likely with so many people around.' I told him about the valet's absences. 'What about the rooms above and below? Any sign of ropes or wires?'

'Hard to tell. The stone's old and there are some grooves. But if someone took him, they could have used some kind of padding and the marks wouldn't be obvious.'

I thought about that. 'Maybe he wasn't taken – maybe he went voluntarily.'

Davie extracted a piece of gristle from his teeth. 'In that case, he'd have got the equipment from somebody.'

'I didn't say he was flying solo.'

'Flying solo's pretty close to the bone. He's an old man and he carries a fair amount of weight. Can you really see him abseiling down to the back garden? Anyway, how would he get out of there without being seen?'

'Good points. The smart money's still on at least one of his staff or bodyguards being in on it.'

I got up and went to the counter, where I obtained a less artery-clogging plateful of vegetable stew and – there was no way I could resist – black pudding.

'We'll keep at them,' Davie said, when I got back to the table. 'What about you?'

I went through what I'd learned from Rory Campbell.

'Do you think he's involved?' Davie had never been a fan of the revolutionaries, even though he'd lost faith in the Council by the end. Campbell, in particular, he reckoned was as slippery as a conger eel. 'You fancy taking a look at this warehouse?'

I did.

Davie drove the short distance to the Pleasance. The warehouse was a three-storey building behind the festival venue. During the Enlightenment period, the complex had been too far out of the centre to be safe for tourists, but since reunification it had been restored and hosted comedy shows, during none of which had I ever laughed. Either I was losing my sense of humour or what counted as comedy these days was a foreign country.

Davie parked the four-by-four outside the dingy block. All the windows were covered by steel shutters. We went to the door, stepping through slush and shivering in the chill, and examined the sign. All three floors were attributed to the same company, EmbraSafeStore – spaces between words seemed to be going out of fashion. I hit the buzzer.

'Who's that?' came a disembodied voice from a small panel.

'ScotPol,' Davie thundered. 'Get this door open now!'

After a few seconds came the sounds of bolts being pulled and keys turning. The door opened a few centimetres and a bearded face appeared between two chains.

Davie held up his ID card.

'Warrant?' said the guard.

'In your dreams, wee man.'

I tried a different tone. 'Rory Campbell sent me here. Call him if you like.'

The door closed. Davie stepped back and raised his booted foot.

'Hang on, Steel Toes,' I said. 'You're not in the Guard now.'

He glowered at me till we heard the chains being disengaged and the door opened fully.

'All right, Mr Dalrymple,' said the diminutive figure in dark-blue overalls. The cap on his head was crooked and his beard could have done with a wash. 'Just you, though.'

After Davie gave him a two-second death stare, he backed away and moved to a staircase. 'Follow me. It's the first floor.'

'Give us the keys,' Davie said.

Resistance was brief. We left the guard – according to the badge on his chest, his name was Kennedy, D. – and went up. Davie opened the three locks and the door creaked like one in a horror film. The smell of paint and glue washed over us.

I hit the lights. All the objects in the large space were covered by white dust sheets – they were an array of static ghosts.

'Where are we going to start?' Davie said with a groan.

I pointed. There were labels pinned to each sheet. The first ones were marked *Thrie Estaitis*, so I left them untouched. Then I struck lucky and lifted the dust sheet up carefully.

'What the—'

I was amazed Davie hadn't sworn because what I'd just revealed was a grade-A stomach-churner. Slightly less than my height, a green-headed hare or rabbit in a coat was holding some kind of pike or halberd over its right shoulder; a male body whose ankles had been fixed together was hanging from the shaft of the weapon, with painted flames and black smoke emanating from a large hole in its belly.

'Fuck,' said Davie at last. 'Any idea what that means?'

'I've got an encyclopaedia of symbols at home, but I'd guess that the hare or rabbit – probably the former because of its long ears – suggests lust. You know how much those creatures procreate. As for the exploding gut, you tell me. Onwards.'

We went down the line, lifting and looking. I found a pig in a nun's headdress making advances to a naked man, and a small creature with a large helmet and armour, but bare thighs, embedded in one of which was an arrow. Its tail looked as if it came from a large lizard. More lust, cut with religious corruption. Was the latter significant? I remembered the Lord of the Isles's chief of staff saying that his boss was a Christian.

'Bloody hell,' came Davie's voice.

'That's the general idea,' I said, the smile freezing on my lips when I saw what he'd uncovered. Two dogs with scaly skins, one with what looked like an aerial coming out of a dish on its head, were at the throat of a naked man with his head thrown back. The trio was strikingly lifelike, and I held my breath before I convinced myself that the figures weren't breathing.

'Nice,' said Davie. 'That Campbell's a twisted bastard.'

'Hieronymus Bosch holds the copyright.'

'Aye, but I can't kick his arse.'

I moved on to the next sheet. It was over an object that came up only to the middle of my thighs, though the bottom part extended outwards. I moved to the side, tugged gently and the figure was laid bare.

'Aw, come on,' said Davie from behind me.

The woman's skin was pale and pasty. She was seated, her legs together and stretched out to the front. Her blonde hair hung below her shoulders, but it was what had a grip on her that made me freeze. Two thin arms were on the front of her torso, each with four long fingers; one hand rose up from the left and clutched her small right breast, the other came from the right and pointed to her groin.

I knew immediately – from the texture of her skin, from the slight smell of decay, from the glassy eyes – that this was no prop.

'Is that a—'

'Real woman? Yes.' I bent forward, looking at the leaf on her upper chest.

Except it was no leaf. It was dark congealed blood around and in a deep, wound about two inches wide.

I heard Davie talking on his mobile but could pay attention only to the corpse. I wanted to close the poor woman's eyes, but I knew Sophia would deride that departure from procedure. So I held her lifeless gaze and hoped against the evidence that she'd left this world without pain.

FIVE

After I'd taken photos with my phone, we got out of the warehouse space and waited for the SOCO team and the pathologist. Sophia wasn't on duty till eight a.m., so I'd have to put up with her smartarse boss. Davie told me that Hel Hyslop was on her way too. Great.

In the meantime, we questioned Kennedy, D., the security guy. It turned out that the 'D' stood for Denzil, not exactly a common name in these parts.

'Right, when did you come on duty, son?' Davie asked, with more bellicosity in his tone than was necessary.

'Eight o'clock yesterday evening,' the man with the beard said. It made him look older than he was. I reckoned he was in his late twenties.

'Anyone been in here since?'

He shook his head emphatically. 'The people who rent space have keys and twenty-four-hour access, but it's rare for them to show up when I'm on.'

'You always work nights?' I put in.

He nodded. 'The pay's a wee bit better and I like it on my own. During the day there's a lot of coming and going.'

'What do you do with yourself when you're not on rounds?' I continued, giving Davie a warning glance. Robust interrogation methods were no longer legal – worse, they often made people clam up.

Denzil Kennedy shrugged. 'I'm doing a distance-learning course from Inverness University. Computer science.'

The northern city was well known for its innovative digital pedagogy.

'Good for you,' I said. 'So, do you go into each floor's locked spaces?'

He nodded. 'Have to; it's in the protocol.'

We hadn't told him what we'd found. 'When were you last in the Theatre of Life's area?'

He dropped his gaze. 'I . . .' He looked at his phone. 'I have to log my visits on this. Two twenty a.m.'

Something was clearly getting at him. 'Are you sure?' I said.

'Aye,' he said rapidly.

I gave him an encouraging smile. 'And what does the protocol require you to do on each visit?'

He was still looking at the concrete floor. 'Em, you have to walk up and down, checking that everything's as it was on the last round. Which was at ten p.m.'

Davie had had enough. 'What are you hiding, you wee shite?'

I raised my eyes to the ceiling. Fortunately, the outcome was positive.

'I don't like that place,' Kennedy said. 'All those sheets, they're like shrouds over dead people. I looked once. It was horrible. Two great big ears with this huge blade sticking out between them. Creepy.'

I took his arm. 'Is that all you saw? How about tonight? Did you look under any of the dust sheets?'

He shook his head. 'No way.' He looked at me. 'Here, what did you find?' There was the sound of approaching sirens.

'If I find out that you know . . .' Davie didn't need to spell out the threat.

Vehicles pulled up outside and uniformed ScotPol officers rushed in.

'Take this specimen to HQ,' Davie said, pushing Denzil Kennedy forward.

'Give him something to eat and drink,' I added.

'And don't let him out of your sight,' finished Davie.

I watched as the bearded man was led away. A second after he went out the door, in came Hel Hyslop.

Davie and I looked at each other and then for an emergency exit. There wasn't one.

'Over here,' said the director of ScotPol, motioning to the far corner.

'I'll handle this,' I said.

Davie grinned. 'Just like old times. I've got your back.'

'Well?' she demanded, arms akimbo.

I was tempted to reply, 'Not bad. You?' but decided to stay alive.

'What have you heard?' I asked.

'Very little. Start from the beginning.'

I did, then passed the middle and reached the end.

Hel tugged on one of her unruly curls. 'Might the attempted strangulation in Leith be connected to the Lord of the Isles's disappearance?'

'That's a big jump at this time.'

'All the same, you'd better liaise with the detectives you put on that case.'

'Will do,' said Davie, backing away to make the call. Hel Hyslop was keen on immediate action. My worry was that she was about to immediate-action me.

'What next, Quint?' she demanded, which was a victory of sorts.

'Check this place for other bodies – I hope not including his lordship the leader of the opposition. Then try to identify the poor woman upstairs, work out why she's here, who killed her and why, then investigate Matthew Barker in depth, see what the SOCOs discover here, talk to Rory Campbell again . . .'

Hel raised a hand. 'Be careful with that individual.'

I locked eyes with her. What the hell? Live dangerously. 'Any particular reason?'

'He has a problematic history.'

'You mean he revolted. So did I.'

There wasn't a hint of humour in her smile. 'Don't worry, that has been noted.'

'I remember your and Andrew Duart's histories, too,' I said, going for broke. She and her boss had several things they didn't want trumpeted about in the now free press of Scotland's capital. They had Glasgow's editors in their pockets.

'Rory Campbell is a suspect in a major case,' Hyslop said.

'And what's that?'

She chewed her lower lip to give the impression of reluctance before telling me something big. 'He's been having secret meetings with representatives of Nor-England.'

Although Lachie MacFarlane had mentioned our friends in the south, I feigned surprise. I'd learned only to share the minimum with Hyslop and Duart.

'Does that have anything to do with the Theatre of Life props upstairs?' I asked.

'How would I know?' Hel could play the same game as me,

but I was better at it. 'Let me know immediately if you find an English connection.'

I had the feeling she wouldn't mind if the Lord of the Isles went missing permanently.

Hel looked at her phone. She had a flash model with a big screen. I'd seen her typing notes on it. 'I don't get this. The props and the woman upstairs are from *The Garden of Earthly Delights*, but the tree-fish attacker in Leith was from another painting, *The Temptation*—'

'*Of Saint Anthony*,' I completed. 'That didn't escape me. Maybe anything by Bosch goes.' I gave her a tight smile. 'Or maybe there are different assailants reading from the same catalogue raisonné.'

That made her head shoot back. Goal.

'There's the pathologist,' Hyslop said after a brief silence. 'Keep in touch, Quint.' She narrowed one eye. 'After all, we know where you live.' Then she went over to greet the medic.

Davie came back and I told him the little I'd heard.

'This is beginning to stink,' he said. 'It really is like old times.'

'Fish rotting from the head down.'

'Even tree-fish. I spoke to my people. They'll be at HQ in half an hour.'

'I take it they haven't made any significant progress.'

'You take it right. Going up with the pathologist?'

I nodded and we walked over.

'Ah, Dalrymple,' the short, plump doctor said, his bulbous nose in the air as if I hadn't washed.

'Ah, McKirdy,' I returned. He was from Dundee, which used to have a renowned teaching hospital, but he'd got away before the anarcho-syndicalists took over. They'd have had his bowels for bootlaces. 'Glad we're still on surname terms.'

'Don't worry, I call your wife by her first name,' he said, with a smirk.

I'd get him for that before the night was out.

A SOCO handed the pathologist, Davie and me coveralls and bootees. On the first floor, a space had been cleared around the body. All the dust sheets had been removed and technicians were at work on the props. Only four had Bosch connections that I recognized. We hung back and let McKirdy carry out his preliminary examination. He had a large silver case and numerous pieces of equipment, some beyond my ken. Eventually, he got off his knees and turned to us.

'Right, then – ask your predictable questions, Dalrymple.'

'The answers to which will be "I need to run more tests".'

'Not necessarily,' he said through his mask.

'Cause of death?' said Davie, ratcheting up the volume.

The pathologist gave him a quick look and straightened his back. 'I do, of course, have to run more tests, but I'd say the wound to her chest was fatal.'

I took out my notebook. 'Any thoughts on what caused it?'

'A flat-headed object approximately five centimetres in diameter. Wielded with considerable force, as it went through the sternum and almost broke through the skin on her back.'

'Flat?' Davie repeated. 'Not sharp.'

'No. Something like a steel bar.'

I conjured up the painting. There were several weapons of that shape in the right panel of the triptych. I decided not to share that with Sophia's boss.

'Time of death?' said Davie.

'I'd hazard between eight and ten hours ago. I'll have to—'

'Yeah, yeah,' I interrupted. 'Was she killed here?'

'I'd say not. There's no blood on the floor beneath her.' McKirdy started to pack up his equipment. 'I'll tell you something else.' Nothing was forthcoming.

I realized I was expected to supplicate him. 'Very good of you. What?'

'The victim was a drug addict. There are numerous puncture marks between her toes. She may well have been unconscious when she was murdered.'

'Couldn't have been an accident?' Davie said.

The pathologist snorted. 'Highly unlikely with a flat object, Detective Leader.'

'Just checking, Doctor.' Davie gave him a slack smile. 'See, we're the ones who decide if this is a murder case. After you've run further tests, of course.'

McKirdy stalked away. I hoped he wouldn't take his irritation out on Sophia.

*　　*　　*

After talking to the SOCO leader and taking a slight detour, we went back to the four-by-four.

'No obvious signs or traces of the victim's arrival at the warehouse,' I said. 'The timing that Dundonian arse gave us covers the change of shift. You'd better bring in the security guy who was on before Denzil Kennedy.'

'Already organized,' Davie said, starting the engine. 'While you were giving your attention to that jukebox.'

The ground floor had been rented by a pub chain that was storing vintage pinball machines and the like.

'Great music on it,' I said.

'Sonny Blue Catshagger? Hound Dog Dalrymple?'

'Drive, fool.'

'Yes, sir. Where to, sir?'

'I'd like to say "home, David, and don't spare the horses", but I guess we'd better go to your place of work.'

'Brilliant. I'm hungry.'

'Again?'

He ignored that.

The snow started again, thick flakes floating slowly to the sodden roads and pavements. The wind had blown itself out. Drifting would soon be a problem.

'Shit!' Davie gasped, swerving towards the kerb.

A large silver car of the kind that the richest business people drove had passed us and forced us to the side of Jeffrey Street. Davie was out of the four-by-four in a flash, his truncheon fully extended. Then, as the window came down, I saw who was in the rear of the other vehicle.

'Jesus, Billy,' I said. 'Davie!'

Too late – he'd already got the chauffeur on the road and was cuffing him. I wasn't inclined to intervene.

'Get in, will you, Quint?' Billy said with a frown. I knew for sure that he wasn't concerned about the fate of his driver.

I got into the car, smelling the sumptuous leather interior.

'This'd better not be about my Icelandic royalties.'

'You haven't sold there yet.' He opened the compartment on the floor between us. 'Twenty-five-year-old Talisker, Detective Leader?' he said to Davie, who was peering in the window.

'No bloody chance, *Mr Geddes*.' The name came out like a curse.

Davie had never had any time for Billy and his scheming. He went back to the four-by-four, dragging his victim.

Billy handed me a cut-crystal glass containing a large measure, adding a few drops of water with his shaky hand. I could have declined, but that malt was way out of my price range.

'You want to pick my brains, don't you?' I said after I'd taken a sip of the nectar.

Billy took a slug rather than a sip. 'Of course I fucking do. Where's the Lord of the Isles?'

'Angus? Can't you tell me? You're in bed with him on numerous money-making ventures, aren't you?'

'So what?' he snarled. 'He has plenty of other business partners, you know – not all of them well-intentioned like me.'

I took in his misshapen features. It seemed he wasn't being ironic.

'Names?'

He raised the glass again. 'Not so fast. What have you found out?'

I looked at him sceptically. The thing was, Billy could be a useful source – by now he knew everybody who mattered across the country – but he expected plenty in return. I decided to play his game, confirming that the Lord of the Isles was missing. I also told him about Matthew Barker's link to the Lord of the Isles – not that the SOCOs had found any sign of the missing man in the prop-maker's house, we'd heard – and about the dead woman. But nothing about Rory Campbell or the finger, let alone Hieronymus Bosch. I was still trying to make sense of that.

'Shit,' he said in a low voice, propping his chin up with his good hand. 'This is a fucking disaster.'

'Which part of it?'

'Angus being absent, of course. There are deals to be finalized, clients to be whiskied and dined.'

'I'm sure you'll manage in his stead.'

'Ha! They don't show me off to visitors like that. I'm the greedy goblin, remember?'

A long-dead senior member of the Enlightenment had called him that.

'Any idea what might have happened to Angus Macdonald, Billy?' Flattery was always a good idea. 'He trusts you as much as anyone.' I was repeating what Billy had told me a couple of months back.

He sniffed. 'I thought he did.'

'No secret lovers? Opium dens? Blackmailers? Kidnappers?'

'That puffed-up old prig? You're kidding. His idea of a good time is standing in a freezing river up to his balls, trying to catch a fish for his tea.'

I thought of Barker and the kippers the pair had eaten – he hadn't caught those.

'Besides, he's got a large staff and a security detail,' Billy continued. 'How could he have slipped away unnoticed?'

'I don't know. Yet.' Then I remembered what Lachie MacFarlane had told me. 'Here, is it true that there are people from Nor-England in the city?'

Billy's eyes were immediately veiled. I'd hit pay dirt. 'Pardon?' he said, his voice taut.

'I'll take that as an "aye". What are they like, the English?' I hadn't spoken to one since a hair-thinning trip to Oxford ten years back.

He glared at me. 'They've got two heads and three eyes. Christ, Quint, what do you think? They're like anyone else.'

'Self-centred, money-grabbing hedonists with bad haircuts, worse facial hair and abysmal tattoos, then?'

'Pillock. There are only three here, apart from their bodyguards. Hel Hyslop forced the latter to give up their weapons. Apparently, they were armed to the teeth.'

'And you've met them?'

'Two – a big bugger called Nigel Shotbolt—'

'You're kidding.'

'He's the leader of Nor-England – one of his titles is Warden of the Marches.'

I took out my notebook and scribbled the title down.

'He's a big mouth and a blusterer,' Billy continued. 'The brains belong to his aide, a woman by the name of Gemma Bass.' He leered, which was a frightful sight. 'Blonde and extremely well upholstered. Knows her commodity trading.'

I kept writing. 'And the third?'

'Another guy, seems to be the aide to the aide. Geoffrey something . . . can't remember . . . oh, yeah, Lassiter. Skinnymalink who defers to the others in a big way.'

'The media have been remarkably quiet about this Nor-England,' I said.

'The government will have been pulling their chains. It's only recently come into being. Apparently stretches from what were, when we were kids, Northumberland and Cumbria, to Durham and North Yorkshire. The purveyors of chaos that were in charge have been eradicated, according to Shotbolt.'

'And you're crapping yourself because the contracts you've been working on with them have to be approved by Angus Macdonald.'

'I already told you that.'

'But he's the leader of the opposition. Why can't the energy minister sign on the dots?'

He laughed uproariously. 'You think the government's in charge of everything in our freshly reminted country? You get younger every birthday.'

'Incorrect. I'm permanently sixteen. Andrew Duart thinks he's in charge.'

'Not when it comes to oil and gas. The Lord of the Isles can turn off the taps any time he wants.'

'If that's true, Duart's more likely than anyone to be behind the disappearance.'

'Don't be an idiot. Duart's economic strategy relies on oil and gas being pumped every second of the day.'

I smiled. 'You've told me about the Nor-English because you think they've got Angus Macdonald.'

I got a twist of the lips in return. 'It's certainly a possibility. They haven't used him as a bargaining tool yet, but it would be handy if we found him before they do so.'

Sitting back in the soft leather, I considered the situation. Duart and Hyslop could have put me on the case because they had the same concerns as Billy; they hadn't given me the background because living in democratic Glasgow had made them careful about managing the flow of information. But they also hadn't authorized me to question the Nor-English, let alone drag them in chains to ScotPol HQ. Davie would have encouraged me to do that. To him, English meant bloodthirsty, shoot-first-and-don't-bother-asking-questions criminals – which, to be fair, were the only kind we'd encountered during the drugs wars.

'I trust you'll act on what I've said,' Billy said, lighting one of his noxious cigarillos.

'You seem to have become indispensable to those in power. Why don't you pull Hel Hyslop's chain yourself?'

He laughed. 'For some reason she's never taken to me.'

'Despite the deals you worked on with her boss before the Enlightenment ended?'

'Maybe she hates cripples,' he said, blowing smoke over me. 'She wouldn't be the only one.'

I opened the door and got out. Maudlin Billy was unbearable.

'Here,' he called, 'don't think you can pull the fleece over my eyes. You didn't tell me about the severed finger.'

Bastard. I waited till my gut had stopped trampolining. 'Need-to-know basis only,' I said, in as normal a voice as I could manage.

'Strange coincidence, though, isn't it?' he said, in full sly mode. 'It's the same one you're missing.'

I kept quiet, confining myself to raising the stump at him. He didn't know the truth about how I'd been mutilated, but he'd always had an active imagination.

I managed to talk Davie into letting the chauffeur go with a warning and a boot up the arse.

'What did that bawbag want?' he asked, as we continued down Jeffrey Street towards the building site that would become the reactivated Waverley Station next year.

I gave him the gist.

'English from the North? Here? First I've heard of it.' He drove through the gates of ScotPol, after activating them with a remote control. The uniformed personnel didn't stand to attention or salute. Hel Hyslop had removed as many authority markers as she could. Davie didn't approve.

'Me too, but I suppose it's inevitable that the government, not to mention the business-hungry opposition, would want to make money out of them.'

'The Borders have been back in the Middle Ages for decades. Do you really think they're under control on the English side?' He pulled up in a space marked 'D.L.'. 'I know for a fact they aren't on ours. The Defence Force is holed up in castles and forts and we haven't any traction south of Kelso and Selkirk. From what I've heard, Hawick is in ruins.'

I got out of the vehicle and my legs almost gave way. I was too old for this kind of case. I had to get some sleep and told Davie so.

'All right, you fader,' he said, punching me what he thought was lightly on my arm. 'Let's see where the various lines of enquiry have got and make a plan. Then you can get to your bed.' He laughed. 'For a couple of hours.'

'Even you need to get your head down,' I protested.

'Got a sofa in my office, remember?' He slapped his belly. 'As long as I fill the beast.'

We headed for the operations room on the second floor of the glass building. That was another of Hel Hyslop's requirements – ScotPol officers had to be visible when they were at their desks. I hadn't asked if the glass was bulletproof.

Davie was immediately surrounded by subordinates. I found a chair and watched him handle them. In five minutes he had a collection of brown folders. The younger staff all worked with portable computers but Davie and a couple of other old-timers from the City Guard preferred paper.

He waved me into his office. It was a soulless box with glass on all sides, though senior personnel were provided with blinds. It wouldn't do for the populace to see them with their heads on their desks or crashed out on sofas. The only personal touch that Davie allowed himself was a photo of the Hume Barracks rugby team, which he'd captained for seven years. It had won the inter-barracks cup every time he led them out. I preferred darts.

'So,' he said, swinging round in a chair that looked comfortable, though nothing like as much as those in Billy's car. 'Where do you want to start?'

'Matthew Barker.'

'Insists he knows nothing about the Lord of the Isles's disappearance and that the last time he saw him was a week ago.' He drank from a large mug of coffee that a young female officer had brought him. I wasn't touching the stuff as it would keep me awake.

'What about the nature of his relationship with old Angus?'

'Claims it was just friendship. When pressed, he said they both felt out of place in the capital and wished they were back in the northwest.'

'Did he get the lawyer he wanted?'

'Aye. We'll have to cut him loose this afternoon.'

'Cut him loose now, but put a tail on him.'

'Right.' He made a note.

'Denzil Kennedy.'

'The security guard at the warehouse?' Davie opened another file. 'He held firm under heavy-duty questioning. The feeling is that he's clean. His record's been checked and there's nothing out of the ordinary.'

'Let him go too, with a tail.'

'Right. He took over from one Ricky Fetlar. He's being brought in as we speak – apparently, he went to visit a friend in Dalkeith.'

'How did he get there?' The town was seven miles to the south.

'He has a motorbike. His record's not so clean – a couple of drunk-and-disorderly arrests, admittedly over five years ago, and involvement in a hit and run. It went to court but the verdict was not proven. A witness recanted.'

'Interesting.'

'I'll interview him myself.'

'Check the warehouse records first. We need to know when the dead woman was brought in.'

He gave me a sharp look. 'Amazingly, my people thought of that and are on it.'

I smiled. 'You run a tight – no, *sober* ship.'

Two fingers were raised in my direction. 'The other prop-makers have been located and are waiting to be spoken to. Their records are clean.'

'I'll talk to Rory Campbell later on. According to Hyslop, he's involved in talks with the Nor-English. Lachie MacFarlane might be too.'

Davie grimaced. 'Rather you than me.'

I thought about the local leaders. It wasn't beyond the realms of possibility that they wanted the Lord of the Isles out of the way. Leith, Edinburgh's port, was being redeveloped as an oil and gas facility for tankers, much to the chagrin of Angus Macdonald, who wanted to run pipelines all over Scotland. Perhaps he was also thinking of extending them into Nor-England, not that Billy had said anything about that. As ever, he knew more than he'd told me.

'What about the tree-fish case?' I asked.

'It was back-burnered, as you know, but I put a competent team on it after we found the dead woman. That witness, Ann Melville, is sticking to her story, but not saying anything more. And she's got a lawyer.'

'She was scared, I remember.'

'Guess who her lawyer is.' His grim look gave it away.

'Not that tosser Adamson.'

'The very one.'

Since the Truth and Reconciliation Hearings, the law had allowed suitably qualified individuals to work as both solicitors and advocates. The fact that Peter Adamson was willing to take on a seemingly minor client like Ann Melville was suggestive. Then again, he'd had a fall from grace.

'I didn't think the booze had destroyed his professional standing to that extent,' I said. I was disappointed it hadn't after what he put me through.

'It did, but since last year he's been working for some big guns again.'

I wondered about that, then moved on. 'What about the assailant? Any other sightings?'

Davie shook his head. 'I suppose it could be a coincidence. Or someone having a go at the Theatre of Life. After all, the costume's from a different painting.'

'Hm.' Rory Campbell was popular with the voters of Edinburgh, but his role in the revolution meant that the more extreme supporters of the Enlightenment hated his intestines.

Davie got up. 'I'm going to eat. Coming?'

'No, thanks. I'm going to run home.'

That provoked a belly laugh. 'You'll do yourself an injury.'

'It isn't far.'

'Far enough. Remember, maintain an even pace and keep your breathing regular.'

'That's rich, coming from a guy who never runs.' His knee didn't allow that.

'I exercise in other ways,' he said with a wink as he walked out.

Within seconds he'd started talking to a statuesque blonde officer in plain clothes. Typical.

Then again, there was a blonde waiting for me in our bed. Not that she'd showed much interest in inter-sheet exercise recently.

I was panting hard, my calves and thighs on fire and my mouth drier than the deserts that had reportedly swallowed Las Vegas. I came round the corner of Great Scotland Street at a limp and was confronted by two individuals I knew to my cost.

'Quint,' said the female member of the pair, her brown hair pulled back and her medium height enhanced by heels that must have hurt even more than mine. 'Good morning.'

I stopped, caught my breath with a struggle and looked at my watch. 'It's five thirty, Miss Thomson,' I said.

'In the morning, aye.' She smiled, her lips painted a bright purple. 'How many times do I have to tell you to call me Charlie?'

'Twenty-three million,' I said, taking out my keys. 'Now, if you don't mi—'

'The Lord of the Isles,' she said. 'I hear he's disappeared and you're looking for him.'

Not for the first time, someone in ScotPol had leaked. Or maybe someone in the missing man's staff. The Scottish media had deep pockets these days. Charlotte Thomson worked for SignalScotland, a group that owned a TV channel, numerous radio stations, both national and local, and a long list of news platforms, print and online. Her byline often appeared on the front page of the *Scottish Observer*, a paper that purported to be highbrow but filled its Sunday magazine with scantily clad models of both sexes.

'No comment,' I said, slipping the key into the street-door lock.

'Which means you are,' the journo said. 'You getting all this, Andy?'

The man with the camera on his shoulder nodded.

'No, it doesn't,' I said, pushing the door open.

Thomson came up the steps. 'What were you doing in ScotPol HQ half an hour ago, then, Quint? Traffic offence?'

'Correct. They kept my car.'

She turned and looked at our battered four-by-four, then faced the camera and pointed out that I was being frugal with the truth.

I took the opportunity to close the door. Shit. With the press on my back, the job just got even more difficult. I laboured up the stairs and tried to get into the flat. The keys turned but the chains were all engaged. Sophia was making me do this the hard way. I called her name as softly as would carry to the bedroom. Eventually, she arrived, gave me a sharp look and closed the door. I heard the chains being undone.

'Thanks,' I said.

'For nothing,' she replied, turning away. 'Heck's just woken up.'

I went into the wee lad's bedroom and picked him up. He promptly kicked me in the gut. At least he was barefoot.

'Let's play cars,' I wheezed.

'Yay, Dad!' he trilled, writhing around till I put him down. He then emptied a box of toy racers on the carpet.

I managed ten minutes, before Sophia rescued me and pointed to the bed. I managed to get most of my clothes off, then burrowed under the quilt and sank into the abyss of Morpheus.

I awoke, shaking all over, thanks to Sophia, Maisie and Heck.

'Wake up!' said our son.

'You look like a corpse,' said our daughter.

'Can you take Heck to playgroup?' said my wife.

My body creaked as I sat up. They scattered, with a mixture of laughter and groaning. I stumbled into the kitchen.

Sophia was putting her coat on. 'I have to go. I gather there's a new . . .'

'I'm not a fool,' Maisie said. 'You've got a fresh cadaver.'

Heck sniggered. 'Cad . . . a . . . ver,' he said, over and over.

'Thank you, Maisie,' said Sophia, with a disapproving look. She turned to me. 'I imagine I'll see you shortly.'

I nodded and watched her walk out with her head high. What had happened between us? She'd been known as the Ice Queen when she was first appointed Medical Guardian, but I'd broken through to the soft and generous woman below. Now I was being frozen out again.

'Cars, Dad!' Heck said, wiping jam across his face with the back of his hand.

Maisie sighed and got a wet cloth.

'I'll watch him while you shower,' she said. 'You need one. Have you been smoking?' Her voice was almost as chill as her mother's.

'No,' I replied. 'Billy tracked me down.'

'Billy Geddes?' It sounded as if she was chewing a slug. 'I don't know what you see in that awful man.'

I didn't bother trying to explain. After I'd cleaned up and put on fresh clothes, Maisie kissed my cheek on her way to the door.

'Come on, old man,' she said with a smile. 'Make her feel wanted.'

So it had come to this: marriage guidance from an eleven-year-old, admittedly one with the wisdom of a professor.

'Thanks,' I muttered. 'Have a good day.'

She departed with a wave, her schoolbag covered in patches with the names of ancient blues bands. At least I'd managed a degree of indoctrination.

'Cars!' shrieked Heck.

'All right!' I screamed back.

We collapsed in hysterics.

I walked to ScotPol HQ after I'd taken the wee man to playgroup round the corner from the flat. My legs were still complaining, but at least the snow, which had nearly brought me down numerous times when I was running, had melted. The pregnant clouds over the city suggested there would be more of the white stuff along soon.

I found Davie crashed out on his sofa, boots on the floor next to him. His mouth was open and he was snoring like a grampus. I noticed his flies were open and wondered who was responsible for that. The blinds were down on all sides of his glass box and he could have had company. I decided not to enquire. He was less open about his dalliances with staff now, not least because inevitably they were all junior to him and regulations were strict. Unless he'd been dallying with Hel Hyslop . . . No, not even Davie would do that.

I held his nostrils shut and waited for the explosion, stepping back when it happened.

'Bastard,' Davie said, when he'd caught his breath. He looked at his watch. 'What are you doing here so early?'

'Heck,' I said, starting to pull up the blinds to show we were open for business.

'Oh, aye.' He pulled on his boots – City Guard-issue steel-toe-capped clodhoppers that he'd managed to find in a surplus shop. 'Breakfast,' he said, his expression lightening.

There was a knock on the glass door.

'Come in!' Davie shouted. 'Ah, Eilidh. I mean Officer Mackay. You know Citizen – Mr Dalrymple?'

We nodded to each other. I reckoned Eilidh – who must have been in her late twenties – and the zip were intimately connected, the spots of red on her cheeks a dead giveaway.

'Several things, Detective Leader,' she said, looking at her clipboard. 'The pathologist is most insistent that you attend the postmortem he's carrying out in . . . eighteen minutes. Director Hyslop wants a briefing at ten a.m. And' – she took a deep breath – 'there's been a suicide in the holding cells.'

My heart skipped a beat. 'Who?' I said.

Officer Mackay checked her notes. 'Ricky Fetlar.'

'The security guard at EmbraSafeStore who was on before Denzil Kennedy.'

'Shit,' said Davie. 'You should have woken me, Eilidh.'

'It was only discovered twenty minutes ago, sir. The doctor's still in there.'

We headed for the stairs at speed.

'Eilidh?' I said.

'Piss off.'

I let it go.

Davie cleared a path through the gathered officers and went through the open cell door. He swore loudly.

I managed to contain myself, taking in the heavily built man lying on the floor, his head hard against the wall, the cranium misshapen and blood, bone and brain matter around it. There were marks on the white-painted bricks above, as if he'd lowered his head and run into the unforgiving surface.

The doctor was an elderly man I'd worked with in the past.

'Dalrymple,' he said, with the weariness of one who had seen it all but could still be surprised by the actions of his fellow humans.

'Craigie,' I responded. 'You think he rammed his head into the wall himself?'

'Almost certainly. There are no signs that he's been held or swung like a battering ram, though we'll have to wait for the PM to be sure. Bruises might still appear, but I doubt it.'

'Who was on watch?' Davie yelled.

A tall young officer stepped forward. He told his tale. Nothing seemed out of the ordinary. He had checked all cells, as required, every half-hour, and the dead man hadn't been on suicide watch. No sounds had travelled to his desk in the middle of the corridor, but the walls were thick and the doors heavy.

I left Davie and went to the gate through which prisoners were brought in. A female officer opened it for me and I went to the office beyond.

'Mr Dalrymple,' said the middle-aged male officer behind the desk, getting to his feet.

'Tom,' I said. He used to be in the City Guard's gang unit but was injured in the shoulder by a spear. Edinburgh's criminals had used any weapons they could fashion before guns became available. 'Can I take a look at Ricky Fetlar's personal possessions?'

He opened a filing cabinet and took out a brown envelope, then emptied the contents on his desk.

I ran my eye over them. Watch, belt, shoelaces, wallet – containing twenty-five poonds in notes, a few coins and a bank card – they had been introduced the previous year, but credit was still only available to those better off than me. There were two bunches of keys, the first with a ring bearing the name of the warehouse. The second ring had three keys on it and made me think. I'd forgotten to bring my Hieronymus Bosch book from home so I couldn't check, but I was almost certain that the three-headed brown bird delicately moulded in plastic was from the central panel of *The Garden of Earthly Delights*.

What the paradise was going on?

SIX

I told Davie about what I'd found as we drove the short distance to the morgue. It was a new facility in the Cowgate, near where the pre-Enlightenment one had been. A serendipitous circularity, one typical of Edinburgh across the years.

We were led through the vestibule and given pale-blue scrubs. Although the facility was municipal, ScotPol provided part of the funding, giving it more sway than most of the staff, including Sophia, liked. Then again, the pathologists were paid by Hel Hyslop's outfit when crimes were involved, so complaints were *sotto voce*.

'At last,' said McKirdy, looking up from the desk that was at the entrance to the cutting room. 'Though I hear we're about to have a new customer from ScotPol HQ. Tut-tut, Detective Leader – very careless of your people.'

Davie scowled and pulled up his surgical mask. I smiled at Sophia before doing the same. She was at the second table, on which lay a small object that didn't make me feel great. Neither did the blank look she gave me.

'Doctor McIlvanney,' said McKirdy – it occurred to me I didn't know his first name and had never tried to find it out – 'Sophia . . . have you reached any conclusions about the finger?' He led us over.

I followed, trying to disguise my reluctance.

'I have,' said Sophia sharply. It was obvious she had little time for her superior. 'Right forefinger of a male aged between thirty and forty, severed three-quarters of a centimetre from the proximal interphalangeal joint by a sharp, non-serrated blade that widens from the initial cut in the epidermis. Sufficient pressure applied to cut through the bone. Likely to be a chef's or a hunting knife. Blood tests show no presence of drugs or alcohol. The cut was made between twelve and eighteen hours before the discovery of the digit. The condition of the nail and skin suggests that the victim engaged in manual labour. There is also sustained exposure to a petroleum product that I have narrowed down to heavy fuel oil.'

'As used in ships?' I asked.

'I believe so.'

Davie and I exchanged glances. Was the victim a sailor? The Lord of the Isles owned oil tankers.

McKirdy was looking over the papers on the clipboard he had taken from the table. 'That seems in order, Doctor.' He turned to Davie. 'Are there still no reports of people missing said finger from hospitals or clinics in the city?'

Davie looked at the file he'd been given by Eilidh Mackay. 'None – that includes East, Mid and West Lothian facilities.'

'Perhaps the victim was given first aid by someone who'd been trained but isn't a medical professional,' I said. I couldn't repress the memory of what happened when I lost my finger. I'd gone to the infirmary after cleaning myself up and was vague

about what had happened, feigning drunkenness. The doctor was
suspicious and alerted the City Guard, but I was lucky. The investigating officer had served under me during the drugs wars and
buried the report when I told him I'd been attacked by a tourist.
He didn't believe me, but that didn't matter, thank Plato. Afterwards,
I said I'd been hyper-careless with a kitchen knife. Anything but
the truth . . .

The senior pathologist's eyes narrowed. 'Or perhaps he was
tortured, and more digits will turn up. Strange place that this one
was found.'

Davie and I didn't pass comment.

'Very well, let's look at the unfortunate woman,' said McKirdy,
moving to the other table. 'Doctor McIlvanney, will you take the
lead?'

The bastard was trying to catch her out in front of Davie and
me. I hoped Sophia wouldn't give him the opportunity.

As it turned out, she didn't. She performed the necessary preliminary checks, examining and photographing the corpse all over, noting
the needle marks between the toes, and pointing out older tracks
on her inner forearms. The woman was in the same position as
when we found her, still stiff from rigor mortis. The four-fingered
hands were around her midriff, one on her breast and the other
pointing to her groin. They were carefully removed and placed in
transparent plastic bags. They appeared to be wood that had been
painted black. Again, I wished I had my Bosch book with me. Heck
had distracted me as we left the flat.

Sophia was leaning over the woman's upper abdomen, looking
at the round wound in the sternum. The body had been washed
so there was no blood around the edge any more, but there was
something odd about it, something related to the colour inside the
deep hole. Sophia adjusted the magnification of the surgeon's
glasses she was wearing and picked up a retractor.

'Oh, my God,' she said in a low voice.

'Let me see,' said McKirdy, bending forward. 'There's something
inside.'

Between them they tried to lever out whatever it was, without
success.

'We'll have to make an incision,' Sophia said, and her superior
nodded agreement. She took a scalpel and cut a circle in the skin

about five centimetres from the edges. Then she clamped the flaps of skin and bared the hole.

I peered in and saw something black, with spots of white on it. I had no idea what it was, but I felt sweat erupt all over my body. Something from the Bosch book was hovering just beyond the limits of my memory.

McKirdy took over, waving Sophia back, and dug at the hole with forceps. Then he levered the object out.

There was a general intake of breath, drawing the fabric of the masks into our mouths.

'Is that . . . is that a frog?' Davie said.

'Toad, I think,' said the chief pathologist. He moved the creature, which was motionless, into a kidney bowl. 'It appears to be dead.'

'I hope it was in that state when it was inserted,' said Sophia, shaking her head.

'It's been painted,' I said. 'Those white spots aren't natural.'

'Correct, Dalrymple,' said McKirdy.

Then I remembered the close-up from the third panel in the Bosch book. The skeletal hands round the woman belonged to a black demon, while there was a toad sitting on her upper chest. It came to me that toads were seen as demonic forms in the Middle Ages.

'What's going on here?' asked the chief pathologist.

I decided to leave him guessing. I'd tell Sophia something of what I knew later.

After an hour we were armed with the knowledge that the woman had died of shock from an overdose of heroin that had been cut with an as-yet-unknown ingredient. The time of death was between twenty-four and twenty-six hours, meaning she'd been delivered to the warehouse during the day shift, before Denzil Kennedy was on duty. She was malnourished and had undergone at least one abortion. Her teeth were in poor condition, the black fillings dating from Enlightenment times when dentistry was very basic. There were no distinguishing marks – scars, tattoos or disfigurements – so initially we'd be relying on someone reporting her missing.

The toad. It gave me a very bad feeling – though not as bad as the finger.

*　　*　　*

Eilidh Mackay was waiting for us in the vestibule.

'You haven't been answering your phones,' she complained. 'The director sent me to find you. She's going . . .'

'Round the U-bend?' I suggested.

'And down the *cloaca maxima*,' Eilidh said, with a tentative smile.

'You did the Latin option at school in the old days,' I said.

'I didn't,' Davie said, walking on. '*Cloaca* what?'

'The main sewer,' Eilidh said.

Davie grinned. 'I love it when you talk dirty. Now get back to HQ.'

As we exited in two four-by-fours, an ambulance crew was unloading a covered body on a stretcher. The remains of Ricky Fetlar, I presumed. I didn't envy Sophia having to examine the head. Maybe McKirdy would bag it.

Hel Hyslop was pacing about the ops room when we arrived.

'Ten o'clock, I said,' she hissed, looking at her watch. At least she hadn't torn a strip off us at high volume. She knew that would have been seriously counter-productive.

In Davie's office she sat on the sofa, which made me smile. The cover had been replaced – presumably by Eilidh – but the thought of the ScotPol director's posterior in close proximity to where there had been flagrant dereliction of duty was delectable.

'Something amusing about this mess, Quint?' Hyslop demanded.

'Someone, more like. Someone's having several laughs at our expense.'

'Explain.'

'Hold on a moment.' I went to Davie's desk and logged on to his computer. He'd given me his latest password some weeks ago – ?EatDRINKBEMERRY69! – and I found it strangely memorable. I accessed ScotNet and found an image of *The Garden of Earthly Delights*, then swung the screen round to Hel and Davie.

'Bosch?' she said.

'Hieronymus of that ilk, yes.' I took the plastic bag from my pocket. 'See this?'

They scrutinized the three-headed bird on the key ring I'd taken from the duty officer at the cells.

'This belonged to Ricky Fetlar,' I said.

Davie grunted. 'The headbanger.'

'That's inappropriate, Detective Leader,' said Hyslop.

'It's accurate,' I said. 'But not what I'm getting at. Why would a security guard have a key ring with an unusual and unusually well-made figure from the Imaginary Paradise panel?' I zoomed in and pointed to the strange bird with my middle finger.

Hel Hyslop got up and examined the screen. 'You're right. It's the same. What does it mean?'

'In terms of late medieval iconography or the investigation?'

'Don't be a smartarse, Quint,' she snapped.

I deserved that. The problem was that I didn't know the answer on either count. Then again, I could speculate, not least because seeing the painting again had reminded me of elements I'd read about.

'According to some scholars, the central panel is a utopian vision of life on earth – not paradise as represented on the left-hand panel. As you can see, people of all races are engaged in various pleasurable activities, in complete harmony with the animal world. Look, there's a hoopoe, *Upupa epops*, one of my favourite birds. They haven't reached as far north as Edinburgh, but with the Arctic ice cap almost completely gone it's only a matter of time.'

'What are you on about?' Davie demanded.

'Sorry. I think the three-headed bird – and those other weird creatures – would normally be seen as monsters, but in the Imaginary Paradise they're as natural as any other being.'

Hyslop had sat down during my homily. 'Fascinating. Why's it on the dead man's key ring?'

I wasn't so keen to speculate on that, but I had a go. 'Figures from this painting are all over this case, or concatenation of cases. The Lord of the Isles's friend Barker made copies of figures, the dead woman was posed as one . . .'

'And there was a toad in her chest,' added Davie.

Hel raised an eyebrow and he told her about the post-mortem.

'That's in the painting, too,' I said, zooming in on the Hell panel, 'though the toad's *on* rather than *in* her chest. Don't ask me what that's about.'

'And Rory Campbell's putting on a show using these props?' Hyslop said, her tongue flicking between her lips like a boa constrictor's. She'd be very happy to nail Edinburgh's deputy leader and former revolutionary leader.

'I don't think his connection to this is suggestive,' I said, 'though of course we'll be talking to him.'

'No,' said Hel firmly. 'I'll do that.'

I looked at Davie and then shrugged. 'Whatever you think will do the job. Of course, Rory will clam up with you and you'll get—'

'I said, I'll do it. Now, back to this Bosch bollocks.'

I gave her a tight smile. Alliteration was an advance for her. 'Then there's the attempted strangling in Leith by the tree-fish from *The Temptation of St Anthony*.'

'Anything on why a different painting's involved?' Hyslop asked.

I shook my head. 'It could be a coincidence. Maybe there are two sets of Bosch fans at loose in the city.'

Hel gave me a dubious look. 'You don't really believe that.'

'We need to find out.'

She looked at her notes. 'The finger that was found in the Lord of the Isles's bedroom?'

Here we go, I thought. I told her what Sophia had found, speaking clearly but at speed. She didn't seem to notice the unease I was disguising.

'And still no men lacking a right forefinger reported?' Hyslop asked.

Davie stepped out, then returned quickly – Eilidh Mackay was standing outside with a large folder. 'No,' he said. 'Checks are continuing.'

'What are you going to prioritize?' Hel asked, looking from Davie to me.

I wasn't going to tell her, and I had the perfect distraction.

'There's been a leak,' I said. 'Charlotte Thomson was outside my place early this morning. She knows the Lord of the Isles is missing. I claimed ignorance.'

'Fuck and shit,' said the director of ScotPol. 'I'll talk to her editor.' She stormed off.

'Right, let's get out of here.'

Davie peered at me. 'Where are we going?'

'Magical mystery tour.'

'Oh, great,' he said, having been on the receiving end of several such calamities.

This one might turn out to be the worst of all.

*   *   *

'Ramsay Gardens?' Davie was driving up the High Street in second gear. There was only one vehicle lane, the rest of the road being used by stalls selling tourists local specialities – lowland whisky in old ale barrels, anyone? – and even more serious tat such as hats in the shape of the castle's half-moon battery. Perfect for assault and . . .

'Correct.'

'Are you sure?'

'One hundred per cent proof sure.'

'The Nor-English?' His voice lacked its usual vigour. 'Hyslop will go Vesuvius.' The Italian volcano had erupted a year earlier, destroying much of Naples and killing thousands.

'You can drop me off, if you like.'

'Piss off.' He accelerated past the Heart of Midlothian, where some tourists were following the old tradition of spitting on the stones set into the surface, to the applause of a flouncing guide in a kilt. 'Are you sure it's worth breaking protocol? We're not supposed to go near official guests.'

'That's why I'm curious.'

Davie parked on the steep side street.

'Let's see. They sound like people of interest.'

'Right,' he said, opening his door. 'Get intae them.' He went over to the black door that isolated what was once among the most expensive living spaces in the city. Under the Council it had been turned into luxury guest accommodation and was now owned by the Scottish state, much to the irritation of Lachie MacFarlane, who wanted to use it for poor Edinburgh citizens to experience how the nobs had lived.

The door was opened by a hulking security guard in black clothes.

'Who are you?' he demanded.

Davie showed him ID.

'Aye, but you cannae come in here withoot a government permit.'

The guy, who looked as if he'd been in the City Guard, was in his fifties and out of condition. Davie went up close and spoke into his ear. That was only going to end one way.

'Come in,' the chastened guard said, looking up and down the street. 'I'll need you to sign in.'

'I'll pretend I didn't hear that,' said Davie.

'There's CCTV in the reception area.'

'Turn it off and wipe the recording.' Davie ordered. 'We were never here.'

The guard nodded keenly, making we wonder what Davie had said. I asked as we headed to the suites on the first floor. He just gave me a slack smile.

'Gently does it,' I counselled, knocking lightly on the newly painted green door marked *Number One*.

Nothing happened. I tried again. Zilch.

'So much for that great idea,' said Davie, turning to leave.

My mind had gone into hyper-drive. 'Get the master key from reception,' I said, ear against the green panel. 'Not necessarily gently. While you're there, check the records for any appearance by his lordship.'

Even his large boots made little noise on the thick carpet. I listened intently but could hear nothing from inside the suite.

Davie reappeared, brandishing a large key. I took what was either a real Georgian specimen or a convincing copy. 'Don't worry,' he said. 'No one will talk. And old Macdonald hasn't been here since this lot arrived last Wednesday.'

'You like threatening people far too much,' I said, as I slipped the key into the lock. It turned smoothly. I pushed the door open. The pile of the carpet in the suite was even thicker and there were paintings on the walls that I was sure I'd seen in what had now become the National Gallery again.

We moved into the main room. It was so large that Heck and I could have played hide-and-seek for hours around the antique furniture and aspidistras. Then there was the view. Even in the dull winter light, the gardens below and the New Town straight ahead was eye-grabbing.

'Here,' Davie said, handing me a pair of latex gloves. 'Wouldn't want to leave any prints, would we?'

The carpets were dark-coloured, including a particularly fine one with lions leaping on deer against a dark-blue background, so our damp boots weren't leaving obvious traces.

'What are we looking for?'

I glared at him. 'Has Eilidh Mackay melted your brain? The Lord of the Isles, of course.'

'What? You think the Nor-English are behind his disappearance?'

I shrugged. 'Now we're in, it's definitely worth checking. You go left, I'll go right; one of us should make it.'

He snorted and headed away.

'Not just him,' I called. 'Anything Bosch-oriented, anything . . .'

'Aye, got it.'

I went round the living room, checking the presses – shelves behind locked doors where Edinburgh burghers once stored their prized possessions. Fortunately, they were all unlocked. Plenty of alcohol, board games, poker chips and so on, but nothing germane to the investigation. The paintings – David Wilkies, Allan Ramsays, Henry Raeburns – were magnificent, but not Bosch. I went back to the hall and into the first bedroom on the right. It was furnished with a large bed and looked out over the inner courtyard with its trees and bushes. There were large walk-in spaces, which could easily have contained a suitably restrained lord – but didn't. There were some extra-large suits in agricultural colours that I guessed belonged to Nigel Shotbolt, the leader that Billy Geddes had mentioned. But there were surprisingly few personal effects. Even his toilet bag was small and contained only a shaving brush, soap and a cut-throat razor. No toothbrush, and the suite's complimentary one was still in its wrapper. I looked under the bed and the mattress, as well as behind the paintings – a standard place to stash papers. Nada.

The second bedroom was smaller, with women's clothes in the walk-in space and on the backs of chairs. This was where Gemma Bass laid her head. Billy would doubtless have paid plenty to be here.

'Nothing,' Davie said from the doorway. 'There are men's clothes in the room opposite but bugger all else.'

'That'll be the sidekick Lassiter's place,' I said, impressed that I'd remembered the surname, but disappointed the first name had fallen into the abyss. 'Maybe they're nomads and carry their gear wherever they go.'

Davie pointed at the chairs. 'She doesn't.'

'No.' I went to the nearer chair and lifted a black evening dress. What I saw made me bend forward and peer from close range.

'What is it?' Davie said, approaching.

'A belt,' I said. 'Lady's, brown leather, pretty poor quality, but look at the buckle.'

'Is that a mermaid?'

'It is,' I confirmed. 'Blonde hair, naked upper body, scaly lower abdomen and tail, the latter going over her head. She's holding one end of the forked appendage with her left hand.'

'Right.' Davie straightened up. 'Spit it out, then.'

'Like the bird on the headbanger's key ring, it's from Imaginary Paradise, the central panel of *The Garden of Earthly Delights*.'

'Bloody Bosch again.'

I nodded, trying to get my head round what this meant. There was no sign of Angus Macdonald, which was good, but the Bosch connection was worrying.

'Take a photo or six of that, will you?' I said to Davie, who whipped out his phone and fired away.

Of course, the Nor-English could still have taken the Lord of the Isles and stashed him elsewhere. As honoured guests, their movements would be monitored but not too much. Besides, they might have allies in the city, such as the tree-fish impersonator in Leith.

Davie's phone rang. 'Shit,' he said, after cutting the connection. 'That was the guard on the door. The residents have returned.'

We ran to the door and locked it behind us, then headed down the corridor in the opposite direction. There were convenient alcoves opposite each other, one with a large spiny plant that must have come from the Botanic Gardens – Davie went behind that – and the other with a bust of an ancient warrior with his helmet pulled back. There was enough room for me to hide. A loud voice came up the stairs, followed by a gust of laughter. I decided to risk a look.

Nigel Shotbolt, at the front, was corpulent; his hair was like a hedge in a hurricane. The suit he was wearing was ill-fitting and blinding yellow. Geoffrey – I'd remembered – Lassiter was carrying a heap of files, his expression that of a dog that got beaten more often than fed, while Gemma Bass was even more of an eye-full than Billy had suggested. I pulled my head in before it melted. Then I heard the door bang and looked across to Davie. He must have looked at the woman too: his eyes were still wide.

We waited and then went down the corridor at speed. Davie growled at the various service personnel and we were let out by the cowed security guard.

'Curiouser and curiouser, cried Alice,' I said, as we got back into the four-by-four.

'Whit?'

The Enlightenment had banned the works of Lewis Carroll as over-imaginative and potentially subversive, so there was more than a generation of Edinburgh folk who knew nothing of the Red Queen, the Cheshire Cat or Humpty Dumpty. I was old enough to have read the Alice books before the UK fell apart. They were weird, but not as weird as what had been going on in the city for decades.

'What's her name?' said Davie, sounding worryingly smitten. 'Bass?'

'Which,' I said, the thought having just struck me, 'sounds rather like Bosch.'

Davie swore under his breath and slammed the brakes on at the Mound junction to shake me up.

Had our illegal jaunt been worth it? We'd found nothing concrete enough for Hyslop – who in any case wouldn't be able to get beyond our infraction of protocol – but the belt buckle was suggestive.

'Bugger Bosch,' said Davie.

I could only applaud.

Back at ScotPol HQ, we were met by Eilidh Mackay.

'You did it again,' she said reproachfully.

'Oh, shit,' said Davie, taking out his phone and turning it back on. I followed suit. 'What's going on?'

'Hyslop's waiting for you in her office.' Eilidh drew closer. 'The presiding minister's with her.'

Davie and I exchanged glances and groans.

'Do you think she knows where we've been?' I asked, as we walked to the lift.

'Anything's possible,' Davie said, his jaw protruding like the prow of a battleship steaming at full speed towards the enemy. He had no positive feelings for Andrew Duart whatsoever. I'd pointed out after the election that the alternative was the Lord of the Isles. He had thrown an empty beer bottle at me.

We were whisked up to the top floor in the executive lift.

'Say no more than you have to,' I counselled. 'I'll take the heat.'

'My hero,' said Davie.

We walked over the polished parquet floor towards a silver steel door. The white-haired officer at the desk outside got to her feet and opened it, giving us a look that made it clear what she thought of people who were late. I gave her my most winning smile, while Davie provided a scowl. Soft PI, hard cop.

As we got closer, I saw from the rear the top part of a male figure on a sofa to the left of the desk. I recognized the balding head immediately. The Glaswegian presiding minister.

Hel's lair would have done for the biggest of dragons. There were floor-to-ceiling windows on three sides of the space, looking up at the obelisk in the Old Calton Burial Ground to the north, the burgeoning station to the west and the shore beyond Musselburgh to the east. The only part of the capital that she couldn't see was the Old Town, including the parliament building – which was highly appropriate as she regarded lawmakers as pains in the arse. Unless their name was Duart.

The pair sat on white leather armchairs by the northern windows, a green slate table between them bearing a cafetière and cups, the latter adorned with the insignia of ScotPol – an open eye above the scales of justice. Hel Hyslop had changed into uniform, the dark-blue combat trousers and blouson clinging to her body more than must have been comfortable. She was also equipped with a pistol, in a holster on her belt – she had been granted an open-carry permit, the only officer on the force to have one. Even senior staff like Davie had to get permission every time they needed to be armed, thanks to parliament. She was sending a message I didn't like and the fact that neither of them rose at our approach delivered another.

'Detective Leader Oliphant,' she said waspishly, 'that's the second time today you've been out of contact. What have you been doing?'

Davie kept his cool. 'Sorry, director. I didn't get much sleep last night. It won't happen again.'

'It'd better not.' Hel's gaze was turned on me. 'What about you, Dalrymple?'

Andrew Duart raised a hand. 'Quint isn't a member of ScotPol,' he said, giving me an expansive smile. 'And we have a serious situation to deal with. There's unrest in the western Highlands and Islands about the Lord of the Isles. He was supposed to be opening a resort hotel for energy workers on Lewis yesterday morning, as well as speaking to school head teachers in Oban in the evening. I've had several senior people from the opposition raising questions.' His brow furrowed. 'As you know, although Scotland has recently come together, there's still a lot of suspicion between the regions. He must be found immediately.'

Hyslop got to her feet. 'Don't worry, we've made your job easier. The presiding minister has provided me with an executive order authorizing the use of any and all kinds of force in the interrogation of witnesses, staff members and anyone else we deem worthy of investigation.'

My jaw had headed floorwards. 'You . . . you must be joking,' I managed to say.

Predictably, Davie was more sanguine. 'Just like the good old days.'

'That doesn't mean you can beat people within an inch of their lives,' said Duart.

'Oh, right,' I said. 'How about two inches?'

'There isn't time for this,' Hyslop said, going to her desk and pressing a button on the phone. 'Keep your mouths shut, both of you.'

The door opened and the lawyer Peter Adamson came in. He walked with his chest out like a male pigeon trying to attract a mate, his fleshy lips formed in a self-important smile.

'Presiding minister,' he said with an almost imperceptible nod. 'Direct—'

'Hands in the air!' Hel shouted, her pistol in both hands and pointing at Adamson's now suddenly less extended upper abdomen. 'Detective Leader, cuff this suspect immediately and sit him on the floor.'

Davie looked at me, shrugged, then did as he was told.

Although I had history with the lawyer and didn't trust him an inch, he was an officer of the court; unless Hel had found out something we hadn't, he was entitled to due procedure, as well as a modicum of respect. There had been no mention of arrest and I suspected there wouldn't be.

'What . . . what are you doing?' Adamson said, still defiant, though his cheeks were flushed deep red. 'I'm a—'

'You're nothing,' Hyslop said, re-holstering her weapon. 'The presiding minister has issued an executive order, as he is entitled to do.'

'Only in time of national crisis,' the lawyer said.

'This is one,' Duart said, coming closer. 'Tell us what you know about the Lord of the Isles.'

'Like this?' Adamson said, looking up. 'On the floor in handcuffs?

You can whistle.' He turned to me. 'Are you part of this, Dalrymple?
I thought you had some honour.'

I wouldn't have made such a claim, but he had a point. 'I'm
not sure this is the best way to proceed,' I said, catching Andrew
Duart's eye. 'Mr Adamson will cooperate when he understands
what's going on.'

'He's a suspect,' Hel said, coming closer, hand on the butt of her
pistol. 'He has two choices – spill his guts or I'll do that for him.'

I wouldn't say Duart looked hugely enamoured with the situation,
but he had great faith in Hyslop.

Adamson started to laugh, stopping abruptly when Hel squatted
in front of him, racked the slide and jammed the muzzle of her
weapon into his soft belly.

'What do you know about the Lord of the Isles?' she said, her
voice softer but no less threatening.

'I . . . I don't understand the question.'

'Yes, you do.'

The lawyer started to pant. 'The Lord . . . of the Isles . . . is the
elected leader of the opposition and—'

Hyslop whipped the pistol away from his abdomen, held it about
twenty centimetres from his left ear and pulled the trigger. It was
no blank – the bullet ricocheted around the room, making the rest
of us duck. This was getting way out of hand.

'Hel,' I said, stepping closer. 'Let us take him to an interview
room. This will have consequences.'

She glanced at Duart and smiled. 'The only consequence will
be that Mr Adamson stops talking shite and tells us what we need
to hear.'

I knelt by his other side. 'Do what she says,' I advised. 'She's
deadly serious.'

He nodded, tears falling to the floor, but he was gasping so much
that he couldn't get any words out.

'Here's another question,' I said, hoping that Hyslop kept off.
'You've been hired by a number of people that have come to our
attention.' I took out my notebook and turned pages. 'Ann Melville
and Jack Nicol.'

Adamson relocated his voice. 'The . . . the latter was attacked
by a person in a tree-fish costume. He's a victim. So's the witness.
They're both in fear of their lives.'

Hel was looking at a typed page. 'What about Ronnie Lyall, Amanda Dunure, Gerald Wills, Alexander Buccleuch and others?'

I recognized those names.

'Many of the Lord of the Isles's staff feel they are unjustly suspected of knowledge of or involvement in his . . . in his disappearance.' The lawyer seemed to have got his confidence back until the stutter at the end.

Hyslop raised her weapon again and placed the muzzle against the side of Adamson's head. 'I do hope you haven't been talking to anyone else about the leader of the opposition.'

'No . . . no, I haven't. Honestly.'

I believed him, even though lawyers and honesty were a problematic pairing.

'Very well,' said Duart, signalling to Hel to lower her pistol. 'I'll leave this with you.' He headed for the door. Having dropped his executive order, he didn't want his hands dirtier than they already were.

I glanced at Davie. He was looking less enthusiastic than he had done.

'Detective Leader,' Hyslop said. 'I'm taking personal control of this case. Mr Adamson will be helping me with my enquiries indefinitely. You and Dalrymple – who's only still here on the presiding minister's express wish – will follow up the lines of investigation you have initiated. Update me by phone every four hours. Dismissed.'

I could have argued, I could have told her that extreme methods of interrogation were counter-productive, I could have refused to serve. But the truth was that we were suddenly back in Enlightenment Edinburgh, where anything was permitted if it produced results. I didn't condone such methods in democratic Scotland, but I'd let them go in the past – in fact, I'd taken advantage of them, and I would do so again now. There went whatever honour Adamson thought I possessed.

'What about Charlotte Thomson?' I asked, remembering the journalist outside my door.

Hyslop gave a lupine grin. 'She's been read the cease-and-desist act.'

So much for freedom of the press in the new republic.

*　　*　　*

'Notice she's keeping us away from the interview rooms,' I said, as we went towards the lift.

'Worried about your conscience, no doubt,' Davie said, grinning.

'It wasn't me who twisted people's arms and other things,' I pointed out.

'Anyway, Hyslop's effectively cut off our arms and our legs – we haven't got anywhere with the leads we've followed.'

Davie pressed the call button and then looked at me. 'We haven't followed them all up completely, though, have we?'

I thought about that. Matthew Barker had a lawyer – not Adamson – but maybe Hel would drag them both in. She was going to question Rory Campbell, which put the Theatre of Life off limits. She was dealing with the Lord of the Isles's staff. What else was there?

'The tree-fish,' I said.

'What about it?'

We were now moving downwards at speed, which struck me as a perfect metaphor for the investigation.

'Your boss has deprived Jack Nicol and Ann Melville of their lawyer. Maybe they'll be more inclined to talk to us now.'

'Aye,' Davie said, 'it's worth a shot.'

We checked in with Eilidh Mackay, who, for a change, had nothing for us. I asked her to find Jack Nicol's address. She nodded, then gave Davie a look I envied. It was some time since I'd had one like that from Sophia – or directed one towards her.

We got into the four-by-four under lowering grey-black skies.

'No wind,' Davie said, starting the engine. 'If it dumps now, there'll be drifts everywhere.'

'Have you heard the forecast?'

'You don't pay attention to that, do you?' It was the case that ScotMet, a government agency, was notoriously inaccurate. Then again, with climate change all bets, even educated ones, were off.

My phone rang.

'Two/three Henderson Street,' Eilidh said. 'He lives with his mother, Jennifer Nicol.'

I thanked her, rang off and told Davie. He knew the street.

We pulled up outside a row of tall tenements that would once have been decent housing but, after three decades of Enlightenment spending restrictions, were now in serious disrepair. The odd flat had obviously been bought by the residents under the Transfer of

Ownership scheme set up after the end of the regime, and the window frames of those had been replaced and were freshly painted. I had a feeling Jack Nicol and his mother didn't live in one of those. I was wrong. They lived in paradise.

SEVEN

The street door was open, the lock mechanism absent. Leith and neighbouring Portobello had been the breeding grounds for violent gangs in the later years of the Enlightenment. ScotPol had cracked down, but it would take years for the damage to properties to be repaired. Meanwhile, the gangs had become more sophisticated.

We walked up to the second floor on worn stone steps that smelled less than salubrious. Flat Three was impossible to miss. It had a red door, with a tree the height of Davie on each side. I looked at them. They were surprisingly green for deciduous specimens, despite the change in the temperature. They turned out to be plastic – there were even small oranges among the luxuriant pseudo-foliage.

Davie peered at the door knocker, before using it. It was a large brass strawberry. I was beginning to pick up a theme.

'Who's that?' said the voice belonging to a woman who was presumably observing us through the spyhole.

'ScotPol,' Davie said, holding up his ID card.

'Is this about Jack?'

'It is, Mrs Nicol,' Davie confirmed.

'Ms. You have to talk to his lawyer.'

'We just have,' he said, glancing at me.

'Och, all right.'

There was the sound of locks being undone. The lack of one on the street door had obviously driven at least this resident to invest in her own security. The door opened at last and we were invited in. Ms Nicol – she introduced herself as Daphne, an unusual name in Scotland – was tall and slim, her blonde hair pulled back tight, the long ponytail falling nearly to her backside. She was wearing a white robe-like garment that almost reached her feet.

They were bare – the temperature in the flat must have been in the mid-twenties.

'I'll wake Jackie up,' she said.

'Don't worry,' I said. 'We'd like to talk to you.' I introduced myself.

'I remember you,' she said, giving me a dispassionate look. 'Haven't read your books.'

'You're in the majority,' I said, trying to put her at ease.

'Uh-huh.' She led us down the dimly lit corridor into a room that took my breath away. She turned round when we were past the door and opened her arms. 'Welcome to the Garden of Earthly Delights.'

I took in the walls, which were covered in wallpaper patterned by various of the upbeat sections of Bosch's painting. But they were only the beginning: on the floor were thigh-high models of the strange structures in the work – blue fruit pods, pink buildings with spiky excrescences and towers, naked figures of both sexes in unusual poses. There was a heavy smell of fruit-flavoured incense that almost made me sneeze.

'You're a fan of Hieronymus Bosch, then?' I said.

'A fan,' she scoffed. 'I worship him.' She bowed her head and started speaking what I recognized as Latin. I didn't have a clue what the words meant. My father, a classicist, would have been disgusted.

'This is a shrine,' Daphne Nicol said, pointing to the far right-hand corner, which appeared initially to be a heap of rubbish.

I looked closer. There were objects I remembered from the central panel – fruit, mussel shells, fish (fortunately plastic), birds. On the top was a wooden panel bearing the letters *H.B.* above a mermaid. I instantly recognized the latter – it was the one on the belt buckle I'd found in the Nor-English representatives' flat.

'You're a worshipper of Hieronymus Bosch?' I said.

'I am,' she confirmed proudly. 'He is the supreme prophet, not only of the life to come but the life we can live now if only we love our fellow humans and everything in the natural world.'

I glanced at Davie, who was staring at the image of a male figure on the wall with his rear in the air and flowers sprouting from it.

'Is this a personal belief or are you part of a' – I paused, unwilling to use the word 'cult' – 'a group?'

Daphne Nicol looked at me solemnly. 'I am one of the Followers of H.B. the Prophet,' she said. 'It's been on the religions register since last February.'

Reunified Scotland was home to many religions and cults, though the historical churches had shrinking flocks. The authorities' attitude was generally benign but, aware of the dangers of sectarianism, required all faith-centred organizations to register and submit to regular inspections.

'Are there many of you?' Davie asked, having finally removed his eyes from the images.

'Over thirty in Embra,' Ms Nicol said. 'Nearly two hundred and fifty across the nation. Would you like some tea?'

I hesitated, wondering what kind of concoction she would serve, then decided to chance it. Daphne Nicol was providing information voluntarily and I wanted that to continue.

'The woman's crazy,' Davie said, when she left the room. 'Let's get her son in.'

'In due course, big man. Bull in china shop is not always the best move.'

He glowered at me, then started taking photos of the room with his phone. The furniture was discomfiting – the sofa was covered in salmon-pink throws and had feet like testicles with short hairs on them. Everything was about fertility and fecundity. Not that there was anything wrong with those, as long as people kept their clothes on outside – something they had signally avoided in the painting.

Ms Nicol reappeared, bearing a tray with cups shaped like birds' heads – no hoopoe, unfortunately – and a round blue pot like one of Bosch's edifices. She poured us a liquid that smelled strongly of fruit but had hardly any taste.

'Jackie will be here in a minute,' she said. 'He loves his tea.' She settled into what I'd learned was a lotus pose, though I couldn't see exactly where she'd put her feet under the voluminous gown. Yoga, banned by the Council as mumbo-jumbo, was now a fad in Edinburgh. Sophia and Maisie went regularly.

'So, what is it the Followers of H.B. do?' I asked.

'We spread the word,' Ms Nicol said, as if that was obvious.

'What word would that be?' I said. 'Bosch wasn't a writer.'

'No, but we derive our doctrines from studies we have made of the painting.'

'The three panels of *The Garden of Earthly Delights*?'

'Yes. For us that is the only source.'

Which again raised the question of the tree-fish and its origin in another Bosch painting. I turned to Davie and inclined my head towards the door. He moved with surprising speed.

'There's another group that follows Bosch, isn't there?' I said, catching and holding Daphne Nicol's gaze.

'They are heretics,' she said, her voice suddenly shrill. 'One of our founders left because he thought we were too hedonistic.'

There was a pounding of boots and Davie reappeared.

'He's not here and there's no other way out unless you can fly.'

Ms Nicol was unperturbed. 'Perhaps he never came back, though I thought I heard the door. That boy, he uses this place like a hotel.' The smile she gave us suggested that she was happy playing hotel keeper.

'What's his work?' Davie demanded.

'The clubs,' she said. 'That's why he keeps irregular hours.'

'What does he do in the clubs?' I asked.

She raised her elegant shoulders. 'I don't know exactly. Sells drinks, acts as host, helps people enjoy themselves. He's good at that kind of thing.'

'Does he preach the word in these clubs?'

'No, Mr Dalrymple, he does not. Such places are not appropriate for sensitive work.'

'Uh-huh,' said Davie, his patience clearly having run out. 'Your Jackie got himself attacked by a strangler dressed as a tree-fish. He obviously got up somebody's nose.'

Daphne Nicol glared at him. 'The Church of Bosch. It can only be them.'

'Did your son tell Mr Adamson about that?' I asked.

She nodded. 'We both did. He said not to involve ScotPol because he was still gathering evidence.'

'Which is our job, not his,' Davie growled. 'We need names. Who runs this Bosch Church?'

'Church of Bosch,' Ms Nicol corrected. She paused. 'Och, all right. Jackie kept his mouth shut, but it's about time you heard about his attacker. His name's Monteith, Laurence Monteith. It isn't hard to find him. He runs a café on Baltic Street. Of course, he won't have been the tree-fish himself – he's in his sixties and a lard bucket. But he's got some very nasty members. Ex-gang headbangers.'

'Charming,' I said. 'Tell me, Ms Nicol, do you have any connections with the Theatre of Life?'

She looked at me blankly – a pretty convincing blankly. 'Never been there. I don't go to the theatre or cinema. They're corrupting influences.'

'So,' I said, watching her closely, 'you're unaware that an upcoming play will have props based on images from *The Garden of Earthly Delights*?'

Daphne Nicol went white and then bright red, which was a rare talent. She spluttered for a while and then gave up trying to speak.

I stood up and said to Davie, 'Stay here while I have a look at the son's room.'

The notable feature was that there was hardly anything related to Bosch on the walls or elsewhere. The posters were of Scottish power-folk bands – that was the current hot listening potato – and fantasy novels; they were popular too, especially in Edinburgh, where reality had been grim for decades. I looked out of the window. Although it wasn't as far to the ground as the Lord of the Isles's bedroom, you still wouldn't get away with your bones intact. There was no sign of a rope having been used. Maybe his mother really had been confused about when he came in, though I doubted it.

'I need the names of the clubs where Jack works,' I said, going back into the sitting room.

'The Hermitage and the Whiteout.'

'Both in Leith,' Davie said.

'Thank you, Ms Nicol,' I said. 'We may need to speak to you again.'

'Mr Adamson will be the judge of that.'

I let her go on believing that. The only thing Peter Adamson would be judging in the near future was the distance between the dung pail and his bed. But his involvement with the Nicols, the witness Ann Melville and members of the Lord of the Isles's staff nagged at me. He wasn't the kind of lawyer to take on low to medium earners. Someone had put him up to it. That person's name was probably being beaten out of him right now.

The afternoon was swiftly being eaten by night, even though it wasn't much past three. Far too early to hit the clubs, so our next target was obvious.

'Laurence—'

'Monteith,' Davie completed. 'I'm not thick.'

'Except of muscle. Anyway, how did you know I wasn't going to say "of Arabia"?' I got into the four-by-four.

'Was he a follower of the prophet H.B. too?' He slammed his door and started the engine.

'No idea. I think he was a follower of himself. This is the wrong side of outlandish, big man. One band of Boschites I could accept, but two warring factions?'

'It isn't just them,' he said, skidding across the snow, which was indeed drifting. 'Why is Rory Campbell interested in the artist? And the Nor-English woman? And the Lord of the Isles?'

'We don't actually know that the old man is a Bosch fan, though it's obviously a possibility. Maybe one of the sects grabbed him. But why?'

'His pal Matthew Barker might know.'

'In which case Hyslop's goons will get it out of him.'

Davie nodded, turning on to the main street in the old centre of Leith. 'I don't believe it,' he said, peering through the windscreen.

'Baltic Barracks,' I said, similarly taken aback. 'It's now Monteith's "Coffees and Cakes".' The building had been a City Guard base during the Enlightenment, and we'd had several cases connected with it. Leith had gone up in the world since the end of the regime, but it was still a roughhouse on Friday and Saturday nights.

'What a waste,' Davie said, shaking his head as he parked with the near-side wheels on the kerb.

'You haven't even tried the coffee and cake,' I observed.

His expression lightened. 'Good point. Come on.'

I followed him in. Laurence Monteith's café took up the whole of what had been the barracks' ground floor. There must have been at least fifty tables and most of them were taken. I wondered what was in the coffee.

I joined Davie at the end of the cool cabinets. He'd sent a waitress off in search of the proprietor, having first managed to obtain two slices of cake and an éclair. He was already digging in.

He said something.

'Pardon?'

After swallowing, he repeated, 'It's good. This fruitcake is really good.'

I got a fork and tried it. He was right, but I still smelled a rodent. A massive café in Leith with high-quality products and dozens of customers? The area wasn't that upmarket.

A large man in baker's whites appeared, wiping his hands. Daphne Nicol was right about the lard he was carrying, but if he was eating what he made, I couldn't blame him for expanding. There were worse ways to go.

'Detective Leader Oliphant,' he said, squinting at Davie's ID through small, round glasses. 'An honour.'

Davie introduced me and that produced more protestations along the lines of not being worthy. I waved them away.

'What's the secret?' I asked.

The café owner looked alarmed for a second. 'What do you mean, Mr Dalrymple?'

'Call me Quint.' I'd got that from *Moby-Dick*. Then again, Quintilian was an even weirder name than Ishmael. 'Is there somewhere private we could go?'

Monteith's doughy face fell. He was either as guilty as hell of something or he was expecting a shakedown. He raised the counter and led us to the rear of the café. There was a large office with the barred windows that had been a feature of the barracks.

'Something stronger, gentlemen?' he said, lumbering to a side table covered with bottles.

'No,' I said firmly, raising a hand to Davie. 'We're investigating a serious crime.' I wasn't going to go into detail yet as I wanted to see how he would react.

'Oh, aye?' Laurence Monteith had poured himself a large measure of a dark liquid. He downed it in one, which suggested nerves. 'What crime would that be?'

'Attempted murder,' I said.

'Really?' He managed not to pour himself another drink, but his right hand was on the bottle. 'What's that to do with me?'

I moved closer and cast a single word at him.

'Bosch.'

He almost stood to attention, but his face remained impressively impassive. 'Pardon?'

'Don't extract the urine!' Davie yelled, moving quickly across the room. 'You're in charge of the Church of Bosch, aren't you?'

We waited till the fat man nodded.

'I have nothing to hide. The church is registered and has passed all inspections.'

'Uh-huh.' Davie stepped up to the café owner. 'So have the Followers of the Prophet Hieronymus Bosch. How would you describe the church's relations with them?'

Monteith was duly goaded. 'They're heretics. They have twisted the old master's message. They deserve . . .' The words trailed away.

'Strangulation?' I suggested.

'I don't know what—' He broke off, realizing there was no way we'd believe he hadn't heard about the attack on Jack Nicol. 'Oh, you mean the tree-fish?'

This was promising.

'I'm all ears,' I said.

'That's all I know,' he said, pouring another huge measure and gulping it down.

'Davie,' I said, stepping back. Monteith needed the third degree. While Davie got into the zone, I looked around the room. The desk was covered in piles of paper and a large hand calculator, suggesting the café hadn't taken advantage of the minimal-interest loans banks were offering for business development. Then again, someone who worshipped Hieronymus Bosch was unlikely to be a digital whizz. On the wall at the rear of the room were team photographs of young men in green-and-white shirts. The legends proclaimed them to be the Hibernian Third Development XI. Monteith was present, wearing a tracksuit that had got tighter as the years passed. In the most recent photos, he was in a suit and the team's shirts bore the strapline of *Monteith's Coffees and Cakes*. He seemed to have gone from trainer to sponsor. Then, in the 2037 photo, I saw someone else I recognized. I looked closer. There was no doubt about it. The woman in the back row in a green tracksuit and carrying a bag marked *Doctor* I'd last seen in the mortuary, and previously in the warehouse with demon-hands around her and her chest pounded open.

'Davie!'

The shouting from the other end of the room stopped.

'He's admitted he set his dogs on Jackie Nicol.'

I took the photo off the wall and carried it to the fat man. Monteith was wiping his mouth with a cloth. The blood kept flowing.

'Who's this?' I said, pointing to the woman.

He smiled, despite the onslaught his ears had sustained. 'That's Janey, my daughter. Love of my life since her mother, Hilda, died. Well, that's no' true. She was the love of my life the second she came into this bastard world. She's not really a doctor; she just looks after the players' strains and bruises.'

I was avoiding Davie's eyes. 'And . . . when did you last see her?'

'Last week. She comes round every Wednesday for her tea.'

'I see. What does she work at?'

Monteith's smile disappeared. 'She never really found her way. She used to work here, but last year she went travelling around the country. Met some people . . . some people I don't like.'

'Why was that?'

'I think they were taking drugs. Not Janey, she's no' that stupid. I bawled them out and haven't seen them since.'

'Can you remember what they looked like?' I asked hopefully.

'Naw. Young, spotty, hair all over the place. Two of them were from Glasgow.' For many Edinburgh locals the big city was still the den of iniquity the Enlightenment had proclaimed it to be. 'Janey,' he continued, 'she's smart. She just needs a bit of support. Won't take it from me, of course. Too proud.'

'Was she a member of the Church of Bosch?' I asked.

The fat man nodded. 'Aye, but these last few months she's not been turning up to services. She's been different since she came back to Embra.'

He was either covering up her drug use or he didn't know about it. In any case, a decision had to be made. Davie stayed in the background, waiting for me to make the running.

'Mr Monteith, I need to ask you to come with us,' I said, speaking quietly.

'What for?' he demanded. 'I've got a business to run.'

'I have to insist,' I said. 'You're not under arrest, but that can change.' I hoped that would nip his resistance in the bud.

'Och, all right.' Monteith took off his apron and threw it on a chair. 'I haven't done anything wrong.'

He'd forgotten admitting that he'd authorized the attack on Jackie Nicol, but that could wait. We'd have to put out a search order on the young man – I was certain he knew more about the Bosch cults than he was saying. It also seemed likely he would have known Janey. Could he have been involved in her murder?

We put him in the back seat of the four-by-four and headed back to the centre. He'd only start wondering what was going on when we drove past ScotPol HQ on the way to the morgue.

Sometimes what we did made me sick.

Monteith was wailing by the time we pulled up outside the morgue. I couldn't make out the words that were spilling from his quivering lips, but it wasn't hard to get the gist.

Davie took hold of him and I led us in, telling them to wait in the small, grey-walled reception area. I went inside and found Sophia working on a male corpse. She'd just removed the top of his skull.

'Quint,' she said, in a mixture of surprise and irritation. 'I'm up against the clock.' She peered at the brain.

'Don't worry, I'm not here to see you.' The moment the words left my mouth, I realized I'd said the wrong thing. 'I mean . . . we've got the father of the woman with the hole in her chest. He's outside.'

Sophia put down her scalpel. 'All right, I'll arrange for her to be wheeled to the identification window.'

'Thanks,' I said, with a tentative smile. 'See you later?'

'You know the address.' She turned on her rubber-boot-covered heel.

Shit. I really did need marriage guidance. I went back into the reception area, where Davie was sitting next to Laurence Monteith. As I got closer, I heard them talking about football. Well played, Davie, not least because he was a diehard rugby supporter. And, for some reason, a Jambo.

'Please, tell me why I'm here,' Monteith said, when he saw me. The spell was broken and his face was lined like a recently ploughed field.

'I have some more questions,' I said, hoping to distract him again.

'Fucking tell me!' he yelled, spit flying from his lips.

'There's someone here we'd like you to . . . look at.'

The fat man fell on to his knees, then prostrated himself on the tiled floor, weeping and moaning. Davie and I looked at each other helplessly. When the middle-aged female clerk came, she knelt by Monteith's side and spoke words that resulted in him getting to his feet after a couple of minutes. I found myself wishing that the dead woman wasn't his daughter – but I was sure she was.

We stood by the curtained window, Laurence Monteith wiping his eyes inadequately with the backs of his hands. The clerk handed him tissues, then knocked on the glass. The curtain opened. On the other side lay the dead woman, only her head visible. Her skin was utterly bereft of all signs of life now, but her features were still recognizable. Her father hit the floor again, this time unconscious.

'Och,' said the clerk. 'I really need a few words of confirmation.'

I opened my mouth but wasn't quick enough to get even one word out. The door at the end of the corridor slammed open and Hel Hyslop appeared, still in black, beret jammed over her unruly curls.

'I take it that's the café owner and Hieronymus Bosch worshipper Laurence Monteith,' she said. Armed personnel slipped past her and struggled to heave the fat man to his feet. Under a minute later the men were gone, the clerk shooing them away with her clipboard.

'You may have got there first, but I'm taking over this line of inquiry, Dalrymple,' Hel said, with a tight smile. 'We've got Daphne Nicol too.'

I didn't ask about the son, Jack. He was probably still on the loose, given the ScotPol director's tendency to brag.

'I'll leave you to it,' Hyslop said.

'To what, exactly?' I demanded. 'Have you forgotten that you and Duart specifically wanted me on this case?'

She laughed. 'It's getting far too complex, even for an investigator of your . . . experience.' The pause was long enough to make it clear just how much she rated my work.

'What about Davie?' I said. 'Surely you want him on your team.'

'No,' she said, walking past us with her head high. 'His loyalty is questionable.'

Davie's eyes widened.

'I think I'll call the presiding minister,' I said, taking out my phone.

'Call who you like,' she said, over her shoulder. 'I'm in charge.'

That made me think. There was no chance that she'd deposed Andrew Duart, but it was entirely possible that she had some dirt on him and was threatening to fling it into the public arena.

'Looks like it's you and me against the world,' I said to Davie.

He grinned. 'Worked often enough in the past.'

'We're going to have to use off-the-wall methods.'

He slapped his hands together. 'Great. And the fourth degree?'

'You never know. In the meantime, move out.'

'Where to?'

Good question. Fortunately, I didn't have to answer it. My phone rang and what I heard made me choke on my own saliva.

Davie pounded on my back till I could breathe and speak again.

'What is it?' he asked, as I headed for the exit.

'The Theatre of Life,' I said, standing by the four-by-four's passenger door. 'Rory Campbell's found the Lord of the Isles.'

'Alive or dead?'

'The former. Uninjured but terrified.' I held my left forefinger against my lips. He got the message.

We got in and he drove down the Cowgate. It was only five minutes to the theatre, which was enough for me to get some things straight with him. In writing. I found it unlikely that Hyslop, having frozen us out of the investigation and impugned Davie's honour, would have left us with the ScotPol vehicle unless it was bugged, and may have been from the start. There might have been a camera too, but that would be harder to hide and there was no sign of one. I shielded what I was writing in my notepad to be sure. More worrying was if there was a tracking device.

BUG IN HERE? ACT NORMALLY. PULL IN.

Davie did so and we both got out, closing the doors.

'I'm way ahead of you, Quint,' he said. 'I check every morning.'

'Found anything yet?'

He shook his head.

'Maybe they're using something sophisticated and very small.'

He put his hand in a pocket and took out what looked like a pen.

'This is state-of-the-art. I got it from a pal in Technical Services. It picks up everything, no matter how smart or small.'

'Run it over the vehicle again.'

It made sense as Hyslop and her people had recently been in close proximity. Soon enough there was a low beep when he pointed the device at the rear windscreen.

'Son of a female dog,' he said, pulling open the rear hatch.

The sound got more frequent as he scanned the housing of the windscreen wiper. He looked closely and then took out his City Guard service knife – something that was definitely not approved for ScotPol officers. A second later he brought the point of the knife in front of my eyes. The object on it was the size of the nail on my pinkie. Davie drew his forefinger across his throat, and I nodded. He dropped the mini-device to the asphalt and brought the heel of his boot down on it hard.

'There'll be a transmitter too,' he said, continuing to search with the locating device. 'Bingo,' he said a few minutes later. There was a black box under the rear wheel. He crushed that too.

'Wasn't that liberating?' I said, as we got back in.

'We still stick out like a sore cock. There aren't so many ScotPol four-by-fours in Embra, and only one with P23 painted in big letters on the roof.'

'We've bought ourselves some time, big man. That may be exactly what the Lord of the Isles needs.'

Davie parked round the back of the theatre. It was dark now, so we were less visible for the next sixteen hours or so. I hammered on the stage door. It opened on the chain and I saw Rory's face, as well as the pistol he was holding.

The door closed and opened more widely. He waved us in urgently, then slammed it shut again.

'Good to see you, Quint,' Rory said. He gave Davie a less than friendly look. 'And your sidekick.'

'Never mind that,' Davie said. 'Where's the leader of the opposition?'

'Having a lie down in my dressing room.' Rory led the way, up poorly lit stairs and down dingy corridors. Theatres were the Jekyll and Hyde of buildings, done up in a dinner jacket out front and rough as a murderer's hands in the back.

We went into his room. To my surprise, Angus Macdonald didn't wake up at the sound of our boots on the wooden floor. Whatever he'd been up to must have exhausted him. His clothes – a greenish-brown tweed suit, checked shirt, clan tie and brown brogues – were in pretty good condition. The only sign of tension were the lines on his forehead, which was furrowed even as he slept.

'He was famished,' Rory said, angling his head towards a pile of plates on his desk. 'I couldn't get much out of him, except that someone very nasty's after him.'

'Anyone see him coming in?' Davie asked.

'It was still light then, but he found his way to the door you used. He's been here often enough on first nights. And we're between productions, so there's hardly anyone about.'

'Two questions,' I said. 'One, why did he come here? And two—'

'Have you called ScotPol?' put in Davie.

Rory gave him a stony glare. 'No, I bloody haven't. Your boss spent three hours last night interrogating me. One of her gorillas even gave me a couple of slaps.'

'What did she want to know?' I asked.

'About the Bosch play and the props. Accused me of killing that poor woman. Unfortunately for her, the logs kept by the security guys at the warehouse show I wasn't there.'

'You know that the guard on duty when the corpse was brought in killed himself by running into his cell wall?' Davie said.

Rory nodded. 'I didn't know him well – Ricky was his name, wasn't it?'

'Ricky Fetlar,' I said. 'How did the so-called interview end?'

'With me repeating what I know – which is only to do with the play and the ordering of the props – for the nth time. Eventually they gave up.' He grinned. 'My reputation as the bravest of the brave went before me.'

Davie failed to swallow a laugh. He was out of order, as Rory had been an exemplary revolutionary leader. But he did, like many actors, have an exaggerated view of his talents.

'And Lachie put pressure on Duart, who put pressure on Hyslop to cut you loose,' I said, with a knowing smile.

'Well, there was that,' Rory admitted. 'Quite right – I'm a senior elected member of the Municipal Board.'

'Uh-huh,' said Davie. 'Which gives you no more rights than any other citizen.'

'That's enough,' I said, loud enough to make the Lord of the Isles stir. He didn't wake up fully, though. 'We need a plan.'

'Hyslop told me that you and beefy here are off the case,' Rory said, giving Davie a smile that was asking for retaliation. 'You're going to need a plan of extreme subtlety.'

'Quite,' I said. 'You haven't answered my first question. Why did old Angus come here?'

Rory Campbell suddenly looked less sure of himself. 'Like I said, I didn't get anything very coherent out of him. Something's really put the shits up him. He didn't go to parliament, so presumably he doesn't trust either Duart's people or his own.'

I thought of the visits the Lord of the Isles had made to Matthew Barker. The latter was no doubt back in a ScotPol cell, but the visits were still suggestive. Had the old man been planning his own escape rather than been abducted? I hoped he would be compos mentis enough to explain that when he came round.

Rory was still talking.

'Sorry,' I interrupted, 'say that again.'

'He knew about the Bosch play.' The actor frowned. 'He said something about how the saviour would protect him.'

Davie grunted. 'That's it?'

'He was begging to eat, then he passed out,' Rory said. 'I think he'd been confined somewhere.'

'All right,' I said. 'We'll take him off your hands.'

'Are you sure that's a good idea?' Rory said, eyeing Davie. 'How do you know Thunderboots won't keep Medusa advised?' Hel's curly locks had led to that nickname being used by the few, like Rory, who weren't scared of her.

I moved quickly to put myself between them. 'We're all on the same side here. Something dirty's going on in the city – maybe the whole country – and we need to stay united.' I wasn't going to ask them to shake hands – that would have been asking for trouble – but I used my eyes on them enough to achieve an unspoken truce.

'Which is why I can help,' said Rory. 'You don't imagine that when the revolution succeeded, we disbanded our network?'

To be honest, I hadn't given much thought to the issue, but what he said made sense. In the period leading up to the referendum on the reunification of Scotland and the early years of national government, there had been plenty of disagreements, some involving violence on the streets – not much in Edinburgh, but plenty in Glasgow (especially when it didn't become capital city) and in Dundee, where the anarcho-syndicalists were ideologically opposed to dealing with what they saw as capitalist robber barons. It occurred to me that they might have been after the Lord of the Isles – he was their number-one hate figure.

'Wakey, wakey,' said Rory. 'I can direct you to a safe house and provide you with armed guards.'

I looked at Davie. 'Let's stick to the first for the time being. And don't tell anyone else where we are.'

Rory nodded, but didn't speak. I suspected he would share information about us with his closest subordinates but had to hope it wouldn't go further. We didn't have many options. I could hardly take the Lord of the Isles back to the flat on Great Citizen Street and have him play chess with Maisie. Shit. Me disappearing now would go down like a lead airship with Sophia.

'I'm guessing you arrived in a ScotPol vehicle,' Rory said.

'What of it?' Davie said. 'It's clean.'

Rory smiled. 'I'm sure it is. So clean that it'll be seen by ScotPol's helicopter, as well as showing up like a shining star on every traffic camera.'

'Have you got an alternative?' I asked.

'Yes, but you'll have to wait a bit.' He picked up his phone and walked into the corridor.

'Do you really trust this bandit?' Davie whispered.

'Yes,' I said simply. 'You should too. We haven't got many friends right now.'

As if to argue that point, his phone rang. He looked at the screen. 'It's Eilidh,' he said.

'Keep it short. They may be tracking us.'

Davie listened, then signed off. 'Hyslop's tearing bits of people since we went off the grid. We're now officially "wanted".'

'Wonderful. Turn that off and take the battery out.' I called Sophia and told her that I'd be away for a while. She'd already been informed of our status – our photos were on TV. She asked what she was supposed to tell the kids, and I struggled to answer. I told her I loved her before I cut the connection, but was only told to get home as soon as I could.

I dismantled my phone and put the pieces in my pocket.

Rory came back. 'Transport in half an hour.' He looked at us. 'You know, I think you need new costumes. I'll do some work on your faces too.'

Davie stood there with his head lowered like a bull about to charge.

Again I got between them. Changing the way I looked could only be a good thing. Maybe Rory could get rid of my belly too.

Then the Lord of the Isles woke up with a wail.

EIGHT

I t took the old man a couple of minutes to calm down, after looking around and blinking, clearly confused as to where he was. Rory gave him a glass of water and he gulped it down.

'Is that you, Dalrymple?' he said, putting on his glasses.

'It is, my lord.' That was the first and last time I was going to address him by his title. I thought it might soften him up.

'What are you doing here?'

'Looking for and finding you.'

Angus Macdonald was staring at Davie now. 'I know you. Elephant, isn't it?'

Davie sighed. During the Enlightenment he'd only been known by his barracks number or, to the likes of me, by his first name. 'Oliphant,' he said. 'Detective Leader.'

The old man looked as if he was about to have a heart attack, his eyes bulging and his right arm clutching his left.

'Don't worry, we've been shut out of the case by Hel Hyslop,' I said. 'Despite the fact that she and Andrew Duart begged me to get on board.'

'Ah,' he said, relaxing his grip. 'There was an informal agreement among the party leaders that if one of us went missing, you were to be involved.'

'Flattering,' I said. 'Shame nobody bothered to tell me.'

He gave a weak smile. 'Don't take it too personally. At that stage there was limited faith in ScotPol.'

'Duart stuck to the agreement, but its informality appears to have let Hyslop off the hook.'

The Lord of the Isles nodded and then tried to get to his feet. He sat back down rapidly.

'Are you all right?' I asked. 'Should we get a doctor to check you?'

'I . . . I was generally well treated. Except for . . .' He raised the bottoms of his trousers. There were bruised lines above both ankles.

'Footcuffs?' asked Davie, smothering a grin. He'd never trusted

Angus Macdonald. Then again, neither had I, but I had the feeling
he'd found himself well out of his depth, despite his power and
wealth.

'They were attached to a chain that went through a ring in the
floor.'

I raised a hand. 'Let's start from the beginning. How did you
leave the house in Ainslie Place?'

'Ah.' He lowered his head like a naughty schoolboy. 'Well, they
got me out.'

'They?' I said.

'My . . . captors.' The old man was still looking at the floor.

I exchanged looks with Davie and Rory. This was like extracting
blood from granite.

'And who are they?'

Angus Macdonald's head jerked up, his face suffused. 'If I knew
that, I'd have told you, man.'

I took a deep breath. 'Let me get this straight. You don't know
who extracted you from a house full of security and other staff. Not
to mention your valet, who will have been put through seven kinds
of extreme interrogation on your behalf.'

'Ach, the poor man.' His lordship looked genuinely upset. 'There
. . . there was no other way.'

'Spit it out, then,' Davie said. I initially thought that was deeply
unhelpful, but it got the old man going.

'I . . . I got a text message the day before they came for me . . .
They . . . they have my wife.' He broke off and wiped his eyes with
a dirty handkerchief he'd pulled from his jacket pocket. 'They sent
me a photograph of her holding that day's *Scottish News*. I . . . I
spoke to her too. She was frightened, awfully frightened, but they
hadn't hurt her.' He started to sob.

'Your wife . . .' I said, searching my memory for her name. 'Lady
Margaret. She stays in your house outside Oban, doesn't she?' I
remembered hearing that from Billy, and it made me think. Could
he have one or more of his fingers in this purulent pie? It didn't
seem particularly likely – he'd been worried about the Lord of the
Isles's absence from deal making – but with my lifelong friend-
cum-enemy you never knew.

'Yes,' the old man said. 'There's a small security detail, of
course – clan members rather than ScotPol officers. It seems . . .

it seems they weren't up to the job. Either threatened or bribed
– whichever, they absented themselves when Margaret was taken.'
'And nobody noticed?' Rory said.
Angus Macdonald shook his head. 'It was done in the middle of
the night. I was forced to cover the disappearance by telling the
staff in the house up there that my wife had come down to Edinburgh.'
'So what happened?' said Davie. 'You're free. Judging by your
demeanour, her ladyship isn't.'
'No, she isn't.' The Lord of the Isles was gasping for breath now.
He really did need to be seen by a doctor.
I asked Rory if he had one in his team.
'Aye, but she's no expert. Battlefield medicine's her strongpoint.
She does have a medical qualification, though.'
'Bring her here,' I said. He went off to make contact. 'So, what
happened at Ainslie Place?'
'They . . . they told me to get up to the rear bedroom on the
third floor at three in the afternoon. I slipped away when Douglas
was down in the kitchen.'
I thought about that. 'The door to your room was locked on the
inside.'
Angus Macdonald's eyebrows shot up. 'Obviously I didn't do
that.'
Someone must have turned the key after the door was broken
down. That individual would either have already been broken
by Hyslop's sidekicks or would be soon. Maybe he or she had
been bribed or threatened to do it in order to confuse the
investigators.
'There was a masked figure wearing black waiting for me,' said
the old man. 'To . . . to my horror, I was forced to slide down a
rope to the garden where another masked figure was waiting. The
security squad was conspicuous by its absence.'
'What happened to the rope?' said Davie.
'I looked round as I was led out of the garden. It was untied and
thrown down. The figure in black came down on the drain pipes.'
One or more of the security people must have been in on the
operation, but it didn't matter, even if they were broken by Hyslop's
people. The abductors knew what they were doing. They'd have
kept their appearances and identities hidden.
'Then . . . then a hood was put over my head and I was shoved

into the back of a vehicle, a large four-by-four, I'd say. My phone was taken immediately. We drove for over an hour. I was led out of the car and taken inside, up two flights of stairs and my feet cuffed. I pulled the hood off as soon as I could, but I was alone. The room was cold and damp, pale brown wallpaper peeling and the windows shuttered. I couldn't hear any sounds except birdsong.'

'Outside the city, then,' said Davie.

I considered that. 'They could have been driving in circles. There are parts of Edinburgh with minimal traffic noise and in proximity to parks, but you're probably right.' Then I thought of the outer suburbs. Some of them, especially the southern ones, had been devastated during the drugs wars and were only now beginning to be rebuilt. He might have been out there.

'What did they want from you?' I asked.

'That's . . . that's confidential.'

I raised a finger to keep Davie back. 'We're your only hope.'

He eyed us dubiously. 'How will you find Margaret?'

'I've never failed,' I said, which was true when it came to missing persons cases. My strike rate when dealing with homicidal maniacs was lower, though I usually still got them – but often there were fatalities along the way. The question was, were his erstwhile captors maniacs? There wasn't much evidence of that so far.

'But,' I continued, 'I need to know why you were taken. It obviously wasn't because you tell side-splitting jokes.'

Davie guffawed, adding to the aristocrat's discomfort. I felt sorry about his wife, but this wasn't the time for prevarication.

'All right . . . all right. You'll be aware that my companies provide Scotland and several other countries with energy of various kinds. There's been heavy competition for extra oil and gas supplies because of the much severer winter that's hitting most of the northern hemisphere. I've been scrupulous about sticking to the terms of signed contracts. But some countries have started to play dirty. First it was attempts to talk down the companies' share prices, but rather to my surprise ScotExchange proved strong enough to resist such tactics.'

I remembered something about that in the papers a few months ago, but I'd paid little attention, assuming that the Lord of the Isles and his people, paragons of capitalist efficiency, would sort things out. As, apparently, they had.

'Then . . . they went right over the top.' The expression sounded strange coming from the old man's cracked lips.

'Who's they?' asked Davie.

Angus Macdonald gave him a searching look – he was probably wondering how much a detective would understand about such matters, forgetting that detectives were past masters at the comprehension of greed in all its manifestations.

'At first we thought it was the South Africans – with the approach of the icebergs from Antarctica, the country's mean temperatures are dropping fast.'

'Except it's summer down there now,' I said.

'Indeed. Then we looked at the recently reformed state of Finland. There was some evidence of malfeasance, but we took the appropriate steps.'

'Who was it, then?' Davie said, his impatience manifesting itself in bulging eyes and a furrowed forehead.

Rory rushed in. 'ScotPol vehicles at the main entrance. Get out the back now! The driver's waiting. Brown van.'

I took the Lord of the Isles by the arm and led him to the stage door, Davie pounding behind. I opened the door and had a look. The police hadn't arrived yet. We went down the narrow passage to Buccleuch Street. The van was on the other side of the road. I pulled the old man in front of a bus, which slewed to the side, and got him in the open side door. A few seconds later we were moving southwards.

It was dark and the snow was coming down again, making a mockery of the streetlights. With any luck we'd get away unnoticed.

Then what?

The driver was a young woman with a black woollen hat pulled down to her eyebrows. Wisps of light brown hair had escaped. She had a striking nose, bent high up and longer than most men's. It was curiously attractive, as were her high cheeks and full lips. Unfortunately, they were pressed tightly together in a straight line that smacked of serious disapproval. I was in the back with Angus Macdonald, so I left Davie to charm her.

After five minutes he gave up. She declined to give her name or say where we were going. When he asked if she knew who we were, she let out a long sigh and nodded once.

She took a left off Causewayside and drove around the side streets.

'None of you have phones that are turned on, I hope,' she said, her accent not local. It wasn't rough enough to be Glaswegian, so I guessed at somewhere between the cities.

'We're all completely turned off,' said Davie, which prompted not even the slightest response.

Then we were on Dalkeith Road and heading south at speed, until she took another left and headed for what had once been Prestonfield, a flash hotel and restaurant; my parents had taken me there once when I won the English prize at school. Since the drugs wars it had been a ruin. As we pulled up in front of the old lodge, I saw in the headlights before they were doused that it was still in a state of devastation.

'Out,' said our driver, moving to the side of the collapsed walls and disappearing into the murk.

'Charming young lady,' said the Lord of the Isles.

'If you're lucky, she won't turn out to be a class warrior,' I said, immediately wishing I hadn't. The old man looked as if he'd just seen a guillotine in the light of the torch that was approaching us.

'Gentlemen,' said a bearded man in dark coat and pulled-down balaclava. In his other hand he was holding a pistol. 'Let's get you inside.'

Other figures appeared to our sides and took our arms gently. We were led to the right, then down uneven steps. We went through an open door into pitch darkness. When the door was closed and bolted, lights came on.

'Plato's bollocks,' said Davie, looking around in astonishment.

We were in the basement of the old building, which had sustained little damage and was done up like a military base, with dark-green paint on the walls and metal bunk beds all over the wide space. Desks had been placed by the brick support columns and people in dark clothes were working at computer terminals.

A tall man with short white hair came up to us.

'Quint Dalrymple,' he said, extending his right hand. 'I served with you in the Tactical Operations Squad.'

That was a blast from the distant past. I tried to get my memory into gear. A ghostly figure with lustrous black hair appeared before me.

'Andy Bothwell,' I said, shaking the proffered paw. He had very large hands.

'That's right, sir.' He laughed. 'Bet no one's called you that for a long time.'

'The last man who did was Jimmy Taggart.'

Bothwell's face fell. 'Shame what happened to him.'

I nodded. 'Though he'd probably have wanted to go down fighting.'

'Right enough. Christ, the TOS. Brings back a lot of memories.' Andy Bothwell's cheeks reddened. 'Sorry, sir, shouldn't have mentioned that.'

'Don't worry – just seeing you had that effect.' I looked around. 'So, what have you got going on here exactly?'

A young woman with a friendly face had approached the Lord of the Isles and led him away.

'Manda will look after the old man,' Bothwell said. 'Besides, he doesn't need to hear this.' He gave Davie a sceptical look. 'Nor does the detective leader.'

'Hume 03, as was, has been at my side since 2020. You can rely on him. Besides, we've been given the arse's rush by Hel Hyslop.'

The white-haired man was studying Davie. 'Hume 03. I remember you. Thunderboots.'

I put a hand on Davie's arm. 'That nickname's not a favourite,' I said. 'Remind me, which barracks were you in, Andy?'

'Raeburn, of course,' he replied, with a grin. I might have known. That barracks was located in the old Lothian and Police headquarters by the ruins of Fettes College. Its proximity to the wild northern suburb of Pilton led to it being staffed with the City Guard's most enthusiastic headbangers. 'I was known as Knee Tae The Nuts. Knee for short.'

'Knee it is,' I said. 'So, what's going on here?'

'Lachie and Rory set up this base in the year before the revolution. I deserted two years before that, so I've got more experience underground than most.'

'But why do they need a hidey-hole and a bunch of washed-up revolutionaries?' said Davie. He was still smarting from the use of his nickname, as well as being confronted by a former Raeburn auxiliary. Hume Barracks fancied itself as the toughest in Edinburgh.

I'd seen some epic rugby matches between the two, with Davie very much to the fore. I had a vague recollection of Andy Bothwell playing on the wing, not a real position for a steamrolling forward like Davie.

'We're not washed up,' Bothwell said, smiling as he refused to take offence. 'Lachie isn't a hundred per cent convinced that democracy will hold across Scotland, so we're the backstop. Edinburgh can survive whatever comes at her.'

I glanced at Davie. He showed no sign of knowing about this nest of freedom fighters. I felt a fool for not having suspected its existence. The truth was that Scottish democracy was vulnerable because of the uneasy cohabitation of regions that were run in very different ways. And then there were the Nor-English. If they were wealthy enough to be doing energy deals, they might be eyeing Scotland with an acquisitive eye. It wouldn't be the first time in recorded history.

Then I saw a stocky man in camo gear walking across the basement. My eyes moved automatically to his right hand, which was holding a green file. The forefinger was missing below the lower joint. My gut did a passable imitation of flung dung.

'Who's that?' I said to Knee Bothwell.

'That's Jinky MacGuphin. Used to be a hell of a football player.'

'Is that how he lost his finger?' I was doing my best to keep my voice level.

Bothwell laughed. 'No, he was a builder. Had a run-in with some kind of power tool years ago.'

It had been obvious from the start that he hadn't provided the recently severed finger that had been found in the Lord of the Isles's four-poster. I considered asking the old man if he knew anything about it – or if fingers were removed in the Highlands and Islands as punishment. I'd heard worse.

'Come and have something to eat,' said Andy Bothwell.

'Now you're talking,' said Davie. 'I could eat a moose.'

'None of them here, though I've heard they're trying to breed them somewhere up north. Here, what's this with the Lord of the Isles? Rory told us to look after him.' He led us to an alcove at the rear, where there was a wood-burning stove with a large pot on it. 'Stew.'

Davie craned forward. 'Smells all right. Any meat in it?'

'Shug?' said Bothwell to the man in a dirty apron, who was brandishing a ladle.

'Aye, there's loads ae meat in it. Squirrel, rook, rabbit . . .'

I forced down a small bowl while Davie wolfed three big ones. Twas ever thus. Maybe this would be the first time he got gut rot, but I wasn't counting on it. Barracks fare had been pretty dire in the early days of the Council.

'What now?' said the big man, after we'd retired to a pair of battered leather armchairs. 'Sit on our hands?'

I shrugged. 'At least Hyslop can't get *her* hands on us here. We need to talk to the Lord of the Isles at length, but that'll have to wait till tomorrow.' The medic had told us the old man was suffering from exhaustion and was out for the count.

'Copulate this for a game of revolutionaries,' Davie said. 'I want to go home.'

'To meet Eilidh?'

He smiled. 'Possibly.'

I thought about Sophia and the kids. I had to get a message to them.

Knee Bothwell appeared at Davie's side. 'Fancy going out with us?'

'Naw,' Davie said. 'You're so, so far from my type.'

I gave him the eye. 'What are you doing?'

'Rory wants us to go down to Newhaven. There are some smugglers to be dealt with.'

Davie sat up. 'That's a job for ScotPol.'

Bothwell laughed. 'No, no, I mean dealt with in the sense of doing a deal with.'

'You taking the pish?' Davie demanded.

'Mildly. Hume people never did have a sense of humour, ha.'

'All right,' I said, raising a hand. 'It's a bit late to be holding grudges from the Enlightenment. Are you saying that the deputy convenor of the municipality of Edinburgh is receiving illicit goods?'

'Kind of.'

I glared at Davie, who looked as if he was about to blow his cranium. 'Why? What are these goods?'

'Wait and see.' Knee shrugged. 'You don't have to come if you don't fancy it.'

Rags, red, bulls for the baiting of. We got up swiftly.

Whatever transpired, it had to be better than a smoky crypt filled with snoring revolutionaries. But on that, as so often in recent days, I was completely wrong.

We set off in another van, this one black with small white letters claiming it belonged to a bespoke house painter called R.W. Forsyth. Bothwell was driving, with Davie and me making the front seat a tight squeeze. There were a couple of guys in dark-coloured overalls in the back.

'I've got to get in touch with Sophia,' I said to Davie.

'We can't reactivate our phones,' he replied. 'The woman from hell will nail us.'

'You want to make a call?' Knee said. 'Hey, Ralphie, give them a flamer.'

'A what?' I asked.

'Phone with a temporary number. Untraceable.'

I took the device I was handed and rang Sophia.

'Hello?' she said uncertainly, not recognizing the number.

'It's me,' I said. 'I . . . I won't be back tonight.'

'What's going on, Quint? Hel Hyslop was at the morgue, asking where you were. At least I didn't have to dissemble when I told her I had no idea. Have you done something?'

'Other than get up her nose? No. But there have been developments. There's something rotten in the state of Scotland.'

'Amazing. I don't suppose you can talk about it.'

'Better not, so you can carry on not having to dissemble.'

'Fine,' she said sharply.

'Can I talk to the kids?'

'Is that a good idea? You'll only upset them.' She was right. Heck would demand my presence immediately, while Maisie would tear numerous strips off me for what she called 'doing my dirty business'.

'All right.' I lowered my voice. 'I love you.'

'What?' She may have been playing deaf.

I said it again, louder.

'Really? I love you too, but you're driving me round the bend. We have to talk when you get back.'

That was something not to look forward to. 'OK,' I said. 'Stay safe.'

'You too, you old romantic.' She cut the connection.

Knee and Davie were studiously looking to the front as we went down the Pleasance.

'Maybe you should call Eilidh,' I said, elbowing him.

'No, you're all right.'

'In case she has anything important to pass on.'

'Oh, I see.' He was handed another phone and made the call.

I drifted away, trying to make sense of what was going on. Hel Hyslop, presumably with Andrew Duart's approval and no one else's, was squeezing the nuts of the people we'd gathered to interview – and no doubt more that she and her minions had tracked down. Why had the case taken such a turn? Were the two Bosch cults the surface-level manifestations of serious malefaction? It was when we began to find the links between the tree-fish attack, Rory's upcoming play and the cults that Hyslop got her extra-judicial authority. The Lord of the Isles must have known something about the cults – maybe along with his fellow Highlander Matthew Barker. The latter was probably in serious pain right now. I'd be talking to the old man in the morning. In the meantime, what was going on in Newhaven?

Davie gave the phone to the men in the back of the van. We were now heading down Broughton Street, not far from the Destructor in Powderhall. Many of the city's illicitly executed drugs gang members had ended up in the giant incinerator, which was still operating despite its advanced age.

'News from somewhere,' Davie announced.

'William Morris would be very proud.' I was impressed that he knew about the Victorian writer and artist. The Council had regarded him as a frivolous thinker – maybe because *News from Nowhere* was a functioning as opposed to deeply flawed utopia.

'What?' the big man demanded. 'I'm talking about HQ.' So much for his cultural knowledge. 'Eilidh says they're all talking, the people we brought in, as well as others the boss-lady has picked up.'

'Hope there aren't too many finger and toenails scattered around,' I said. We'd done a fair amount of the third degree ourselves over the years, but never resorted to torture. Well, rarely.

'She didn't say. One of the Lord of the Isles's security detail admitted to turning the key in the lock of the bedroom door after it was knocked down. Said he was told to by the people who paid

him, but he never saw their faces or heard their voices. Another
one made sure there was no one on duty in the garden when the
intruders came in through the back door, which had been left
unlocked.'

'So old Angus was telling the truth.'

'Aye. Shit!' Davie stuck his hands out as Bothwell hit the brakes
on Goldenacre. I managed to follow suit; just as well, because the
seat belts didn't do much to hold us in our seats. A kid ran up
the pavement, one hand and its middle finger raised. The future
of Embra.

'Can we maybe get there and back in one piece, Knee?' I said.

'Sorry. Running late.'

I turned back to Davie. 'What else?'

'Matthew Barker. Apparently, he held out till this afternoon.
Claimed that he and the Lord of the Isles had been friends since
they were kids and don't have anything to do with either Bosch
cult. The old man was just homesick.'

'Any news of Lady Margaret?'

'Nope. Oh, and the heat's off us. Hyslop's been trying to get in
touch to tell us we're welcome back on the case.'

'Balls to that, at least for the time being. What happened to Rory?'

Andy Bothwell gave me a worried look.

'He didn't say a thing. Hyslop didn't have the nerve to let the
dogs loose on him. Lachie MacFarlane was in the building, creating
havoc. They left together, not long ago.'

'Thank God for that,' said Bothwell. 'Hear that, boys? Rory's OK.'

There were shouts of approval from behind.

'What about Daphne Nicol and Laurence Monteith?'

'Talking, but not saying anything we didn't know. I still think
the fat man's dirty.'

'Me too, but there's not much we can do while he's off the streets.
I take it he hasn't been released.'

'You take it correctly.'

'Any sign of Jack Nicol?'

Davie shook his head. 'You think he's a player?'

'Could be. What about the other Bosch prop-makers?'

'Clean. They're not cult members.'

'Right, gents,' said Knee, as we went past the old merchants'
houses in Trinity. I had a flash of my old man when he lived in a

retirement home down here, which gave me a stab to the heart. 'We'll be at the harbour soon. Balaclavas on.'

Davie and I exchanged looks, then put on the woollen hats we'd been given, pulling them over our faces. It wasn't impossible that ScotPol officers might turn up.

Bothwell turned on to Starbank Road and parked. The snow had stopped, but down here on the shore the wind was stronger, whipping the last leaves around the windscreen.

'Me and my men need to check what's going on in the harbour,' Bothwell said. 'If the boat's arrived, I'll come back for the van.'

'We're coming too,' I said.

'Your funeral. Do you want handguns?'

'No,' I said, getting a thump from Davie, who missed the weapons he'd had access to in the City Guard.

'No problem, we're carrying plenty.'

'Brilliant,' I muttered, wondering what we'd got ourselves into, but – as ever – overwhelmed by curiosity. What was Rory up to?

We took cover behind a heap of empty fish boxes. The harbour was still used by Edinburgh's fishermen, though a new dock had been finished for them to the west at Granton. Apparently, old habits died hard with the salty canines.

For a quarter of an hour nothing happened, apart from my hands losing circulation, even though they were gloved. A few cars drove along the road to our rear, but most locals were in their beds by now. Then a light flashed three times over the water.

'We're on,' said Bothwell, beckoning us forward.

The pier was narrow and slick, and Davie grabbed my arm to stop himself skidding. That did nothing to slow my heart rate. There was a single lamp at the end of the dock, but we didn't get that far, stopping behind Knee and his men. Davie and I held back. Gradually, out of the murk appeared a small fishing boat showing no lights.

I looked over my shoulder. No vehicles had pulled up, though that didn't mean ScotPol weren't waiting in the backstreets. I didn't think that our welcome back to the case would last long if we were found with smuggled goods, whatever they were.

The sound of the boat's engine, low and thrumming, came through the cold air. I watched as it passed the pier end and

swung towards the quayside near where we were standing. Then
the engine was cut and the old tyres on the side of the boat squeaked
against the fenders on the wall. Lines were thrown ashore and
Bothwell's men ran to tie them round bollards.

There was now a dim light in the wheelhouse, but it was hard
to see what was going on. A pair of figures in dark clothes, one of
them hooded, was led to the side of the boat by a long-haired
crewman in yellow waterproof gear. Knee Bothwell extended a
hand, only for it to be ignored by the first figure, who stepped up
to our level in a rapid movement. The other almost fell over and
was grabbed by the sailor, who got him or her ashore with a shove.
Then the lines were loosed and the boat reversed away, disappearing
round the end of the pier and into the night.

So much for smuggling goods. Rory was dealing in people, which
was curious as there was free movement across the country. Then
it struck me. Maybe these individuals were from beyond Scotland's
borders; maybe they were from Nor-England. But I dismissed the
thought. The border to the south was notoriously porous, despite
the presence of numerous Scottish Defence Force squads. Going by
boat was the worst option.

Bothwell and the pair came up to us.

'Who are these, then?' said Davie, his jaw dropping as soon as
the words left his mouth. 'Jesus.' He pulled up his balaclava.

My voice went AWOL for longer than was polite, then I revealed
my face too.

Andy Bothwell gave a low laugh. 'Rory said you'd be surprised.'

He'd be even more surprised the next time I saw him.

'Hello, Katharine,' I said, taking off my glove and extending
my hand.

My former lover hesitated, then took off her own glove and
squeezed my hand – hard.

'Quint,' she said, her voice huskier than it had been when I last
saw her six years ago. 'I didn't expect to run into you here.'

'Join the club.'

'Move, please,' said Bothwell. One of his men went past us at
speed.

As we passed the fish boxes, the van came towards us. In a few
seconds we were inside, Katharine, Davie and I having got in the
back.

'Well, Davie,' she said to her old partner in bickering. 'Your muscles have run to fat.' She pulled back her hood.

'Want to test that assertion?' he said with a growl.

I was studying Katharine Kirkwood's face. We'd been together for over ten years until she'd drifted away, first from me and then from the city. The skin was drawn tight over her high cheekbones and her once-full lips were cracked, revealing yellow teeth. Her hair was short and grey, making her look even more etiolated. But her green eyes flashed brighter than ever in the glow from the street-lamps. It was obvious she had a cause to believe in.

'Are you back in Stirling?' I asked. 'I heard you had a hard time before reunification.'

'Fucking feudal land-grabbers from Perthshire,' she said. 'They drove us out for a time, but we gave better than we got and now we're back. Dougie here's from Dundee. They gave us asylum when we needed it.'

'So feminism still rules in Stirling,' Davie said snidely. 'And anarcho-syndicalism flourishes in Juteopolis.'

'Been a long time since we had anythin' tae dae wi' jute. Anyways, what are you? A servant of capitalism?'

Davie's chest swelled.

I tapped his arm. 'We're all friends here,' I said. 'I hope. What's going on?'

'None o' your business, pal,' said the Dundonian.

'How about we introduce ourselves?' I said. 'Quint Dalrymple. And this is Davie Oliphant.'

Fortunately, there was no comment about Davie's surname, which Katharine wouldn't have known.

'Dougie. We don't have surnames.' He was in his mid-thirties, with a pasty face, unwashed long black hair and a wispy beard, though any impression of fragility was dispelled by his unwavering dark-brown eyes and heavy accent.

'No surnames?' I said. 'How do you avoid confusion?'

'Everyone knows each other in each syndicate and that's facili-tated by single names. Self-activity and management mean that everyone has equal responsibilities and equal rewards.'

Davie grunted. 'Aye, but you still take handouts from the Scottish state.'

'Why shouldn't we? Capitalism owes everything tae the workers.'

'All right,' I said. 'Let's leave the politics for a while. What are you both doing here?'

'Need-to-know basis,' said Dougie, with a sharp grin. 'I'm dealin' with Rory Campbell and no one else. Besides, I've remembered who you are. Your books aren't banned in Dundee, but they're no' popular either. You served the fascists here.'

Again, I put my hand on Davie. 'No politics, remember?'

'Politics are everywhere, Quint,' said Katharine. 'You of all people know that.'

'Look, Rory arranged for me to be here. That must mean something.'

'Could mean he's givin' us a look at the enemy,' said the Dundonian.

'Indeed it could,' I said, resisting the temptation to let Davie loose on him. I turned to Katharine. 'Where are you staying?'

Andy Bothwell looked over his shoulder. 'Rory thought you could sort that out, Quint, given your, er . . . history with Ms Kirkwood.'

'Did he, now?' A splinter of ice entered my heart. If Sophia laid eyes on Katharine, whom she knew of old, my marriage would be flimsier than Andrew Duart's conscience. 'Why can't she stay in one of the city's numerous hotels?'

Katharine let out a long sigh. 'We're not here officially. In fact, if we're identified, the consequences will be severe.'

'All right,' Davie said. 'I can go to Eilidh's. She'll no doubt have more to tell me from HQ.' He dug in his jacket pocket and pulled out a set of keys. 'You know your way around.'

I nodded. There had been several late-nighters in recent months that ended with me on his sofa, replete with malt whisky.

'But I'm not having that long-haired anarchist in my place.'

'Don't worry,' Knee Bothwell said, 'Rory's looking after Dougie. Where to, then?'

'Dean Village,' said Davie.

'Oooh,' said one of the revolutionaries up front. 'Made a mint and bought a duplex, have we?'

'I pay rent for a one-bedroom ground-floor flat,' said Davie, glowering.

I leaned towards Katharine. 'I'll come in and get you settled, but I have to get back to the family afterwards.'

She gave me a tight smile. 'Don't worry, I know you married

Sophia. I'm happy for you, and that you have a child. A daughter would have been better, of course.'

'I have one of those too.'

'But she's not really yours.'

'Yes, she is. Have you got kids?' She'd never been interested in the past.

'We share childcare duties, so I'm not an ignoramus on the subject. But no, I haven't birthed.'

The verb grated, but I couldn't resist smiling. One of the reasons I'd loved her was her commitment to what she believed in, even when I – and many others – couldn't agree with those beliefs. That had been one of the reasons we'd eventually parted.

'So you don't have any men at all in Stirling,' Davie said. That provoked a snigger from Dougie.

'Oh, we have men,' Katharine said, piercing him with her gaze. 'After all, our eggs need fertilizing, though IVF is being phased in. Plus, we prefer to contract out our heavy labour – we have better things to do.'

'Drop me here,' Davie said, as we approached Queensferry Road.

'Aye, run away, yah big chicken,' said Dougie, unaware of how close to obliteration he was.

'Got any more of those flamers?' I asked. Four more were handed over from the front seat. I took two and gave the others to the big man. 'Call me in the morning.'

'Right,' he said. 'Don't wreck the place.'

I bit my tongue. A minute later we crossed the Dean Bridge and turned down towards the village. What had been mills and warehouses were being turned into flats that ranged from luxury to comfortable.

'Here will do,' I said.

The van stopped and Katharine slid the door open. I followed her out and stopped as she sniffed the air.

'Edinburgh. Still smells of beer.'

'You thought reunification would make people teetotal?'

'It has in Stirling.'

'Just how authoritarian is your regime?'

She ignored that and kept silent as I led her down the narrow street towards the Water of Leith. It was flowing fast over the rocks.

Davie's flat was in one of the first buildings. I let us in through the street door and then turned the keys in his own. Fortunately, the heating was on, a wave of warmth washing over us as we stepped inside. There was also a less than healthy odour.

'Socks,' Katharine said authoritatively. 'Not washed properly.'

I tried to remember when I'd last had a shower. As a metaphor for the case, it did the job.

We went into the main room. She immediately removed the socks and other garments from a drying frame. I picked up newspapers from the sofa and plates from the table. At least the goldfish was still alive. I went into the kitchen, found an extra-large pizza in the freezer and turned on the oven. Then I raided Davie's whisky supplies, taking two decent malts and a couple of reasonably clean glasses.

Katharine had removed her coat and over-trousers. I was shocked. She was as thin as a libertine, her legs in tight jeans particularly hard to look at. Of course, she realized what I was doing.

'What is it? The gentleman doesn't like what he sees?'

'Come on,' I said, putting the bottles and glasses down. 'Are you OK?'

'We have doctors and hospitals in Stirling, you know.' She pulled the cork from the fifteen-year-old Macallan and poured herself a large measure. 'I work all the hours I'm awake, Quint. Unlike when I was here, there's a purpose to my life.'

'Obviously not looking after yourself,' I said, helping myself to the other whisky, the standard Laphroaig.

She grimaced as she sat down. 'That's not how we think. If you really want to know, I have a stomach ulcer. And don't say whisky's not a good idea. I don't have many indulgences.'

I sat back and looked around the living room. There was a wall covered in Hume Barracks rugby XV photos, and a framed print of the famous portrait of David Hume. A one-track mind, Davie's.

'Why are you in Embra,' I asked, 'and why are you sneaking in the back door?'

She looked at me but didn't answer.

I began to feel uncomfortable. 'Yes, I know I'm fat and old. Are we even?'

'No,' she said firmly. 'We don't encourage the reading of fiction, just as we've restricted access to television – they both rot people's minds. But I've been through your novels.'

'Ah.' This wasn't going to be pleasant. I'd reduced Katharine's role in the action, partly because I didn't want to draw attention to her but also because I knew Sophia would be on the lookout.

'I don't blame you for minimizing my role,' she said. 'In fact, I wish you'd cut me and my brother out completely.'

Things hadn't ended well for Adam Kirkwood. I'd considered creating a replacement, but eventually I left him as recognizable, at least to people who'd known him. I rationalized that it was a kind of immortality, but I wasn't going to risk telling Katharine that.

'My biggest problem was with the other stuff you cut.' She got up and went into the kitchen. I heard the oven door bang as she put the pizza in.

'For instance,' she said, when she came back in, 'the full horror of the corruption in the Council.'

'I thought I was pretty open about that.'

'You didn't say much about your mother.'

She had me there.

'And, even worse, you cut the ENT Man.'

The stump of my forefinger immediately started to throb. I swallowed the bile that shot up my oesophagus.

I had some explaining to do.

NINE

'Tell me all about it,' said Katharine, after we'd finished the pizza and settled on the sofa with charged glasses.

'All about wha—'

She raised a hand and I saw calluses and deep scores. Apparently, not all the heavy work was done by males in Stirling.

'All right,' I said. 'But how about you tell me what you're doing here?'

'Gentlemen first.' She smiled and for the first time I caught a glimpse of Katharine as she had been – warm and generous beneath the tough carapace.

So I went through the case, leaving nothing out except the fact that Rory had the Lord of the Isles. I had the feeling he'd be wanting to tell her that himself. I felt comfortable talking to her – after all, we had worked together for years, as well as being lovers. Her mind was as sharp as ever. She took no notes and asked questions that cut to the quick.

Including: 'A right index finger?'

I'd been telling her about what had been found in the Lord of the Isles's room in the house on Ainslie Place.

I might have known she'd stick on that.

'And no idea who put it there?'

'Maybe the old man himself. I haven't had a chance to question him. Anyway, how did you know he'd gone missing? There's been no official announcement or press reports.' I'd asked that question earlier and she'd ignored me.

'For the love of Bruce,' she said, her temper fraying as it used to. It was interesting that she'd used the expression favoured in the nationalist media. Maybe Stirling claimed the victor of Bannockburn as one of their own because the battlefield was in its territory. But as far as I knew, there had never been any doubts about his sex.

'Not Wallace?'

'And him. Stirling Bridge, remember? Anyway, how do you think I know? I'm on the governing council. We have contacts in parliament.'

'But parliament doesn't know.'

'Sometimes you're very naive. Of course people at Heriot's know. Why do you think you and the beast are back on the case?'

'Don't call Davie that,' I objected. 'You're in his flat.'

She looked around disapprovingly. 'I wish I wasn't.'

'I suppose you live in Stirling Castle.'

'No, that's where the council meets – open to the public, I hasten to add. We're in what used to be the university, along with plenty of sisters.'

I wanted to know how the region worked, but this wasn't the time.

'You're saying that parliament put pressure on Andrew Duart to rescind his executive order?'

Katharine nodded. 'That's what we told our members to do as soon as we heard about it.'

'I suppose I should thank you.'

She emptied her glass. 'Never mind that. I haven't forgotten the finger, Quint. Why do you think it was there?'

I disposed of what was in my own glass, the mild burning in my throat entering the acid house that my stomach had again become. 'What are you getting at?' I asked, playing for time.

Her eyes widened, always a sign that her patience was at an end.

'I don't know,' I said, which wasn't far from the truth.

'Don't you dare call it a coincidence.'

I saluted, which went down like a concrete balloon. 'You think it's something to do with me?'

Katharine stood up and threw her glass at me. It was on target – my face – but I moved to avoid it. There was a thump on the wall, but the receptacle didn't break. Davie would be pleased.

'You've been making things up too much, Quint,' she said, arms akimbo. 'Remove the plank from your eye.'

'You read the Bible up there?'

'It's not exactly a text brimming over with feminist principles. Speak, man!'

'All right, wait a minute.' I thought seriously about the finger for the first time, having been too worried to do so earlier. 'It seems like a pretty abstruse way to attract my attention. Why not send it to my flat if that was the aim?'

'How would you have reacted to that?'

I took her point. 'With fury,' I said, imagining what would have happened if Maisie or Sophia had found it. Heck would probably have treated it as a fake cigarette. Which would have made me even more uncontrollable.

'Which they didn't want. Whoever planted it wants to put a very strong wind up you. They also knew that you'd be involved in the case.'

I shrugged. 'It's common knowledge that ScotPol use me as a consultant.'

'Yes,' she said, catching my eye, 'it's even on the back of your books.'

'Not my doing. Billy's.'

She shook her head. 'I might have known. That scheming slime-ball's no doubt thriving in the new Scotland. Anyway, think about this. You made no mention of the ENT Man in *The Body Politic*, just mentioned your lover Caro as a casualty of the drugs wars and made up another connection to the woman I—'

'All right!' I shouted. 'What's your point? That someone's pissed off I didn't mention that piece of shit? No one knows what happened to him.'

'Are you sure about that?'

I swallowed hard. In truth, I wasn't – not a hundred per cent.

After a protracted silence, Katharine said, 'Right, I need to sleep. I'll take the sofa. I don't fancy the beast's – sorry, the big man's bed.'

I should have gone home but I felt completely bereft of energy. At least Sophia wasn't expecting me, though I didn't think that through. I shuffled to the bedroom and crashed down on top of the covers, sure I wouldn't sleep.

The problem was that I did.

. . . the Ear, Nose and Throat Man appears in Princes Street Gardens, his hulking form moving slowly, relentlessly, along the asphalt path beneath the sloping grass. The figure is darker than the darkness the Council imposes in the few hours the tourists are inactive, but I catch the odd reflection from the knives he's holding in the few lights on the castle. He doesn't know I'm tracking him; the lure I used was too subtle for the man his fellow gang members call Little Walter – they're all blues fanatics – but behind his back the Slaughterman. He's a killer, not a thinker. But he was smart enough to lie in wait for my Caro during the Tactical Operations Squad raid beyond the city line. Strangled her with a rope before I got to the dilapidated farm building, tightening so hard that she bit off her tongue. Caro. I swore then that I'd catch him myself; this wasn't something I could leave for the Public Order Directorate. I smell him as I get closer, rotting teeth and unwashed clothes, impregnated with the body fluids of the people he murdered, cutting off their ears and noses, stuffing their mouths with soil or pieces of fabric. But he becomes aware of me too; he hasn't survived so long without honing his senses. Stops and waits without turning his head, just extends his arms with the knives. And I run at him, leaping on to the great back and circling his thick neck with the E-string from my guitar, pulling tight the way he did with Caro, hearing him grunt. Then he shakes his body like a dog trying to cast off a flea; shakes and I struggle to hang on, my feet off the ground, my brow banging against the back of his head. *Die, you fucker*, I'm gasping, *die, you piece of shit*. But he's too strong, and he eventually casts me off. I land on my feet and crouch, then run at him again and drive into his belly with my head, sending him flying backwards, unaware that he's sliced my finger off until I feel blood on my hand. I pick the digit up and put it in my pocket. Because I'm looking at him, motionless on the asphalt, lying on his side. I roll him over and see that he's landed on one of his knives, stabbed himself in the heart, which explains the lack of jerking or drumming of boots. The ENT Man is dead. I know exactly where I am; my plan has worked. I drag him to the newly poured concrete in the stand that's being built for the hippodrome over the railway lines, drag him into the still wet mix and submerge him, wait till the body stays down, find a rake and clear up the mess, smooth over the surface. Rain is forecast and it has already started. It'll wash the blood from the grass and asphalt. I remember my finger. I push it into the concrete to lie with the serial killer for eternity, along with my E-string, which is still round his neck. Then I slip away into the night, the stump of my finger now screaming with pain. I have a carving knife in my flat. I'll say I cut myself. I have to get blood on it before I go to the infirmary. I'm away, free as the wind, heart flying. And then I see what I've never noticed when I've rerun the scene before: a pair of eyes glinting above a railing, a figure that disappears into the darkness, a witness . . .

I was woken by the ring of my mobile.

'Are you still at my place?' said Davie.

'Aye.'

'Are you decent?'

'Piss off. What time is it?'

'Just after seven. Rory wants La Kirkwood somewhere as yet undisclosed as soon as possible.'

'And you've volunteered to drive?'

'Why not? I'm in so deep with this . . .'

'All right, can you drop me at home first?'

'My thinking. I'm at the top of the road.'

At least he hadn't blundered in. Katharine would have loved that, his flat or not. I went into the living room. She was standing on her head.

'Morning,' I mumbled.

She performed an impressive flip and stood up. 'Quint. I take it we're on the move.'

'No time for breakfast.'

'I don't eat it.'

'Quelle surprise.'

She gave me a sharp look as I headed for the door.

There was a thick haar over the Dean Village. Davie nodded to me as we got into the four-by-four, raising an eyebrow at Katharine.

'I still don't know where I'm to take her,' he said, pulling away.

'Her is here,' she said from the back seat.

Davie ignored that. 'You'll be looking forward to telling Sophia who you spent the night with, Quint.'

I wasn't. Katharine didn't comment.

'Ah, Edinburgh,' she said, as we went through the western New Town. 'I've heard property prices in the centre are beyond ordinary citizens. The benefits of capitalism.'

'I suppose you have communism,' said Davie, looking in the mirror.

'A version of it, yes. Utopianism didn't die with the Enlightenment.'

That shut him up. I was thinking about what to say at home and didn't notice we were there until we'd stopped outside.

'There's a plaque to J.M. Barrie a few houses down,' Davie said. He was really getting his pound of flesh. 'Peter Pan here is about to meet his Wendy.'

I jammed my elbow into his side, hurting myself more than him.

'See you later, no doubt,' I said to Katharine, who was now lying on the back seat. 'Thanks for taking cover.'

She gave a single laugh. 'I'm not doing it for you, Quint. I'm not officially in the city, remember?'

I stalked off after slamming the door, hoping the pair of them had a challenging conversation. As I went up the stairs, I heard Heck in full scream mode. Good – that would be a useful diversion. I tried to let myself in but the chains were on. Well done, Sophia – or, more likely, Maisie.

The latter did the necessary.

'Good morning, Quint,' she said formally, presenting a cheek to be kissed. That was unusual.

Heck appeared at ludicrous velocity, his legs bare.

'Come here, you,' said Sophia, on his tail and laughing. She stopped when she saw me, then rallied and gave me a medium-strength smile. 'What are you doing here, Quint?'

'Er, this is where I live.'

She came up and kissed me on the cheek. 'I don't mean that. You told me you were going undercover.'

Heck burst out laughing. 'Undercover, undercover, in the bed, lazy Dad!' Then he grabbed my leg and started jumping up and down. I took the hint, grabbed him and swung him above my head.

'Careful,' Maisie warned. 'He's had half his breakfast.'

Vomit-hair I could live without. I brought him down to my chest and planted kisses over his face and neck. He squirmed and squealed satisfactorily.

I'd come to a decision. 'Dearest, can I have a word?'

Sophia looked at me impassively. 'Of course.'

'No,' I said, 'on our own.'

'Secrets, eh?' said Maisie, taking Heck from me. 'We know when we're not wanted.' She carried him into the kitchen.

In our bedroom, I sat down on the bed and patted the area next to me. Sophia complied, but warily.

'What's going on, Quint?'

I took the plunge off that cliff in Acapulco I remembered from the TV when I was a kid, hoping to avoid a belly-flop.

'Katharine Kirkwood's in town.'

Sophia stiffened. 'Is she now?'

'And I spent the . . . we slept . . . oh, for the love of God, we had to talk about the case and I was so tired I passed out on Davie's bed but she was on the sofa. And nothing happened.'

My entrails were all over the Pacific Ocean.

'That was convincing,' Sophia said, standing up. 'Why did you have to talk to *that* woman about the case?'

Good question. I wasn't going to say it was because I felt at ease doing so. 'She's here in secret. There's something dodgy going on, but I'm not sure where it ends yet.'

'Oh, well, as long as you and she aren't getting cosy.' She bent over me. 'Because that would lead to great unhappiness.'

At which point Maisie and Heck came in, picking up the acidity in her tone. Maisie raised her eyes ceiling-wards and my son ran headfirst into my groin.

When I got over the agony, I remembered something I should have followed up.

Davie came back to pick me up. I had to endure a fraught half-hour getting Heck ready for playgroup – Sophia was taking him this morning – as he had turned into a homicidal maniac. He was very defensive of his mother, the little tyke. Maisie was working on scorn. She scored ten out of ten.

'By the way,' Sophia said, as she led Heck towards the front door. 'The Boschean woman – Hyslop's had her corpse removed; don't ask me where.'

Great. The day could only get better.

'Why are you snow white?' asked Davie, after I'd got into the four-by-four, covered in flakes.

'Why are you Dopey?'

'Huh. My favourite dwarf was Sneezy.'

'Don't. Where did you take Katharine?'

'I'm afraid that's classified.'

I gave him the evil eye.

'Oh, all right. Number twenty-three, Arden Street, third floor. Four of Rory's rebels were there, with guns. Lucky bastards.'

'What about Rory?'

'Not that I saw. Where to? HQ?'

The haar was lifting but the dull light was being soaked up by the blackened walls. During the Enlightenment, coal was the main source of energy and Edinburgh had become Auld Reekie again. I suspected there was more snow on the way.

'Not for the time being. Let's leave Hyslop to stew. We've been remiss about a couple of things.'

'Oh, aye?' He slammed the vehicle into first gear at the top of Dublin Street. 'Such as?'

'Ricky Fetlar,' I said, my groin still aching.

'The security guy who was on duty when the dead woman was delivered?'

'Right. Why was he so desperate that he repeatedly rammed his head into the wall?'

'I asked Eilidh that,' Davie said proudly. 'Apparently, it hasn't been followed up – seen as a waste of time.'

I looked ahead as we came on to Princes Street. 'I don't suppose she gave you his next of kin?'

He stuck a paw in his pocket. It came out with a folded sheet of paper.

'Maureen Duff, mother, eight-B Blacket Avenue.'

'Does she even know he's dead?'

'Aye, someone went round. She was stoical. A female officer stayed with her for an hour. She didn't hear anything, not even a single cry, before she was turfed out.'

Davie had crossed Waverley Bridge and was heading up Cockburn Street. Some tourists were already out and about, trawling the trendy shops for what they thought would be bargains.

'This is going to be fun,' I said gloomily.

'At least it isn't the death knock.'

'Not far off it.'

'What else have we been remiss about?'

'Questioning the Lord of the Isles.'

'We can go on to Prestonfield; it's close enough.'

'Assuming he's still there. Maybe Rory's taken him to Arden Street.'

Davie grinned. 'Well, we can gatecrash their little party.'

'Down, boy.'

The rest of the drive to Newington passed in silence.

'Ms Duff?' I said, when the street door opened. The detached building had originally been a town house, but during the Enlightenment it had been split into flats.

'Mrs,' corrected the short plump woman, who peered up at me through thick glasses. 'Though ma man's long gone. Who are you?' Even if she had normal eyesight, she wouldn't have seen the four-by-four as I'd got Davie to park further down the road. I left him there with instructions to pick Eilidh's brains about ongoing developments.

'Name's Dalrymple,' I said, eschewing the usual 'Call me Quint'. I was hoping for a degree of anonymity to put her off her guard.

'Oh, aye? Whit do ye want?'

'It's about your son.'

'What about him?' The woman was showing no emotion.

'My condolences,' I said, following her into the living room.

It was poky and smelled of cats. She sat in the tattered armchair and picked up a magazine. She was either in denial or she was Scotland's most callous mother.

Above the fireplace was a photo of Ricky Fetlar that I recognized from the file. He must have been about twenty when it was taken, his hair short and shoulders broad. I couldn't help noticing that his head was unusually square.

'If you don't mind, how come he didn't have your name?'

'Changed it himself aboot a year ago; don't ask me why,' she said, drinking from a plastic flask. I caught a whiff of cheap whisky. 'Anyway, who are ye? Whit de ye want?'

There wasn't a single book in the room. Maybe she was one of the Enlightenment's citizens who'd resented being required to attend evening classes. Lifelong education meant lifelong tedium for many.

'Insurance,' I said, hoping she didn't have my novels on her bedside table, or was about to remember me from appearances on TV, radio and in the press.

'Is there money in his death?' Her face was instantly transformed. Now she was lusting for life.

'There may be.' In fact, there definitely would be, as some money-grabbing lawyer would soon tell her. Suicide in custody was on ScotPol. I was surprised a queue of the bastards hadn't formed outside. The death obviously hadn't been made public. 'I need some information, though.'

'Fire away, son,' she said, smacking her lips.

I glanced around the room, guessing that she'd lived here for a long time.

'Do you own the property, Mrs Duff?'

'Aye,' she said proudly. 'Had a windfall.'

'Good for you. What happened?'

She was suddenly suspicious. 'Is this . . . whit de ye call it? Relevant?'

'I'm afraid so,' I insisted, with a smile.

'Right, well, aboot six months ago Ricky came home wi' a cheque for fifty thousand poonds. Whit de ye think ae that?'

I was definitely interested, but I looked at her impassively. 'Where did he get that?' A cheque suggested a reasonably legitimate source.

'He wis a bit . . . a bit vague aboot that. Said it was a deposit ae some kind. From his work.'

I studiously noted that down, wondering if Hyslop's team had pulled in the warehouse owner.

'Mrs Duff, forgive me, but you know how your son died?'

'Course. Ran himself intae the wall.' Definitely Mrs Callous 2038.

'Did he have a history of behaviour like that?'

'Naw, he wis a tough guy. Nivver backed doon in a fight.'

'Did you ever meet anyone from his work?'

She shook her head.

'How about his friends?'

'I knew his pals when he wis wee, but after he left school he nivver brought anyone hame.'

'He did live here?'

'If ye call dropping in frae time tae time wi' his washing that, aye.'

'Do you mind if I have a look at his room?'

'Naw. But ye willnae find anything. I've cleared it oot. Got a lodger comin' tomorrow.'

I went to the back of the flat. When Maureen Duff said cleared out, she meant exactly that. The room was completely empty, the walls freshly painted pale blue, the smell making a pleasant change from that of cat elsewhere. All the floorboards were solid – no places to hide stuff that I could see. Then I had a thought.

'Did Ricky have anything on his walls?' I called.

The woman snorted. 'For a start, they were red – the colour ae blood, kin ye believe it? Took the painter three coats to cover it. Then there was the muckle great poster.'

That got my attention.

'What was it?'

'Some old painting,' Mrs Duff said scathingly. 'Religious, it was, and ah dinnae hold wi' that. Some kindae gardens – paradise, ah suppose – and the pits ae hell on the side.'

I accessed the photo archive on my phone, went back into the front room and showed her Bosch's *Garden of Earthly Delights*.

'Aye, that's it. Awfie nonsense. Ah tore it up and put it in the bin.'

'Did he have anything else like that? Maybe a belt buckle?'

She shook her head. 'Ah put him right from the start. He could have the poster but nothin' else.'

'When did he put it up?'

'Och, I dinnae ken. Not long after reunification, it must ae been. He used to have that framed photo of the City Guardians. Proper wee wannae-be auxiliary, he was.'

After establishing that she had no time for the Enlightenment, the conversation meandered and I rapidly lost interest. I was tempted to tell her who I really was. Still, the link to Bosch had made the visit worthwhile.

She didn't get up when I left. It was good to escape the stench of cat piss and greed.

'Bosch again,' said Davie, as he drove back to the centre. 'Doesn't explain why Fetlar boshed his brains out. See what I did there?'

'Very funny. What was it that Rory said?'

'To get you over to Arden Street sharpish. There's a big meeting about to take place.' He sniffed. 'Doubt I'm invited.'

'I'll insist.' I took out my phone and accessed ScotWeb. 'The dead guard changed his name a year back. Ah, right – Fetlar's one of the Shetland Islands. The word comes from Norse, meaning "shoulder-straps".'

'Very illuminating.'

'What was it I heard about Shetland on the news last year?' I rummaged in my memory as we turned on to Kilgraston Road.

'No oil up there any more,' said Davie.

The clutter in my mind disappeared. 'That was it. Apparently, a South African company has found new reserves. Not huge, though.'

'I never heard that. Anyway, what could that have to do with Bosher changing his name?'

'Haven't the faintest idea. Aye, aye, what's going on here?'

There was a wooden barrier blocking the entrance to Arden Street. The brown van that we'd been in was on the left, black-clad personnel toting machine pistols standing on the asphalt. Which made me wonder. Would any local resident contact ScotPol?

'Those buggers have got guns,' Davie complained.

I got out and was told to sign against my name on a printed form. 'He's with me.'

The female rebel looked dubious but she let him pass after he gave her his best death-glare.

There were more characters in black outside number twenty-three. I could see another van, this one dark red, at the far end of the street.

I had to show ID. Davie managed to talk himself through. We were searched. They let me keep my propelling pencil but took Davie's favourite cosh.

A woman in a trouser suit led us upstairs. It was a standard tenement with the standard smells – cabbage, pee and watered-down disinfectant. She knocked on a door that needed more coats of paint than had been applied to the walls of Ricky Fetlar's room.

Rory Campbell opened it. 'Quint, welcome.' He stared at Davie. 'Does he have to come in?'

'It's both or neither,' I replied.

'Fair enough. Be diplomatic, Detective Leader.'

'Does that mean "shut up"?' asked Davie.

'Yes.' Rory went down a corridor, the floor of which was covered in new high-quality parquet. The inside of this safe house was a lot classier than the outside. I heard voices, one of which was Katharine's.

Rory led us in. Everyone I expected was present – Dougie the Dundonian, Lachie MacFarlane and the Lord of the Isles, as well as my former lover.

'Quint,' Lachie said, raising his hand. 'I see you've brought your loyal sidekick.'

'You can trust him.'

'I hope so.' Edinburgh's leader turned to the Lord of the Isles. 'As agreed, Quint Dalrymple will act as guarantor of your safety.'

'Good of you to ask,' I said. 'Just as well I brought the big man.'

'Who needs a weapon,' Davie put in.

'Quint and his companion will also look after you, Katharine, and you, Dougie.'

'I don't need lookin' after,' said the Dundonian, shaking his greasy locks.

'We're experts in self-preservation.'

'My city, my rules,' said Lachie. 'Why don't we all sit down? Drinks, please. We have a particularly fine Lothian malt.'

'Not for me,' said Katharine, taking a red leather armchair. 'We don't drink alcohol in Stirling.'

'I'll have hers,' said Dougie, spreading his legs on one of the two matching sofas. 'In Dundee we only drink alcohol.'

The Lord of the Isles, seated in a plush armchair, was following the exchange in bewilderment. I wondered if he was fully fit. Lachie was in an antique chair that must have been made for a child, while Davie and I took the other sofa. Rory sat next to the Dundonian.

'What exactly's going on?' I asked, sipping the malt after I'd dribbled water into the glass. It was excellent – light but flavoursome. Brandy barrels, I suspected.

'All will be revealed,' said Rory. 'Lachie's put me in charge of this . . . what shall I call it? Counter-enterprise?'

'What does that mean?' said Davie, receiving a frown from the actor-director.

'We brought our friends down from Stirling and Dundee to share information and decide on a course of action,' Rory said.

'In response to an action or actions initiated by someone else, yes?' I said. 'Who?'

Rory smiled. 'That's where you come in, Quint.'

'What, when I'm not being your visitors' bodyguard?'

'You can put Detective Leader Oliphant in charge of that, if you like.'

'Duly delegated,' I said, nodding at Davie. It was exactly his kind of job.

'As long as I get a weapon,' he stipulated.

'Very well,' Lachie said. 'On your way out.'

Davie emptied his glass, smacked his lips and beckoned to the waiter – who was in black combat fatigues – for a refill.

'Are you sharing information with the Lord of the Isles, too?' I asked.

'Indeed,' said Rory. 'Of course, that's a two-way street.'

I guessed that they'd been in contact for some time, given that the old man had turned up at the Theatre of Life.

'This is about oil and gas, isn't it?' I said.

The Lord of the Isles looked at me thoughtfully. 'Primarily, yes.' He controlled a wide range of businesses – maybe they were all involved. 'Gentlemen' – he turned to Katharine – 'and lady, the nation is facing a serious threat.'

There was a pregnant pause.

I broke its waters. 'In that case, why isn't Andrew Duart here? Why is this meeting taking place in secret, with no elected members present and no representatives from the other regions?'

'Good question,' said Lachie. 'Let's hear more from his lordship first.'

Angus Macdonald took a sip of whisky and then rubbed his hand over his head, making a mess of his normally perfectly combed white hair. 'Where to start?' he said, looking down.

I managed to hold my tongue, glancing at Davie to make sure he did the same.

'The people who took me from Ainslie Place . . . I never saw any faces and they spoke to me with balaclavas on, so I can't tell you anything about their accents. I'd say they were all male. My head was pushed between my knees after I got in the vehicles, some kind of four-by-four, dark-coloured. We drove for . . . I don't know . . . at least an hour – not much more than that. Faster as the journey went on, I presume because we were out of the city. They'd put a balaclava over my head too, but back to front so I couldn't see. I . . . I struggled to breathe . . .'

'Take your time,' said Lachie.

The Lord of the Isles took another sip of whisky. 'The car stopped and I was pulled out. Almost immediately, I was inside a building, my shoes dragging over floorboards. They took me upstairs – still bare boards – and pushed me into a room, pulling the balaclava off as I stumbled forward. There was no light. I felt around the walls with my hands. It wasn't a very large room. I eventually bumped into a bedstead with nothing on top of the springs and sat down. I didn't find anything else. Fortunately, I was able to wrap myself in my kilt, but I still thought the cold would be the end of me.'

He sat back, breathing heavily.

'Then what happened?' Rory asked.

'I . . . nothing. I don't know how long I was there – they'd taken my watch and phone. At least twenty-four hours, I think. At one point the door opened and a big bottle of water and a loaf of bread were put on the floor by a person with their head covered. I asked if I could get a heater and use a toilet, but the door was slammed shut. I . . . I'd already had to relieve myself in the corner.' He swallowed a sob. 'I felt like an animal.'

'But they finally let you out?' I said.

Angus Macdonald nodded. 'My head was covered again. I was taken downstairs and sat on a chair. It was warm in that room and I could hear rooks cawing outside. No one said anything for a long time, even though I was asking what was going on, promising them money, anything . . .'

Katharine got up and went over to him. To my surprise, she sat on the arm of the chair and took his hand. 'Don't worry, we'll get to the bottom of this,' she said. 'We'll find your wife and bring her back to you.'

She must have been briefed by Lachie and Rory. I was taken by the sudden return of her compassion. I'd assumed that character trait was reserved for women in Stirling.

'Thank . . . thank you, my dear,' said the Lord of the Isles.

She tried not to wince at that term of address and went back to her place.

'It was then that one of my captors started to speak. Again, the voice was muffled, but I have a feeling it was a woman's.'

I immediately thought of Gemma Bass, the Nor-England representative.

Would she and her colleagues really have kidnapped one of the most important men in Scotland?

'She . . . she told me they had my wife. They played a recording of her begging not to be hit again. I stood up but was immediately pushed down. I swore at them and was punched in the stomach. I . . . I started to cry . . .'

'Anybody would,' I said.

The old man nodded, then put a hand to his forehead. 'It's of no account. I was told what I had to . . . *have* to do.' He turned to Lachie. 'Would you mind taking over? I . . . I don't feel at all well.'

'Would you like to lie down again?' Rory asked solicitously.

'No, thank you. I need to hear the discussion.' Angus Macdonald took a larger hit from his glass and lowered his head again.

Lachie, always organized, had a maroon file, which he opened. 'Lady Margaret will be returned unharmed, providing that all his lordship's shares in energy companies are made over to a company called BirdMammon, which is registered in Luxembourg.'

The tiny state between what had been Germany, Belgium and France was still operating, having survived the outbreak of extreme violence across Europe thirty years ago by hiring the most experienced mercenaries it could find. It was now operating as an onshore haven for companies that wanted no one to know their details – Billy had told me that.

'And,' Lachie continued, 'as you may know, getting information out of that poisonous statelet is pretty much impossible.'

I let the others comment first.

'It's clear,' said Katharine, 'that losing control of Scottish oil, gas and renewable-based energy would be a catastrophe for all of us. We can't let this happen.'

'Too true,' said Dougie, who was now several mainsails to the wind. 'Dundee will fight this any way we can.'

Rory nodded. 'We'll certainly do anything to oppose this move.' He glanced at the Lord of the Isles. 'Though we will first return Margaret to you safe and sound.'

'Indeed,' said Lachie. He looked at me. 'We need your help with this, Quint. You've had plenty of experience of crisis management.'

Suddenly, I was the saviour of the nation rather than a novelist and part-time investigator.

'I still don't understand why Andrew Duart, elected representatives and leaders of the other regions are absent.'

Katharine gave me a tight smile. 'Because we suspect that he and the regional chiefs are involved in this.'

'Suspect?' said Davie, frowning.

'More than suspect, Detective Leader,' said Rory. 'Stirling has been accessing their communications, while Dundee has raided the local government buildings in Perth, kidnapping key personnel.'

'Who have all talked,' said Dougie, raising his empty glass again and grinning. 'There wisnae too much torture.'

'Glad to see the law's been observed,' I said ironically. 'Why are they collaborating? That seems the appropriate word.'

'Why d'ye think?' bawled the Dundonian. 'Filthy lucre, ya fool.'

I thought about that. It wasn't inconceivable – the Lord of the Isles's companies distributed large dividends to shareholders, but ordinary Scots still had to pay for their energy, even though prices were subsidized. I'd learned never to underestimate how greedy people could be.

'I suppose Hel Hyslop's in on this too,' I said.

'Everywhere that Duart goes, she is sure to follow,' said Rory, with a slack smile.

'We've promised to support Stirling and Dundee,' said Lachie. 'Katharine and Dougie will go back and contact sympathizers in the surrounding regions. Rory and I will deal with Glasgow, while his lordship handles the western Highlands and Islands.'

'When I get Margaret back,' said Angus Macdonald.

'That's your priority, Quint,' Rory said.

The problem was that I didn't have the faintest idea how to find the missing woman. On the other hand, I had some pressing questions to ask.

TEN

'**I**s there a deadline for the shares to be reassigned?'

The Lord of the Isles gave me a bleary look. 'Yes, Mr Dalrymple. Tomorrow at six p.m.'

Great. Little more than a day to save the leader of the opposition's wife, then the country.

'No problem,' said Davie, with the gung-ho attitude he always displayed in such circumstances. 'We'll have everything fixed by teatime.'

'What do you need?' asked Rory.

'Answers, but I don't think any of you can provide them.'

'Try us, Quint,' said Katharine. 'No more whisky for him,' she ordered the waiter. Dougie scowled but kept his mouth shut. She'd always been able to do reginal.

I took out my notebook. 'All right.' I decided to beard the lion, even though I didn't know where her or his den was. I looked at Angus Macdonald. 'Why was a severed finger left in the drawer under your bed?'

His eyes shot open. 'What? First I've heard of it.'

I believed him. So it hadn't been put there to frighten him – the abduction of his wife had been enough to do that.

Katharine's gaze was on me. 'You know what I think, Quint. It's something to do with you.'

The Dundonian leaned forward. 'Oh, aye. Why's that?'

'What are you suggesting, Katharine?' I said. 'That secreting the right forefinger of another male – who hasn't yet been located – would pique my curiosity?'

She raised her shoulders. 'You have to admit it's a curious . . . coincidence.'

'Do I?' I asked, though she was almost undoubtedly right. I didn't want to consider that right now. Instead, I told them about the Hieronymus Bosch connection to the security guard Ricky Fetlar, and then went for gold. 'We found a belt buckle with a Bosch design in the bedroom of the Nor-English representative Gemma Bass in Ramsay Gardens.'

Lachie exchanged glances with Rory. 'I take it you didn't have authorization to go there.'

'You take it correctly. Just as well we went, though. What are those people doing in Edinburgh?'

The Lord of the Isles roused himself. 'We're negotiating energy supplies with them. They're eager customers – or were. I hope my absence hasn't put them off.'

I turned to Davie. 'Check if they're still around, will you? As well as getting a general update. Also, see if your colleagues have found out who owns the warehouse.' I looked at Rory, who shrugged his ignorance.

'They took my phone, remember?' Davie said.

'Use the landline,' said Rory. 'They can't trace it.'

Davie left the room, followed by the waiter. I hoped the latter was trustworthy.

'Any Bosch cults in Stirling or Dundee?' I asked.

Dougie laughed raucously. 'We don't have cults at all, pal. Bourgeois bollocks.'

Katharine shook her head. 'If there are any, we haven't found them. I hear there are two in Edinburgh.'

'So far,' I said. Maybe there were cells of Bosch-related activists all over the place. Which made me think of Jack Nicol. We urgently needed to track him down. I had a feeling there was more to him than had met Tree-Fish's eye.

I looked at Lachie. 'Are you sure the leaders of Aberdeen, Inverness, Fife and so on can't be trusted?' Perth didn't need to be mentioned because it had become semi-feudal, despite the best efforts of central government.

'Trust me, Quint,' said Edinburgh's leader. 'We have people in all the regions.'

'I still think involving parliament should be considered,' I said.

'No, it shouldn't,' said the Lord of the Isles. 'My party will do what I say, while the government will do what Andrew Duart says. And my wife . . .' He broke off.

I saw his pain. We'd have to do it Lachie's way.

Davie came back. 'The Nor-English are still here. Apparently, they've been threatening to leave, but the energy minister has been entertaining them.'

'What about the warehouse?'

'Get this. The owner is one Morris Gish, a.k.a. Morrie the Nut – so called because of his habit of smashing rivals' noses with his head. Suspected gang boss, but nothing's ever stuck, thanks to his lawyers.'

'The Edinburgh kiss,' said Dougie, sniggering.

'Ever heard of him?' I asked Rory.

'Not a whisper,' he replied.

'Me neither,' added Lachie.

The Lord of the Isles shook his head when I turned to him. One large blank drawn.

'Anything else?' I asked Davie.

'I'm keeping the best till last. A couple of hours ago, a ScotPol patrol found a guy on the pavement in Saughton. He recently lost his right forefinger.'

That got me to my feet. 'Is he in the infirmary?'

'Aye.'

'Time for all of you to go,' said Rory. 'Katharine and Dougie are due in Newhaven in an hour. Detective Leader, will you accompany them with my people?'

The big man nodded.

'What about Margaret?' Angus Macdonald asked plaintively.

'Don't worry, I'll find her,' I said.

My only hope was the man with nine fingers. Maybe he'd be a kindred spirit when he spotted my stump. Then I thought of another question.

'Where were you released?' I asked the Lord of the Isles.

'My head was covered again and I was driven back – the trip was shorter that time. Maybe forty minutes. I was pushed out of the vehicle after being told not to take the balaclava off until I'd counted to a hundred. When I did, I found myself in a suburb I didn't recognize. Fortunately, a taxi appeared. It was just before five in the afternoon. I got the driver to drop me on Causewayside. I kept the balaclava pulled low on my forehead to avoid being recognized. I walked to the rear door of the Theatre of Life, checking that I wasn't being followed.'

He would have been conspicuous in his red kilt – not many people in Edinburgh wore them, apart from young people of both sexes who took pleasure in letting it all hang out.

I briefly wondered if the leader of the opposition went underwear-free, then got back to business. It was time to move.

Downstairs, Davie got his cosh back, as well as a .45 Colt automatic that looked old but well maintained.

Katharine came up behind me. 'So this is farewell, Quint,' she said, mouth close to my ear. 'For the time being.' Then she put her hand on my arm, pivoted and kissed me quickly on the lips. She walked to Davie and Dougie without looking back.

I didn't have time to think about the kiss because Rory arrived at my side.

'What's your plan?' he asked.

'Need to know—' I broke off as I noticed an old man on crutches moving awkwardly along the pavement across the road, his head bowed. He was wearing a beret and his clothes were ragged. Something didn't ring true.

'Davie!' I yelled, racing forward as best I could.

The gunshots were rapid and loud. The old man had ditched his crutches and pulled out a large pistol. Dougie the Dundonian fell to the ground like a felled pillar, having not even managed to move his arms from his sides.

'Don't kill him!' I screamed.

The shooter – clearly not old at all – had set off down the street like a sprinter.

Davie raised his weapon and fired once.

The target crashed to the pavement and clutched his lower left leg. Rory's people ran to disarm him.

A pool of blood was already forming around Dougie's head and upper chest. He wouldn't be seeing the silvery Tay again.

'Katharine has to catch that boat,' Rory said, catching me up. 'Inform your contacts in Dundee, please,' he said to her. 'Try to keep them calm.'

'You know I can't guarantee that.'

'Come on, then,' Davie said, opening the rear door of the van that had pulled up beside us. He and Katharine got in, the doors closed and the van departed at speed.

'We need to clear the area,' I said.

Rory nodded. The other van had stopped to pick up the wounded assassin, while a black estate car arrived for Lachie and the Lord of the Isles.

'Come on, Quint,' Rory said. 'Let's get this piece of shit back to base.'

We got in the front of the van, while five black-clad personnel leaped in the back with the captive. As we drove down Grange Road, we heard ScotPol sirens approaching from the north.

After a couple of quick turns, we disappeared into the rapidly descending night.

Once we were in the basement at Prestonfield, I used a flamer to call Sophia.

'Can you talk?' I asked.

'I just open my lips and blow.'

'I'm serious.'

'Hold on.'

I heard her rubber boots squeak on the morgue floor.

'Fire away.'

'That's what just happened.' I gave her a condensed version. 'I hear there's a guy missing you-know-which finger in the infirmary.'

'Yes. I was asked to match the digit to the stump.'

'And did it?'

'Yes. Hel Hyslop arrived after he was treated and took him away.'

'Shit. We may need you to look at the killer Davie shot.'

'Have you forgotten the kids, Quint?' There was ice in her voice.

'No. By the way, Katharine's gone back to Stirling.'

'Good. I hope they let her past the Fife coast.'

'It was all right on the way down.' She had a point, though. The former Kingdom of Fife had always ploughed its own furrow and had a reputation for doing as little as it could for the newly reformed nation. Maybe Stirling's women, who didn't exactly play democracy by the rules as parliament expected, were kindred spirits.

'Can I go now?' Sophia asked.

'Course. You know I love you.'

'Define "know".'

'Later, darling.'

She cut the connection.

Rory gave me an amused look that I discouraged with a frown.

All friends in the fight to safeguard the nation.

The wounded man was put on a scrubbed table in what passed for a sickbay in the basement and curtains were drawn around. A female medic who looked as if she'd only just left school cut off the leg of his trousers and examined the wound, holding the limb down until other personnel strapped the struggling man down.

'Straight-through wound,' she said. 'Was it a forty-five bullet?'

I nodded.

'I can patch him up, but he needs proper attention. Can we get him to the infirmary?'

'Not yet,' I said. 'Do what you have to, but keep him conscious.'

She didn't look happy about that, but Rory gave her the nod.

He took my arm and led me through a gap in the curtains. 'Listen, Quint, we haven't much time. Hyslop will be investigating what happened on Arden Street.'

'She's already got the guy with the missing finger.'

'Hell's teeth.'

Neither of us laughed.

'I may have to go back to ScotPol HQ and rejoin the official investigation,' I said. 'Davie, too. We're too far out of the loop.'

Rory nodded. 'Let's see what we can get out of the shooter first.'

'He's not the only lead we've got. Remember Morrie the Nut, the owner of the warehouse where you stored your creepy props?'

'Aye. We've got untraceable access to ScotWeb, if that's any help.'

'It's a start.' I paused. 'Tell me, Rory, why did you decide to use Bosch imagery in your play?'

He shrugged. 'The man was a genius. His vision fits perfectly into a satirical vision of the city under the Council.'

I wasn't buying that. There were plenty of other artistic geniuses he could have used – Brueghel, Goya, the moderns . . .

'You were aware of the Bosch cults, weren't you?' I watched his face carefully – he was a consummate actor.

'True enough. One of the company's brothers was involved in the Church of Bosch. Said they were a bunch of lunatics, but persuasive ones.'

Which made me think of Jack Nicol, even though he was attached to the other cult.

'Hang on,' I said. 'The other guard at the warehouse – Denzil Kennedy. We reckoned he was on the level, but I don't trust anybody now. We need to track him down too.'

'Maybe he'll lead us to Morris . . . what was his surname?'

'Gish. He might. Take me to a computer.'

I spent the next twenty minutes in front of a scratched and worn screen that must have been liberated from the old City Guard. But it and the tower worked well enough to tell me, via the Election Archive, that Denzil Kennedy lived in West Pilton. So, to my satisfaction, did Morrie the Nut. Then I realized what we were up against. I waved to Rory. He came over with Knee Bothwell, who was sporting his usual smile.

'What do you need?' said the latter.

'This one you can trust,' Rory said. 'He's been with us from the start.'

'Kennedy and Gish both live in West Pilton.'

Suddenly, Bothwell looked as happy as a man facing a firing squad.

'You want to get into Edinburgh's biggest no-go area?'

I nodded. 'Morrie Gish is a gang boss too.'

'Hardly a surprise,' said the tall man. 'Everyone there either leads or is a member of some gang or other. ScotPol only patrol in daylight. At night the wolves come out.'

I looked at Rory. 'Very dramatic. We'll have to think of a way to trap them.' I hit the keys again. 'Looks like young Denzil's got another job on his nights off, this one working the door at a club on Leith Walk called Salt and Chilli.'

'No doubt owned by Morrie the Nut or a proxy,' said Rory. 'Still, Leith Walk's not so bad.'

'The bottom end of Leith Walk,' I said.

'Bugger that.' Knee Bothwell stepped back. 'Do we have to do what this jumped-up snooper says, Chief?'

Rory's gaze was unwavering. 'If I go with him, yes.'

For a moment I thought Bothwell was going to question that, but he held back. Still, I wasn't sure how trustworthy he was.

'Mr Dalrymple?' called the medic.

We went back through the curtains.

'What have you got, Angie?' Rory asked, re-establishing the pecking order.

'Like I said, this man needs hospital treatment. I've managed to control the bleeding and given him pain medication. The bone's smashed. I doubt he'll be running in the future.'

I gave her an inquisitive look.

'Andy told me what he did,' she said, her cheeks colouring. It was pretty obvious they were a couple.

'Anything in his clothes?' I asked.

Angie shook her head. 'No ID, no phone, no helpful pieces of paper.'

'Right, let's get the bastard to talk,' said Rory.

I raised a hand. 'That's my area of expertise. Stand back, all of you.' I went to the head of the bed and squatted down. The man had blond hair and his face was suntanned – he definitely wasn't a local. His eyes were a piercing blue and his nose looked as if it had been repeatedly broken.

'I'm Quint. What's your name?'

His lips formed into a malignant smile and he made a strange sound, almost as if he was being strangled. I checked that his neck wasn't constricted.

'You knew who you were shooting, didn't you?'

Again his mouth moved, but only the grating sound came out.

'As you've probably gathered, we aren't the police.' I glanced at Bothwell's waist. He got the message and pulled his combat knife from its sheath. 'This can only end with you losing more blood.'

Angie the medic opened her mouth to protest but shut up when she saw the look on Rory's face.

'But why not be civilized?' I said. 'We can get you to hospital and then back to your people. Who are your people?'

The same noise came out, but this time louder. Then the wounded assassin opened his mouth and roared as best he could. All that remained of his tongue was a shrivelled stump.

'Fuck's sake,' said Rory, when we were back at the computer. 'Shall we take him to the infirmary?'

'After I've gone through his clothes. Get Angie to check if he's got any tattoos or other marks.'

I called Davie on a flamer. He told me he was on his way back in the rebels' van, having seen Katharine's boat disappear into the dark. I could only hope that the Scottish Coast Guard and Navy's patrol ships didn't pick it up on their instruments. Then again, maybe Lachie had pulled strings.

Rory came back with a plastic bag and emptied the contents on a nearby table. Angie was right. There were no tell-tale clues. The clothes and work boots could have been picked up at any second-hand shop in the city. And there was nothing of interest in the pockets or sewn into the seams. Which made me wonder. Without money, how had he intended to make his escape? Perhaps he'd resigned himself to capture or death, which suggested he was a serious hard case.

Angie called for me. We went over and found her and two male rebels holding the shooter down on his front, not that he was struggling particularly hard. He started to roar again, defiance in spades.

'Jesus,' said Rory.

'Nope,' I said.

Tattooed across the centre of the man's back was a grotesque image that I recognized immediately. The blue bird-headed figure was stuffing a naked human figure into its open beak, while black birds flew from the figure's smoking backside. The main bird was wearing a cauldron as a helmet and sitting on a wooden chair that obviously had a hole in the seat, because in a blue balloon the birdman was excreting more naked human figures into a pit. Another human had its arse bent over the pit and was shitting out gold coins. I pulled up *The Garden of Earthly Delights* on my phone and zoomed in. Yes, there was no doubt about it – the assassin had the Prince of Hell, as some scholars posited, inked on to his back. Just below the birdman's thin legs, which ended in green pitchers, was the woman with the toad on her chest and the four-fingered hands wrapped around her.

This case was stranger than truth, but at least there was some consistency emerging.

Davie came back soon afterwards. I told him about West Pilton. He was up for a fight, which was typical but not hugely helpful.

'What do you think about rejoining the ScotPol investigation now we've stopped being Typhoid Quint and Plague Davie?' I asked.

'Dunno. Are we better in than out?'

It was a reasonable question. He had a reliable source in Eilidh, though no doubt Hyslop would throw the regulation book at him for going walkabout, and I had no desire to further her career. Still, going into West Pilton with a team of ScotPol officers was tempting.

'Let's stay with the rebels for the time being,' I said.

'We could always slip into Pilton on our own under cover of darkness,' the big man said, with a worrying grin.

'Uh-huh. I'm not suicidal yet. Besides, young Denzil's on the door of a club called Salt and Chilli in Leith. There's a decent chance it's Morrie the Nut's and maybe he'll be there too.'

'I'm up for that,' said Davie, parting the flap of his jacket to display the butt of his automatic. 'Any more clips?'

Knee Bothwell handed him a couple.

I looked at my watch. It was coming up to eight – too early to hit the club. That wasn't a problem as there were two places I wanted to visit first.

Bothwell was driving the brown van into the centre, with four of his people in the back, and Davie and me up front. The tongueless man had been taken to the southern suburb of Liberton in another vehicle and an ambulance called to collect him.

'What are we supposed to do while you're carousing?' the driver complained.

'Discuss the French Revolution?' I suggested.

'That's *vieux chapeau, mon brave.*'

'Bravo, André.'

Davie turned to me. 'Did he just make a joke?'

'Even rebels can have a sense of humour.'

'Aye, and pigs might form their own air force.'

I laughed, then got serious, thinking of Ricky Fetlar, who'd broken his own head open for a cause I couldn't fathom. There was also the blond guy with the Prince of Hell on his back. Was there a connection between them? I knew someone who might be able to help.

'You can come in, if you like, Davie,' I said, when we turned on to Great Citizen Street. I had an ulterior motive. 'Knee, go to the address I gave you and make sure the occupant doesn't leave. If he tries, bring him round here.'

'Yes, sir,' the driver said, with an insolent smile.

I couldn't think of a smartarse reply so I got out and went up the steps to the street door. Davie followed and then overtook me on the stairs. More fool him. I started panting, my legs burning; I really had to do something about my carcass before it imploded. I put the key in the lock and opened the door. It took Heck about five seconds to hit Davie round the knees with what might have been called a rugby tackle by someone with a very loose understanding of the laws, especially the one about biting.

'Ooyah!' Davie exclaimed.

I managed to pull the wee bamstick off. He accepted a cuddle, then struggled free.

'Muuuum!' he yelled. 'The fat man's here!'

'Thanks a lot,' said Davie, rubbing his leg. 'Do I need an anti-tetanus jab?'

'Definitely,' said Maisie, appearing from her bedroom with a large textbook draped over her arm.

'Biology?' I asked, catching a glimpse of a skinned animal.

'The year after next's set book,' she said. 'How soon can I go to university?'

'Tomorrow.'

'Really?' Then she realized she'd been had and stomped off.

'Neat parenting skills,' said Davie.

'Here comes Heck again.' I watched as the imp drove Goliath into a corner.

Sophia came out of the kitchen. 'Didn't expect to see you tonight,' she said, looking at the pan of sliced carrots she was carrying. 'Oh. I forgot to peel them.'

'Little bit of boiled dirt won't do them any harm,' I said, leaning forward to kiss her on the lips. She didn't resist.

'I take it you and Davie – Heck, leave him alone! – aren't staying for dinner, then.'

'Busy, busy. I need to ask you something, though.' I followed her into the kitchen, which was in a state of chaos.

'Do I need a live-in maid?' Sophia said. 'Yes, urgently.' She started to brush the bits of carrot, then gave up.

'I'll see what I can do. Tell me, the warehouse guard who smashed his skull in—'

'Fetlar, R.? What about him?' Sophia put the pan on the ring. 'Is this something to do with his tattoo?'

'So he has got one?'

She nodded. 'A black boat with a red sail, on his left shoulder.'

I pulled up the Bosch painting on my phone, zoomed in and showed her.

'That's it.'

The said boat was on a yellowish-red expanse of water towards the top of the Hell panel, an army crossing a bridge beneath it and a cliff with a ladder leading to a tunnel above.

'What is it about that horrible work of art?' she said. 'The dead woman had the toad and branchlike hands.'

'We've just sent a guy without a tongue to the infirmary. He's got the Prince of Hell bird on his back.' I showed her that part of the panel. Then I made a connection. 'Hang on, the blue birdman and the other guy shitting gold coins. We've come across a Luxembourg company called BirdMammon.'

'And we don't believe in coincidences, do we?' Sophia said.

'Generally not. Well, well.'

'I need the room,' she said, waving me away. 'Heck will have driven Davie round the bend. Kids! In the kitchen now!'

'Si, Mama,' called Maisie.

'We need to have a serious talk about her education,' I said.

'When you can afford the time,' Sophia said, with a tight smile.

Davie walked in, hands under Heck's arms and extended so his midriff was out of range of the kicks being directed there.

'Yours, I think,' he said, presenting her son to Sophia.

'His, too,' she said, angling her head towards me.

I beamed with pride.

'Let's walk,' I said to Davie. On the way to Heriot Row – Billy had managed to keep hold of the double flat he'd had during the Enlightenment, even though it was on Edinburgh's most expensive street – I told Davie about Ricky Fetlar's tattoo.

'Shit,' he said, 'Eilidh should have told me about that.'

'Who knows how much Hyslop's sharing with her?'

'True enough.' He slipped on the slush-covered pavement. 'Bugger this. I wish it would snow properly. I can't stand this soggy mess.'

'Be careful what you desire.'

'Aye, right.' He glared at me. 'About time you trained that nipper of yours.'

'I have been training him – to nip.'

He raised his right arm and I took evasive action, which landed my left leg in chilly water up to the calf. That made him laugh. End of conversation.

We stopped outside the brown van.

'He's up there,' said Knee Bothwell, nodding at the lights flooding from all the windows on the second and third floors. Unlike most houses in the street, this one had a lift, put in by Billy when getting auxiliaries to carry him up and down was no longer an option. 'And he's got a lady friend. Lovely-looking young woman.'

At least Billy's company was young. He had been known to go for grannies, though that taste might have been stimulated by compulsory sex sessions with randomly assigned partners during the Enlightenment. Then again, I'd managed to control myself on that count, usually by having a cup of tea with my intended partners instead, before they went on their way. Farewell, my lovelies.

'Right,' I said, 'you lot stay down here.'

'Aw.' Davie was crestfallen. 'Are you sure you don't want me to beat the crap out of that thieving scumbag?'

'Yes. He's a cripple, for Plato's sake.'

Bothwell laughed. 'You're not still reading that old fascist?'

'No.' The truth was I knew numerous passages of the Enlightenment's favourite thinker off by heart. Weekly debates on his work had been obligatory in barracks. Davie seemed to have forgotten all he knew, despite the fact he was in the City Guard till the revolution, while I got demoted in 2018. I remembered because of Socrates, as he was presented in Plato's dialogues. He was a great example to a private investigator – play dumb, then come up with questions that tie your interlocutor in Gordian knots. Though that technique didn't work with Billy.

I crossed the road and pressed the intercom buzzer.

After a lengthy silence came a screech.

'Who the fuck is it? Go away, ya cunt!'

'It's me,' I said. 'Urgent business.' I stressed the last word to tantalize him.

There was a pause. 'Oh, all right.' The lock clicked and I pushed my way through. The hall smelled of furniture polish and the scent of flowers that were definitely not local. Billy liked to fly them in from African countries to impress visitors.

I went up the stairs, trying not to pant. On the second flight I passed a seriously attractive redhead in clothing that would have been inadequate during the Edinburgh summer. She gave me a cool look that warmed me up in a second.

'What the hell do you want?' came the cracked voice from his open door. Billy was in his wheelchair, wearing a silk dressing gown that showed more than it covered up. 'What is this business?'

I walked past him, but he quickly overtook me on the teak floor.

'You interrupted me at a very juicy moment, Quint.' His lips twisted lewdly.

'Spare me,' I muttered, heading for the drinks table, which was huge. 'Want something?'

'I'm all doped up and Rowena will be back as soon as you're gone.'

Way too much information, especially given the disarray of his single garment. A pharmaceutical company in one of the many ultra-religious American state-nations – with typical hypocrisy – had produced a pill that gave you 'an erection St Simeon Stylites would be proud of', according to the ad. Billy had obviously been convinced.

'Where to start?' I said, pouring myself a decent dram of something in Gaelic that I couldn't pronounce. The old language had been compulsory in schools in the Lord of the Isles's domain since reunification. He'd tried to make it compulsory across Scotland but had been told by parliament where he could insert that.

'You're the bloody storyteller,' said Billy scathingly. 'Which reminds me. The Finnish contracts have come in. You need to sign them. They want to make a TV series out of *The Body Politic*.'

'I thought Finland only recently reconstituted itself. Have they got the money?'

'What do you think? Everyone needs wood.' He cackled. 'Except me.'

I groaned. 'All right, listen. This is for your ears only, definitely not Rowena's.'

'Don't worry, pillow talk's not my thing.'

'Why am I not surprised?' I told him about the reappearance of Angus Macdonald and the pressure that was being exerted on him.

Billy watched me carefully. 'Why hasn't that been on the news?'

'Care to hazard a guess?'

He gave his lopsided smile. 'You've finally found out that the new Scotland is about as united as that Manchester football team, have you?' The English city was notorious for longstanding gang warfare and had recently become part of Merseyside. As far as I knew, the area wasn't in Nor-England.

'How much do you know?'

'What's in it for me?'

I took out my phone and called Davie. 'Hey, Thunderboots, Billy wants—'

'No!' screamed my host.

'Stand by,' I said, then cut the connection.

'Bastard,' Billy hissed.

'No, I think his parents were married.'

'Ha fucking ha. All right, I'm glad old Angus is back in town. I heard his wife's been kidnapped.' I nodded. 'If he doesn't sign those deals, the Nor-English will get nasty. Good sources have reported that they've got an army fifty-thousand-strong.' He grinned. 'Another thing that hasn't been mentioned in the media.'

I stared at him. 'I thought the place was a gang-haunted wasteland until recently.'

'It was. Then Nigel Shotbolt took over. He'd been a gang leader himself, of course, but he has more . . . what could it be called? Not nous, but animal cunning. He's also a very effective demagogue. His speeches about Nor-England's destiny being to reunite the country go down like . . . well, Rowena.'

'Get a grip, you old libertine. Where did he get the money to create an army?'

'Where do you think?'

I took in his expectant expression, like a devil's sick for sin. 'What, from here?'

'Bravo. The bankers in the shiny new financial centre that the Enlightenment built lend to anyone they think has a future.'

I was shocked and it must have showed, because he laughed. 'Does the government know?'

'Duart and a select few of his cronies, yes.'

'What about the Lord of the Isles?'

'Not sure, but I'd say he doesn't. I doubt he'd countenance that kind of deal, even though he's a major shareholder in most of the banks.'

'So Andrew Duart might be behind the kidnapping of Lady Margaret.'

'I wouldn't put it past him.'

'And the contracts that are to be made over to BirdMammon – that company's a front for the principal minister and his circle?'

Billy shrugged, his shoulders uneven. 'Could be.'

'How do you know all this?' I demanded. 'Have you got shares in the banks? Were you involved in those loans?'

'Yes. And no. We need to stop Angus making his energy shares over to that company, no matter who's behind it. Scotland needs to keep control of its energy sector. The economy will collapse without it.'

I still smelled rodent. 'You've got shares in the energy companies too.'

He nodded. 'I'm a businessman. What do you expect?'

'Certainly not any trace of morality.'

He cackled. 'Don't get on your big stallion with me, pal. How do you think I was able to pay the advances you happily pocketed?'

I might have known. As ever, I was complicit up to my oxters.

'Doesn't Duart know about the military threat from the Nor-English?' I asked, draining my glass and denying myself a refill.

'Of course. He thinks we can beat them.'

It was my turn to cackle. 'What with? The Scottish Defence Force is half the size of the army you're talking about, and most of them are guarding the oil and gas installations.'

Billy wheeled himself closer, his face unusually serious. 'You haven't heard of the secret weapon?'

My stomach decided it didn't like whisky any more. I managed to swallow the liquid that had suddenly filled my mouth.

'Tell me.'

'I can't.'

I reached for my phone again.

'No, it's not that I won't. I can't because I don't know.'

'You're not a whoring friend of the defence minister?'

'Believe it or not, that arsehole's happily married. He's terrified of his boss. In fact, he might not even know about whatever it is.'

'Where did they get it, for fuck's sake? Is science and technology that advanced in Glasgow?'

'Aberdeen's the armaments place, I hear.'

Which explained that city's failure to join Katharine and the late Dougie on their mission to Embra.

Billy smacked my thigh. 'What are we going to do about the Lord of the Isles? He's got to sign the papers with the Nor-English.'

'I doubt he'll do that. Lady Margaret's his priority.'

'Where is he, anyway?'

'I told you, Lachie's got him.'

'Bloody interfering dwarf.'

'He's got principles. You don't even know what those are.'

He laughed, but his expression remained sombre. 'What to do?'

'That's what I came to ask you.'

We sat there like a pair of salmon who had spawned and were waiting for the end.

'I need to talk to Angus,' Billy said. 'I can talk sense into him.'

I decided against asking how he imagined he could manage that. 'OK, I'll get a message to Lachie.'

Billy snorted. 'I bet he's hiding like a timorous beastie.'

'He led the revolution.'

'So what? Life goes on, fuelled by the lust for profit. I'll make contact with the Nor-English – butter them up and keep them here.'

'You could always take them to your favourite massage parlour.'

He laughed creakily. 'I doubt Gemma Bass would go for that. She's a very driven woman, not given to the pleasure of the flesh. I tried.'

I considered telling him about her Bosch belt buckle but decided against it. In the past, information I'd passed to Billy had come back to bite me in the groin.

My phone rang. Davie came on, breathless.

'Get down here. Rory says the base is being attacked.'

I stood up and headed for the door. 'Who by?'

'I'll give you one guess.'

'Hyslop.'

'Is the correct answer. Now run.'

I did my best.

ELEVEN

A t the van, I stopped by Knee Bothwell's open window.
'Get in, man,' he said, revving the engine.
'Come on, Quint,' added Davie.
I shook my head. 'I don't think so.'

'Fuck's sake!' yelled Bothwell. He grabbed his phone and punched buttons. 'Rory? Dalrymple's turned yellow.' He handed me the device.

I heard gunshots before Rory Campbell's voice came on. 'What's going on down there?'

'Frontal attack by ScotPol armed units. I'm getting our people out the back. You need to be here, Quint.'

'Shit. Can you see who's in command?'

'No. They're advancing behind armoured vehicles.'

'And you haven't heard from anyone? Hyslop, for instance?'

'No, this is a kill mission.'

I took a few moments to think. 'If it is, make sure you get out. I don't see the point of Bothwell and his men walking into a wall of bullets. Besides, this shows that Hyslop and Duart are rattled. I need to keep probing elsewhere.'

Rory was quick-witted. 'You're right. Stay away. Give me Andy.' I handed the phone back.

Bothwell listened, his forehead lined, then cut the connection. 'Fuck!' he screamed, glaring at me. 'We're to stick with you. Rory must have lost his wits.'

'No, he hasn't. He's getting your people out.'

'Let's hope the polis haven't surrounded the place. What's so important here?'

'Leave the bigger picture to me, Knee. Get in, Davie.' I waited and then joined him in the front seat.

'Where to?' demanded Bothwell.

'We can't wait for Morrie the Nut to head to the Salt and Chilli Club. We have to get to West Pilton.'

The rebel's face was split by a grin. 'Now you're talking. Break out the machine pistols, boys.'

Davie looked happy too. 'I need one of those, thanks.'

I shook my head despairingly. This was like the prelude to the combat missions we used to run against the drugs gangs. They had been armed to the teeth and completely unforgiving. I hoped the suburb wasn't like that any more, but its reputation suggested it might be.

As the van slalomed down Howe Street, I had a flash of the ENT Man during my struggle with him. At least he no longer walked the earth. But the sick bastard who'd planted the severed forefinger in the Lord of the Isles's four-poster did.

'How do you want to play this?' Davie said to me.

'Fast in, fast out.'

'What's the target's address?' asked Andy.

I squinted at my notebook. 'Twelve West Pilton Grove.'

He handed Davie a map. 'Find it, will you?'

As they discussed the best approach, I looked through the windscreen. Snow was coming down again. At least that would discourage the lads and lassies who roamed the streets looking for trouble in the northern suburb. We might manage to get close without mayhem erupting. Then again, there would be sentries posted around Morrie the Nut's place. Speed was of the essence. As we traversed the trendy area of Stockbridge, I tried to make sense of what was going on. Even if Hel Hyslop wasn't at Prestonfield, she must have given the order for the attack. I could only hope that Rory and his people got out, and that Lachie and the Lord of the Isles were hiding somewhere that no one else knew about – even Rory would crack under the fourth degree. I was sure whoever was behind the abductions of Angus and Margaret Macdonald was in the city. Billy had mentioned the arrival of a Finnish trade delegation. Finns had blond hair . . . Then again, so did lots of people.

'Weapons check,' Bothwell said over his shoulder. He turned on to Crewe Road.

As the sounds of magazines being removed and then slapped back into pistols of varying shapes and sizes filled the van – Davie making more noise than he had to in his excitement – I looked to the right. What had been Raeburn Barracks – the old headquarters of the pre-Enlightenment Lothian and Borders Police – was now being turned into luxury flats. Raeburn had been where the City Guard's biggest headbangers were posted to counter the threat from the gangs in Pilton, though Davie's lair, Hume Barracks, would have disputed that, fists to the fore. Then we passed the tree-shrouded rubble that was the remains of Fettes College, whose most notorious alumnus had been the last prime minister of the UK before it fell apart in fury and flames. To my surprise, the site wasn't being reused. Perhaps the soil had been permanently poisoned by the man who would be the messiah's presence. Still, not even he deserved to suffer the same fate as William Wallace after the mob crashed into Downing Street.

'Balaclavas!' ordered Bothwell.

I pulled mine down, nudging Davie. He could have gone in undisguised, as the city's smarter villains knew who he was. Which begged the question, why hadn't Morrie the Nut been picked up before? Maybe Hyslop was protecting him. That wasn't a reassuring thought.

We turned left at the roundabout, on to Ferry Road and then into the estate. It had been devastated during and after the drugs wars, though the municipal leaders had done their best to finance new apartment blocks. Morris Gish had taken over an entire building.

Bothwell floored the accelerator and the van skidded in the slush. I couldn't see any people on the streets, but that didn't mean we hadn't been spotted. We pulled up with a screech outside number twelve and leaped out, leaving one heavily armed rebel to guard the vehicle and sending another to cover the rear of the building.

'Here, whit are ye—'

Davie silenced the man in the sheepskin coat with a right to the jaw that was definitely not permitted in ScotPol regulations. Then again, neither was sending armed units without Municipal Board approval, which Lachie obviously wouldn't have given for the raid on Prestonfield. Rules were for suckers in reunified Scotland.

Davie charged in. 'Come on, I know where he'll be.'

So did I. Gang bosses always took the top floor so they could see assailants coming and have time to get down the fire escape or specially mounted ropes. We raced up the stairs, ignoring the lifts, which were potential deathtraps. Fortunately, this block only had three storeys. As we reached the third flight of stairs, bullets

started to fly. Bothwell and his men laid down covering fire while
we dashed on. I could have been back in the Tactical Operations
Squad – if my thighs weren't burning, my lungs bursting and my
throat drier than Andrew Duart's soul.

'Drop it!' Davie shouted, firing at the floor in front of two guys
dressed in red uniforms like those worn at Waterloo. Gish was
clearly even more of a nut than his nickname suggested.

I took the key from one of the now-kneeling men and slipped
it into the hole in the door. Bothwell and his men arrived, having
dealt with gang members on the lower floors.

I turned the key and Davie rammed the door open, leading with
his shoulder. I followed, as did Bothwell. His men stayed on the
landing, firing down the stairs.

'No, you don't!' Davie yelled, loosing off a burst around the
window that a large man was partially through. He came back in
with surprising agility.

'He shot Denzil,' Morrie the Nut said.

I looked down. Davie had indeed terminated the former warehouse guard's life. Kennedy was lying on his back, his chest a field
of blood. One fewer to question, though I wished the young man
was still alive. I had the feeling he was easily led, rather than a
reprobate like his boss. But who had given the order for him to be
released from custody at ScotPol HQ?

'Sit down,' I said to Gish.

Davie thrust him into a pink leather armchair, then raised an
eyebrow at me. 'Are we not getting the Hades out of here, Quint?'

'Can't be sure we'll make it, never mind him. I need to give his
balls a preliminary squeeze.'

'Allow me,' Davie said, with a grin. He tossed me his machine
pistol, leaving the Colt in his belt. He leaned forward and stuck his
hand in the prisoner's groin.

Morrie the Nut squealed, his voice rising as the pressure
increased. We were back in City Guard mode, but there was no
time to feel bad.

'Right, Mr Gish,' I said, moving closer. The gunfire outside
started again and Knee Bothwell went to have a look. 'You have
one minute to spill your guts. My friend has a Guard-issue combat
knife. Remember those?' I looked round the room, which had been
decorated by someone with too much money and no taste. There

was a frame on the wall with at least ten knives mounted inside it. 'Yes, you do.' I smiled with as much encouragement as I could muster. The place smelled like a brothel that catered for creatures from the black lagoon.

'What is it ye want?' Gish squealed, tears streaming down his face into a beard that had been incompetently dyed red.

'You own the warehouse where Ricky Fetlar and Denzil Kennedy worked,' I said, noticing that he had no lobes on his ears. It wasn't clear if they'd been cut off or had never existed.

'So? It's all legal, I've got the . . . stop! . . . got the papers.'

'How much did you pay under the table?' I asked. Lachie MacFarlane ran a tight municipality and corrupt civil servants were dealt with firmly, but there would be some festering apples.

'A . . . a thousand poonds. Tell him . . . to stop . . . please!' The tears were a torrent now.

I nodded to Davie, who pulled his hand away and sniffed it cautiously.

'Come on!' shouted Bothwell. 'There's too many of the buggers.'

I heard shooting from the window.

'Who's your backer?' I said, mouth close to Gish's ear.

The question took him by surprise and he started mouthing inaudibly.

'Davie?'

'No! I cannae tell ye. They'll rip me to pieces.'

'And you think I won't?' Davie said, pulling out his knife.

'All right, all right. BirdMammon, they're called. I don't know—'

This time Davie didn't need to be told what to do. He whipped off the tip of the gang boss's nose. The scream almost broke my eardrums.

'Who runs BirdMammon?' I yelled. 'Now!'

'Mr . . . Mr Sebastian,' Morrie said, hand over his nose. 'Mr Edward Sebastian. He's a—'

There was a blinding explosion and bullets flew around the room.

'Stun grenade,' Davie mouthed. 'Come on.'

I followed him to the window, my ears ringing as if I was next to the biggest bell ever made, my legs unsteady. Morris Gish was lying back, shot through his left eye. I saw Andy Bothwell stagger in.

Davie pointed downwards. The rebel we'd sent round the back

was on one knee, his head bloodied, engaging a group of armed men and women with rapid fire. I slid down the escape rope and grabbed the wounded man's pistol from his belt. The shots I fired hit some of my targets. Then Davie thumped down beside me and let loose with his machine pistol. Bothwell made it to the ground, but he went over on his ankle. I grabbed him, while Davie picked up the other rebel, continuing to fire after he swiftly changed magazine. We headed round to the front of the building. The rebel there was in the van, firing from the front seat. We piled into the back, Davie clambering between the seats to take the wheel. He reversed rapidly and ran into bodies. Bullets stitched lines across the van's bodywork. The tyres were shot out and the vehicle's wheels screeched across the snowy asphalt, swerving violently. The noise of gunfire increased, and I reckoned we were done for, but somehow Davie managed to pull off a 180-degree turn while moving and accelerate away. Bullets still came through where the windows had been, but soon there were fewer of them.

'Clear!' Davie shouted, as he turned out of the estate. He looked at the man next to him. His skull had been blown apart.

'Fucking shit!' Knee Bothwell was holding a piece of fabric over the crown of his head. Blood pulsed through it immediately. 'That stunt cost us three men. I hope it was worth it.'

I didn't reply. It wasn't clear that it had been. I was unscathed, which made me feel a fraud. Then again, Davie was untouched too. Not that he'd be beating himself up about that. Good for him.

We had to split up. Bothwell said he would hijack a car and take himself and the other wounded men to a hospital in one of the neighbouring towns. Davie and I ran down Crewe Road, stopping a taxi by standing in the middle of the road. The driver was aghast – both of us had blood on our clothes – but the fifty-poond note I waved had an effect.

'Where to?' he asked.

I glanced at Davie. Bothwell had told us three rendezvous points that had been set up for those in the Prestonfield base if it was attacked. I decided against going to any of them till I could contact Rory or Lachie.

'Hanover Street,' I said. We'd be able to disappear into the crowds of drinkers and diners in the city centre.

On the way, I considered our options. It was clear that either of us rejoining the official enquiry wasn't an option now. Nor was going home. Hyslop was no doubt having the flat watched. Would it be possible to get Sophia and the kids out? I decided the risk was too great. There was no alternative entrance or exit to the tenement, and we hadn't the means to set up a rope like the Lord of the Isles's kidnappers had done in Ainslie Place, not to mention the late unlamented Morrie the Nut in West Pilton. But how was I to find this Edward Sebastian? I knew the first person to ask and redirected the driver.

'Wait, please,' I said, when we pulled up outside. 'Both of you.'

Davie shrugged.

This time there was an immediate answer.

'Who?'

'Quint.'

'Was that you?' Billy's voice screeched through the intercom. 'Hell of a mess, even by your standards.' He buzzed me in.

I took the stairs one by one, low on energy.

He was waiting for me on the landing. 'There's a TV crew down in Pilton. Seems there was a modern version of the gunfight at the O.K. Corral.'

'That only lasted thirty seconds,' I said. I was a fan of the films made about the shootout before Hollywood became its own disaster movie. 'This went on for . . . it seemed like hours.'

'So it *was* you,' he said, closing the heavy wooden door behind me. 'No doubt Thunderboots was there too. I don't suppose he took a bullet or six?'

'You don't suppose correctly. He's downstairs. Shall I fetch him?'

'No!'

I staggered to an armchair and slumped into it.

'When did you last eat?'

Good question. I couldn't remember.

'I'll bring your belly sustenance.' Billy wheeled himself out of the room and soon returned with a tray on his knees. 'Oatcakes, Camembert from Aberdeenshire, wind-dried beef from Fife, haddock mousse made by my own fair hand and smoked aubergines from the Carse of Gowrie.'

The hot summers had enabled farmers to experiment with fruit and vegetables that never grew in Scotland before.

'The Carse of Gowrie's in Dundee territory, isn't it?' I said, as I heaped mousse on to a triangular bannock.

'Yes, I think the loony left managed to take it from the feudalists next door.'

'This is amazing,' I said, spraying crumbs.

'I thank you. My talents are, as you know, legion.'

'Speaking of which, where's Rowena?'

'Her work is done,' he said, with a smirk.

'All right,' I said, after swallowing a slice of aubergine. 'Try this on for size. Who's Edward Sebastian?'

Billy's ears pricked up, despite the damage they'd suffered under the horses' hooves. He suddenly looked warier than a cat padding through Dogville.

'Ah-ha,' I said. 'You know him.'

There was a long silence, during which I cleared most of the plates and bowls. Billy had also brought a large glass of no doubt extremely expensive red wine. I emptied it.

'Edward Sebastian,' I repeated, wiping my mouth.

More taciturnity. Billy looked scared, which was unusual – his *modus operandi* was to stare the world out and abuse anyone who got too close.

'All right,' I said. 'I'll hazard a guess. He's an overweening and ultra-powerful businessman, whose companies you've invested in and are scared shitless you're going to lose out on. Correct?'

He shook his head. 'It's not that.'

'There's worse? For a money-grubber like you?' I was using the standard tone of our conversations, but he wasn't returning serve. 'That bad?'

'Yes, Quint,' he said firmly, avoiding my gaze. 'Where did you hear the name, anyway?'

'Morris Gish – the guy in West Pilton. Have you heard of him?'

'Course not. I don't hang around with gang bosses.'

I laughed. 'You hung around with plenty in the past.'

'That was different.'

'Oh, aye? Because the guardians knew Plato, that made them better than Morrie the Nut? I don't think so. It made them worse, you idiot.' I got up.

'Where are you going?' Billy said, alarm in his voice.

'To wave at Davie. He'll be up in a flash.'

'For fuck's sake. All right, I'll tell you.'

'Yes, you will. And then you'll help me sort out this burgeoning nightmare. Right?'

No answer, which I took as a 'yes'.

'So, Edward Sebastian.'

'Mr Edward Sebastian.'

'Yes, that's how Gish referred to him too. What is he, a surgeon?' I was just tossing out ideas, but the look on Billy's face told me I'd drawn blood. That was the first profession in which 'Mr' was an honorific that had come to mind. I gave Billy the eye and this time he didn't avoid it.

'He's not just any kind of surgeon,' he said. 'Not a urologist or an ear, nose and throat man.'

My blood turned to ice. I presumed he hadn't chosen the second example deliberately – he knew about the ENT Man back in the day, but not what I'd done to him. This case was raising phantoms I'd never wanted to see again, the main one being the psycho-killer who took Caro from me.

'What is he, then?' I asked, keeping my voice level.

Billy paused. 'He calls himself a teratologist.'

Although I never studied the classical languages in depth, my old man – who was a professor of rhetoric – had made sure I knew plenty of word roots. 'Teras' was the ancient Greek for 'monster'. I had a bad feeling about Mr Edward Sebastian.

'What do you understand by that?' I asked innocently.

'I know what it means, though I had to look it up. You?'

'I seem to remember the old man going on about the *terata* in the Council.'

'Aye, well, this guy's a special kind of teratologist.' There was a combination of distaste and delight on Billy's face now. He was going to try to shock me. I put my hands over my full stomach. 'He fixes people with genetic and other disorders. Works all over the world – highly respected, I've heard.'

'Other disorders?' I said. Many nuclear power stations had been destroyed by drugs gangs or terrorists in continental Europe. There were rumours of people being born with all sorts of abnormalities.

'You know, legs fused together, missing fingers . . .'

He broke off. I hadn't told him about the finger in the Lord of the Isles's bed, but he was now staring at my stump. It was still a source of fascination after all these years. Then again, Billy had some interests that were much more perturbing than the put-upon Rowena.

'Uh-huh,' I said, returning his stare. 'What can this surgeon possibly have to do with a gangster in West Pilton?'

'Search me.'

I believed he was ignorant of that aspect of Sebastian, but that wasn't the whole story. 'How do you know him?'

'What makes you think I've met him?' he said, suddenly defensive.

'Because you almost shat yourself when I said his name.'

He opened his mouth but nothing came out. Eventually, he spoke again. 'He was in Edinburgh a couple of weeks ago looking for investors. He wants to build a specialized clinic in southern Finland.'

'Did he find the funds?'

'What are you, a pestilent poet?'

'Ha. What kind of a hold has he got over you?'

'None.' He rubbed his forehead, which was even more furrowed than usual. 'He's the creepiest-looking man I've ever seen. Must be six foot six, thin as a scaffolding pole, black hair flattened to his scalp, and teeth . . . I don't know why he doesn't get them fixed.'

'What's the matter with them?'

'The canines are long and yellow and he's missing at least one front tooth between them, top and bottom.'

'Sounds like Nosferatu.' Billy, Caro and I had seen the old Murnau film before the Enlightenment. We'd required several drinks afterwards.

'Much worse than that human rodent. He's got weirdly long fingers too, now you mention it. Good for operating, I suppose.'

'Have you seen him since?'

Billy shook his head. 'He's not been back. I'd have heard. Now piss off and solve your case on your own. What am I? Your personal databank?'

I declined to answer and stalked out. The idea that one of the undead had been in the city was unsettling. Then again, vampires generally didn't have dealings with mid-level gangsters.

*   *   *

'Wakey, wakey,' I said, opening the taxi door.

Davie's head jerked back. He looked at his watch. 'Where have you been?'

'Eating the finest food and drinking the—'

'Hanover Street,' he said to the driver. There were restaurants that stayed open late there.

I needed to contact Rory and Lachie, though they wouldn't be answering their usual numbers.

'Pull up over there,' I said, pointing to the public phone under a plastic cover. There were fewer every year. I got out, put a coin in the slot and tried Lachie's reserve number, one that I had memorized after the revolution; it was likely he'd set up a forwarding programme. There was a series of clicks and buzzes, then a woman answered.

'Tadnon House, who's speaking, please?'

I sighed in relief. 'Skrytot.'

The names, anagrams of two leading revolutionaries, had been agreed soon after the Council fell, when the political situation was highly volatile. Rory's codename was an anagram of Bakunin.

'Hold, please.'

There were more noises on the line, which I took to mean that security measures were being applied. Then Lachie spoke.

'We can't be overheard, Quint,' he said. 'What's happening?'

'I was rather hoping you'd tell me. Rory said it was a kill mission. Is he OK?'

'Yes. He and his people got out with only minor casualties. I think Hyslop was actually trying to scare and disrupt us. For the time being . . .'

'How about Angus? Has he met the Nor-English?'

'Tomorrow.'

'I hear there are Finns in town too.'

'Also tomorrow. I don't suppose you've found any trace of Lady Margaret?'

'Afraid not.' I told him about Morrie the Nut, but he'd already heard from Bothwell, who was in hospital in Falkirk, recuperating. I mentioned the teratologist.

'Yes, I'm aware of him. He's not an immediate issue – banking business, though I'm also trying to talk him into building a clinic here. No, the problem is that our friends in Dundee have taken

Dougie's death very badly. There's a boatload of them on the way and they want blood.'

'Superb. When are they due?'

'They're not saying. They may stop off and pick up the few malcontents left in Fife.'

'Does Hyslop know about this?'

'Of course. Duart, too. They're panicking.'

'Good. I'll see what I can do about Lady Margaret, but she could be anywhere.'

'You think? I'd say she's in the vicinity of Embra; she might even be in the city.'

'Why?'

'I reckon the Nor-English are behind her and Angus's kidnappings. Before you ask, I haven't got any evidence, but when you've been a rebel for as long as I have, you get a nose for bad apples. The tosser Shotbolt is definitely one of those.'

'But you're negotiating with him.'

'Not me – I'm just watching Angus's back.'

'All right, leave it with me.' I cut the connection.

The fact was that I did have evidence that the Nor-English were potentially connected to serious wrongdoing; or at least Gemma Bass was: her belt buckle with the Bosch mermaid symbol. It was high time I followed that up.

'Food,' Davie said desperately.

We went to a pizza place on Hanover Street. He ordered two pies, both with eggs on top. Billy's feast was heavy on my stomach even though I was only going to be a spectator.

'No wine,' I said, as he was about to order. 'We've got work.'

'Oh, aye? I was hoping to see Eilidh.'

'Later, my friend.' I told him what Lachie had said. The bit about the Dundonians made his eyes flash. 'Maybe you could ring Eilidh for an update.'

He did so, while I gulped water. I still felt twitchy after the shootout.

'Right,' Davie said, putting his phone down. 'Hyslop's crapping herself about our quasi-friends from the north. She's also pissed off about a certain incident in West Pilton – let's hope the locals had stoned all the CCTV units. As for the rest, nothing's moving. No new leads on the dead woman, nothing significant from the poor people who've had the seventh degree. She's wondering where we are, though – the queen wasp, I mean. Eilidh heard her talking about putting us on the wanted list again.'

'Bollocks to that. Then again, we have been consorting with revolutionaries.'

'Consorting, eh?'

His food arrived and there followed an exhibition of gluttony that Fats Waller and Domino would have admired. Fortunately, it was over quickly.

'So what are we doing?' he asked.

'Talking to the Nor-English.'

'Great. Gemma Bass is something else.'

He was right there, but I wasn't thinking about her body. Was she something other than a trade representative? It was time to find out.

We walked up the Mound to Goose Pie, as Ramsay Gardens were known. There were lights on in the flat we'd broken into. Davie repeated his trick with the guards and we got up the stairs without our names or images being recorded. I stood outside the familiar door and rang the bell. Heavy footsteps came down the corridor beyond.

'Who's that?' said a man with a deep voice.

'The name's Dalrymple,' I said. 'Quint Dalrymple.'

The lock was disengaged and the door opened at speed.

'The writer?' This time Nigel Shotbolt was in a blue suit with yellow lines crisscrossing it in squares and a check shirt. 'I love your books. Come in, come in.' He turned away. He had a strong accent, but I couldn't locate it. Definitely northern English – maybe Yorkshire, if such a county still existed.

I looked at Davie, who shook his head. 'You're my secretary,' I whispered, getting a growl in return.

We followed the Nor-English leader down the corridor and into the sitting room. The full-length red velvet curtains were drawn. On one sofa sat the striking Gemma Bass, her hair pulled back from her strong features; she was wearing a black evening dress that rendered the imagination superfluous. I hoped Davie wasn't drooling.

'This is my number two, Gemma Bass,' said Shotbolt, going to the drinks cabinet. 'The famous Quint Dalrymple.'

The woman remained seated. I approached her and took the hand she extended.

'Famous for what?' she asked, her voice almost as deep as her boss's.

I was certain she was dissembling, not because my books didn't sell beyond the border – Billy had proudly announced that they did, though he complained about how hard it was to get payment – but there was a knowing look in her unusually large eyes, the irises of which were pale green. I got the feeling she knew I was an investigator and was playing dumb.

'Who's your friend?' she asked, giving Davie a sultry look. 'Your amanuensis?'

'How did you know I look after his garden?' quipped Davie.

Gemma Bass laughed and a shiver ran up my spine. I told my anatomy to behave itself.

'Here you are,' said Shotbolt, holding out a tray with four glasses on it. 'We make our own firewater,' he said. 'I was keeping a bottle for the Lord of the Isles, but he seems to have gone AWOL.' He smiled humourlessly. 'I hope he's not off with the bloody Finns. We should take priority. After all, our shared heritage is British.'

I looked at Davie to shut him up. 'Well,' I said, struggling to be diplomatic, 'you could say that.'

'And we'll all be together again!' The Englishman raised his glass. 'To a further union, a deeper communion!' I recognized the line. The guy wasn't the complete buffoon he appeared to be.

We all drank.

'Good stuff,' said Davie. 'I didn't know you people were Christians.' I suspected he hadn't recognized where the words came from.

'We're not exactly devout,' said Shotbolt, 'but we respect the old country's religion. We're business people, aren't we, Gemma?'

The woman, who was now standing, nodded. 'Indeed we are, Nigel.'

'What do you have to trade?' I asked, feigning ignorance.

'We're in the process of re-establishing the shipbuilding that the Northeast was famous for, as well as getting back into steel manu-facturing. We've got a lot of the mills in the Northwest running an' all.' He raised his broad shoulders. 'What we need is investment and we're offering generous terms. Most of all, we need dependable sources of energy. As you probably know, the oil and gas fields off our coast are no longer operational. We'll get them going again, but in the short to medium term we need what Scotland exports.'

'I wouldn't have thought you need whisky, given you have this flammable little number,' said Davie, taking the bottle, offering it to everyone else and then filling his glass. I knew what he was doing – playing the fool to see if they dropped their guard. 'Is it just the two of you, then, in this gigantic flat?'

Gemma gave him a thoughtful look. 'No, there's our colleague Geoff – Geoff Lassiter.'

Shotbolt laughed. 'Yes, he's standing in the corridor with a submachine gun, waiting to see if we need help.'

Davie went for a look. He returned, shaking his head.

The landowner lookalike's eyes were fixed on me. 'What is it that you want, Quint?' He raised his right hand – I noticed that the fingers, all present, were thicker than rustic sausages. 'I know you consult as an investigator for ScotPol. I also know that the big guy's your sidekick, as well being in charge of this city's detectives. So why the visit long after office hours?'

It was time to turn the heat up to twelve.

'Do you mind if I ask some questions?' I said, with an ingratiating smile. Always soften them up before inserting the blade.

'I'm not promising I'll answer them,' said Shotbolt.

Davie gave him a malevolent grin. 'Then we'll draw our own conclusions.'

'No need for that,' the Nor-English leader said, in a hurt voice. Good start.

'Do you know Morris Gish?' I watched him carefully.

'Who?'

I got the impression he was playing for time. 'Morris Gish, also known as Morrie the Nut.'

Gemma Bass laughed, but I kept my eyes on her boss. Shotbolt wasn't comfortable, though the only giveaway was a sudden onset of blinking.

'Morrie the Nut?' the woman said. 'What is he? A naturalist?'

'A gangster,' I said, pausing. 'Or rather, ex-gangster. He was killed earlier this evening.'

The blinking slowed. Shotbolt seemed to be relieved by that news.

'I'm sorry to hear that,' he said, taking a sip of firewater. 'But no, I've never heard the name.'

I kept up the attack. 'How about a company called BirdMammon?'

The rapid blinking started again. 'BirdMammon?' He turned to his colleague. 'Gemma's our financial expert. Do you know that name?'

She shook her head slowly, her eyelids motionless. 'No. What kind of company is it?'

I moved on, convinced only that Gemma Bass was better at dissembling than her boss.

'How about Mr Edward Sebastian?'

'Sebastian?' said Shotbolt. 'I know him. He's some kind of surgeon. Wanted us to finance a clinic in York.' He wasn't blinking rapidly, but he seemed ill at ease.

'He calls himself a teratologist,' I said.

'I don't even know what that is,' the Nor-Englishman said, less than persuasively. He was scared.

Gemma Bass stood up and held her glass towards Davie. 'Congenital deformities, that sort of thing – he fixes them.'

I began to wonder if Shotbolt was a mouthpiece and she was the real leader. Nothing seemed to provoke questionable reactions from her. I had an ace down my trousers.

I caught her eye as she took back her charged glass. 'Are there any Bosch cults in Nor-England?'

'What?' she said, mouth opening before she got it under control. Gotcha.

'Cults inspired by the paintings of Hieronymus Bosch.'

'Oh, them,' said Nigel Shotbolt. 'There are one or two. Harmless fools. We have freedom of religion, as long as it's related to some aspect of Christianity. No Muslims, Sikhs or Hindus in Nor-England! My people looked into it and confirmed Bosch was a believer. I'd never heard of him.'

I was still concentrating on Gemma Bass. For the first time, she'd been rattled. It was time to strike again.

'You have a belt buckle with a design from *The Garden of Earthly Delights*.'

'How do you know that?' demanded Shotbolt, but I ignored him.

The woman looked as if she was going to throw herself at me, one hand raised and the fingers bent forward like claws.

'The cleaners,' I lied. 'Are you a fan of the painter or something more?'

'None of your business, arsehole.'

Davie and I looked over our shoulders. The tall young man who had spoken was standing in the doorway, a submachine gun raised in each hand.

'Geoff,' said Gemma Bass. 'Where *have* you been?'

'I'm here now, aren't I?'

No love lost there, I thought.

'These gentlemen are leaving,' said Nigel Shotbolt. 'Now.'

I smiled at him. 'A message from the Lord of the Isles. He'll see you when he gets back what he's missing.'

The Nor-English leader and his business chief exchanged glances.

'No idea what you're talking about, Dalrymple,' he said. 'If you're really in touch with Angus, tell him we'll be here tomorrow, but then we're going home. He knows what will happen then.'

The 50,000-strong army would invade, which would provoke our leaders into using the mysterious secret weapon. Armygeddon? The Dundonians were on their way towards Edinburgh too. This was even worse than when the Council was in charge.

TWELVE

'That was fun,' said Davie, as we went downstairs. 'I could have taken him, you know.'

'Really? I'll grant you there was no sign of a weapon under La Bass's dress, but how do you know Shotbolt wasn't armed too?'

He harrumphed. Back on the street, I considered our options. Adrenaline still gripped me, so I thought about charging into Hel Hyslop's office. In all likelihood, she'd be there or at Duart's official residence. I talked myself down, which made Davie peer at me.

'You all right?'

'Thinking aloud.'

'Aye, well, I think you've done enough of that tonight. Let's get some sleep.'

'What, here?'

He grinned. 'Tempting, but I'd prefer my mother's.'

'You have a living mother?' I was amazed. Although auxiliaries under the Enlightenment were not allowed to maintain family ties, many did in secret – and those, like Davie, who didn't, made contact again after the revolution. Which he must have done. 'Why didn't you tell me?'

'She's . . . difficult. Besides, she disapproves of me.'

'Can't imagine why.' That got me an elbow in the ribs.

Davie grabbed my arm. 'Come on. The good thing is she told me never to reveal the family connection to anyone.' He stopped. 'Shit. Oh, well, that'll be your lookout. At least no one will know where we are tonight.'

A cab came down the steep street and we both raised an arm.

'Holy Corner,' Davie said to the driver.

I looked at the city as we headed southwest. The streets were in better condition than they used to be and the buildings, many of which had been left to crumble under the Council, were gradually being done up, especially those within walking distance of the centre. House prices and rents were rising due to the parliament and the financial area, and many locals had been forced to move to the outer suburbs, which were still in poor condition. Things were improving, but not fast enough for plenty of people. I wondered if that was the same across Scotland. If so, the newly reunified nation might quickly fall to pieces, especially if the Nor-English decided to take on the Scottish Defence Force. Maybe Shotbolt had a secret weapon too.

We got out at the junction where four churches were built. They'd been converted into a barracks during the Enlightenment and now were being turned into luxury flats. Davie gave the driver a big tip and winked. He looked around, then led me down Colinton Road. The street lights weren't as bright or as frequent out here, even though the area was up-and-coming. We passed a large building site on our right. It had been part of Napier University, an institution that had been used as a Council education centre and was now re-establishing itself. Davie turned right. Napier Road had been one of Edinburgh's most desirable streets, though the merchants' and bankers' houses had been turned into workers' flats in the 2010s.

Checking we were alone, Davie took out a set of keys and let us into a shared hallway, then into a flat at the back.

'She never puts the chain on,' he complained. After we were in and the door closed and secured, he turned on the hall light.

'Is it you, David?' The voice was high-pitched and croaky.

'Yes, Mrs Oliphant,' he said. 'She insists I call her that,' he whispered.

Then more lights came on and a tiny figure with dyed red hair appeared at the end of the corridor. She was holding a rolling pin.

'You didn't put the chain on,' Davie said.

'Of course I did. Have you broken it?'

Davie raised his eyes to the ceiling.

'Who's this?' the old woman demanded, slapping the wooden implement against her hand. 'It isn't the famous Quintoliam Delrumple, is it?'

I heard Davie stifle a laugh. Smiling, I advanced, my right hand extended. Not for long – she took a swing at it, missing my fingertips by millimetres.

'Pleased to meet you, Mrs Oliphant,' I mumbled.

'What?' she screeched.

I upped the volume and repeated the sentence.

'Who said that's my name?'

Davie had his hand over his eyes.

'I'm sorry,' I said.

'It was him, wasn't it? That oaf of a son of mine. Well, what are you waiting for? The whisky's on the table.'

I gave Davie the full benefit of my death stare as he walked past me.

We were handed large measures of a decent malt in chipped crystal glasses. I tried not to cut my lips but failed. At least the whisky was dark-coloured and the blood disappeared into it.

'What do you want then, David?' his mother demanded, emptying her glass.

'Em, a bed for the night?'

'I'm not having two men in the same bed,' the woman squalled.

'I'll take the sofa,' I volunteered hastily. 'Mrs . . .'

'Only my son is allowed to use my married name,' she said sharply. 'Ronnie Oliphant was taken into the Guard and wounded in the head on the border. He was never the same again. It was a mercy when the cancer took him.' She closed her eyes briefly and I saw faint evidence of tears. 'It's *Miss* Lemon to you, son.' She picked the rolling pin up again. 'And don't you dare laugh.'

It was a challenge I just managed to pass. I wondered if she was an Agatha Christie fan.

'So,' she continued, pouring herself another dramatic dram, 'what are you boys wanting to do? How about a game of poker? I've got the cards.'

'No, Mrs Oliphant,' Davie said. 'I need to use the phone. And don't worry, we've eaten. We'll get to bed as soon as we can.'

'Leave some money!' Miss Lemon called after him. 'Incredible, the cost.' She looked at me through half-closed eyes. 'Here, were you two down in Pilton earlier on? I saw there was a shootout and young David's awfie keen on them.'

I raised my shoulders. This was not a woman to be messed with. Nor was her flat. It was so tidy that the ornaments looked as if they'd been glued down and dust banned with extreme prejudice.

'Em . . . we were following a vital lead.'

'And now you've got that cow Hyslop after you, eh?'

'That's true, though we didn't fire first.'

'Hard to prove that kind of thing.'

'Tell me, Miss Lemon,' I said, taking my life in my hands. 'What did you do during the Enlightenment?'

'What do you think? I fought like everybody else.'

'You were in the City Guard?'

She squealed with laughter. 'Of course not. I couldn't be doing with all that discipline. Fascists they were at heart; you know that as well as anyone. I've read your books.'

I waited for criticism, but she obviously wasn't interested in my literary talents.

'No, I was in the fire brigade. I drove the trucks and crawled into the places the big men couldn't manage. They gave me a row of medals, but I sold them to a collector after the revolution. No time for that kind of thing.'

Davie came back.

'Right, out with it, David,' said his mother. 'What did the lassie say?'

He gave me a dejected look. 'She's been sidelined. Hyslop must have guessed she was in touch with me.'

'That wasn't what I meant,' Miss Lemon said. 'Did she say she loves you?'

I'd never seen Davie so awkward. His face was red and he struggled for words.

'Aye,' he said eventually. 'She did.'

'Then she's a romantic with cotton wool for brains. Dump her before you make an even bigger fool of yourself.'

Davie's head dropped. 'It's my life,' he muttered.

That went down like a barbed-wire sandwich. His mother stood up and moved towards the door.

'You can both spend the night in here,' Miss Lemon said. 'I cannae be bothered to clear the clothes off the spare bed.' She smiled tightly. 'You can arm-wrestle for the sofa; loser gets the armchair. The eejits in the fire service did that. I always won – by kicking them in the shins.' She departed with all the dignity a woman in fluffy pink slippers could manage – which in her case was sufficient to silence any laughter.

'Bloody hell,' I said, after the door to what I assumed was her bedroom was closed.

'Keep your voice down,' Davie hissed. 'She'll be listening at the door.'

'I need a piss.'

'Do you really want to face her again?'

I braced my bladder. I'd taken the armchair because I'd never beat Davie at arm-wrestling. I could have pulled rank, but I hadn't had one for decades.

Davie quickly fell asleep. I was haunted by the battle of West Pilton before my mind shut down.

'You awake?' came a whisper.

I hadn't been. I looked at my watch, a flash number that Sophia had given me when I got my first publisher's advance from Billy.

'It's half past four, big man.'

'Can't sleep any more. This sofa's made of a whole horse, not just its hair.'

I swallowed laughter and nearly peed myself.

'I've got to get to the bog.'

'Go ahead, she takes sleeping pills.'

I went to the freezing bathroom and pumped ship for over three minutes.

'Why doesn't she have the heating on?'

'Doesn't need it, she says. The last thirty years made her hard.'

'So why does she treat you like a schoolboy?'

'Because that's what I was the last time we spent time together. I only tracked her down a month ago. At first she didn't want to let me in – said I was part of the past she didn't want to remember. Our relationship's what you might call a work in progress. All work and no—'

'I wouldn't say that. She seems to care about you – admittedly, deep down.'

'Deeper than the *Titanic*.'

I pulled my coat around me. 'Since we're awake – thanks for that, I can't imagine what your mother would have done to me if I'd soaked her chair – we should formulate a plan of action.'

Davie switched on the small reading lamp on the sideboard. In the chill, his breath exited his nostrils like smoke from a dragon's.

'We should ask my mother,' he said. 'She's much smarter than me.'

I decided against pointing out how difficult that wasn't. 'What's her first name, by the way?'

'You don't want to know.'

'Yes, I do.'

'You really . . . oh, all right, but don't ever say it to her. It's—'

'Squeeze My?'

'Grow up. No, Clementine.'

I managed to control myself. Just. 'And Lemon's her real surname?'

'Her mother's. My grandfather ran off and is never spoken about.'

There was a silence that was ended by more sniggers. Then I got down to business.

'Right, the Nor-English. Did you believe anything they said?'

'Only the bit about the guy in the hall with the gun.'

'That – and the fact that they know Edward Sebastian. That name put the wind up Nigel Shotbolt.'

'As did your mention of the Bosch belt buckle with gorgeous Gemma.'

'True. So we don't trust them?'

'In triplicate. I'll get that tosser for holding those submachine guns on me.'

'I'm sure you will. But exactly how will you achieve that? We can hardly go storming in and arrest them. I'd rather not cause a diplomatic incident, let alone a war.'

'True enough. What do we do, then?'

'First, we question the father of the dead woman from the warehouse again. I bet we'll find a connection to Morris Gish.'

'He doesn't live in Pilton; I remember that from the file.'

'Doesn't matter. Why don't you put Eilidh on it?'

'Good idea. She's sick of filing.'

'Tell her to be careful. Morrie the Nut was connected to Sebastian. If the gang boss provided the dead woman to whoever killed her, maybe he also provided live specimens for the surgeon. Who may well be her murderer.'

'I'll get Eilidh to take a squad.'

'Making sure Hyslop doesn't notice.'

'Aye.'

'Shotbolt got nervous when I gave him my made-up message from the Lord of the Isles. Do you think the Nor-English have got the old man's wife?'

'We're not exactly drowning in other suspects.'

'No.'

'So do we tail them?'

'I doubt they'll go anywhere near where she is.' I broke off and gave that some thought. 'But they also said they'd be leaving soon. I need to talk to Lachie again. Do you think Clementine will mind?'

The door opened at speed.

'What's going on here?' demanded Miss Lemon.

'I don't feel well,' I said, putting my arms round my midriff. 'Can I call a doctor?'

She glared at me, then shrugged her bony shoulders. 'Make sure you leave money.'

I looked at Davie, trying to get across to him that he needed to detain her as long as he could. As I left the room, she started on him, complaining about his manners. Maybe I'd have time after all.

* * *

'You'll be wanting breakfast, I suppose,' Miss Lemon said, after I came back from the phone.

I was about to decline, but Davie got in first.

'Yes, Mrs Oliphant, that would be wonderful,' he said.

We were led into the kitchen.

'Bacon in the fridge, eggs in that basket, bread in the bin,' the old woman said, pointing at a large clay container with a wooden lid. 'Nothing for me, thank you.'

She sat at the small table as we prepared the meal. I nudged Davie to make him hurry.

'You're right, he eats far too much,' Miss Lemon said, mistaking my action. 'I've told him to watch his weight.'

I reduced the fried eggs to two each and the bacon to three rashers between us. There was no toaster, so I sawed at the less-than-fresh loaf with a blunt knife, ending up with two doorstoppers.

'No butter, it's far too expensive,' said Davie's mother. 'And I cannae eat margarine. Reminds me of the rubbish the Supply Directorate produced.'

We ate in silence and rapidly. As we were wiping our plates, she dropped a large bombshell.

'You know, Quintessence,' she said, 'your books leave out more than they tell. For instance, the finger you supposedly cut off with a sharper knife than mine – I never bought that line.' She fixed her gaze on me and I was aware that my lower jaw had dropped, even though there was still food in my mouth. 'See, I was at a fire in Leith – must have been in the early Twenties, after you'd been demoted from the Guard. This guy – he was a gang leader, we found out after – he was trapped by collapsed roof beams and the fire was heading towards him. We couldn't move him, there was just too much weight on his legs. "Kill me," he says. I told him I couldnae – we didn't do that kind of thing, especially not for criminals. So he told me.' She looked at me with a mixture of triumph and pity. 'He beckoned to me as the others were leaving and I put my ear close to his mouth. "That piece of shit, Quint Dalrymple – Bell 03, he used to be – he's a murderer," he says. "I saw him kill Little Walter . . . in the gardens under the castle . . . knifed him and buried him in the concrete." Then another beam fell, this time on his chest, and he was done for.' Miss Clementine Lemon looked at me, then at her son. 'I never told anyone. You know what it was like. Sometimes wee acts of rebellion were all that kept you going. Besides, Bell 03 was a hero; the city would never have beaten the drugs gangs without him. Tell you the truth, I forgot about it. Till David here mentioned that he worked with you.' She smiled hollowly. 'What do you think about that, big special investigator man?'

I was having trouble keeping my breakfast down. I felt Davie's eyes on me but couldn't look at him. No one said anything for a time, and then Miss Lemon did a strange thing.

'Don't worry, son,' she said, touching my cheek with a scaly palm. 'I'm sure the bastard deserved it. I wouldnae tell anyone after all this time.'

I had a small amount of fight left in me. 'Thanks, Clementine,' I said, getting up and moving rapidly to the front door.

We stopped fifty metres down Napier Road.

'Jesus, Quint,' Davie said, putting a heavy hand on my shoulder. I looked round at him. 'I know, I should have told you.'

'No! You called her Clementine! You're out of your mind, man.' I glared at him. 'You know what I'm talking about.'

Snow was falling, even more heavily than in previous days.

'Course I do.' He put his arm round my shoulders. 'Look, I always knew there was something off about how you lost your finger, but I was a kid when I first knew you and you were a legend. Or leg end. After that, I let it lie.' He smiled. 'You really did kill that murderous fucker?'

'Yes! But shut up about that. I spoke to Lachie. Rory and his guys are going to pick us up at the end of the street in the next few minutes.' I hurried on, thoughts flashing across my mind like shooting stars. We had to focus on the case before things got seriously out of control. Fortunately, I'd had a lot of experience of that during the Enlightenment.

A van, this one blue, pulled up not long after we reached Colinton Road and the side door slid open.

'Quint,' Rory Campbell said, from the front seat. 'Detective Leader.'

'Morning, Spartacus,' Davie said, referencing one of the actor-director's most successful roles.

'I'm Spartacus,' said Knee Bothwell, from behind the wheel, provoking laughter from the three men with us in the back, two of whom I'd seen at the base.

'Everyone got out?' I said to Rory.

'Just. Lost a lot of equipment, though.'

'Weapons?'

He shook his head. 'We took what we had. We have other stockpiles.'

'Good,' said Davie.

I disliked guns, but I could see they might be needed again before the end of the case. 'Where are we going?'

'Lachie wants to see you. All of you back there, put on balaclavas and turn them back to front. Stop the van, Andy, and join them. I'll drive.'

He was right to be secretive. If any of us were taken, we'd be broken easily by Hyslop or any of her people skilled in eliciting maximum information with maximum pain.

It must have been about twenty minutes later when we stopped. I couldn't tell if Rory had doubled back; we could have been beyond the suburbs, though not by far. The door slid open and we got out gingerly. Waiting hands led us up a short flight of steps and inside a building. A heavy door slammed and we were told to uncover our heads.

'Gentlemen,' said Lachie, standing across a tiled hall at the bottom of a curved ceremonial staircase. 'Welcome to the house with no name.'

I looked around. There were portraits of men in kilts and women in long tartan dresses.

'Late Victorian?' I asked.

Lachie nodded. 'Follow me. We're running out of time.' He looked over his shoulder. 'Andy, take your men downstairs. There's food.'

We did as were told. Lachie moved upstairs with surprising speed and opened a panelled wooden door.

'Nice,' said Davie, once we were inside.

Instead of antique sofas and armchairs, there was a collection of plastic outdoor furniture. In front of the ornate fireplace, in which a heap of logs was ablaze, stood a long table that was ten years old at the most. It was piled with papers, and as I got closer, I made out a map of the city and the surrounding area, its corners held down by wax-encrusted candlesticks. Light came from naked bulbs dangling from the ceiling.

'Not your official residence, then,' I said.

'Well spotted,' Lachie smiled beneath his extravagant moustache. 'Right, it's decision time. I've been advised that the boat carrying the Dundonians is still in Anstruther, but it can get here in a couple of hours. Rory, you'll need to stand by here and then get down to the shore as soon as we know their ETA. Let's hope you can talk some sense into them. I'll give you a note for their leader.' He thought about that. 'If they have one. Whatever – a note for all of them.'

'And in the meantime?' asked Rory.

'Let's see about that. Quint?'

I glanced at Davie. 'We've got people trying to find out if the dead woman in the warehouse had some connection to Morrie the Nut.'

Lachie gave me a quizzical look.

'The point being that she might also be a link to this Sebastian guy – the teratologist.'

'He gave me the willies,' said Lachie. 'Peered at me like a specimen to be dissected.'

I'd told him on the phone that the Nor-English also knew Sebastian. There was no telling if that was significant.

'Do you think Shotbolt would really start a war if the energy contracts aren't signed?' I said. 'Billy Geddes has been known to exaggerate.'

Lachie opened his hands. 'Who knows?'

'I think Gemma Bass wears the trousers in that trio,' Rory said.

'Not when I last saw her,' put in Davie.

I gave him the eye. 'We need surveillance on them.'

'Already arranged,' said Rory. 'My people are in a room on the other side of the street so we can see if they leave.'

'Isn't there more than one exit to Goose Pie?' I said.

'They're all covered,' he said.

'No ScotPol presence?'

He shook his head. 'They've got other things to worry about, Quint.'

'You realize they'll be tracking the boat from Anstruther.'

'Aye. And they'll be down in Newhaven.' He grinned. 'But we've already told the Dundonians to head for the marina at Silverknowes. They've got a second boat that'll act as a distraction.'

'You've got closer ties to other regions than you've let on, haven't you, Lachie?'

'Essential in this problematic democracy, wouldn't you say, Quint? The guys from Dundee are pissed off enough, but it's not us they want – it's Duart and the rich scumbags who fund his party.'

'But we don't know it was them who shot hairy Dougie,' said Davie.

Lachie smiled. 'No, but Dougie's pals think they did.'

Edinburgh's municipal leader had always been devious, but he was excelling himself.

'Is this another revolution?' I asked.

'Not exactly. There's a decent malt over there, Davie.' Lachie pointed to the far corner. 'No glasses.'

'No worries,' was the response.

Despite the hour, we all took a swig and then gathered round the map.

'Is the Lord of the Isles here?' I asked.

Lachie raised a finger and placed it on his lips vertically.

'Fair enough,' I continued. 'Lady Margaret – our only hope is that the Nor-English lead us to her. But they may leave her wherever she is and head back south. They said they'd do that if Angus doesn't sign the contracts.'

'Lady Margaret is undoubtedly a problem,' said Lachie, 'but not the most important one.'

'Really?' I said. 'What else have you got?'

'The Finns. Until recently we've had good relations with the Norwegians, the Swedes, the Danes and the north Germans.'

'Until recently?'

'Yes, Quint. They need energy. You know the Norwegians' reserves ran out two years ago. We have oil, gas and sustainable technology. We've done separate deals with each country or federation, but the Finns – sick of having to fend off murderous Russian gangs – have been pushing for a union of the countries.'

'Like the old EU?' I said. It had collapsed in 2003 after most of its members' governments fell, initially to far-right nationalists and then to organized and later disorganized crime.

Lachie nodded. 'Yes, but much more selective about who can join. The Finns have wood and mineral resources, so they think they're eligible. There are several differences, though – for a start, they want joint armed forces. It doesn't take a genius to work out that sooner rather than later someone's going to convince the rest of them to invade us and cover their energy needs for free.'

'Bloody hell,' said Davie. 'Where are our friends?'

'Good question, big man,' said Rory. 'Andrew Duart's been negotiating with various states – at least so he says – but he won't confirm which ones. And in any case, no one else in Europe has significant armies, navies or air forces.'

'And the Americans and Canadians have split themselves up into micro-states,' said Davie, who was party to that kind of information in ScotPol. 'There's no shortage of weapons, but they mainly use them against their fellow citizens.'

'There are Finns in Edinburgh now,' I said.

'I'm talking to them,' Lachie said, 'but they're stalling.'

'Do they know about the Nor-English?'

'And their army? I don't know. I wouldn't be surprised.'

'For Plato's sake,' I said, reverting to Enlightenment speak. 'Hang on, do you think the Finns might have taken Lady Margaret? Do you think they're behind BirdMammon?'

'The Luxembourg shell company?' said Rory. 'Don't be funny.'

Lachie shook his head slowly. 'It's not even mildly amusing. That must be a possibility, Quint. The Finns only arrived yesterday, but they could have had local scumbags working for them.'

'What about the tongueless man who shot Dougie?' I said. 'He's got blond hair. Maybe he's a Finn.'

'Maybe,' said Lachie.

'So we follow them too,' said Rory, anxious to please his boss. 'And monitor their communications.'

'Do you know how many people in Edinburgh speak Finnish?' Lachie asked acidly.

Given the lack of free movement during the Enlightenment, I guessed the number would be closer to one than ten.

'Plus,' Lachie went on, 'they're speaking a dialect that the woman we found working as a prostitute in the New Scotland Hotel says is incomprehensible. Any thoughts?'

'Only one,' I said. 'Do they have Bosch cults in Finland?'

No one replied. Then an unpleasant thought surfaced in my mind.

'How about this?' I said.

I spoke for long enough to persuade them. It wouldn't have been longer than a minute.

Lachie nodded.

'Let's go then,' I said to Davie.

We went.

'Are you sure about this?' Davie said, at the wheel of the ancient Land Rover that was waiting for us when we were dropped off in Morrison Street. 'It seems reckless even by your standards.'

'You're drooling at the prospect of using that machine pistol Rory gave you.'

'True. I mean, only if I have to. Which, let's face it, I probably will.'

'Uh-huh.' I watched as he turned down Lothian Road. 'Just keep it concealed when we go in. We won't have much time.'

He was smiling in anticipation. My gut was tying itself in a European death knot.

A few minutes later Davie pulled up in front of the New Scotland Hotel. It had been built at the junction with Princes Street, where the Independence used to be till it was burned down in 2020. Which made my internal organs tighten even more. The arsonist had a connection to the ENT Man. Why had that finger been left in the Lord of the Isles's bed, and by whom?

'Come on, Quint,' Davie said, waving his ScotPol ID at the taxi driver and the kilted doorman who'd come up to protest. He stormed to the reception desk.

Under a minute later we had the room numbers – four single rooms and a suite.

'Might as well go for broke,' I said, as we set off up the stairs to the second floor.

'The suite, then?'

'Aye.'

My breathing was rapid by the time we made it to the door. Fortunately, there was no sentry. I knocked on the door lightly. There was no spyhole.

'Hello?' said a female voice.

'Complimentary champagne,' I said, hoping that Finns were like most northern Europeans – very keen on booze.

There was a brief conversation that I couldn't make out. I raised two fingers at Davie and he nodded. We both knew there could be more people inside.

Then the door was opened. Davie piled through, landing a tall young woman on her backside. I stopped to help her to her feet, then pulled her forward by the arm – it wasn't the time for good manners. He kept going, into a large sitting room. Three men were sitting round a blazing fire, glasses in their hands. Davie had the machine pistol in one of his.

'What's this?' said the oldest of the three, though he was probably only in his early forties. His hair, like those of all four Finns, was blond.

'What does it look like, pal?' Davie said.

'Robbery?' said another of the men.

There was no sign of weapons, which made me suspicious. I pushed the woman towards the nearest sofa and checked the two bedrooms and their en-suite bathrooms. I even checked the walk-in cupboards. No one and nothing. I pulled all the phones I found from the wall and crushed the plugs under my heel.

There was an uneasy silence in the main room when I returned. I saw why – one of the guys was holding the side of his head, blood coursing between his fingers.

'Tried it on,' Davie muttered. 'Which one?'

I'd taken a name badge from the suit jacket that was on a chair in the larger bedroom. It had a photo on it. The older guy turned out not to be the 'Delegation Chief'. That was the bleeding one.

'Him,' I said, pointing.

Davie grabbed him, handing over the weapon. 'Cover me,' he said.

I did my best, brandishing the gun with its long silencer at the remaining Finns as Davie manhandled the chief, whose name was Aku Koskinen, to the door. Then I remembered.

'Mobile phones,' I said. 'All of them.'

The woman was sobbing now. I felt sorry for her, but at least we hadn't done her serious injury. I gathered four mobiles, then found another in a discarded jacket pocket.

'If you make a sound,' I said, looking at the red fire-alarm box, 'any kind of sound, he dies. Got it?'

They nodded avidly.

I left at speed and caught Davie up on the stairs. He took back the machine pistol and jammed the muzzle into Koskinen's side, covering it with a jacket he'd picked up in the suite.

'You really don't want to draw attention to us,' Davie said to the Finn, as we reached the ground floor.

The blond man held his head high, showing no sign of fear. That made me apprehensive. Did he have a plan?

We walked at regular pace through the reception area towards the main doors. The guy in the kilt saluted Davie and ushered us out, raising an eyebrow at the Finn's lack of coat but saying nothing.

The Land Rover was where we left it, but there was a uniformed ScotPol officer by the driver's door. That was not good, especially as he recognized Davie with a nod. We were about to find out if Hyslop had put a red star against our names.

I moved closer to Koskinen and opened the rear door. Now was his chance to call out, but he didn't take it. The officer opened Davie's door for him. We were in, seatbelts on and away in a matter of seconds.

'Whew,' I said.

'That'll get back to the queen wasp,' Davie said, driving down a back street. 'Here,' he said, handing me the weapon between the seats.

'That really isn't necessary,' said the Finn. 'I didn't resist when I could have. Why would I do so now?' His English was perfect and without an accent. 'But I'm curious. Why have you abducted me?'

I decided to be civilized. 'This isn't an abduction. Davie up front is a senior police officer.'

'And what are you?' Aku Koskinen's pale-blue eyes took me in, his gaze unwavering.

'A consultant.'

'I thought as much. You're that fellow Dalrymple.'

Davie stifled a laugh. I knew the word 'fellow' would be cast in my direction for weeks.

'I read one of your books in Swedish. Was it really like that during the dictatorship?'

We passed the Tomb Builders, a pub notorious for raucous folk music and lethal lock-ins.

'Wasn't a dictatorship, pal,' said Davie.

'He's right,' I said. 'The Council was at heart benevolent, at least after order was restored. There are citizens who would like it back.' That was true, but I would do anything I could to prevent such a development. In any case, once the genie of commercialism had been let out, people lived to shop. Unless they were from Dundee. I wondered what was going down on the shore of the Forth.

'Balaclava on,' Davie said.

'Sorry,' I said, pulling mine back to front over the Finn's face. Ten minutes later we arrived at a detached house off Newington Road. It was one of Rory's alternative bases.

And in the basement, I soon learned, was a makeshift torture chamber.

Koskinen was led down the stairs by two rebels. Lachie stood watching from the other side of the hall. Near the ceiling was a frieze depicting Scotland's celebrated authors – Scott, Burns, Douglas and so on. I was surprised it had survived the Enlightenment, which was dead set against symbols of national pride. Everything was about Edinburgh, not the country. Maybe the presence of Robert Fergusson had saved the wall painting.

'They'll put the fear of Odin up him,' Lachie said, once the door was closed.

'Did the Finns worship the Viking gods?' I asked.

'Who cares?' said the wee man, with a smile that made his moustache move oddly. 'Rory's made contact with our friends from Dundee. They're holding back for now. We've got a place near the landing site where they can eat, drink and sleep.'

'We've got decisions to make,' I said. 'Any movement by the Nor-English?'

He shook his head. 'Sitting tight.'

Davie was on the phone to Eilidh. When he'd finished, he came over. 'You were right, Quint. The dead woman, Janey Monteith, got her drugs from one of Morrie Gish's dealers.'

I thought about that. It explained how she'd ended up dead in the warehouse the scumbag owned, but not much else. Why her?

'Ah, something, or rather someone, I forgot,' said Lachie, his tone making clear he was telling what the Council used to call 'untruths'. He looked to his left, where a door had opened.

'I'm back,' said Katharine.

'Magic,' muttered Davie.

I was thinking of Sophia and how she'd already given me my head in my hands to play with.

* * *

'He isn't talking,' said one of Lachie's men. He was wearing a
leather apron on which, I was glad to see, were no spots of blood.
Yet. 'He also has no tattoos or suggestive symbols on any of his
possessions. He wants to see you, Mr Dalrymple.'

'I'm coming too,' said Davie.

I raised a hand.

'Maybe I can get him to speak,' Katharine said. 'Lachie told me
about your rather desperate plan. How do you even know the Finns
are involved with the abduction?'

She was wearing a dark tartan jacket and matching trousers, and
I had to admit she looked good. Her hair was down and the sharp
angles of her features were less pronounced. Then again, she was
still wearing heavy boots.

'Take our esteemed guest along, Quint,' said Lachie. 'Davie, you
can tell me more about what you heard from your ScotPol contact.'

There was a high-pitched scream from the basement. Katharine
was first to move towards the open door and Davie second. I let
the man in the apron sprint past me and brought up the rear.

THIRTEEN

'Is he going to be all right?' I asked.

'The maniac bit a great chunk out of the sentry's cheek,'
Katharine said, in disgust. She'd knocked Aku Koskinen out
with the butt of her pistol. He was on his right side on the floor
in the chair he'd been tied to, his mouth and lower face covered in
blood.

The wounded man had been taken upstairs by his colleague.

Davie was shaking his head. 'Maniac's not strong enough. He's
a fucking psycho. You were right though, Quint. The Finns aren't
simply traders.'

So it seemed, but I took no joy from that. Besides, a psychopath
would be unlikely to break easily.

'I don't suppose you've got a truth drug,' said Katharine.

'We did have,' I said, 'but it was destroyed. It killed the people
it was given to.'

Davie grunted. 'Would have been just the thing for this piece of shit. I suppose we'll just have to beat the hell out of him now.'

'We haven't got time,' I said. 'Katharine, do you want to try?'

Koskinen was beginning to come round. He looked up at us and laughed, a chilling sound. He was actually enjoying himself.

'Fuck you all,' he said, spraying blood from his lips. 'You might as well put my corpse in the bins.'

'That can be arranged,' Davie growled.

'Let's get the chair back up,' I said. We manhandled the piece of furniture and its cargo till all four legs and both feet were on the floor.

'I'll go and see how the guy you tried to eat is,' Davie said, making to headbutt the Finn, but stopping just before their brows met. Koskinen bellowed out laughter.

'Your turn,' I said to Katharine.

'Do you know who I am?' she asked the confined man, keeping about a metre away from him.

'Should I?' the Finn said. 'You're too old to be an escort. Those Edinburgh girls, Dalrymple. They're really something.' He leered at me.

'Because,' Katharine continued, '*I* know *you*, Aku Koskinen. You're a criminal.'

That was interesting. I listened more intently.

'You visited Stirling last July.'

The Finn's eyes narrowed. 'So? A perfect shithole of a place.' He laughed harshly. 'Women in charge, men doing the donkey work.'

'You weren't so dismissive at the time,' Katharine said, cracking the joints of her fingers. I couldn't remember her doing that before. 'In fact, you offered funding for a forestry college.'

Koskinen looked at her more closely. 'I recall. You were one of the leaders. You argued against our offer.'

'I still am one of the leaders,' she said, 'and I wasn't the only woman to take against you.'

The blond man didn't speak – it was obvious he'd lost some of his confidence.

'As we discovered after you left, all three male members of your delegation assaulted local women. Only you raped your victim, though what the others did was no better. I have a warrant for your arrest.'

'Lies!' Koskinen shouted.

'That will come out in the trial,' Katharine said dispassionately. 'The problem is, Stirling's a very law-abiding state. We only have court hearings every three months and we recently had one. Still, our one and only prison isn't too uncomfortable. Though the last prisoner – a man, of course – contracted a life-threatening condition caused by the rats that nibbled his hands, feet and face every night.'

The Finn turned to me. 'Dalrymple, you can't allow this to happen! You brought me here illegally. I demand to see Hel Hyslop. She will—' He broke off when he saw the gleaming short knife that Katharine had taken from her jacket pocket. 'Dalrymple!'

'The warrant empowers me to bypass the trial process and personally carry out the punishment deemed appropriate if getting you to Stirling is impractical.' She glanced at me. 'Which it clearly is.'

'Definitely,' I said.

'What . . . what is this punishment?' asked Koskinen, his voice almost as high as the scream he'd elicited from the sentry.

'Castration,' Katharine said. 'Hold his legs open, Quint.'

The blond man broke before I reached them.

'All right, we can do a deal, yes? What is it you want to know, Dalrymple? I'll tell you anything as long as you call off that bi— that . . . woman.'

I looked at Katharine. She nodded almost imperceptibly.

'Where's Lady Margaret Macdonald?' I said.

His head dropped till his chin was in contact with his chest.

I repeated the question. 'You were behind her kidnap, weren't you? And that of her husband?'

'Yes,' he admitted, in an almost inaudible voice. 'But I can't tell you where she is for one simple reason.' He looked up at me with damp eyes. 'I don't know.'

'Legs, Quint,' Katharine said, brandishing the knife.

'No, no, no!' squealed Koskinen. 'I'll tell you, I will.'

We waited in silence.

'Arniston House by Gorebridge,' he said, with a desperate gasp, as if he'd confirmed his own execution.

I nodded, then went up the stairs as quickly as I could.

Lachie dispatched Knee Bothwell and two squads of male and female rebels within minutes of me advising him. One of them was from that part of Midlothian and said the old Georgian house was still unoccupied, having been badly damaged in the drugs wars. Davie wanted to go, but I needed him in the city, much to his annoyance. Out in the country he'd have been able to fire his machine pistol.

Katharine appeared at the top of the stairs. There was no sign of her knife.

'Is he still in one piece?' I asked.

'For the time being.'

'That stuff about the court and summary punishment was make-believe, yeah?'

Her expression was grave. 'No, it wasn't. In Stirling we control men and their animal appetites strictly.'

I looked at Lachie. 'Have you heard that?'

He nodded. 'I'm thinking about doing it here.'

Shit. Not even the Council had castrated men who abused women. At least not to my knowledge.

Lachie, Katharine, Davie and I were sitting in the sitting room at the back of the house off Newington Road, having just finished a dinner consisting of haddock in mussel sauce and fresh vegetables. One of the rebels had trained as a cook during the Enlightenment, not that we got decent fish and veg then. There was a barrel of beer that he'd brewed too, as well as several good whiskies. The fire was keeping us warm and making us comfortable, at least physically.

'The Nor-English haven't left,' Lachie said, putting the phone down. 'I doubt they'll make a move tonight. The snow's getting even worse.'

'Where's the Lord of the Isles?' I asked.

Lachie gave me an inquisitive look. 'Why do you want to know?'

'I was wondering if confronting the Finn with him might lead to even more spilling of his intestines.'

Davie laughed, earning himself an icy glare from Katharine.

Edinburgh's leading politician gave that some thought, then shook his head. 'We can't risk Angus's security right now, Quint. I'll probably have to bring him out of hiding to do some kind of deal with the English tomorrow.'

'Aren't you under serious pressure from Andrew Duart to produce the old man?' Lachie had told me on the phone that he'd informed the presiding minister that the Lord of the Isles was safe, but unavailable.

'Why do you think I'm hiding out here rather than lounging in my official residence? Parliament's in uproar too, but the members don't know the dangers. One of the problems of democracy is that your average elected representative hasn't got anything approaching the skills to handle issues of national security, never mind the temperament.'

I considered Westminster before the last election in 2003. The House of Commons had been full of people who represented interest groups that stopped at nothing to get their way. Soon enough the people got theirs – to hell with the lot of you – but they should have been careful what they wished for. In my experience, hell had a capacity for endless deterioration. Which made me think of Hieronymus Bosch and *The Garden of Earthly Delights*.

'Something doesn't add up here,' I said. 'There are supposedly no Bosch cults in Finland. I didn't get the impression the people in the hotel were dissembling about that, and the lack of tattoos and images on and about the biter downstairs suggests that's reasonable. There are Bosch cults in Edinburgh, but they don't appear to be of any significance beyond the spiritual, despite the bad relations between them.'

'Right,' Davie said. 'Eilidh managed to talk to a colleague who's been monitoring the cults. The members aren't involved in criminal or revolutionary behaviour.'

'Except perhaps for Jack Nicol,' I said, remembering the young man who'd almost been strangled by the person impersonating the tree-fish. 'Any sign of him?'

Davie shook his head.

'I'm beginning to think he might have been in with Morrie Gish.'

Davie raised a finger. 'He wasn't on the list of dead or wounded from West Pilton.'

'Which doesn't mean he wasn't there. You didn't manage to hit everyone in the area.'

'What are you saying?' said Katharine. 'That this Nicol is involved? How?'

'I don't know, but I'd like to.'

'How can we locate him?' asked Lachie.

I looked at Davie and shrugged. 'I'll think about it.'

'What else?' said Katharine.

I was still wondering about Bosch. The Nor-English had cults but claimed they were unimportant, we had them but ditto, the Finns didn't have them. What about the Dutch? After all, the painter was from the Low Countries.

'Lachie, have you heard anything about what's going on in the Netherlands, as were?'

His moustache did its usual trick when he laughed. 'Still Dope Central as far as I know – individual cities and communities either run by drugs gangs or supplying them.'

'We don't engage in trade?' I asked.

'Not that I've heard. There's no government. They probably burn witches to keep warm.'

Katharine turned her electric eye on the small man and his smile disappeared.

'How about Luxembourg?' I persisted.

'You're thinking of the BirdMammon company?' Lachie asked. 'They don't send people outside their borders – everything's done by computer. As to whether they have Bosch cults, no idea. I do know that they get their energy from coal mines in the German statelet nearby. The Lord of the Isles mentioned that once.'

I took that in. Luxembourg was a tiny state and it didn't have energy problems. Apart from the company whose name hinted at *The Garden of Earthly Delights*, the place didn't seem worthy of further consideration. Something was still gnawing at my mind and memory, but at a level I couldn't reach.

'Remember the guy with no tongue?' I said to Davie.

He nodded. 'Dougie the Dundonian's killer. He had Bosch-related tats all over his back.'

'He did. And he was blond. Pity we haven't got a photo.'

Davie took out his mobile and fiddled. 'Here you are.'

I took the phone and went down to the basement. Aru Koskinen seemed to be asleep, his head down, but he rallied when he heard my footsteps.

'Do you know this man?' I said, thrusting the phone in front of him.

He peered and then shook his head. 'I don't – and he's not a Finn, if that's what you're getting at, Dalrymple. No Finn has suntanned skin like that, even with climate change.'

I went back to the sitting room. 'Negative, and I believe him. He pointed out how suntanned the dumb man's skin is.'

'One of the southern states of what used to be the USA?' Lachie said. 'They're hot enough and some have got their economies going again.' He shook his head in disgust. 'Using slavery. But none have sent delegations here. Trust me, I'd have heard.'

I couldn't argue with that. Then I remembered Ricky Fetlar, the security guard from Morrie the Nut's warehouse who had smashed his head to pieces in his ScotPol cell. Fetlar – it was an island in Shetland. And there was oil and gas exploration in that independent state . . . A high-intensity light came on in my head.

'South Africa,' I said, raising the forefinger on my left hand.

Katharine looked at me quizzically. 'What about it?'

'Lachie, is there a South African delegation in town?'

'No,' he replied, 'but there was. They left last week. Signed a big deal for oil and gas supplies – they've been building huge tankers to transport them both.'

'What do you know about the country?' I asked, adrenaline coursing through me.

'They keep their politics to themselves, but I could see what they are,' said Lachie. He paused infuriatingly.

'And what are they?' I said, struggling to control the volume of my voice.

'Fascists and racists,' he said, as if the words had been dipped in dung. 'One of them got drunk one night – he was blond, now I come to think of it. The Boers – remember them from history lessons? – took control five or so years back. They haven't reimposed apartheid, though – they've gone right back to slaves in chains. They've sunk new gold and diamond mines and found tons of the stuff. That's how they can afford our oil and gas and the ships.'

Several thoughts shot across the firmament of my mind.

The first: 'If they've enslaved the blacks and other coloured people, they must have a lot of weapons.'

Lachie nodded. 'And a large standing army. They make so many arms that they export them to any state that can pay.'

The second: 'The Nor-English could have got arms from the South Africans.'

He shrugged.

The third: 'Boers speak a version of Dutch. They're likely to be interested in Dutch culture and art.'

'Bosch,' said Katharine.

The fourth: 'They're using the Nor-English as a surrogate invasion force.'

No one commented, but I could see they saw the sense in what I'd said.

Then I had a fifth thought: 'The Scottish Defence Force's secret weapon. Where did it come from?'

Lachie MacFarlane suddenly looked like the child he wasn't.

'The South Africans,' I surmised. 'Pressing that red button will result in precisely nothing.'

There was a long silence.

'Where does all this leave us, Quint?' asked Davie.

'We have to find Lady Margaret,' I said. 'Then her husband can refuse to sign the shares over to BirdMammon. I'm willing to bet all my blues and rock albums that the South Africans own the company. Why fight, even with a surrogate army, if you don't have to? I'm sure they'd rather have a compliant but organized Scottish state as their vassal than a rag-tag coalition of regions led by Nigel Shotbolt.'

The landline phone rang. Lachie spoke the prearranged words and then listened. After he cut the connection, he said, 'The Finn downstairs has got bigger balls than we thought.'

'Not for long,' hissed Katharine.

'That was Bothwell. Arniston House is empty. They're not sure when they'll get back. The snow's drifting out there.'

'Let's give the blond arsehole the eighth degree,' said Davie. 'Come on, Katharine.'

She gave me a questioning look.

'Please yourselves,' I said. 'I don't think he'll say anything more. Even if he does, how can we trust him?'

Lachie nodded. 'And I'm running out of personnel.' He looked at the others. 'I know the situation's critical, but I don't want the Finn damaged irreparably. If we survive this, we'll need to negotiate with the northern European states. Chopping one of their representative's balls off isn't in any protocol I know.'

We watched Katharine and Davie head off without much of a spring in their step.

'So,' Lachie said, 'you think the South Africans are behind all this? You might be right, but what can we do about that? It doesn't help us find Lady Margaret.'

I nodded, thinking back to Aku Koskinen's behaviour after he'd

bitten a hole in the sentry's cheek. When he came round, he was
still channelling the Mr Hyde side of his being. What was it he had
said? Something that wasn't as well expressed as his English usually
was. I tried to remember.

'What about you?' I said to the small man. 'You can't stay hidden
for long. Edinburgh needs to see its leader. Andrew Duart will
already be gathering your enemies to find a replacement.'

'True. My people are holding out, but I don't know how much
longer they'll be able to. It doesn't help that Rory's down with the
Dundonians.'

'Why don't you bring him back?'

'And let loose those bloodthirsty brutes?'

I smiled. 'Use them. You could put them on to Duart or have
them barricade parliament.'

He thought about that. 'At this rate Scotland's going to fall apart
again. We're all going to end up in the dustbin of history.'

And there it was. Dustbin. Bins. That was what Koskinen had
said: 'You might as well put my corpse in the bins.' It was hardly
something a well-educated foreign speaker of English would say
– he wouldn't have used the plural 'bins'.

Heart pounding, I went to the table and ran my gaze over the
map of the city's environs.

'What is it?' asked Lachie, getting up on a chair.

I laughed. 'The bastard. He told me straight out and I didn't spot
it.' I pointed at a location to the west of the city. 'The House of the
Binns.'

Lachie peered at me. 'Bit far-fetched, isn't it? And why would
he tell you?'

'Only one way to find out.'

'What about the snow?'

'We're Scottish,' I said over my shoulder as I strode to the door.
'Snow's our natural habitat.'

The bravado of the words echoed in my head as I went down to
the basement. Was I about to make an even bigger fool of myself
than the Finn already had?

The only available vehicle was a decrepit Land Rover from the
earliest days of the City Guard. Davie groaned when he saw it, and
not just because it was already covered in a layer of the white stuff.

'I thought these had all been scrapped,' he said, opening the rear door and pushing in Aku Koskinen. He was shivering despite the coat we'd found him, handcuffs on his wrists. Maybe he was in shock. Katharine had her knife a few centimetres from his groin when I arrived and Davie had his neck in an armlock.

'Guess where we're going,' I said to the Finn.

'Fuck you, Dalrymple,' he gasped.

I was aware we were potentially on a wild ptarmigan chase and wanted to see his reaction. Miraculously, after Davie had managed to fire up the engine, when I hit the switch the internal light came on.

'The House of the Binns,' I said.

There were no signs of either surprise or gloating. Maybe he wanted us to go there, which made me immediately apprehensive. Perhaps there was a gang of heavily armed headbangers waiting. Too bad – we needed to find Margaret Macdonald and this was the only lead we had.

Davie decided against using the recently reopened bypass to the south of the city. It was always jammed by crashed vehicles in these conditions because drivers didn't reduce their speed. Then again, Davie's own velocity was making the Land Rover fishtail round corners. In five minutes he'd struck glancing blows on three parked cars and shoved one slow driver to the side.

'It would be good to get there in one piece,' Katharine said mildly.

'Prefer to walk?' was the response.

We went along Princes Street because it was always the first road to be cleared. At this time of night and in this weather, there were few people around – only the occasional staggering drunk, one of whom was being helped by a uniformed ScotPol officer. No one wanted frozen corpses to be found by visitors to the city. Shandwick Place had been gritted as it was the route for tourist buses to get to the airport – not that flights would be taking off tonight. Corstorphine Road was a test for the Land Rover's worn tyres, but we made it. As we passed the turn to Matthew Barker's house, I thought about the Lord of the Isles's friend. Was he still in a ScotPol cell, body and mind in pieces?

'What do you think?' Davie said, straining forward to see through the snowstorm. 'The fast road to Glasgow?'

'It's the best option,' I replied. 'At least it's wide, though you'll no doubt have to weave better than a . . .' My brain declined to complete the metaphor.

'Weaver?' suggested Davie, accelerating past a snowplough, which gave us the benefit of its klaxon.

'The smart thing would have been to stay behind that,' the Finn observed.

I looked over my shoulder. 'The smart thing would have been to keep quiet about the House of Binns, Aku. Why did you drop the hint? Is there an execution squad waiting for us?'

He lowered his head.

'It's obviously a trap, Quint,' said Katharine. 'But those can sometimes be sprung without too much cost.'

'I'm all ears,' I said, leaning closer.

'Me too,' said Davie, swerving past a minivan that had stopped in the central lane. People were waving from the windows.

Katharine sniffed. 'No, you're not, big man. You're all arse.'

So much for the three musketeers, I thought, though her idea was interesting. Shame we only had two knives, three pistols and a machine pistol between us. Davie argued, but I allocated the latter to her.

Somehow we made it to the exit that would lead to the Binns. Not much further on, two cars had collided. Davie slid open his window, ordered the passengers out and then bulldozed his way through.

'Those people will freeze,' said Katharine.

'They can get back in now,' said Davie. 'Don't worry, if this works out the way I'm hoping, there'll be plenty more cars coming down here. They'll get help.'

'You think so?' said the Finn, with a manic cackle.

I looked at Davie and he kept his mouth shut.

'How much further?' Katharine asked, racking the slide on the machine pistol and applying the safety.

'About a mile,' said Davie. 'But the estate's big. I'll tell you when to bail out.'

'Do you think there'll be a gate?' I said. 'With guards?'

'Who knows?' he replied. 'But this heap is in better condition than I thought. It'll get us through.'

Visibility couldn't have been much more than five metres. Davie had the headlights dipped, which reduced the chances of us being spotted. I hoped.

'Oh, shit,' I said, wiping the windshield with my sleeve. 'Gate. Guards.'

'Oh, goodie,' said Davie, with a worrying grin. He increased speed. 'Hold on!'

Katharine grabbed my thigh, which hurt. I managed not to squeal – until the front of the Land Rover hit the single-barred gate and crashed through. There was a burst of automatic fire and the rear window cracked all over and then fell in. The Finn gave a series of high-pitched laughs. We drove on.

I eventually made out a faint blur of lights. 'That must be the house.'

Davie hit the brakes and we slithered to a halt. 'Good hunting, Mrs,' he said, as Katharine got out. She slipped away into the snow-filled dark. 'Maybe we should all do that, Quint,' he said. 'We can put a sock in the cheek-biter's mouth.'

I considered that. 'No, what we can do is use the Finn as a bargaining chip. Keep your pistol jammed in his side.'

'*Mon plaisir*,' Davie said in his atrocious accent, driving on.

The lights got brighter and other vehicles became visible: all were under snow, but I could make out a pair of vans, a four-by-four, and a tractor with a snowplough fitted to its front. That explained why the last section of the road hadn't caused Davie too many problems.

'This'll do,' I said.

We stopped about fifty metres from the house. I'd been once before, towards the end of the drugs wars. A gang of recalcitrant madmen had holed up in the house, which had been in the Dalyell family for centuries. The old four-storey building had been badly damaged, but from what I could see it was in good order now.

Davie and I got out and looked around. There was no one in the vicinity, though the gatekeepers had surely raised the alarm.

'You know what?' I said. 'We *should* gag the Finn.'

'I'm not using my socks,' Davie said. 'Fortunately, I have a handkerchief. Used, but that's too bad.' He went to the rear door, opened it and hauled the prisoner out, jamming the handkerchief into his mouth before he could make a sound. Koskinen rolled his eyes but came along without resisting, the muzzle of Davie's pistol in his side.

There were at least ten external lights on the front of the house, two of them on each side of the main door. The Scottish baronial towers and battlements gave the place an appropriately Gothic atmosphere. I had a flash of Poe's House of Usher before it slid into the tarn. Was there a Roderick inside? Was there a Madeline? I'd settle for a Margaret.

The thick double doors were pitted by bullet holes rather than studded with iron nail heads. Very encouraging. There was no sign of Katharine or anybody else, though the snow was coming down like a curtain. I turned the circular handle and the lock disengaged.

'They're waiting for us,' I hissed to Davie.

'Bring them on,' he said.

I pushed the heavy door open and went slowly into a wide hall from which the flooring had been removed. We walked on frozen earth. It was a disquieting effect – the outside of the house in good condition and the inside more like Poe's creation. There was also a strange smell about the place.

'Someone's not been using the bins,' Davie said, holding Koskinen tightly to his left side.

I swallowed a laugh. 'Do you think that staircase is safe?'

The structure was missing numerous boards, the wall alongside it dotted with the remains of plaster that looked as if it had contracted leprosy.

Davie glanced around. 'Let's stick to this floor.'

'Yes, you should,' said a thin, piping voice from a door that had just opened to our right.

'Indeed you should,' said another voice, deeper than the first but oddly similar in tone – which was a mixture of satisfaction and something less easily definable. The hairs on the back of my neck rose.

Aku Koskinen started to make a keening noise through the handkerchief and Davie jabbed the pistol into his side.

'Don't hurt the Finn,' said the first voice.

'No, don't hurt him,' said the second. 'He's ours.'

The accent of both voices was hard to pin down, but it definitely meant something to me. Once again, my memory let me down.

'Come in,' said the first voice.'

'You're quite safe,' said the second.

I exchanged glances with Davie. 'Is Lady Margaret Macdonald here?' I asked. 'We're not going anywhere until we know.'

'Of course.' The second voice dissolved into laughter that wasn't exactly hysterical but was disturbing enough. 'Come in. She's waiting for you.'

I saw no armed men in the brightly lit hall, though that didn't mean they weren't waiting for us in the room.

'Let's do it, Quint,' said Davie. He pulled Koskinen forward.

'Yes, do it!' said the two voices, like children about to get a treat. 'Do it, quickly!'

I lagged behind for some moments, wondering if we were about to make a terminal mistake. But I was also afflicted by the investigator's curse: curiosity. Who were the owners of those eerie voices? They had kept themselves out of sight. There was only one way to find out. I moved forward.

Davie went through the door, pushing the Finn ahead of him so that there was room for them to get through. 'Whoa,' he said breathlessly. 'Quint, get in here.'

At least he wasn't warning me off. I walked on and crossed what turned out to be the threshold to a world of wonder. The first thing I saw was a large reproduction of Hieronymus Bosch's *The Garden of Earthly Delights*. The second made me stop in mid-stride, then almost collapse.

'Hello, Quintilian Dalrymple,' said the voices in unison.

I stood open-mouthed at the sight before me, after managing to regain my balance. Standing on the faded Persian carpet was a woman. Two women. A woman with two heads. She . . . they had black trousers on their two legs and a pink blouse over a single upper abdomen that was wider than usual. I managed to raise my lower jaw.

'Hello,' I said, my voice little more than a croak.

'I'm Amber,' said the head on the left.

'And I'm Penny,' said the head on the right. 'Penelope really, but I don't like that.' There was suddenly an edge to the higher of the voices.

'You're Davie, aren't you?' said Amber, looking at the big man, who had lowered his weapon. 'You can take whatever that is out of Aku's mouth. He's no danger to you now.'

Koskinen went to the conjoined twins and dropped to one knee. 'I brought him to you, mistresses. Are you happy?'

He was struck in the chest by the left of the two feet and let out a squeal.

'Brace up, man,' said Penny. 'Go and sit in the corner.' She pointed with the arm on her side.

He did as he was told. It was then that I saw the figure in an armchair, ropes around her chest and legs, with her mouth taped. I recognized Lady Margaret from her short, pure-white hair. Her skirt was the tartan that her husband wore.

I saw that the door had closed behind us.

'Don't worry, Quint,' said Amber. 'Come and sit down. We want to get to know you.'

They both smiled and I took in their faces, which were well formed and attractive, as well as very similar. Both were wearing makeup, Amber's laid on thick and Penny's much more minimal. The hair on both heads was black. Amber's was in a short bob, while her sister's was in long plaits. I began to grasp that they were quite different personalities. But who were they?

'What's your surname?' I said, sitting on their right on a large sofa.

'He's curious,' said Penny. 'Shall we scratch his itch, dear?'

Amber looked past her sister and gave me a broad smile. Her head was more angled outwards. 'We agreed we would.'

Evidence of a plan.

Davie went to the door and turned the handle. 'Locked,' he said, raising his pistol. 'Want me to break it down, Quint?'

'No, no,' said the twins, in harmony. 'We're all friends here.'

'Uh-huh,' said Davie. He stood near the door so he'd be concealed when it opened.

'Pringle,' said Penny, whose voice was the higher. 'That's our name. Penny Pringle, that's me.'

'Amber Pringle, at your service,' said the other twin, again leaning forward and smiling.

'At our service?' I said. 'In what way?'

They looked at each other, suddenly serious.

'You really don't know why you're here, Quintilian Dalrymple?' Penny said. Her tone was formal now, like that of a prosecutor. 'You really don't know?'

'We gave you so many clues,' said Amber.

I tried to ignore my somersaulting stomach. 'The finger,' I said.

'Of course!' they said together, enthusiastic again.

'That made you think; admit it,' said Amber.

'It certainly did. Why on earth was it in the drawer under the Macdonalds' bed?'

The twins looked at each other again.

'To make you realize that your actions have consequences,' said Penny, her head held high.

That wasn't encouraging, but curiosity was still my master.

'Which actions?' I asked.

'Can *I* tell him?' asked Amber.

Penny gave her a sharp look. 'No, that's my job.' She turned her almost black eyes on me. 'We hereby charge you with the murder of our father.'

Bile immediately filled my mouth. The witness to the death must have talked. The Ear, Nose and Throat Man had been such a psychotic slaughterman that it never occurred to me that he might have had children. Given the number of women he and his fellow gang members raped, I saw now that there were bound to be offspring. But these poor souls? A wave of sorrow crashed over me and I almost moved to embrace them. Then I saw the look on Penny's face.

'Quintilian Eric Dalrymple, we hereby sentence you to death by hundreds of cuts.'

The door banged open and several burly men rushed in, one of them laying Davie out with a single blow as soon as he showed himself. I stood up, but stayed where I was when a machine pistol was pointed at my chest.

'And here's your executioner,' said Amber, with a chilling laugh.

A tall man with short hair walked in. He was carrying a wide black leather bag. I didn't need an introduction. This was Mr Edward Sebastian, the surgeon who called himself the teratologist, and I was clearly the monster in his view.

'We're dicephalic parapagus,' said Penny conversationally.

I was watching the surgeon. He pulled on latex gloves and started laying stainless-steel operating instruments out on a rubber mat he'd put on the slate table in front of the sofa. My mouth went drier than a vermouth-free martini.

'Yes,' said Amber. They got up and walked without awkwardness towards the log fire. 'We're fused at the abdomen and pelvis. We have one liver, three kidneys, one bladder and two breasts. Each of us has our own heart, stomach, spine, lungs and spinal cord. We're twenty-eight.' The last sentence was spoken with pride.

I studied them. They were shorter than usual, probably around five feet, but otherwise were startlingly average in appearance – excepting the two heads, which were both angled slightly outwards, Amber's further.

'Bosch,' I said, pointing at the reproduction of *The Garden of Earthly Delights*. 'What's the interest?'

They laughed, the contrasting tones discomfiting. Penny gave me a mordant smile.

'You know perfectly well, Quintilian.'

'Are there conjoined twins in the triptych?' I didn't recall such figures, though there was no shortage of grotesques in Hell; there were also naked people standing close to each other in the central panel who could have been linked physically.

'If you want there to be,' said Amber.

Penny gave me a lubricious look that made my cheeks burn. 'Well, do you?' she asked. 'Want us to be there? Or here?'

I closed my legs as the teratologist picked up a saw-edged blade that glinted in the firelight.

'We had a third arm,' said Amber. 'But Edward got rid of it for us.'

I decided to play hardball, maybe for the last time.

'Put it in the bin, did he?'

There was more jarring laughter.

'Honestly, Quintilian,' said Penny. 'You were so slow.'

'How do you think I could have worked out that Lady Margaret was in this house, let alone you?'

The twins shrugged, a disconcerting movement.

'Not our problem,' said Amber. 'Admit it. Since you found the finger, you've been quivering with fear.'

I snorted. 'In your double dreams. I killed your father. Do you think a finger, even a right forefinger like the one I lost, would bother me?'

'Yes,' they replied, Amber loudly and Penny considerably less so.

'How do you know the ENT Man was your father?'

'Guess,' said Penny. 'Though that doesn't seem to be your strong point.'

Finally, I identified their accent. I hadn't heard a similar one since the Truth and Reconciliation Hearing – the dignified old black South African judge.

'How about this?' I said. 'Your mother – poor woman – was one of the Howlin' Wolf gang's sex slaves. When she found she was pregnant, she managed to escape; I can't imagine how. I'd hazard she was injured. And, even more amazingly, she managed to find somewhere safe to give birth – somewhere with a functioning hospital. I imagine your birth wasn't straightforward.'

'Portsmouth,' said Amber. 'Sailors defended the city centre from the criminal gangs, at least until we were healthy enough to travel.'

'Then your mother took you on a ship to South Africa.' That was pure conjecture. I didn't know whether ships had been sailing anywhere in 2010, let alone to the southern hemisphere.

'Wrong,' said Penny. 'You were right about Mother. She succumbed to her wounds and loss of blood three hours after we were born. She'd stolen some gold from Father's gang and arranged for a young woman to accompany us to Cape Town. It was as far away from Edinburgh as she could afford. Diane stayed with us till we were nineteen. She was killed during the civil war.' She sobbed once. 'Such a kind woman. She wouldn't have liked the new regime, though. The poor cow was sorry for the blacks.'

I looked up at the teratologist. He had pulled on green scrubs and tied an incongruous scarf decorated with vibrant colours over his head. He eyed me like a lizard about to consume a fly. I had no interest in being a fly; I wanted to be a male Scheherazade – the longer I talked, the longer I would stay in one piece. But I had little expectation of lasting one night, never mind a thousand and one.

Where was Katharine? Would Davie ever come round? I was on my own and, for once, I wasn't enjoying that in the least.

FOURTEEN

'You know who he is, don't you?' I said, pointing at the surgeon. 'Of course,' said Amber. 'Mr Sebastian's been our consultant for ten years.'

'Nine and a half,' said Penny, with a frown.

Amber gave her a cool look. 'He removed our third arm when

we were eighteen. And don't say nineteen, dearest. I remember the year clearly.'

I picked up animosity between the sisters, which could be useful. 'You know what he calls himself?'

The surgeon's eyes locked on mine.

I kept going. What did I have to lose? 'The teratologist.' I spoke the word in a doom-laden voice.

Both twins looked at me, their eyebrows rising.

'What is that?' said Amber. 'I don't know what it means.'

'I do.' Penny turned away from her twin.

I went for broke. 'A monster specialist – that's what he is.'

'What?' shrieked Amber.

'That is incorrect, miss,' said Sebastian. 'Teratologists are experts in physical abnormalities.'

'And "teras" means monster in Greek,' I added. I didn't say that it also meant marvel – that might come in handy later.

Amber stared at the surgeon, eyes bulging. 'You think we're monsters?'

'Of course not,' said Sebastian dismissively. 'Have I ever done anything to harm you?'

Amber's cheeks were red. 'You want to separate us.'

'Stop it, darling,' said Penny firmly. 'Can't you see that Dalrymple's trying to rile us?'

And succeeding, I thought – at least fifty per cent.

'That must be a dangerous procedure,' I said.

Penny kept her eyes off me. 'It is. That's why we haven't agreed to it.'

'And we like being together,' said Amber.

The surgeon was now holding a scalpel in his right hand. 'Shall we get started?'

'Hold on,' I said, masking my terror. Flattery was one of my few remaining weapons. 'You ladies must be powerful to be here in Scotland. Do you let him order you about?'

'Of course not,' snapped Penny. 'For your information, we're the republic's principal trade advisors. Mr Sebastian is our personal consultant.' She smiled thinly. 'And deliverer of pain. I know exactly what you're doing, Quintilian. It amuses me to toy with you.'

'Me too,' said Amber. 'Toy with you.' Her head was twitching;

she resented not being the dominant twin. 'We want Scotland's energy and we aren't going to pay a rand for it.'

'Dearest,' said Penny. 'Be careful.'

'You've financed and armed the Nor-English to squeeze our government's balls.' I chose my words carefully because I wanted to see how worldly they were.

Amber laughed, while Penny raised her eyes to the ornate ceiling. I noticed that it was dotted with bullet holes, presumably dating from the drugs wars.

'You've got someone working for you in Nor-England, haven't you? Someone who's in Edinburgh right now. Someone with an interest in Hieronymus Bosch.' I paused for effect. 'Gemma Bass.'

Penny turned to her sister and they started to clap hands. They'd clearly worked at it, but the movement was disconcerting. It looked as if they each controlled their own side of the shared torso.

'Maybe you're not as foolish as we thought,' said Penny.

'And your country is behind BirdMammon in Luxembourg, yes?' They nodded, Amber more energetically.

'This is rather entertaining,' Penny said. 'Go on.'

'There are Bosch cults in South Africa, but you aren't members.' Amber looked at her sister, clearly hesitant.

'No, we aren't,' said Penny. 'They . . . they don't want us.'

'I'm sorry,' I said, with genuine sincerity.

'We don't care,' said Amber. 'Besides, they need us to advise on their deals. We're mathematical geniuses.' She frowned. 'But they won't let us meet anyone from the other delegations.'

I saw how Sebastian was looking at her, wondering if he wanted to separate them so that Penny would be without her naive sister. If Amber's head was removed, would Penny survive without her twin? I resolved that, if I could save myself, I would save them from the teratologist too. He was the real monster in the room.

'How did you find out that I killed your father?'

Penny gave Amber a warning look. 'We read your novel, Quintilian,' she said. '*The Body Politic*. Good title, but full of lies and evasions. The man who saw you kill our father made it known that he would share important information with people able to pay for it. We heard about that and extended feelers. You cut the Ear, Nose and Throat Man out of your novel and we're going to cut pieces out of you.'

My heart missed several beats. 'Have you any idea what your father was like?'

'Oh, yes,' said Amber mildly. 'A rapist and killer – the worst kind of man.'

I had few cards left. 'Whose genes made you what you are.'

'That is of no significance,' said Penny. 'Our mother left letters telling us exactly what he was. But he was still our father. In the new South Africa, family is of the utmost importance, no matter what individual members do.'

I remembered the short-lived governments after apartheid. Nelson Mandela had been a hero across the world – until he and most other heads of state were overthrown.

'Cut him, Mr Sebastian,' ordered Penny. 'How about his digits to start with?'

I almost lost control of my bladder. The teratologist put down the scalpel and picked up a pair of vicious-looking shears.

Then the room metamorphosed into an abattoir.

First there was the crack of breaking glass. Through a small parting in the velvet curtains the muzzle of a machine pistol appeared. There was a burst of fire that put down the men who'd dealt with Davie. One of them was only wounded and reached for his pistol. Davie suddenly came alive and grabbed the man's arm. It snapped loudly and the gorilla started screaming. Meanwhile, Sebastian had dropped the shears and picked up a narrow probe. He pulled me to my feet and used my body as a shield. The point of the probe was close to my right eye.

'Drop it!' Davie yelled, aiming the pistol at us. 'You've got five seconds.'

'Drop that pistol,' said the teratologist. 'You'd never allow me to blind your hero.'

I wondered where he'd got that idea. It was the kind of thing Hel Hyslop would say in a mocking tone. I opened my eyes wide in Davie's direction. To my surprise, he took the hint and lowered the pistol.

'You behind the curtains!' Sebastian said, jerking me round. 'Come out now or Dalrymple loses an eye!'

Katharine was on the spot, but I could help her. I jerked my head away from the probe.

A single shot rang out. The teratologist dragged me backwards, then his arm slipped away and he crashed on to the table with his instruments. He wouldn't be needing them any more. Katharine had blown his left eye out.

The twins stood stock still as Davie and Katharine approached. Amber's mouth was open, but Penny was in control of herself. She took in the weapons pointed at her and her sister, then let fall the scalpel she must have picked up when I was being held by Sebastian.

'You're wasting your time, whoever you are,' Penny said. 'The house is full of armed men.' She raised a finger. 'Katharine. You're Katharine Kirkwood.'

'How do you know that?' Katharine shook snow from the hood of her coat.

'We heard you'd been in Edinburgh,' said Amber, turning her head away from the dead surgeon.

'You seem to know a lot,' said Katharine. 'Who have you bribed?'

'Who haven't we?' said Penny, with a caustic smile.

'There isn't time for this,' said Davie, collecting weapons from the blood-drenched men on the floor. He cut Margaret Macdonald's bonds and helped her to her feet. She looked bemused.

'Come with me.' He led her to the curtains.

'You too,' I said to the twins. 'Take those blankets from the sofa.'

I wrapped one around them. I threw another to Davie and he put it over Lady Margaret's shoulders.

'We don't want to,' said Amber, biting her lip.

Penny took a step forward. 'Don't worry, dear. They won't hurt us.'

'We won't,' I confirmed.

There was hammering on the door, which Davie had locked when he got up.

'Take them, Quint,' he said. 'I'll hold them back. Give me that machine pistol, Katharine.'

'Still no manners,' she said, handing over the weapon and taking a pistol from him. 'Thank you.'

'What about Aku?' Amber asked.

'He's made his choice,' I said, disinclined to aid the Finn, who was cowering in a corner.

Katharine led us out, after opening a high French window. 'Run to the first four-by-four. I've demobilized all the others.'

I helped Margaret Macdonald, who seemed only partly conscious.

The twins were able to take rapid steps in the fresh snow that had fallen since we arrived. Heavy flurries filled the air. There were only about thirty metres to go. Several bursts of fire came from the room we'd left. Davie appeared, pounding through the snow, then almost going his length as he took evasive action. On his knees he emptied the machine pistol's magazine at the window and came weaving towards us as shots were fired at him.

Katharine got the engine started. I went in the back door after the twins and Lady Margaret. There was just enough room. As soon as Davie got in the front, she reversed the four-by-four away at speed and then carried out an impressive turn on the move. Before I could compliment her, she put her foot on the brake.

'Out you go, big man,' she said. 'I turned the engine over. The key's in the ignition. I take it you can drive a tractor.'

Davie grinned. 'I take it you can follow without crashing into me.' He disappeared into the snow.

Amber laughed, her expression ardent in the dashboard light, while Penny had her eyes closed. A childlike adventuress and a cold thinker – how did they share the same body? Then again, they were supposedly both advanced mathematicians.

A few seconds later the lights of the tractor came on and it moved forward, the snowplough coming down. Katharine went after it, again demonstrating more skill than I remembered.

'Have you been doing a lot of driving recently?'

'We don't have many vehicles. We use most of them to take supplies to the remote parts of our territory. I do a lot of that.'

'I thought you were a leading light.'

She snorted contemptuously. 'Everyone mucks in, Quint. We don't have ranks or classes.'

'How peculiar,' said Penny.

Katharine looked in the mirror but didn't comment.

I watched as the tractor moved to the side of the road. I wondered what Davie was doing and then saw what remained of the gate and sentry-post disappear into the snow-covered bushes alongside the road.

'That should be it,' said Katharine. 'Coast clear.'

'Where are we going?' asked Amber.

Katharine glanced at me. 'Coast as in . . .'

I got her drift. We were heading for where the Dundonians had been put up by Rory. What kind of welcome would they give the twins sitting next to me?

We were lucky with the roads. There was enough snow to be a problem, not least with the windscreen wipers, but not too much to stop Davie's plough. Margaret Macdonald had fallen asleep – I wondered what the late Edward Sebastian had been drugging her with. We made it to the outskirts of Edinburgh, where there was very little traffic, so not many people saw the incongruous tractor as it headed to Cramond and the Georgian house in a secluded estate where Rory and his crewmates were ensconced. Thankfully, there was no ScotPol presence.

'What is this place?' Amber asked.

'Don't worry,' I said, 'it's safe.'

'That wasn't what I asked.'

Penny looked at her. 'Are you all right, dear?'

'No, I'm not. We've been in a gunfight, kidnapped and now have no idea where we are. Hasn't the seriousness of our situation struck you?'

'Well, no, not really.'

'This isn't one of your stupid excursions! We're not going to see the Eiffel Tower!'

'That was nice,' said Penny. 'Such a shame the top had been blown off.'

'Come on,' said Davie, opening the door. 'Inside, all of you.' He extended a hand to Penny, but she ignored it and the twins manoeuvred past him. Amber smiled tentatively, but Davie's expression was neutral. I woke Lady Margaret up gently and helped her out.

Inside, Rory was waiting. For some reason he was wearing a kilt. I'd never seen him in one. Edinburgh people generally didn't, preferring tartan trews for formal wear. He was the perfect host, bowing to the Lady of the Isles and then the twins, showing no surprise. He hadn't been advised that Amber and Penny were on the way, let alone Lady Margaret, as communication had been hampered by the weather.

There was a lot of noise from the rear of the house; men were shouting and laughing, clearly lubricated by alcohol. Amber looked interested, but Penny was disdainful.

'What's going on?' she demanded. 'Is there a riot?'

'Please follow me,' Rory said, going to a door at the back of the black-and-white-tiled hall. He led us into a small and snug sitting room with Scottish landscape paintings on the walls – made a change from Hieronymus. 'Would you like something to drink? To eat?' he asked.

Davie had stayed in the hall so there wasn't an instantaneous positive response. Amber looked keen but Penny was continuing her impersonation of Queen Victoria on a day when John Brown had called in sick. Margaret Macdonald settled in the armchair I'd led her to, pulled the blanket around her and dropped off.

I took Katharine into a corner.

'Can you stay with them?'

She gave me a dubious look.

'I'll keep you advised of what's going on. Please. I don't want the Dundonians to see them.'

'They learn manners in Dundee, you know, Quint.' Then she nodded. 'All right. I almost froze out at the big house. It'll be good to warm up in front of that fire.'

'Thanks.' I moved closer. 'And thanks for your intervention at the Binns.'

'Couldn't have you wearing an eye-patch,' she said, with an unusually sweet smile. 'You'd look so dashing.'

'Ha. You'll pick their brains? Amber gives more away than her sister.'

'Penny is a strong woman, I admire that. But, yes, I'll try to bring them out of themselves. If that's an acceptable way of putting it.' She squeezed my arm and went over to the twins.

I angled my head at Rory and he left the women with a cheery smile. Back in the hall, he stared at me.

'What the hell, Quint? Who are they? She? I don't know what.'

I explained. He tried to take the story in, but it was clearly a struggle.

'I need to talk to Lachie.' He smacked me on the arm. 'Well done, Quint. You've gone a long way to clearing up this mess.'

I wasn't so sure. The Nor-English and their army were still a major problem, as was the current government. We would be in danger if Duart and Hyslop found out where we or Lachie and Angus Macdonald were. Though we did have the crazy gang from Dundee on our side.

'Any news from Knee?' I asked.

'Not since the last time I was in touch with Lachie. The snow's even worse to the south.'

'Pity they didn't find a snowplough like we did.'

He beckoned to two armed men. They took up position outside the sitting-room door.

'Come on, Quint.' He went to another door and unlocked it. He turned the key on the other side when we were both in what had been a library – all the books formerly on the shelves would have been burned for heat during the drugs wars. 'There's a phone here. The line was terrible when I spoke to Lachie earlier. Let's hope the snow hasn't cut it.' He dialled the number and waited.

'Why are you wearing the kilt?' I asked.

'The crew from Dundee brought it. And insisted I put it on in front of them.' He shook his head. 'They pulled my shorts off too.'

'Good to know.'

He raised a hand and then spoke a jumble of letters and numbers. He was in the fortunate position of having an actor's memory. I had difficulty remembering more than four numbers in a row. Eventually, he started talking comprehensibly, telling Lachie what I'd said to him. It took some time, including pauses from what I imagined were expressions of astonishment from Edinburgh's elected leader. I wondered if ScotPol had a tap on the line. Maybe some local had seen or heard the Dundonian horde, or Rory's people coming and going. It didn't look as if the house had been occupied for some time. Finally, he held the receiver out to me.

'What the fuck, Quint?' said Lachie. 'But good work, all the same.'

'We're not home and dry yet, but at least you can tell old Angus we've got Margaret. Are the Nor-English staying put?'

'They are. I'm not sure what to make of that.'

'Could be that Gemma Bass is pulling a fast one – found some reason to keep them in Embra till the South Africans make contact.'

'Which they won't now.'

'I don't know. The surgeon Sebastian – he was more than just their private doctor. If there are others, they may have realized he's been compromised and press on with a plan we don't know about.'

Lachie laughed. 'Compromised? Your former girlfriend shot him dead. She and Davie dealt with plenty of the South Africans' hired help. We can hope that the snow's making life difficult for the survivors. In the meantime, we have another problem.'

'Go on.'

'My people in parliament are telling me that Andrew Duart's going to declare martial law.'

'Shit.' I thought about the consequences. 'Meaning the Scottish Defence Force will join with Hyslop's ScotPol to lock the country down. Just as well we're already operating undercover.'

'It had better stay that way. We could use those twins to put pressure on the South Africans. Assuming the Nor-English are in cahoots with them, they must fancy their chances of defeating our military.'

'Who's their boss?'

'Good question. I know their trade mission personnel, but none of them are still officially in Scotland. Then again, neither are your twins. There could be any number of blond-haired Boers sneaking around.'

'Thanks for the thought.'

'Hmm. How are you going to save the city like you've done before?'

'I may have lost my touch. Leave it with me.'

'All right, but time's running out. Give me Rory.'

I did so, and then sat down in an armchair that had so much horsehair sticking out that it resembled a porcupine. We could give Amber and Penny the fourth degree, but I didn't have the stomach for that. Then again, Amber at least might react well to a softer touch. They must know about the South African plans.

I heard loud voices approach, then several gunshots that caused more uproar. I ran out of the room and into the hall, but I was too late.

Rory went past me and pushed through the mass of Dundonians wearing black combat fatigues. They were armed with pistols, knives and rifles, and some had grenades hanging from their belts and other straps. Those at the front had broken through to the sitting room where the twins were. There were curses and expressions of disgust.

'Comrades, let me through!' yelled Rory. It took some time, but the fighters complied. I followed. The noise started to die down, then stopped altogether.

'Anyone who takes another step will lose his balls,' Davie shouted. That got to the Dundonians and an uneasy silence continued. Rory and I made it to the door. One of his men had a bloody face.

'What is it?' Penny said. 'You big men aren't frightened of us, are you?'

The twins stood in the middle of the room, both with belligerent expressions. Their arms were raised and fists clenched.

There was muttering from the fighters, but no one answered.

'Never seen conjoined twins before?' Penny went on. 'Think we're freaks? Monsters?' She grimaced. 'You ignorant cowards. There's more in our heads than all yours put together. And get this – without us, you're all going to die horribly. You need us!'

I wondered what she meant and nodded to Davie. With Rory, he herded the fighters out of the room. The sitting room was secured and an armchair pushed against the broken door to close it.

'I'm so sorry,' said Rory to the twins and the Lady of the Isles. The latter looked terrified; Katharine was comforting her. 'They heard there were women in the house and couldn't contain their curiosity.'

'I hope they're satisfied,' said Penny.

Amber laughed. 'They looked like kids who saw the bogeyman . . . women.'

I went over and asked them to sit down, then handed them glasses of water from the table.

'What was that you said about the fighters needing you?' I asked Penny.

She gave me a glacial look. 'None of your business.'

Amber's eyes widened. 'Dearest, don't be like that. Quintilian was on our side.'

'And I'll continue to be, but you have to help me.' I outlined the situation as I'd heard it from Lachie. 'I know the armed men at the Binns were local hired hands. Were there any other South Africans apart from the terat— from Sebastian? Are there any others in Scotland?'

'You've forgotten the salient point, Dalrymple,' said Penny. 'You killed our father and we're going to make you pay.'

I felt tingling in the stump of my right forefinger.

'Come on, Pen,' said Amber. 'There might be war. We could be killed.'

Penny turned on her. 'You're always like this, Amber – soft and stupid. You made eyes at that scheming surgeon who wanted to separate us. Do you really think he had feelings for you?'

Amber's cheeks reddened. 'He said he did. In fact, sister dear, that was why he wanted us to be apart.'

'You think he'd have been turned on by a woman with one arm, one leg, one breast and one buttock?'

'No, he'd have been turned on by a woman with one head.'

'Hold on,' I said. 'Amber's right. War is definitely on the cards.' I leaned closer. 'And your country supplied the Scottish Defence Force with a secret weapon.'

'What is it?' asked Penny brusquely.

'I don't know. Are there any of your fellow countrymen or women in Scotland who would be able to tell us?'

'How should we know?' said Penny, dropping her gaze.

Amber looked past the back of her sister's head and smiled at me shyly. 'Well, there's always Jack.'

I knew it. We should have done more to locate Jack Nicol. There was more to the attempt on his life than rivalry between the Bosch cults. Where was he and who was the tree-fish?

Penny sniffed. 'Jack Nicol's nothing but a pawn.'

Amber was shaking her head at me. 'He's been to our country. He's in charge. Ah!'

I grabbed Penny's arm, which was surprisingly muscular. She'd punched Amber on the chin and her sister's head was lolling back on the sofa.

Amber blinked and came back to herself. 'Just for that,' she said, rubbing her jaw, 'I'm going to tell Quintilian exactly what Jack does.'

'Don't you dare!' Spittle sprayed from Penny's lips. 'He killed our father!'

'I don't care. We both know our father was a pig. Do you think our mother would have approved of all your plotting?' Amber turned to me. 'Jack's a smart operator. He's been South Africa's man in Edinburgh for three years. He knows everything there is to know about our government's plans.'

'More than we do,' said Penny, with a harsh laugh.

'Find him, Quintilian,' said Amber. 'I don't want a war. Not even my sister really wants that. Find Jack and stop him.'

I turned to Davie. He was ready to roll.

'I don't suppose you have any idea where he might be?' I asked.

'No!' screamed Penny, trying desperately to free her arm from my grasp. 'Don't say another word!'

Amber shook her head sadly. 'Honestly, Pen, you have more of our father in you than is healthy.' She looked at me. 'He has a base where his men gather and store their arms. I don't know exactly where it is, but I've heard him call it the Destructor.'

Davie raised a clenched fist and grinned.

I called Rory and arranged with him for people to stop Penny and her sister fighting, whatever form that might take. Then, at speed, we gathered a squad of ten armed men and women and put them in the two vans that had chains on their wheels.

'Good news,' said Rory. 'The snow's stopped in the south and Knee Bothwell's people are on the move.'

'Send them to Powderhall as well,' I said. 'Who knows how many we'll be up against.'

'I'd come with you,' said Rory, 'but Lachie's ordered me to sit on the Dundonians. Don't you want them with you too?'

I shook my head. 'They're our tactical reserve. Have them ready to move at a moment's notice. No more booze.'

'Fair enough.'

'You've got Lady Margaret to look after too,' said Katharine, sliding a magazine into an automatic rifle she'd found somewhere. 'I'm coming with you, Quint.'

'Great,' moaned Davie, as he got behind the wheel of the front van.

'Just like old times,' I said, opening the other door for her.

She didn't reply – just gave me one of the enigmatic smiles she'd been practising over her years in Stirling.

So we headed for the Destructor. It wasn't hard to see how the place could live up to its name.

The snow had almost stopped in the western suburbs. We took the road along the shore and through Pilton to avoid ScotPol patrols. We were well enough armed to fend off unwelcome attention in the housing scheme. As it happened, there wasn't any. Maybe the gunfight with Morrie the Nut's people had done serious damage – not that the locals would be quiet for long. It was as we turned on to Goldenacre that we ran into trouble.

'Told you we should have gone the back way to Powderhall,'

muttered Davie, smiling at the ScotPol officer standing in front of the barrier that had been erected across the road.

'Fob him off,' I said, under my breath.

He grunted and wound down the window of the ancient van.

'Is that you, Detective Leader?' said the middle-aged man in a yellow high-visibility suit.

This was the crunch. If Hel Hyslop had put Davie's name on a watch list – never mind mine – then we were in deep dung. The ScotPol squad were equipped with rifles and pistols, which was a mark of how serious the situation was. The last thing I wanted was a bloodbath – but that would happen to the nth degree if the South Africans' surrogates, the Nor-English, invaded Scotland. Our only lead was what Amber told us about Jack Nicol's base at the Destructor and we had to get there.

'Hold on, will you, sir?' said the officer, taking out his radio.

Tension rose in the front of the van, Katharine gripping a pistol she'd removed from her pocket. I nudged her, but she gave me a furious look. She wasn't taking orders from a man, neither a ScotPol officer nor me.

The man finished speaking and looked back at Davie. 'There's a wee problem, Detective Leader.'

I felt Katharine's body tighten.

'The director wants you at HQ right away. I'm to take you up myself.'

Davie swore loudly. 'I'm on an urgent operation.'

'I thought you might be,' said the officer, looking at the van more closely.

'Go with him,' I whispered to Davie. 'It's our only way through.'

'But—'

'But I'll manage. Now bugger off. And leave that machine pistol behind.'

He mumbled something uncomplimentary and got out.

I waited till the officer moved away before taking the driving seat.

The barrier was raised and we were off, the snow chains gripping the snow effectively. I kept my speed down, unlike the guy who was driving Davie – he'd disappeared down the road at ridiculous speed, lights flashing and siren blaring.

'What do you think will happen to Thunderboots?' Katharine said.

'Don't call him that. He's heavily outnumbered and could be about to have the collected works of Hel Hyslop flung in his face.'

Katharine laughed. 'He'll manage.' She looked ahead. 'The question is, will we?'

'Thanks for the vote of confidence,' I said, keeping my foot off the brake as the van slithered across the road.

'You think you're in charge now?'

I let that go. It didn't matter if she wanted to handle tactics on the ground. I was wondering what we were up against and cursing myself for not having followed up Jack Nicol days ago. Lachie's congratulations sounded decidedly hollow right now.

We crossed the Water of Leith and went through Canonmills. Then I turned left on to Broughton Road. The Powderhall Destructor was only a few minutes ahead.

FIFTEEN

I stopped about a hundred metres before the rubbish disposal site. I knew it was surrounded by high fencing, so we'd have to find a way in. I got out of the van and, with Katharine, went to the vehicle behind.

'Andy Bothwell's people are about half an hour away,' said the middle-aged woman at the wheel. 'It would be sensible to wait.'

I asked her name.

'Linda,' she said. 'I was in the Guard, Citizen.' She grinned after she used my old designation.

'Were you now? All right, let's hold on. I don't know how many people are in there. I'm going to scout the area. I'll take one of the guys in the front van with me – you've all got radios, haven't you?'

She nodded. 'What do you want us to do if any vehicles or people exit the compound?'

'Stop them if you can – though putting this heap in front of a bin lorry might not be a great idea.'

'We'd be able to keep up with it all right, though.'

'True. OK, hold fast.'

'I'm coming with you,' said Katharine, before we reached the front van.

'Knock me down with a wren's feather.' I thumped on the back door and asked for a radio. There was no point in putting more than two of us in danger.

We set off past the tenements towards what had been an incinerator till the mid-1980s, when it had been shut down. I knew about it because my parents had lived nearby when they were recently married, and they often mentioned the stinking smoke clouds it had pumped out. After the Enlightenment, when landfill sites outside the city were no longer accessible, the plant had been recommissioned. There were better filters on the chimney now, but the place still reeked. It had the full range of destruction gear now, including a car crusher. Some attempts at recycling were made, but a private company ran the plant and the media had reported that it wasn't exactly fastidious. Not the municipality's finest hour, but the convenors had a lot on their respective plates.

There were lights on inside the compound and the sound of grinding increased as we approached. There was no one around outside: everybody was trying to keep warm – except us.

I looked at the gate. Oddly, it was less solid than the fencing. There was a metal bar across the inside of the steel struts, but I reckoned one of the vans could break through.

'Shall we call them in?' Katharine asked, having reached the same conclusion.

'Let's hang on a bit.'

'Haven't your testicles got frostbite yet?'

'I didn't think you cared.'

'Neither did I.'

We knelt down, trying to make ourselves as small as possible. That was just as well, because three figures in high-vis suits and helmets suddenly emerged from the main building. I tracked them as they moved towards a large black rubbish collection vehicle.

'That's Jack Nicol in the middle,' I said. 'Give me the radio.'

Katharine paid no attention. She checked the channel and then pressed the transmit button. 'Suspect about to board bin lorry. Stand by.'

'Suspect? You're talking to rebels, not ScotPol.'

'That woman Linda was in the Guard.'

She had me there.

We watched as the engine started with a roar and moved towards the gate. It must have been electronically controlled as it opened without anyone nearby.

'Van One, you have authority to ram,' said Katharine. 'Ram! Ram!'

'What authority?' I protested, too late. The front van was already in motion, whoever was driving having placed a heavy boot on the accelerator.

The bin lorry was only halfway out of the gate when the driver, who wasn't Nicol, saw what was approaching. He hit the brake and the van slowed, eventually stopping a few millimetres in front of the lorry's bumper. Linda had driven up behind the first van to double the weight. That would make it harder for the larger vehicle to shove them back. Unless it reversed and took a run at them, which is what started to happen.

I grabbed the radio. 'Follow them in!' I yelled. 'Don't let them open up a gap.'

The van wheels span in the slush but they quickly got a grip and enabled the vehicles to pass through the gate.

'Here we go,' I said, as the driver of the bin lorry jumped down, a machine pistol in his right hand. 'One firefight coming right up.'

I turned my head, but Katharine had already gone. She fired as she went through the gate, making the guy with the machine pistol dive to the ground. The rebels piled out of the vans and brought their own arms to bear on people who ran out of the buildings.

'I want Nicol alive,' I shouted despairingly, as I ran through the gate.

It was a close-run thing. The guys in the high-vis suits weren't rubbish collectors; they were fully trained and/or experienced head-bangers. Two rebels hit the snow and didn't get up, while at least another three were wounded, though that didn't stop them fighting. Katharine had a new parting in her hair above her left ear, blood dripping on to her shoulder. The man who fired that shot didn't stay on his feet for long. I could see Jack Nicol battling hard, a look on his face that was much more vicious than we'd seen before. He was obviously a chameleon and he'd fooled me completely, which made me even more determined to nail him. I ran towards him and was promptly put on my arse in the gritty snow by a guy with a tyre iron. A rebel knocked him out with the butt of his rifle. I got up

and staggered on, waving my pistol like a drunken clown. Then
Nicol saw me. He grinned like a devil distinctly not sick of sin and
came at me, brandishing a long, thin bayonet-like blade. I slithered
to a stop.

There was a blast on a horn. I looked round, to see Andy Bothwell
lead a group of armed rebels from vans that had just arrived behind
the others. Then Nicol was on me, smashing me to the ground and
bringing the bayonet up to my throat.

'They've . . . disowned you,' I managed to say.

His brow furrowed. 'What?'

At least he hadn't moved his weapon closer, though his weight
made it hard for me to breathe.

'Penny and Amber. How . . . do you think . . . I found you?'

'Fucking bitches,' he said, then shook his head. 'Even more
reason to put holes in your face.' The point of the bayonet went
into my right cheek. I screamed.

Then the weight rolled off me. I had my hand on my face, blood
trickling between the fingers, but I could see Katharine. She had
one foot on Nicol's chest and was blowing on her knuckles.

'A right to the jaw,' she said, between breaths. 'He must have
had a glass one.'

I sat up and looked around. Bothwell's arrival had been better
timed than the arrival of Blucher on the field of Waterloo. The men
in high-vis suits were on the ground, some kneeling, more flat out.
I picked up the bayonet and got to my feet, less than steadily.

'All right, son?' said Andy, who must have been younger than me.

'Aye,' I mumbled. 'Tie that bastard up. We need to talk to him.
Take the others too.'

'There are still some in the plant,' he said. A burst of gunfire
confirmed that. 'Shall we get after them?'

'I wouldn't waste any more—'

The air seemed to compress and then a deafening blast sent us
all flying. A mass of flame rose from the back of the facility's main
building, then bits of metal – most small but some as large as my
head – came raining down. I wrapped my arms round my cranium
and found myself on the Somme. I could hear only a high whining.
Gradually, the aerial bombardment lessened and then stopped.
Clouds of smoke roiled across the compound, rebels covered in ash
and dust stumbling around.

I took my arms away and looked for Katharine. She nodded from not far away to confirm that she was unhurt. Knee Bothwell danced up, a crazy smile on his lips. His mouth opened and closed, but I couldn't make out the words. Then I found I could lip-read.

'The Destructor self-destructs!' he was saying, over and over.

I shook my head. Destructors, whether human or mechanical, never really disappeared. At best we had some temporary relief. But experience had taught me that plotters, profiteers and monsters didn't stay away for long, especially from the fair city of Embra.

The explosion brought plenty of interested parties to Powderhall: fire engines, ambulances and police vehicles first and journalists soon after. I caught sight of Charlotte Thomson on the other side of the fence. She waved at me, but I didn't want to talk to her, at least not yet. My hearing was only slowly coming back and my cheek hurt as if a Bosch demon had skewered it. I saw a grim-faced Hel Hyslop get out of a dark-blue Volvo and wondered what had happened to Davie. As yet there was no sign of him. It would be just like Hel to lock him up and use him to twist my arm. Then again, we'd reached the end of the endgame. Her priority would be to shore up what remained of her position. No doubt Andrew Duart was spinning all sorts of yarns to do the same for himself in parliament.

Hyslop saw me and waved me over. She was wearing ScotPol fatigues and a helmet, a holstered pistol hanging from her belt.

'What have you done?' she shouted.

At least I heard that. 'Me? Jack Nicol's sidekicks were responsible for the blast.'

Knee Bothwell was standing a few yards away. He twitched his head and I understood. Rebels had been involved in the explosion. I needed to change the subject.

'Tell me,' I yelled, redirecting her question, 'what are you going to do now that the Lord of the Isles is back on the scene? Arrest the Nor-English representatives and the Finns? What about the South Africans?' I gave her a knowing smile. 'By the way, the teratologist didn't make it.'

She glared but didn't back down. 'What are you insinuating, Dalrymple?'

'Are you sure you want to have this conversation in public?'

Suddenly, she looked a lot less sure of herself.

'In any case, I'm not saying another word until Davie Oliphant's standing next to me.'

Bothwell knew what was going on; he'd given subtle signals to his people and they were massing behind him, weapons at the ready. ScotPol officers saw them but didn't show much enthusiasm for a fight. I got the impression that Hel had lost them.

She spoke into her radio and a few seconds later Davie got out of a service four-by-four. He looked unharmed and strode towards us, grabbing a rifle from a junior officer.

'You OK, Quint?' he said, as he joined us and faced his commander.

I nodded, putting my hands behind my ears. 'Hearing's turned down to about three and a half; cheek's got a puncture, how about you?'

'Untouched by male or female hand,' he said, looking belligerently at Hyslop. 'But I've been locked in an office without phone or ScotNet, and someone's going to pay.'

His boss looked around for support. None of her officers was closer than five metres away. Then her phone rang. She answered it and listened, her face collapsing in ruins. She closed the connection and caught my eye.

'I've been ordered by the moderator of parliament to surrender myself.'

'Ha,' said Davie, handing Bothwell his rifle and stepping forward. He relieved Hyslop of her phone, pistol, combat knife, ID and truncheon. Then he used her own cuffs to secure her hands behind her back. 'Where to?' he asked me, then repeated the question at high volume.

'All right!' I shouted back. 'My hearing's almost back to normal.'

'Parliament,' Hyslop said.

Davie made a call to confirm and then led her away. No ScotPol personnel made any show of support for her. It was never smart to treat people like dirt.

'Quint?' Katharine said. 'Nicol's coming round.'

So he was. It was time for a question-and-answer session.

That took place in the burgh building on the High Street, in front of Lachie MacFarlane and Rory Campbell. The latter had asked Katharine to keep an eye on the Dundonians. The centre of the city was quiet, and we'd just heard that Andrew Duart had surrendered himself to security staff at the parliament building. A paramedic had put a dressing on my cheek.

I drew the others to one side before we went into the meeting room, which had armed guards on the door.

'We need to get the media involved. I'm not convinced all the people involved in this will stop machinating unless the people are told.'

'Good point,' said Lachie. 'But we need the media *owners* on board.'

I beckoned to Charlotte Thomson, who was standing on the other side of the hall. I'd got her into the van that brought us from the ex-destructor and given her a rundown of what had been going on. Her lower jaw spent the whole journey resting against her throat.

Lachie and Rory knew her, of course, and greeted her warmly.

'I've been talking to my editor,' Charlotte said. 'She's been in touch with the owner. We can publish.'

Lachie clapped his hands. 'And when you publish, everyone else will have to follow suit.'

'Well, I don't care about that,' she said, turning to me. 'I get an exclusive interview with Quint here.'

If Edinburgh's leaders had a problem with that, they didn't show it. Now I was going to test them further.

'I'm going to ask Jack Nicol questions with Charlie present, all right?'

They looked at each other and then shrugged.

'We'll be listening,' said Rory.

'And the same goes for the English trade delegation,' I said. 'Davie's gone to detain them.'

'You're taking rather a lot on yourself, Quint,' Lachie said, punching me on the thigh.

I glanced at the journalist and smiled. 'Sometimes I have to.'

We walked up to the guards. After Rory gave the OK, they opened the doors, and then closed them behind us.

Jack Nicol had been relieved of his clothes and was now wearing a thin cotton jumpsuit. His head with the green-and-white football tattoo was bare. The word *PRISONER* was in large letters across the chest and on the trouser leg. His wrists were cuffed to those two burly security men, who were no doubt rebels.

Nicol laughed as we approached the table and sat across from him. 'Who's this, Dalrymple? Your fancy woman?'

'My name's Charlotte Thomson. I'm writing a story about you that people all over Scotland will read tomorrow. Be nice.'

That shut him up.

'So, Jackie, I spoke to your mother.'

He narrowed his eyes. 'I heard. I suppose you believed her like you believed me.'

'She was worried about you. I'm not surprised. When did you start working for the South Africans?'

'Whit?'

'Give it up, son. Amber and Penny told me.'

Silence again.

'That's better. If you tell me what I want to know, you might not spend the rest of your life in the Bar-L.' The old prison in Glasgow had never closed and was again the biggest in Scotland.

'I'm the Prince of Hell,' he said, head up and chest out.

'You actually believe in that stuff?' Charlie asked.

'Of course.'

'And there was me thinking you were just using the Followers of Hieronymus Bosch the Prophet for criminal ends.' I took a sip from the bottle of water in front of me. My throat was still dusty from Powderhall.

'Well, that too.' Nicol gave me a loose grin and I noticed he was missing a canine.

'What happened to your tooth?'

'In some fucker's leg.' He did his arrogant look again.

'How did you get involved with the South Africans?' I asked. 'Tell the truth without screwing around and you'll get a book of Bosch paintings in your cell. Otherwise, forget it.'

He gave me the hard eye and then started to speak. 'They found me three years back. Told me they were interested in Bosch.' He grinned. 'And in making money. We bonded.'

'Uh-huh. *They* being?'

'Couple of blond guys. One of them couldn't speak. He was a bit . . . scary.'

'He isn't any more. When did you meet the twins?'

'Last summer, July it must have been. I'd proved maself by then. Kidnapped a couple of businessmen, extracted plenty in ransoms.'

'They told you about the South African plan to take over Scotland's energy companies?'

'Aye. Worked for me. Those rich fuckers like the Lord of the Isles, they deserve everything they get.'

'His wife as well?'

'Aye!'

'Remember the Bosch book, Prince of Hell.'

That quietened him down. 'When did you first meet the Nor-English?'

'A week later. I knew the Boers were working them. I didn't care. That guy Shotbolt – what a bamstick.'

'Gemma Bass was your contact.'

'Aye. I suppose the twins told you that too. Whit's got intae them?'

I raised my shoulders. 'Conscience.'

'You're joking! Those freaks are the nastiest people you'll ever meet. I used to think Amber was OK, but she's even worse than Penny.'

A worm of apprehension twisted in my gut. The twins were somewhere in the building, Rory having brought them from Cramond. What might they be up to?

'You know the Nor-English have an army ready to invade Scotland,' I said.

'Let them. Then I won't go to prison.'

'And the Finns? I suppose they wanted guaranteed energy from Scotland.'

'Aye, and they're sick of being bullied by the Swedes and Norwegians.'

I wondered if the twins had told him why they wanted the finger put in the Lord of the Isles's bed, but I wasn't going to ask in front of Charlotte. I suspected they'd kept their plot against me to themselves and the teratologist.

'You knew Morrie Gish, of course?'

'Morrie worked for me,' said Nicol, unable to hide his pride.

I doubted that, but it didn't matter. They were all ordure.

I turned to Charlotte. 'You getting this?'

'Oh, yes. Isn't treason the worst crime of all?' She looked at Nicol as if he was a mass murderer.

'By far,' I said. 'Parliament's going to discuss bringing back the death penalty for it.' It wasn't, but how would he know?

'That's shite!' he said less than convincingly.

I smiled. 'What's your problem? You'll be able to take up your rightful place in the underworld, pecking at souls with your beak and shitting them out for eternity.'

He now looked deflated, which was how I wanted him.

'I can still get you that Bosch book.'

'The Prophet Hieronymus,' he said dully.

'Right. Just tell me who helped the South Africans and the Nor-English.'

'Why should I trust you?'

'Because I'm here, with an independent witness who's going to tell your story to the whole country. You've seen Charlie on the TV, haven't you?'

Nicol looked at her and nodded slowly.

'The names then,' I pressed.

He licked his lips and I nodded to the guards to give him a drink. Then he started to speak.

'Andy Duart, of course – he was told he'd be president for life. That cow Hyslop, she'd be his number two. There was to be no parliament.' He went on to name the head of the Scottish Defence Force and numerous senior officers in all three services. They'd been seduced by promises of modern materiel ranging from ships, planes, missiles and bombs to computer-controlled battlefield systems.

'What about the secret weapon? Ever hear of that?'

He shook his head and let me hold his gaze. Maybe it was only an imaginary threat.

'Am I right, then, pal?' Nicol asked, after he'd named the leaders of most of the other regions.

'One last thing. Why were you attacked by the tree-fish? Everything else we found was linked to *The Garden of Earthly Delights*.'

'And that was from *The Temptation of St Anthony*, eh? Right smartarse you are.' He snorted. 'It didnae mean anything. Just one of the baker's guys trying to put the wind up us. He didn't know anything about what I was really intae.'

'Not everything has to fit together,' I mused, then stood up. 'Come on, Charlie. Let's go and talk to the Nor-English.'

'Give them ma worst,' said Jackie Nicol.

'I'll be sure to do that. Now, to hell with you.'

He roared with laughter. At least someone was having a good time. I was skittish and I wasn't sure why.

I bailed out of talking to Nigel Shotbolt and his sidekicks. Rory took Charlie. He'd had plenty of experience of interrogation when he was a revolutionary. I gave Lachie a list of people to be picked up. It might not be easy as many were far from Edinburgh, but he told me he'd been talking to municipal leaders across Scotland: the message back was that most of the implicated regional heads had disappeared. I was still without a mobile phone. Davie and I had given ours to the rebels days ago, so I couldn't call Sophia. She and the kids would be asleep, so I decided to leave them undisturbed. A vision rose up of Heck with his arms and legs spread out and the covers on the floor beneath his head. That made me smile.

Before signing off and going home, I found out where Davie was. Surprise, surprise – down in the refectory, which was open even at this hour. There was a pile of empty plates in front of him.

'Belly full?'

He nodded. 'Are you not hungry, Quint?'

'No, my system's still full of particulate from the Destructor explosion.'

'Can't you expectorate it?'

'Ha. Come on, let's say our farewells to the twins.'

'Do we have to?'

'Yes,' said a voice from the bottom of the stair.

'Katharine,' I said. 'I thought you were with the Dundonians.'

'I was and I will be again shortly. We're needed back home urgently – at least, they are. Stirling's never had anything to do with the South Africans, but I hear some of the syndicates in Dundee have been acting independently. No oil there, of course.'

'We're going to see the twins,' I said. 'Want to come?'

'No, thanks.' She was standing in front of me now. 'But a word of warning. Those two are evil. Trust me, I've seen it too often. Be very careful.'

I nodded. She knew women much better than I did.

'So, this is farewell,' she said, offering her hand to Davie.

He took it and grinned. 'You'll be back. Like a fly to—'

'Thank you, Detective Leader,' I said. 'I'll see you upstairs.'

He lumbered off, leaving us alone.

'Thank you,' I said. 'I mean for looking out for me at the Destructor.'

She smiled. 'You need someone apart from Thunderboots.' She stepped close and put an arm round my neck.

'For auld lang syne,' she said, pulling my head down and kissing me hard on the lips. 'Say hello to Sophia,' she said, after she'd let go and stepped back. 'And send those twins back to Boer-land on the first rowing boat.'

I watched as she walked away and took the stairs in twos.

Women, I thought. Then I remembered Sophia. I'd be back with her and the kids soon – after I'd washed my hands of the astonishing creatures who had tried to destroy me and my country.

SIXTEEN

'We're honoured, dearest,' said Amber, when the door was closed behind us. They were in a small room on the first floor that must have been a middle-ranking civil servant's office. There was a guard at the door, but none inside.

I looked at the desk. No telephone or computer: they must have been removed, which was a relief. I'd been concerned that the twins could have been in contact with an associate who hadn't been identified or picked up yet.

'Ladies,' I said.

Penny gave me a tight smile. 'Patronizing as ever, Dalrymple.'

Amber turned her head. 'Come on, my sweet. He's looked after us.' She beamed at me and then at Davie.

I remembered what Jack Nicol had said about Amber. If he was right, she was a remarkable actress.

'Tell the truth,' continued Penny. 'We're nothing more than monsters to you, are we? Like our father was.'

That was hard to answer, especially as I had thought of them in that way. Then again, I had behaved monstrously myself, both in the past and recently.

'Who am I to judge?'

'Quite,' said Penny. 'You killed our father, which makes you as much of a monster as he was. You broke the laws of the regime that ran this city too – and covered that up. You're worse than us.'

'In Greek "teras" means both monster and wonder.' I looked at them both. 'I think you're sources of wonder too.'

Penny laughed harshly, but Amber regarded me thoughtfully, before saying, 'I didn't know that. Thank you for telling us.' She took her sister's hand.

'What happens to us now?'

'You'll be taken to the airport,' said Davie. 'Your embassy has arranged a plane. You'll never be allowed back into Scotland. Apart from everything else, you've never appeared in any passenger manifest or list of accredited officials.'

'You came from Nor-England every time, didn't you?' I said. 'Busy, busy, weaving your web around Shotbolt, as well as keeping contact with Gemma Bass.'

Neither replied. I took that as 'yes' several times over.

'You think it's finished, don't you?' said Penny to me, as Davie stepped forward. 'You think we'll let you live.'

The ferocity of her tone froze my blood. And this time Amber was with her, laughing like a demon unlocking a fresh transport of souls. There was no way I could offer them my hand. They showed no sign of doing so either.

Davie escorted the twins out.

I sat down on the desk and tried to get a grip. They would be out of Edinburgh very soon, but they were geniuses. What if they had already set a lethal scheme in motion?

I ran out of the room and cannoned into a middle-aged cleaner, who was pushing a cart with her gear.

'Phone,' I rasped. 'Give me your mobile. It's an emergency. Please. My family . . .'

She nodded and fumbled in her pocket. I hit the buttons for Sophia's number, my heart somersaulting.

After what seemed like a lifetime, she answered sleepily.

'It's me. Are you OK? The kids?'

'Of course. Why?'

'Never mind. Check on them.'

I heard muffled sounds of movement, then Sophia spoke again.

'They're both fast asleep. Quint, you're scaring me.'

'Have you put the chains on and bolted the door?'

'Yes! I'm not an idiot!'

'I know, my love. I'm sorry. It's been a seriously weird case, but it's over. I'll be home soon.'

'I'll stay up for you.' The anger in her voice disappeared. 'I want to see you, Quint. You're my man and I love you.'

'I love you too,' I said, suddenly teary. 'See you soon.'

I handed the phone back to the cleaner, who was smiling broadly.

'Very nice, son.' She shook her head sadly. 'I dinnae hear that often maself.'

I gave her a quick embrace and gambolled down the corridor like a winter lamb.

Davie insisted on driving me home.

'Isn't Eilidh waiting?' I asked, as we got into a ScotPol four-by-four that he'd commandeered.

'Waiting while asleep. A brief delay won't hurt.' He grimaced. 'Don't know about me, though. I'm knackered.'

So was I. The vehicle slid round the corner on to the North Bridge. The snow was melting. Maybe the worst of winter was over.

'You saved the day again, Quint.'

'*We* saved it, big man.'

'Aye, sure we did. Who'd have thought it? Most of Scotland's ruling elite are money-grabbing traitors.' He laughed grimly.

'Lucky that Lachie and Rory are trustworthy.'

He glanced at me. 'You sure about that?'

Wind duly taken from sails, a tsunami of exhaustion crashed over me and I spent the rest of the drive trying to stay awake. The way I managed that was thinking about what I'd have to change when I wrote the novel about the case. *Impolitic Corpses* – that might work as a title. I wouldn't be including the twins in the story, though – they were too closely linked to the great gap in my life that was the ENT Man.

'Want me to come up,' Davie said, as he pulled up on Great Citizen Street.

'Sophia's awake.'

'I'll leave you lovebirds to it, then. Tweet tweet.'

I waved him away.

This time I didn't even try to run up the stairs. I was panting as I reached the second floor. I bent over to catch my breath and only noticed that the door was ajar when I stood up. Adrenaline instantly coursed through my body.

'Sophia!' I shouted, pushing the door open. The chains swung impotently and one of the bolts was on the floor. 'Maisie!'

Our bedroom was empty, the duvet half on the floor. I ran to Heck's room. No sign of him. No Maisie either. Fucking hell. I careened into the sitting room and stopped immediately.

Pages from my Hieronymus Bosch book had been torn out and laid over the carpet and the furniture. *The Garden of Earthly Delights* had been carefully placed on the coffee table.

Then I looked at the mirror above the fireplace. Words bigger than my hands had been written on the glass in what looked very like blood – drops had run down to the bottom of the frame:

THE THRILL IS GONE

The title of B.B. King's most famous song polluted my family home and mocked my impotence. In a cold fury I thought of the twins and rang Davie, then the airport, then Lachie and Rory.

Amber and Penny had been taken from the ScotPol vehicle transporting them to the airport. Five ScotPol officers were dead and three seriously injured.

We searched for the twins across the city and the borderlands. We searched all over Scotland, but we found no sign of them.

Or of Sophia, Maisie and Heck.